To the reader who asked me why my books had to
contain any of that "woke, gay stuff".

Here's more for you.

# WITH WING AND CLAW

## FAE ISLES - BOOK 5
## LISETTE MARSHALL

ASIN: B0CWZ7448Z


Cover design: Saint Jupiter
Editor: Erin Grey, The Word Faery


www.lisettemarshall.com
www.facebook.com/LisetteMarshallAuthor
www.instagram.com/AuthorLisetteMarshall

# CONTENTS

# CHAPTER 1

DISAPPOINTINGLY, THE WORLD HADN'T ended while Thysandra slept.

She woke groggily, unwillingly, from the sounds of clanging chains and shouting voices – *fae* voices, most of them easily recognisable even through the thick alf steel plates on her cell door. Some of them were howling in anger. Others in unmistakable pain. In this underground rebel prison, their presence could only mean one thing: that the war had been lost. The fae empire defeated, the Crimson Court taken at last.

She could no longer manage to care.

A dull headache was pulsing beneath her skull as she pushed herself up from the wooden bench that had served as her bed for the past few weeks, rubbing the sleep from her eyes. Her own chains tingled with the movement. She barely felt their cold weight on her wrists anymore, the white-gleaming alf steel blocking her magic; the throbbing, smarting ache in her chest was a far more urgent injury than the bruises on her skin.

*A traitor's daughter.*

She still saw the letters, black ink gleaming on smooth parchment, whenever she closed her eyes.

Outside her cell, the hubbub seemed to be coming closer, doors banging louder and louder as whatever was happening spread to her side of the corridor. She heard other voices too, now, speaking with the distinctive northern accent of alves and the guttural timbre of vampires ... It seemed they were rounding up prisoners, taking them all at once from the cells in which they'd been locked up over the course of the last twenty-four hours. Public executions, maybe. Trials. Who even knew what the Alliance might come up with, in revenge for a century and a half of life under fae rule?

Thysandra huddled her knees to her chest and slumped against the wall, her wings shivering as they pressed into the cold stone. Presumably, she ought to feel fear at whatever was happening outside her cell. Grief, maybe. At the very least, some sort of desperate anger. Four centuries of slaving away for the empire, four centuries of unwavering loyalty, and now this was all that had come of it – ashes and rubble?

Still the feelings wouldn't come. No matter how hard she reached for them, there was nothing but dull, hollow emptiness in the persistent thudding of her heart.

*A traitor's daughter.*

Perhaps she should never have tried to be anything else.

The knuckles against her door didn't jolt her – she was too numb to be jolted, even her battle reflexes dulled to the point of non existence. The door swung open a long five seconds later, as if whoever stood outside had hoped for a reply or permission to enter.

For one heart-stopping moment, she expected to see the pink, flowery silhouette she would have killed to avoid on this miserable morning.

Instead, the figure stepping into her cell was tall and winged and decidedly male – Agenor, her mind registered a dazed heartbeat later, his familiar face grim, an ink-black snake wrapped around his forearm. She didn't avert her eyes swiftly enough to miss the way his gaze shot over her dishevelled appearance – her tangled hair, the scrapes and bruises on her wrists, the red dress she'd worn since the Alliance had captured her. But no matter what he was thinking, no matter the painful contrast of his own well-groomed refinement on the edge of her sight, all that left his lips was a perfectly restrained, 'Morning, Thys.'

She wished she felt enough to punch him in the face.

At the very least, she wished she felt enough to cry.

She sat motionless, hunched up on her narrow bench, as the male she'd once called her ally nudged the door half-shut behind him and crossed the ten feet towards her. The last time he'd visited her in this cell, he'd kept his distance even with the alf steel blocking her magic, likely for the justified fear she might try and scratch out his eyes. There was none of that caution now. Either he trusted that bloody snake of his to deal with any aggression from her side, or he assumed she would no longer feel the urge to commit violence in the first place.

Even her spite at knowing he was right was not enough to make her move.

A glimpse of light reflected off the key between his fingers. For a moment she thought he would free her entirely, but he merely unlinked her metal cuffs from the chains lodged in the walls – quiet, patient motions as outside the door, the clamour of shouting and crying voices swelled to an increasingly loud roar.

'Can you stand?' Agenor asked in his deep voice, stepping back as the last chain fell to the stone floor. 'They tell me you haven't been eating much.'

She glared at him, unmoving.

He sighed and threw a look over his shoulder, as if to estimate how the rest of the Alliance was faring without him. Then, turning back, he added, 'We're taking everyone back to the Crimson Court, Thys. I figured you might want to come, too.'

Back?

To the *court*?

It wasn't surprise, the small spark of interest that flickered to life for the first time in days. It certainly wasn't curiosity. But it was enough to make her lift her head and frown at him. Enough to make her wonder for a sliver of a moment whether he was joking, or lying, or otherwise tricking her into some elaborate fae scheme only a mind like his could come up with.

He looked fully earnest, though – a glimpse of weary concern breaking through the stoic mask of his face.

'Why?' she croaked.

'Reasons,' he said, absently lifting his arm a fraction to allow his snake to slither onto a silk-clad shoulder. A small smile quirked his lips, there and gone again. 'I've been instructed to, mostly.'

Instructed – *he*? Agenor Thenes himself, former Lord Protector of the Crimson Court, who had promptly become one of the Alliance's leading figures after he'd turned his back on faekind and joined the rebellion instead?

There weren't too many people whose instructions he would follow, even fewer he would smile about. Really, she suspected the number of candidates lay very close to one.

'By that daughter of yours?' she numbly guessed.

Silly little Emelin of Cathra, who had turned out to be not so silly at all, or even so little. Half fae and unbound mage, with newly acquired divine powers to boot. If the war was over, if the little vixen had killed the Mother ...

Her heart squeezed.

Would the Mother have been dead if no one had told the Alliance how to get rid of the magical bindings that had prevented the rest of the world from using magic against her?

'By that daughter of mine, yes,' Agenor said, that same smile flickering across his face again. His snake was cautiously slithering into his hair now, black scales blending seamlessly with equally black curls. 'I would have objected if I'd thought she was planning to harm you, though. So ... are you coming?'

She stared at the calloused hand he held out to her.

Was she coming?

It was a genuine question. Not an unfriendly one, even. It made everything worse, that glimpse of his familiar kindness – because the world had been so simple, so blissfully simple, when she'd been sure one faction in the war was good, the other faction was bad, and she was firmly on the right side of that clear-cut divide. And then that gods-damned letter had arrived two days ago, and here the male she'd thought a devious turncoat stood looking like he was still the same person she'd trusted and respected more than almost anyone else in the cutthroat world of the Crimson Court ...

'If you don't mean to do me any harm,' she said hoarsely, 'then why are my wrists still chained together?'

He pursed his lips. 'Well, just to name one thing – last time we saw each other, you called me a traitor and a disgrace to faekind and threatened to slit my throat as soon as your hands were free again.'

It was hard not to wince. 'Yes, but ... but ...'

*But that was before I talked.*

She couldn't bring her lips to shape the words, even though there was nothing new in them, even if he knew as well as she did what had happened in the past two days. *That was before the Mother abandoned me and cast me away like a used tool. Before bloody Naxi followed me into this cell, all sweet and soothing sympathy. Before I spilled those secrets I should have known would spell the end of the empire.*

*Before I became a traitor, too.*

'Yes,' Agenor said, voice flat, green eyes no doubt reading the thoughts straight from her face. His expression didn't exactly *change* ... but it definitely tightened. 'If you want to know, the main reason I'm not releasing you is that a certain half demon warned me you might feel inclined to apply your suggested treatment of defectors to yourself as soon as you were able to. Which I would highly regret, in case that needs to be said.'

Fuck.

It was one thing to be sick of your own existence. For others to be aware of the fact was something else entirely, somehow. She wasn't sure which demon he was referring to, Creon or Naxi, and didn't even care that much; both options were equally humiliating.

'Go to hell,' she muttered.

'I'm afraid I've got a few more urgent things to do,' he said, unfazed. 'Might consider the trip in the future, though. For now, are you ready to leave?'

She bit out a curse and grabbed his hand.

Her knees were a fraction unsteady when he pulled her to her feet. She gritted her teeth and stood all the same, unwilling to be carried out of her cell like some damsel in distress; by the sound of it, all fellow army commanders who'd survived the last days of the war were gathered in that corridor now, and she'd be damned if she allowed herself to lose their respect so swiftly and easily. If they didn't yet know what she'd done ...

Oh, gods.

What if they *knew*?

But she was paid no particular attention as Agenor hoisted her out of her cell, into the throng of alves and fae and vampires. The familiar faces all around her looked more than occupied by their restraints and injuries; she saw Bereas shaking his fist at an unimpressed vampire, saw Imbros clasp a bleeding arm to his chest, saw Nicanor glare his icy glare at the alf female holding the chain attached to his wrists. The few fae who seemed to notice her at all did not bother to greet her. One or two brisk nods were all she was granted at their first confirmation of her survival since she'd been taken captive.

*It turns out*, the Mother's letter had said, *that Thysandra is perfectly redundant to our court ...*

Her body went numb again.

Had any of them been aware of it? She couldn't help but glance around as Agenor positioned her by the wall and strode off with a last muttered apology – couldn't help but let her gaze wander over the sea of faces she'd known for decades, *centuries*. Had they ever realised just how little the Mother truly cared about her, or for that matter, about any of them?

Would they still have fought for the empire, had they known?

Perhaps they would have. Perhaps only traitor's daughters threw aside centuries of loyalty as easily as she had, ignoring duty for some friendly words and something uncomfortably close to reckless lust.

For the first time, she was glad for the alf steel on her wrists. The weight of the cold metal was unpleasant, of course, but freedom would have been much, much worse; every single fae would have known the truth of her treason immediately if the Alliance had singled her out in such an obvious manner. Now at least there was some limit to the damage Naxi and her soft little hands had done. If she simply never told anyone ...

A coward's thought. She clung to it all the same.

After all, perhaps not *everything* was lost yet, if the Alliance wasn't planning to publicly shame her as a traitor. Perhaps she could just ... keep her head down for a while. Make sure to avoid any blue-eyed half demons causing trouble. Try not to get noticed as she gathered the shards of her old life and figured out what was left for her in this Mother-less world without love or purpose, *if* there was even anything left for her ...

And then she'd see.

It wasn't a plan – not really. But it was enough to set her mind turning again, and for the first time since she'd sobbed out those words she really should never have spoken, the numb hole in her chest seemed a little less bottomless.

Around her, the rebels were finally done lining up their prisoners, nothing but open doors along the length of the corridor. She saw Agenor issue a few quick instructions, and then the first alves took the arms of the fae beside them and disappeared into nothingness – transporting their captives to the Crimson Court in the time it took to blink an eye. A helpful sort of magic to have, Thysandra was well-aware, and the Mother had focused years of experiments on attempts to give fae those fading powers as well ... but even after all this time, the sight of living bodies vanishing into thin air always sent a small shiver down her spine.

'Ready to go?' a voice said, suddenly close behind her.

She *almost* shrieked as she whipped around.

Gods-damned Tared Thorgedson had appeared out of nowhere in the open doorway of her cell – tall and blond like all alves, albeit admittedly a fraction more even-tempered than most of his kind. Blood-spattered and soot-stained though he might be on this morning, an unmistakable edge of triumph glinted in his steel grey eyes, and there was no denying the contentment in his casual stance against the doorframe.

Nor did she think she imagined the hint of satisfaction in his voice as he added, 'You'll be glad to know that I've been told to keep a good eye on you. Need to make sure you don't miss any of the proceedings.'

Oh, gods help her.

She'd been there, after the Last Battle a hundred-and-thirty years ago, when the Mother had forced him to kneel at her feet and taken his magic and the memories of his parents. She'd assisted – eagerly – at his downfall.

Clearly, she was not the only one who remembered.

*Why you, of all people?* she wanted to snap, that tendril of almost-curiosity stirring again. *I don't need to be singled out like this in front of my former allies. Couldn't you have given me another alf – any other alf, really – rather than the bloody leader of the Alliance himself?*

She swallowed the question. In all likelihood, he simply felt like gloating, and who else would he gloat to now that the Mother was dead?

'Where exactly are we going?' she tried instead.

'Bone hall.' He stood straighter and wrapped his hand around her arm. A small, skewed grin slid around his lips. 'Or what's left of it, anyway.'

He faded before she could ask what in the world that was supposed to mean.

The colours of the prison blurred together, as if the canvas of reality crumpled around them – a nauseating whirlpool of black and grey and the palest blue, the scent of mouldy earth and brine, the sounds of waves whipping against cliffs. Thysandra clenched her eyes shut and tried not to feel gravity tugging her stomach in all the wrong directions at once, tried not to hear the eerily loud thuds of her heart as the world whizzed by.

Then, just as abruptly, it was over.

The ground went solid beneath her feet so suddenly she almost stumbled. The noise of a crowd roared into existence around her. Blinking against the blinding sunlight, she forced open her eyes, finding herself standing in an all too familiar antechamber. Red marble and gleaming gold. Open arches looking out over rocky, olive-covered hills and the endless stretch of azure sea beyond.

Home.

Even that coveted sight failed to light so much as a spark of joy within her.

Tared's hand gave a tug at her elbow, and she followed him numbly as she and the other prisoners were guided deeper into the castle, their heads bent, their wrists still cuffed together. Through the rows of alves and rebel fae standing guard around the hall. Past the copper-plated doors hanging askew on their hinges. Into …

The bone hall.

Or what was left of it, anyway.

The heart of the Mother's reign had been a grand, majestic place, built by the god of life and death himself, the walls decorated with thousands upon thousands of bones of the enemies he'd vanquished. The battle of the previous day shouldn't have touched it, having been fought on the other side of the archipelago. And yet the hall was un-recognisable now, looking more like the ruins of the Cobalt Court than the glorious home of her recent memories – arches crumbling down from the ceiling, two large breaches gaping in the walls. A small army of humans – *humans*, for the gods' sakes – was hacking away at the last bone decorations with clubs and crowbars, whooping vigorously at every skull to come tumbling to the ground.

By her side, Tared's grin had broadened to face-splitting proportions.

Around them, the other fae prisoners were looking as dazed as Thysandra felt.

The humans were not the only intruders, although they were the most numerous. She caught sight of a handful of grim vampire kings, nymph queens in their colourful dresses, phoenixes gleefully burning piles of shattered bones to ashes. Allie, Agenor's human lover, stood chatting with a blond, pointy-eared half fae in the corner. Farther into the hall, Lyn, Tared's … something, was hurriedly rescuing a pile of books before the other phoenixes' flames could reach it, her small body teetering under the weight of the stack.

High Lady, having killed the previous one, et cetera, et cetera – I've been told I ought to give all of you a chance to dispute the claim, so here we are. Does anyone wish to offer any objections, challenges, or other attempts to make life harder for themselves? If so, this would be the perfect moment to let me know.'

Deafening silence settled over the hall, as if even breathing too loudly might be taken as an act of rebellion.

Thysandra glanced up anyway, in spite of all her wiser intentions – too tense to keep herself blind to her surroundings when even the sounds no longer gave any hints of possible dangers approaching. To either side of her, clenched fists and tight wings suggested shouts barely kept inside … but Agenor's eyes had narrowed to a threat on the other side of the hall, and against the back wall, Creon was smiling with saintly sweetness as he leisurely turned a knife around between his fingers.

Five, then ten seconds of breathless paralysis ticked by.

'That's settled, then.' Emelin's beaming smile at the prisoners was too bright to be sincere. 'I'm glad you're as thrilled as I am. In that case, since you have so trustingly placed your empire in my hands, I would like to make use of this heart-warming occasion to announce a couple of decisions I've made.'

Tared stifled a chuckle behind Thysandra's back.

'First of all' – an edge of disconcerting hardness snuck into their new High Lady's voice all of a sudden – 'effective immediately, the empire relinquishes its control over all islands not inhabited by a majority of fae. Taxation and tribute obligations are ending as of this moment, too. For your convenience, let's just say I'm handing over the authority to whoever was in power before the Mother's invasion, or to whoever inherits that power according to local customs. Then all of you can sort out for yourself who those lucky rulers might be, alright?'

A few muffled cheers and breathless peals of laughter rose from among the crowd, although most of the audience remained quiet and motionless. They must have known this was coming; even the few nymph queens dabbing away their tears didn't seem particularly surprised.

'Second of all,' Emelin added, her smile at the horde of humans much more genuine than her previous one had been, 'all human slaves living at the Crimson Court are free to go. I'll figure out how to remove your bindings to the island later today, and of course we'll have a few alves available to return you all to your homes as efficiently as possible.'

The cheers were louder this time. Close by, the first disconcerted mumbles rose among the fae prisoners – thousands of servants, their quiet work in the background of crucial importance to the daily operations of the court ...

One of the alves snapped a warning, and the grumbling died away again, leaving only thin-lipped glares behind.

'Thirdly,' Emelin continued, a little louder now to reach over the elated whispers of the newly freed humans, 'and perhaps most importantly, I have decided to split up the empire.'

Thysandra had never heard a silence fall so abruptly.

Breaths caught and jaws sagged throughout the hall, even those who had been grinning in triumph two heartbeats ago – this was news, then, *true* news, an announcement not even the kings and queens of the rebelling islands had been aware of beforehand. The alves around them had stiffened, too. Only Agenor smiled, and next to him, Allie was biting her lip with— Wait, was that—

A *fang*?

Good gods.

Everything was happening far, far too quickly.

'More specifically,' Emelin was saying at an immeasurable distance, 'we will install the three courts as three independent administrative entities. All smaller fae isles may choose for themselves who they will ally with, in terms of taxation and infrastructure and such. The Golden Court will of course be in good hands with my dearest father over here ...'

Agenor's smile broadened into an uncharacteristically wide grin.

So he had known, hadn't he? Thysandra risked closing her eyes for a moment, trying to make sense of the meagre hints he'd given her during that short conversation in her cell. Perhaps he'd been trying to tell her she was welcome to move into the Golden Court if she wished to? Which would mean leaving the Crimson Court behind, of course, the home she'd invested every single hour of her time in for the last four hundred years – but then again, if staying at the Crimson Court meant living under the rule of Creon fucking Hytherion ...

'And since I'm already losing my patience with this gods-forsaken place after spending half an hour in it,' Emelin cheerfully continued, 'Creon and I will be taking up residence at the Cobalt Court.'

Thysandra's eyes flew open.

The *Cobalt* Court?

Around her, the whispering among the gathered fae was growing into unmistakable muttering, and this time even the alves guarding them seemed too baffled to do much about it. The Cobalt Court was in *ruins*. Who in the world would choose three crumbling walls and half a tower as their home for eternity? And more importantly ...

If the two most powerful mages currently alive were not planning to stay here and keep an eye on the court the Mother had left behind, then who the hell would?

Who even *could*?

'As most of you appear to realise, that leaves the hellhole we're presently standing in.' Emelin's gesture at the bone hall had the air of a vexed parent confronted with the room her child hadn't cleaned in months; the look she exchanged with Creon was more than a little exasperated. 'To tell you the truth, I strongly considered burning the whole court to the ground – but apparently you've got a nice library, and also, Zera told me to play nice whenever possible. So we'll have to find someone else to take care of it.'

What in the world?

Thysandra couldn't help but stare now, no matter how determined she'd been to stay far, far away from this mess – because even a twenty-something-year-old, almost-human peasant girl had to know this was an outrageously bad idea, didn't she? Or at least Creon or Agenor must have warned her of the risks? Madness, to think any other fae ruler she might choose wouldn't be rebelling within months or years – although that wasn't Thysandra's problem, of course, and all the more reason to keep her head down—

'Thysandra?' Emelin's voice cut in.

It took her half a heartbeat to realise the sound of her name hadn't merely existed in her own mind.

Another one to realise the rows of hand-cuffed fae had abruptly gone very, very quiet around her – no, that the entire *hall* had gone quiet around her.

Hundreds and hundreds of bulging eyes, staring at her wherever she looked – as if she was some unexpected novelty they had never truly noticed before. As if she hadn't wandered this court for four hundred years, as much a part of it as the hills and the hounds and the twisted trees of Faewood ...

'What?' she managed to force out.

Too loud. The word echoed in the baffled silence.

'The Crimson Court,' Emelin said, her tone alarmingly sweet, her smile alarmingly wide. 'You know it well, don't you? I thought you might like to take over the management of it.'

# CHAPTER 2

BY THE TIME SHE reached the place where the marble floor had cracked open, she no longer knew how she'd ever managed to move her feet.

Tared had unlocked the chains on her wrist without wasting a moment, then nudged her forward, out of the rows of fae and into full view of every mortal and immortal soul gathered in the hall. The audience had erupted in riotous clamour, a hundred shocked, stunned, furious conversations bouncing off the pockmarked walls and ceiling. Thysandra didn't dare to look over her shoulder. Didn't dare to look at the gaping hole in the floor either, which was now emanating an eerie red glow – as if even the Labyrinth below was sharing its opinions on this unexpected development, and unhappy opinions at that.

She kept her gaze trained on Emelin instead, for lack of a better alternative. Agenor's daughter still hadn't stopped smiling – that gods-damned honey-sweet smile that had once convinced even the Mother herself there was nothing dangerous or worrisome about her.

As if she had not just signed Thysandra's death warrant.

As if she had not just outed her as a traitor to the rest of the world, and to what remained of the Mother's most loyal following in particular.

Creon had finally come away from the wall and was now sauntering towards the prisoners, his knife still in his hand, an expression on his face that suggested he was hoping one of them would be stupid enough to challenge him. Thysandra didn't dare to look his way, either. Instead, reeling to a standstill at a safe five feet from the crater's edge, she managed to drag in a shaking breath and stammer, 'But ... but I don't want—'

'Oh, that's not really a factor of concern to me,' Emelin pleasantly interrupted, ambling towards her with still that same unfaltering smile on her face. 'I can't remember you caring greatly about any of my wishes either in the past few months. Any other reasons to object?'

Gods have mercy.

She shouldn't have come here. She should have begged Agenor, Tared, *anyone*, to just slit her throat and be done with it, before this deadly trap could shut around her – but here she stood, alive and well, and somehow she suspected the girl before her would not be terribly impressed with pleas or self-destructive requests. What other way out did she have? It would help little to point out her terrible chances of success or survival, not when those should be perfectly obvious to any soul paying attention; clearly Emelin didn't care much about the possibility of having to sweep in next year to restore order once again.

'Why me?' Thysandra breathed.

Whiny and pathetic. Spoken like the traitor's daughter without a dutiful bone in her body.

Emelin shrugged without making that point. 'Why not?'

'You ... you have no idea whether you can trust me.' It wasn't even a lie. She didn't even know *herself* whether she could be trusted. 'I might attack your own court before the decade is over, for all you know. I might only cause you more trouble. I—'

'Yes,' Emelin admitted, looking not at all discouraged. 'Yes, I suppose you might try all of those things.'

Thysandra stared at her.

Behind her back, someone was howling in pain – one of the other fae prisoners, presumably, after having made just too much fuss over these changes for Creon's taste. Another voice was shouting her name.

It sounded like a demand for her to turn around and explain this madness, for her to justify the apparent trust the Alliance was placing in her.

*Treason*, she would have to say. *Turns out I'm the reason you lost that war.*

Was that why Emelin didn't seem in the least concerned? Did she assume Thysandra's betrayal indicated a complete change of sides, rather than an unfortunate confession blurted out in the throes of emotional turmoil?

Would she be right?

Four centuries of loyalty to the empire, to the courts, to the people living in them ... but did she still have a reason to feel so gods-damned devoted to any of it if the Mother had never been loyal to her in turn?

She had no idea where to even start wondering, let alone who to ask. The Mother's most fervent followers would tear her to shreds the moment she acknowledged her first inkling of doubt. The rest of the empire's courtiers, those who were loyal only to their own interests, would be just as eager to betray her for any small advantage a change in power might bring. Weakness was not permitted at the top, and she'd never been weaker than she was today – she wouldn't last the first month on the throne in this state.

Sweat was trickling between her wings, sticking her grimy, ruined dress to her shoulder blades.

'What if I just ... refuse?' she stammered.

'Wouldn't recommend it,' Emelin said, her voice quiet and polite in a way that alarmingly resembled her father's manner of speaking. When Agenor got that pointedly courteous, things were about to get very, very deadly. 'You see, I have asked the members of the Alliance to remain quiet regarding ... certain pieces of information you've provided us with, in order not to jeopardise your brand new rule of this court. But of course, if there isn't a rule to jeopardise ...'

She let the sentence meaningfully trail away, still looking the height of well-bred innocence as the shouts of fae and the agitated clamour of the audience filled the silence again.

Thysandra barely even heard it.

*If there isn't a rule to jeopardise ...*

So that was why the secret had been kept so far – to wield it as a weapon? Leave it to the alves to make sure the news would erupt in the most explosive of ways when Emelin and her cronies thought the time had come. And then it would be a matter of time until a handful of aggrieved fae loyalists hunted her down and took their revenge for their humiliation in battle; even if she took up residence at the Golden Court, even if she hid away in some cave on some uninhabited fae isle, she didn't think she could hide long enough for them to forget about her.

Death if she refused. Death if she accepted.

She'd thought she no longer cared much about survival, and yet, staring into the gaping maws of that bitter end, she found some last little spark of stubbornness clinging desperately, defiantly, to the drumbeat of her heart.

'Don't worry,' Emelin said, her voice suddenly softer, the forceful cheer moving over for something that looked disconcertingly like genuine concern. 'We're not going to fly off in two minutes to leave you with the mess – we need to unbind the humans and make some other arrangements either way. Take a day to recover. I'm sure the world will look less daunting once you've had a bath and some time to think.'

A *bath*?

Thysandra only just stifled the hysterical laughter welling up in her chest, letting out an involuntary choked hiccough instead. A *bath* was supposed to save her from a knife in the back or a pinch of hemlock in her wine? A day's respite, perhaps, but tomorrow she'd wake up and be all on her own. A single traitor among the vying sycophants and the vicious games for power, with no one to talk to, no one to trust—

'Thysandra.' A glimpse of steely authority – of the girl who had dealt with gods and demons alike and survived them all. 'There'll be time to talk later. Go take a nap.'

Yes.

Gods, yes – *sleep*.

It was almost embarrassing how easily she staggered backwards, away from the gaping crater of the Labyrinth and this nightmare conversation. But her mind latched on to the image of her bed – her own soft, safe bed – and at once she could no longer think of anything else, scheming and secrets be damned ...

'Thank you,' she managed, numbly, not sure what she ought to be grateful for.

Then she was stumbling out of this broken hall, away from the former allies she'd doomed to chains, and the crowd of her enemies obediently parted around her.

The castle hadn't changed since she'd been taken captive, and yet nothing about it still looked the same.

She trudged through the deserted marble corridors, past the splendid halls she knew so well, past the gilded doors and the velvet draperies and the shadowy alcoves, and each and every one of them looked as hollow as a stranger's face. Behind her, the tumult in the bone hall slowly grew distant, then died away. It left only the quieter sounds of the island, the rushing of the sea and the howling of the hounds down in Faewood – none of them loud enough to drown out the haunted screech of her own unwelcome thoughts.

*High Lady of the Crimson Court.*

She wanted to cry.

She wanted to scrub the sound of those words off her skin, the grimy, sticky feeling of them, the guilt and betrayal that only grew heavier as she staggered through the castle that could now be hers.

It wasn't *her* title – that was the problem. It belonged to the Mother, who'd ruled the empire from this seat as long as almost anyone remembered. It was a fact of life, the High Lady's presence on this island, no more changeable than the fact that the sun rose in the east. And now the throne was gone, the bone hall had been smashed to pieces, and what was left was a floundering court, like a ship without its captain ... and Thysandra.

Traitor.

Winner.

All these years she'd dreamed someone, *anyone*, would finally acknowledge the sacrifices she'd made for the empire, that for once no one else would be credited for her own hard work ... and now here it was, the recognition she'd sought, and it felt like a kick in the face. Her betrayal stung worse, somehow, now that she was profiting from it. If she'd simply been banished to the dungeons for the rest of her life ...

Behind her, a door slammed.

A voice she vaguely recognised but couldn't identify from this distance shouted, '*Thysandra!*'

Fuck.

Decisions made themselves in a single panicked heartbeat, the impulse of flight the only reflex still alive in her limbs. Without thinking, she lurched into the nearest room and shoved the door shut behind her wings, reflexively scanning her surroundings for threats and dangers. Some imperial archive, it turned out, mahogany filing cabinets rising to the ceiling around her. Not a place where anyone would look for her. Then again, not a place where she could safely take a nap, either.

Outside the room, the same voice shouted her name again. Who was it – Bereas? The volume gave the impression that the male on her trail was used to shouting across the full length of a racing track.

Had the Alliance allowed their other captives out of the bone hall as well?

Cursing under her breath, she made her way to the window on the other side of the room, drawing a smidge of red from her dress to make the glass vanish. *Red for destruction.* She didn't have the blue at hand to heal the damage again, and couldn't care much about it either; for the first time in weeks, she unfolded her wings, unable to suppress a groan at the cramped stiffness of her shoulder muscles.

Best to take the short route, then.

She clambered onto the windowsill as a handful of doors banged open close-by, her pursuer shouting her name once more. Beneath her, the cliff on which the castle was built descended steeply into the dizzying depths. The tangled, gnarled trees of Faewood stretched out beyond, running from the bare rocks all the way down to the southside beach – a sight that hadn't made her wince for centuries, and yet on this cursed morning, she couldn't even glance at it without remembering …

Father.

Wings clipped, legs broken, shouting her name again and again as they threw him to the snarling hounds below.

*He should have known better than to betray us, Thysandra*, the Mother had told her afterwards, so sweet and gentle, stroking her head as she sobbed in the High Lady's lap. *His death could not be avoided. But we won't let him drag you down with him, sweetheart – we'll find you something to do around the court …*

And then after centuries of loyal servitude, after she'd fought and bled and wept for the empire every single day of her life, that gods-damned letter had arrived, written in the Mother's hand.

*A traitor's daughter.*

She gritted her teeth and jumped.

Her scarred wings were stiff and cramped against the cool morning air, stinging her shoulders as she swept them wide and found her balance on the gentle breeze. But at least she was out of that room, away from Bereas, and—

A cry went up beneath her.

Two winged silhouettes launched themselves from a lower terrace, soaring her way.

Fuck. Perhaps she'd been too quick to celebrate.

She slapped her wings against the air currents with a desperate effort, cursing at the agonised cramping of her muscles but unwilling to slow down and find out what the two fast-approaching fae thought of her recent rise in the ranks. Never mind about the short route, then. If people were looking for her, she was too visible flying. Better to make it to the nearest floor of her tower, take a sprint up the stairs, and hope she didn't run into anyone else before she reached the safe haven of her rooms – assuming, of course, that no one was unhappy enough to break through her defences to have a word with her …

Worries for later. Her assailants were close enough to be recognised now – gods-damned Orthea and some fae girl whose name she didn't know – shouting about traitors and urgent strategies to deal with them.

Not the moment to find out if it was herself they were talking about.

Her landing on the nearest balcony was more of a crash, clumsy to the point of humiliation. She refused to care. A flicker of red into the lock and she swung the double doors open, bursting into the space behind without spending a moment's thought on whoever's private quarters she was entering. She realised her mistake only three steps into the room, as the stark white walls and the stark white floor finally registered themselves in her conscious mind.

She'd stepped into the nursery.

The fucking *nursery*.

The place where her life had fallen apart a second time, forty years after her traitor father's death – where she'd stood beside that stark white cot and stared at the uncannily powerful child sleeping in it, with his rumpled little wings and soft white gloves to prevent him from drawing colour and blowing up the whole damn tower. Cooing courtiers around her. Gifts piling up on the shelves. And no one, not even the people she'd thought her friends, had given her so much as a glance now that the Mother's favour had moved elsewhere ...

It was here, in this very room, that she had wondered whether perhaps the High Lady would notice her again, show her even a fraction of the praise and attention she'd been given before, if someone were to smother her gods-damned son in his cradle and feed his little body to the hounds down the hill.

It didn't matter how swiftly she fled the room. There was no escaping the memories the sight of it brought along, so laughably skewed after all she'd learned in the past few days. She'd been so sure – so unerringly sure – that *Creon* was to blame for her downfall, that *Creon* had cut off her way to the top and stolen the love that was rightfully hers ... And so it was Creon she'd hated. She'd worked harder, sacrificed her sleep and her scruples and her sanity, all in the stubborn hope the Mother would one day realise that her son was a spoiled little arsehole, and that Thysandra was the only person she would always be able to depend upon.

Except it turned out that there had been no love to steal in the first place.

Worse, that the Mother had never really loved Creon, either.

*Of course she knew*, Naxi had said sweetly as Thysandra sat shaking and crying in that underground cell, the words from the letter echoing through her mind. *Of course she saw exactly how desperate you were to regain her favour. But why would she save you when ignoring your pain was only motivating you to work harder for her? Why would she tell you she was the one to blame when you were happy to loathe Creon instead and continue to be her useful doormat?*

And why was she thinking of gods-damned Naxi again?

The twisting staircase and mosaic walls blurred to smudges of black and red and gold around her, tears stinging in the corners of her eyes as she forced herself to keep climbing. Naxi, who had noticed her when no one else had. Naxi, who had understood her pain so impossibly well. Naxi, who had soothed and coaxed and tempted, until at long last Thysandra had talked and told the little vixen exactly what she needed to know ...

And then she'd vanished.

Like demons did.

It was a miracle she didn't stumble as she floundered up the last stairs, hands slipping on the cold golden railing, knees shaking with exhaustion. The voices crying out her name downstairs had gone quiet. Perhaps they had realised she might very well slit their throats if they made the mistake of coming too close now; perhaps they had realised she was a traitor after all, and had tiptoed off to make their plans for violent rebellion elsewhere.

She would find out tomorrow, presumably.

If she even survived the night.

There it was, finally, the door to her rooms – its red wood and carved frame looking no different from any of the other doors in this tower, and yet she almost sobbed with relief at the sight. Finally, *finally*, she could at least get out of this fucking dress. Take a nap. Think things through. Sleep some more and then consider her options without any so-called allies attempting to use her for their own ends ...

*High Lady of the Crimson Court.*

The idea still sounded like a joke.

Casting a last cautious look over her shoulder, she pressed her left fingers to her dress and drew a spark of red, aiming the magic at the secret spot between door and frame. Three soft clicks from beneath the wood told her the lock mechanism had survived the weeks of her absence, that unique piece of fae craftsmanship the Mother had commissioned for her when the nightmares wouldn't fade in the months after her father's death.

A single nudge was enough. The door swept open as if she'd never been gone.

It was as unchanged as anything else about the castle, the safe haven of the room waiting for her beyond. Her plants still stood rustling in the high-arched windows. The sunlight still glinted off her green quartz wall. Her half-read books on the table, her slippers on the plush white rug, and—

Her gaze hit the worn velvet couch.

Her feet froze mid-step.

For one last fraction of a moment she could still tell herself it was the tiredness, the shock, her wrung-out mind playing tricks on her. Of course there was no little half demon sitting curled up on her very own couch. That was patently impossible. The door had been locked, and the windows had not been tampered with, either. She must be seeing things, already half in a dream, and if she just pinched herself—

The phantom image moved.

*Smiled.*

Stretching out lazily in the cushions, looking not unlike a contented housecat after a long day of catching mice, Naxi cooed, 'Morning, Sashka.'

# CHAPTER 3

IF SOMEONE HAD PUSHED a whetted dagger to her throat, her body could not have reacted more vehemently.

It was that sharp-toothed smile. The brush of golden sunlight over pink-blonde hair. Most of all, the sound of that gods-damned nickname from those gods-damned rosebud lips, savoured with a sweetness that glossed over a century and a half of hostility – a sound that after all these years still filled her with a maddening echo of softness, of pleasure, of *safety*.

Her heart leapt into her throat. At once, her hands were clammy, not with fear but rather with the certainty that came one step beyond fear – the *knowledge* of imminent trouble.

Which Naxi had to know.

Those demon senses could register every goosebump, every prickle of cold sweat ... and yet the deadly little creature on her couch was still smiling that same bubbly smile. As if her appearance was the happy surprise of the century. As if she hadn't pulled out all solid ground from beneath Thysandra's feet two days ago, then left her to rot in that prison cell as soon as her games had led to the betrayal she needed.

As if her pretence of kindness had ever meant *anything*.

It was that thought that broke the paralysis, a much-needed flare of anger that had Thysandra turn on her heel, slam the door shut, and snap, 'How did you get in here?'

'Oh, don't be so alarmed,' Naxi breezily said, draping herself over an armrest and tucking her chin into the palm of a small, rosy hand. Her blonde-and-pink curls bounced around her slender shoulders, the result a fraction tousled in the most deliberate of ways. 'Your newly appointed subjects don't know how to open your door, I promise. Creon helped me get in.'

*Subjects.*

Gods help her.

And only then did the next sentence land, impossibly *more* alarming than the disastrous title of High Lady of the Crimson Court that had just been dumped onto her shoulders – because what in the world was Creon doing, helping people get into *her* rooms? Since when did the bastard even know how to open her door? And what in the world had made him think that *this* was the company she needed right now, some treacherous little half demon beaming at her when all she wanted was to take a bath and hide beneath her blankets for the rest of the day ...

Had Emelin known?

Really, what were the chances she *hadn't* known, when her lover and foremost ally had colluded on the plan? Perhaps even Agenor had been aware. Tared, chuckling behind her. All of the Alliance, laughing themselves to stitches over the next curveball about to hit her in the face.

'Get out,' she numbly said.

Naxi snorted a laugh. 'No.'

'Oh, for fuck's *sake*.' It took all she had not to drain the last reserve of colour from her now dark pink dress and obliterate both the couch and the unwelcome visitor on it. As tempting as the impulse might be, she'd likely be too slow to surprise her sort-of-nemesis, and she knew how their last fight had ended. Instead, she clenched her fists and bit out, 'What do you need from me this time, then? More secrets? More treason? More heartfelt confessions you can use against me whenever the time comes?'

'Oh, you wound me,' Naxi drawled, not looking particularly wounded at all as she dreamily twisted a pink curl around her finger. 'Is it that unthinkable that I might just want to keep you company? Now that the Mother has helpfully kicked the bucket and we're technically no longer enemies, I figured—'

'Technically?' A razor-sharp laugh burst from Thysandra's throat. 'You're turning this thing between us into a matter of *technicality*? Never mind the fact that we don't even *like* each other? That we've never spoken an amicable word to each other? That—'

If Naxi hadn't been so gods-damned deadly, the abrupt shift of her expression might have been amusing – from mirthful carelessness to the shocked, indignant pout of an innocent accused. 'I *comforted* you!'

'Yes, until I fucking talked! And then you vanished!'

'Because you told me to!' A newborn lamb could not have looked more blamelessly aggrieved; those wide blue eyes, more nymph than demon, suddenly gleamed dangerously. 'You screamed at me to get out of your sight! So I thought I'd mercifully give you some time alone, even though of *course* I'd rather have stayed with you – I even told the rest of the Alliance not to disturb you while you were coming to terms with yourself ...'

Her voice died away, wobbling with perfectly calculated emotion. Or perhaps there was no calculation behind it at all, and that was an even more disconcerting thought – because fine, there *had* been some mention of being left alone in peace in that cell, and admittedly, the volume of the conversation *had* reached a point that some might hypothetically describe as shouting ...

Oh, fuck.

How did the little terror always manage to twist these interactions into the same tangled arguments, into the constant, inevitable conclusion that Thysandra had no one to blame for her troubles but herself?

'I didn't expect you to give a damn about my requests,' she ground out, unable to think of anything better but similarly unable to back down. 'I told you to leave me alone every single time you visited me these past weeks, and you always came back.'

Naxi's eyes narrowed abruptly – a keen, almost *hungry* motion, like a predator catching sight of its prey. 'Are you saying you wanted me to come back?'

'Not at all! I just—'

'That you were *counting* on me to come back, then?'

'There was a pattern,' Thysandra snapped, her wings whooshing against the air as she whipped around and strode into her bedroom to snatch a hairbrush off her dressing table. Tears sprang into her eyes as she yanked it through her tangled black locks – but at least that simple, physical pain was a much, *much* better reason to cry than the manipulative games of a female who could by her very nature not be trusted to ever care about anyone else. 'And you didn't break the habit until I'd served my purpose, at which point you dropped me like a hot coal – so excuse me for assuming—'

An unexpected giggle followed her from the living room. 'You're angry, aren't you?'

'Don't know how you fucking noticed it!' she bit back, clenching her brush even more tightly. It didn't stop her hand from trembling. 'One would almost think you could magically sense emotions, with those subtle clues you're picking up.'

There was a suspicious undertone of amusement in Naxi's hum. 'If you're angry I didn't come back, that suggests you *did* want me to come back, doesn't it?'

'It suggests I'm sick of being manipulated and lied to!' Thysandra burst out, striding back into the living room and only barely suppressing the urge to fling her hairbrush at the infuriatingly dainty face waiting for her on the couch. 'Weren't you the one who told me the Mother didn't deserve my loyalty? Who told me I might as well abandon her since she had abandoned me first? So how are thing different when it's *your* vile little games we're talking about, exactly? How are we suddenly *technically* former enemies when all you've ever done is exploit my feelings and weaknesses for your own bloody benefit?'

A resounding silence fell.

Only then did she realise she had once again nudged dangerously close to the point of shouting; an uncharitable listener might even argue she had already arrived there. The distance between herself and the couch had somehow shrunk to a mere few steps. Even worse, the target of her ire hadn't moved at all – as if this was nothing but a cosy chat between friends, a matter of routine among old acquaintances.

Of course, they technically *were* old acquaintances. If one didn't mind that they hadn't exchanged so much as a word for most of that time, it *had* been a hundred and thirty years since their meeting at the Last Battle – since the day Thysandra had cut her own wings to shreds to fight that torturous demon magic, the day they ought to have been killing each other but instead had—

A most unwelcome flare of heat ran through her.

Naxi giggled again. 'I'm pretty sure I did some other things to you, too, Sashka. You seem to remember.'

For fuck's sake.

'Get out,' she said through clenched teeth. 'I don't have the patience for this nonsense.'

'That's a shame,' Naxi cheerfully admitted, tilting her head in an unnecessarily inviting manner as she nestled her lithe body more comfortably between the velvet cushions. 'I was just getting started. And honestly, if you did not actually want me to leave the last time you yelled at me, then why should I trust you to actually mean it this time? For all I know you'll scold me in two days for—'

'I just want some time to *sleep*,' Thysandra hissed, realising her mistake only when she saw the radiant grin beaming back at her in response.

'Alone?'

'Yes, alone!' The heated twist of her heart really did not help. 'I don't have time for these bloody games, alright? They just named me High Lady of this gods-damned court, and the first rivals will probably be knocking at my door the moment the Alliance leaves – so the *least* I need before then is a few hours of—'

'Ah, yes,' Naxi interrupted, lashes fluttering innocently against her soft, rosy cheeks. 'Rivals. Intrigue. Backstabbing courtiers. You could probably use someone you can trust on your side, then, couldn't you?'

It took an inhuman effort not to scoff or to throw that hairbrush after all. 'And I'm supposed to believe that I would be able to trust you?'

'Why not?' Again that pout, plump and petulant and so pointedly innocent it was almost aggressive in its harmlessness. 'Have I ever done anything to hurt you?'

'You're a *demon*!' Thysandra sputtered, which was perhaps not as persuasive a point as *remember that time you almost strangled me during the Last Battle?* or *how about when you crushed my every goal and motivation in life by showing me a single short letter?* but seemed more than sufficient all the same. 'You're incapable of feeling empathy! Which means you're incapable of love and loyalty, too! If you haven't harmed me yet, it's because I haven't been in your way enough, and the moment I *do* end up between you and some greater goal ...'

Naxi shrugged. 'What if you are my greater goal?'

Oh, *fuck.*

It was infuriating, the way that simple question – wide-eyed and light-hearted – still managed to make her heart skip a beat. As if she hadn't spent almost a century and a half attempting to squash this reckless, senseless longing. As if she didn't know damn well that a demon's infatuation never reached any further than one's use to them, that as soon as the novelty wore off, she'd be cast aside all over ...

*Again.*

Something inside her shrivelled, a feeling so dark it hurt to even glimpse it.

'You're being utterly ridiculous.' Her voice cracked. 'Just because we fucked once doesn't mean you know anything about me, let alone that I mean anything to you – so for the very last time, *get out of*—'

'Do you need me to prove it?' Naxi suggested, pulling up her knees so that her flowery skirt fell around her hips, revealing far, far too much of her pale, silky thighs. It had to be deliberate, that guileless gleam in her blue eyes – as if her demon senses had gone conveniently blind at this worst possible moment. 'That I really won't betray you to any aspirant High Lords or Ladies if you decide to trust me?'

'I need you to fucking leave! How many more times do I—'

'You see,' Naxi continued, unperturbed, 'the core of the matter is that keeping you alive and healthy *is* in my own best interests, considering that you—'

It wasn't even a plan.

It was a desperate hunch, her only way to save herself from this all too tempting trap drawing shut around her – from those cornflower eyes promising a loyalty she knew did not and would never exist. Three steps and she'd reached the potted begonia by the window. It had been years since she'd hidden that particular dagger, yet her fingers wrapped around the leather hilt as if it had been yesterday, and she pulled it from between the bright red flowers without hesitation.

The blade settled against her own throat the next moment.

On the couch, Naxi froze mid-word.

'There.' Thysandra barely recognised her own voice, so shrill and garbled were the words that escaped. 'That's your chance to prove how much you care. Either you leave, or I cut myself. So if you truly want to keep me alive and well ...'

Naxi's laugh was low and razor-sharp. 'That's a little crude, isn't it?'

'Five,' Thysandra spat out, trying not to notice the thin steel edge trembling against her skin. No time to feel doubt. If she felt doubt, those fucking demon senses would know. 'Four. Three—'

'Oh, *fine*,' Naxi interrupted on a drawn-out wail, rolling her eyes as she hauled herself off the couch and shook her curls down her back. She skipped to the unlocked door like some modest village maiden, her dress fluttering after her. 'Have it your way, Sashka. I'll find myself something else to do in the meantime. Let me know when you realise you're going to need my help around this place.'

*When.*

Thysandra didn't dare to lower the knife as she hoarsely said, 'I think you mean *if*.'

'Oh, no.' There was nothing but wickedness in that sharp-toothed grin, not a glimmer of rosy innocence to be found. 'No, I certainly mean *when*.'

And with that prediction, or warning, or possibly threat, the door slammed shut behind her slender back.

It did not matter how tired Thysandra was. It didn't matter that her knees kept shaking uncontrollably long after Naxi's light footsteps had danced down the stairs and out of hearing distance, or that her heart wouldn't settle even after she'd lowered the dagger from her throat and chucked it into the far end of the room.

Before she sat down, she checked her defences.

She had never failed to do so in the four-hundred-and-thirteen years of her life.

First the door, the ingenious lock system and the russet wood, treated with a sprinkle of the Mother's godsworn powers to prevent anyone from breaking through with red magic. Then the windows, reinforced in the same way. Then the daggers hidden around the room, over a dozen of them, in drawers and books and vases, ready to be grabbed at the slightest alarm. Each blade was where it ought to be, at least; nothing seemed to have been moved.

*Creon helped me get in.*

She'd just have to hope the Mother's traitor son had satisfied his thirst for revenge with that little surprise. Against powers like his, there was no preparing; if he was able to force himself into the sanctuary of her rooms, she would be done for if he decided he'd rather see her dead after all.

A shiver trailed down her spine. Bastard.

But he'd let Emelin name her High Lady of the Crimson Court, and so she had to assume he was planning to keep her alive for now – she clung to that thought as she checked the locks on the doors and windows one last time and shut the curtains. Only then, *finally*, did she strip the grimy red dress off her body. The once-flowy fabric was stiff with mud and sweat and blood, as if the garment had tried to shape itself into armour against her skin.

She dropped it to the floor, then swung a burst of red magic at it. The dress vanished as if it had never existed.

It didn't erase the memory of that cell from her mind.

She staggered into the bathroom and turned the tap fully open, inhaling the smell of lavender salts and clean towels as she waited for the tub to fill. Even that couldn't slow her heartbeat. The minutes were ticking themselves away around her, bringing her closer and closer to the moment the Alliance would leave the court and she would be left to save herself from the viper's den. *If* she wanted to flee, she'd have to do it before that time ... but then again, where in the world would she flee to?

Shreds of voices reached her from outside the room. She held her breath as she lowered her naked body into the warm water, prepared for whoever was out there to break through the walls any moment.

Nothing happened.

*Yet*, she corrected her own thoughts.

By the time she'd scrubbed all the dirt from her hair and limbs, the bath water was as dark as her skin. She rinsed off and dried herself quickly, shot into her nightclothes, then checked the space beneath her bed and the dagger under her pillow one last time. No attackers were lying in wait for her. Her weapons were still where they ought to be.

Fists banged on her door just as she curled up beneath her blankets.

She pulled the sheets up to her ears as if they could protect her from those violent sounds, from the voices yelling her name, the unmistakable thuds of punches thrown between whoever were trying to reach her. Like the little girl who'd been all alone at this treacherous court, the little girl who'd just seen her father torn to bloody shreds, she squeezed her eyes shut and wrapped her wings tightly around herself, willing the world to disappear.

Willing herself to become invisible.

She shouldn't have been able to sleep as the hubbub grew louder around her tower. Centuries and centuries of training, of habitual alertness, should not have allowed her to. But she'd spent too many nights on that hard, narrow bench bed in the Alliance's hideaway, and even her heart had grown exhausted of its own rattling and pounding. Now, hidden between the warm, downy blankets of her own familiar bed, her body pulled her into slumber within minutes, forcing her into a semblance of rest that her mind could not find.

The world had gone dark and quiet when she woke up, the fists and voices vanished. No holes in the walls and doors. No knives against her throat. No demons by her bedside, smiling sweet smiles and spinning tempting fairytales of commitments that she could never, *never* afford to believe in.

Her thoughts, miraculously, had gone equally still.

She felt as if she was still dreaming when she slipped out of bed and made her way back to the living room through the eerie, mournful silence, the floorboards cold beneath her bare feet. But her damp towel was there, proof she truly had taken that much-needed bath. Her tangled, black-and-gold hairs still stuck in her hairbrush. Her dagger still lay where she'd chucked it away after chasing Naxi out of her rooms.

Which meant the rest of it still had to be true as well.

*High Lady of the Crimson Court.*

There was no more disbelief left inside her. No more anger and grief. She sank into the plush velvet of her couch, hollow and cold, and let the words play through her mind again and again, breathing them, exploring their ragged edges under her fingertips.

Thysandra Thenessa. Traitor's daughter. Demonbane. High Lady of the Crimson Court.

In the world she knew and understood, there was not a single way for that sequence of titles to make sense. But the world she knew and understood was gone ... and soon, very soon, the consequences would arrive at this court, not nearly as heroic as bloody battles or trials for traitors, but potentially far more deadly. No more human tributes delivering food. No more servants working to clean, to build, to organise. If no one took up the reins, the court would descend into violent chaos within weeks – and the rest of the archipelago would be all too glad for an excuse to sweep in again and burn the whole place to the ground.

So if the island she called her home was to be saved, *someone* would have to step up and save it.

Could she do it?

It seemed unlikely, when, for all her cunning and godsworn magic, even the Mother had lost the battle in the end. Yet the fear wouldn't stir, even as she rose and padded quietly to the arched windows – the wary movements of her limbs not enough to ripple the flat, almost lifeless surface of her emotions.

The island stretched out below her when she nudged aside the curtains, the familiar landscape serene and strangely unchanged in the silvery moonlight. There was the rugged mountain range at the heart of the territory, running westward from the castle. The spiderwebs of light on the north coast, drawing the outlines of fae and human settlements. The darkness of Faewood in the south and the single brighter blot of Creon's home. She knew every single inch of the view like the palm of her hand, yet tonight, it looked as still and lifeless as the void inside her – as if even the cliffs and the trees were holding their breath, waiting for the world to finish shifting around them.

She could make it stop.

All she had to do was accept it.

It might kill her within weeks, taking the throne ... but then, what alternative did she have? If she ran, the revelation of her treason would end her just as quickly. Falling on her sword to avoid the choice would merely be a swifter path to the same outcome. So if she had no better option either way, she might as well try. She might as well fight.

And if she did ...

36

The glass was pleasantly cold against her skin as she rested her forehead against the window, drawing in the crisp air of the night – deeper and deeper, until she felt her lungs might explode with it. If she was going to try ...

Damn it all, then she was going to do it *well.*

Because she might be a traitor's daughter, she might be a turncoat set up to fail – but she *did* know how to play this game. She had never played anything else. So she would forge the right alliances and make the right bargains and fight the right battles ... and who knew? Perhaps that would save her for a while.

If she was careful, if she stayed far away from meddling demons and their pretty promises, she might even make it to the end of the year alive.

It was as if her thoughts had been in shackles, too, and hadn't been unchained until this moment – until finally, *finally*, the mist and the noise lifted from around her. For the very first time since Agenor had pulled her from her cell, the pieces were moving across her mind again. Not yet playing the game but finding their places on the board – getting ready to strike and strategize.

Tonight, she would think.

Tonight, she would rest.

And tomorrow ...

Damn it all. Tomorrow, she'd be Thysandra Demonbane, High Lady of the Crimson Court, and reap the fruits of her treason.

# CHAPTER 4

DAWN ARRIVED IN SHADES of orange and ruby-red, as if even the sky itself wished to celebrate her wretched rise to power. By the time the sun came peeking over the horizon, Thysandra was out of bed and fully awake – her spine and wings still sore from her prison stay below the earth but her mind almost *peaceful*, and infinitely clearer with concrete goals to focus on.

Save the court.

Save its people.

And maybe, if she was very, very lucky, save herself as well.

Food would have to be the first priority, she had decided after hours of nocturnal rumination; not even the Mother's most vehement loy-alists bent on reconquering the archipelago would want to do it on empty stomachs. So they would have to take stock of the meat and grain stores. Figure out how much food was coming from their own fae isles and how much more they would need to survive the upcoming winter. Then it would be a matter of rationing and perhaps closing some trade deals with the recently separated territories, who would doubtlessly demand outrageous prices for the grain ...

But it would just be for a few months, while they prepared to become self-sufficient. She could probably find support for that. Even if she had no desire whatsoever to start another war, there was no reason to tell the loyalists just yet, and—

Knuckles hammered against her door.

She'd jumped up from the couch before the last sharp thud sounded.

An attack? A warning? With one step, she'd reached her nearest dagger, fingers curling around the worn hilt in a smooth, thoughtless reflex – no one to be seen at the windows, a quick glance over her shoulder told her. Which meant she had an escape route if she needed one. Although of course, she would be more vulnerable in the open air, and—

'Thysandra?'

She froze.

A hushed male voice. Quiet but urgent, slightly out of breath and ... *familiar*.

'Are you awake?' the visitor at her door added after a beat of silence, a little louder now – and it was then, with an impossible burst of panic and relief at once, that she recognised that smooth, elegant lilt.

Nicanor. Commander of the Mother's third regiment.

Not someone who would be trying to murder her in her sleep, that was the good news ... but there was a certain awkwardness to interacting with a male who'd spent time in her bed for entirely different reasons. She'd fucked him only in some desperate attempt to forget about Naxi after the mess of the Last Battle and ended their fling when the effort turned out to be hopeless – but of course she hadn't informed him of her motives, and worse, she doubted he'd be opposed to resuming the affair.

Why was *he* here? An attempt to use that shameful bit of shared history to his own benefit, now that she had unexpectedly risen to a position of power?

Did it matter?

He was a potential ally. She couldn't afford to leave him standing on her doorstep.

'What is it?' she yelled, steeling herself.

'Oh, thank the fucking gods.' A mirthless laugh, or perhaps more of a scoff. She could imagine the expression on his pale face even with a door between them – the hint of a habitual sneer on his lips, the narrowing of his ice-blue eyes. 'We've got somewhat of an emergency at hand. It's the Alliance's demon.'

Her heart skipped a violent beat.

An *emergency?*

With the Alliance's demon. But that meant—

'Which one?' she stammered, grateful that at least he couldn't see her face, that at least her words did not betray the savage pounding of her heart. Fuck. *Fuck.* 'They seem to have multiple, these days.'

A hopeless, pathetic attempt at denying the inevitable. Nicanor wouldn't have described Creon as *the Alliance's demon.* And it seemed unlikely that anyone else had emerged out of nowhere with those cursed powers, deciding for no reason to haunt the halls of her court and torment the people in it ...

*When*, Naxi had said.

Cold certainty was creeping up her veins.

'Whatever she's called. The half nymph one.' A soft thud suggested Nicanor was resting his lithe weight against the doorframe outside. 'Apparently Hytherion and the others left her behind when the rest of them ran off a few hours ago. We didn't realise it at first, but it seems she's gone on ... a bit of a murder spree since.'

The rapid thumps of her heart were blurring to a nauseating drone. *I'll find something else to do*, Naxi had said, with that saccharine, meaningful smile. *Have it your way.*

*When.*

Fuck, fuck, fuck.

'What happened?' Her trembling hands fought with the sash of her morning robe, yanked the dark green silk off her limbs. Green wouldn't do outside these rooms. If she was to be the High Lady of this court, she couldn't look anything less than frightening. 'Who's died? And why?'

'No fucking clue.' Again he let out that sharp, joyless laugh. 'By the time we found the fifteenth corpse clawing out its own eyes, I was no longer really in the mood to go ask her. She's taken up position in the

40

bone hall right now. Figured you might have a better idea of how to approach her, given your history with her.'

Thysandra winced.

He was talking about the history *he* knew, of course, the version of events that had earned her this cursed nickname of Demonbane. As far as the court was aware, she'd spent most of the Last Battle valiantly fighting Naxi, keeping her away from the hundreds of others the demon might have killed on the battlefield instead.

The truth ...

Naked skin. Heated kisses. Yet another secret the Alliance could spread whenever they felt like ruining her reputation among her peers; she'd lived with the shame for so long that she hadn't even realised it yesterday.

'Fuck,' she said, out loud this time.

'Succinct but accurate,' Nicanor sourly agreed. 'Mind opening the door? I promise I don't have anyone else with me, if that's your concern.'

Promises were worth about as much as mud at the Crimson Court ... but it didn't make sense for him to lie if his report of events was true, and the story fit her conversation with Naxi too well for it to be a fabrication.

'Give me half a minute,' she said.

It took a little longer to find her favourite dress from her bulging wardrobe – an ankle-length, mulberry-coloured creation with sparkling red flower patterns stitched up along the left side. The skirts hid two niftily placed dagger sheaths. She filled them both, then opened her jewellery case and snatched out the ring that she'd worn on the day of the Last Battle as well: gold, with two razor-sharp spikes curling elegantly around her finger.

The perfect tool to slash one's own wings, among many other uses.

Her hair was passable, she decided with a single glimpse in the mirror, and she should probably not let Nicanor wait any longer without a very good reason. She swept a last trace of down off the gold-black surface of her left wing. Pulled on a clean pair of boots on her way to the door. Drew in a last deep breath, then braced herself and opened the lock – instinctively scanning the full length of the stairwell before she moved even an inch past the threshold.

Nicanor was alone as promised, leaning against the wall in a most decorative manner, frosty blue wings folded meticulously against his shoulders. His long, silver-white braid was unruffled. His half-smile held its usual unimpressed, derisive edge. But there was blood on the cuff of his silk shirt, and more on his leather boots; the mere fact that he hadn't bothered to pause and restore his usual pristine appearance was in itself a sign of the greatest alarm.

His eyes slid over her in a single impassive – albeit undeniably appreciative – glance as he straightened, adjusted his wings, and added, 'And good morning, Thys.'

She gave him a look.

'Thysandra,' he amended, lips curling ever so slightly into a smile that was somehow both remorseful and full of mocking amusement. 'Or do you prefer the title these days?'

'The title can go to hell,' she muttered.

He sniggered and turned his back towards her as she shut the door – a request she'd made ages ago and that he'd never tried to argue against, even in the midst of their one-sided love affair. He, too, knew how to play the game at court. Trust was a currency, and one far more expensive than simple physical desire or even respect; they could be friends, allies, partners, and there was still not a single reason for him to know the mechanism of her locks.

'Alright,' she added in a low voice as she finished and joined him, heading for the winding stairs. The tower seemed deserted apart from the two of them, although there was plenty of shouting to be heard in the distance. 'Any more details on what's happened?'

'I was alerted some two hours ago,' he said, shifting seamlessly into his no-nonsense soldier's demeanour as he shook his braid over his slim shoulders. 'Took us all a while to realise what was going on, because Bereas and his friends were making the rounds and killing a bunch of Alliance sympathisers at the same time ... but then one of *them* got killed and it became clear they were not the only ones at work.'

*Traitor's daughter.*

She forced herself to breathe slowly. 'Do you know how many she killed?'

'At least forty, from what I've heard so far. We may be finding more of them.' He grimaced. 'By the time we managed to locate her at the end of the trail of corpses, she was already making her way down to the hall.'

Good gods.

Should she have seen it coming? *She* was the one who'd spent decades studying demons – yet another doomed attempt to demonstrate her superiority over Creon and the very blood in his veins. Of course she should have realised that Naxi's ruthless mind would always come up with some new dramatic plan to draw all the attention back to herself. A few lives lost ... well, those were of no consequence, were they? Not for demons. Not for creatures that, by their very nature, could not care about anyone else's feelings.

'Did you find any pattern in the identity of the victims?' she made herself say.

All the right, sensible questions. As if she wasn't half to blame for this catastrophe herself. The Mother's trusted do-all, looking into yet another run-of-the-mill court crime. Who cared that this time the perpetrator was the same female who'd held her as she sobbed in her cell two days ago, the same female whose pretty pink lips she'd felt in her dreams for *decades*?

'Still looking into that,' Nicanor was saying, his footsteps inaudible against the polished tiles as they hurried down the stairs. Around them, shadows lurked in every bay and niche. 'There must be *some* pattern, I figure, because she didn't just take down everyone in her way – she seems to have entered specific bedrooms over the course of the night. The only common factor we've found so far is that most of them were in the army at some point, but there are plenty of soldiers she *didn't*—'

Thysandra stiffened.

He almost bumped into her, wings flaring out as he swivelled off-course just in time to avoid her. 'Thysandra?'

Soldiers.

Oh, gods help her – how could she have been *this* fucking blind?

'None of them were very young, were they?' she choked out through the roar of her thoughts spiralling into more and more alarming conjectures. 'Old enough to have been in the army three centuries ago, at least?'

Nicanor frowned. 'Now that you mention it, I think so? But—'

'And do you know' – she had to fight the urge to close her eyes and crawl away into the nearest dark, dusty corner – 'whether any of them were members of the sixth regiment around that period?'

He stared at her.

'*Nicanor.*' Her voice cracked.

'I'm not sure—' He interrupted himself with an impatient, agitated headshake and started again, eyes narrowing in frustration. 'Well, Theone was, of course. And Cercyon, now that I think of it, and—'

She cursed, resuming their descent twice as fast.

'What the hell is the matter with the sixth?' Unusual, for impassive, calculating Nicanor to let so much of his frustration show as he hurried after her. The ugly sight of demon deaths hadn't been enough to throw him off-balance. Ignorance, on the other hand, was doing the trick flawlessly. 'What do you know that I don't—'

'Mirova,' she said through gritted teeth.

'What?' He caught up with her with two agitated slaps of his icy blue wings. 'The island?'

'Yes. The sixth was the regiment that destroyed it during that retaliation attack three hundred years ago.' An infuriating sign of weakness, to admit she'd looked up every detail she could find after Naxi's accusations during the Last Battle – but then, the male beside her didn't need to know why she'd gathered the information. 'I suppose she must have looked up their names in our archives while the Alliance was here and then simply ... worked down the list.'

'But why in the world would a demon care about some nymph isle that— *Oh.*' The last word came out breathless. 'Oh, fuck. A *nymph* isle?'

Thysandra didn't even bother to answer.

They had reached the foot of the stairs, finally, and hurried into the frescoed corridor that lay beyond. Wild, violent, chalk paintings on the walls, images she knew too well to even glance at them ... and on the black marble of the floor, as if to mirror the artist's vision, the carnage Naxi had left behind.

*Ugly* didn't begin to cover the sight.

There were six bodies in this corridor alone, lying curled up on the red-veined marble, their blood smeared across the tiles. Most had been killed by blades, their own dead hands clutching the hilts of their swords and daggers. One seemed to have ripped out her own throat in her hurry to escape the agony of demon torture, and one had apparently bashed his own head against the wall until he died. Their faces, no matter how different their features, were all the same: lips wrenched open in soundless screams, wide eyes gaping unseeingly into the pits of hell.

Demon victims. No doubt.

She'd seen so many of them over the years of her research. She'd read every book in existence about demon magic, the manipulation of emotions that could reduce the bravest of warriors to a wreck pleading for death within a matter of seconds.

Gall welled in her throat all the same.

Other fae were standing around the victims, their hunched postures and haunted glances a jarring contrast to their sparkling clothes and decadent jewels. The looks they gave her as she passed ... Caution. Envy. Distrust. Resentment. Nothing she hadn't expected from the scheming courtiers who'd still been her peers yesterday, and yet she suspected this hadn't helped – the explosion of violence under what was technically her rule and protection.

*When.*

To think that, ten minutes ago, she'd believed food stores would be her greatest problem.

She kept her expression stony as she strode down the halls and staircases, a shield against every accusing glare, every muffled curse. No one spoke up – not yet. It was a test, of course, all of this. An assessment, even through the shock and the dismay, of just how well she would deal with this unprecedented threat, and how much of a threat that made *her* in turn, whether she'd be best approached with violence or flattery. If she made the mistake of coming across as weak or helpless ...

It would be a matter of days before the vultures descended.

'Could you do me a favour?' she muttered to Nicanor.

She'd pay for it later. Former lover or no, he was too savvy to ignore a promising opportunity like this, the obligations that came with services rendered to the crown. But for now he nodded without hesitation, his expression cool and composed again – the usual haughty, elegant indifference, as if they weren't walking past a handful of corpses with their own nails in their eyes.

'Please keep everyone away from the bone hall,' she said, taking care not to move her lips for the benefit of the gathered fae around her. 'Out of hearing distance, at the very least. Tell them it's to protect them from her demon influence, if necessary.'

His quick side-glance was proof enough he'd noticed the half-heartedness of that explanation. 'You don't want anyone to hear you?'

'I don't want anyone to hear *her*,' Thysandra said, which was true, although he was admittedly not wrong, either. But her own words she could control, at least. Gods knew what Naxi would blurt out, and with a castle poised to turn against her, she didn't need any true accounts of the Last Battle to leak. 'I would like to understand her motives here, and she'll speak more freely if she can't sense anyone near.'

'I see.' If he was suspicious, he hid it well – but then again, of *course* he would hide it well. Yet another factor to worry about at a later time. 'I'll keep them away from the hall, then. If she does attack you, though ...'

'If she does attack me,' Thysandra wryly said, 'all of you put together wouldn't be able to save me. Best to stay far away and send a message to Creon if you hear me scream.'

The expression on his pointy face could not have been unhappier if she'd pushed a rotting fish under his nose. But he nodded once again, tapping a slender finger against his temple in a swift mock-salute, and sourly said, 'As Your Majesty commands.'

# CHAPTER 5

THE BONE HALL WAS unrecognisable.

She'd thought it unrecognisable yesterday, too, with the walls stripped bare and the Mother's throne gone – but it turned out she'd underestimated Emelin's threat to bring the entire place down, or perhaps miscalculated the lingering fury of the crowd she'd left behind. The entrance door was half-collapsed. Soot-black scorch marks covered the walls. The hole in the floor had grown and took up at least half of the hall now, leaving nothing but a narrow strip of marble around the perimeter.

Beneath it, the hollow of the Labyrinth gaped. An eerie pink glow emanated from the bowels of the mountain, shrouding the ruined hall in a dusky light.

It was on the other side of that jagged hole that Naxi was sitting in her flowery dress, bare feet dangling over the edge of the crater, dried blood covering her hands and forearms up to her elbows. She was humming some monotonous song as Thysandra slipped through the crumbling doorway, but she interrupted herself the moment their gazes met – jolting up with a smile so bright and delighted that one might think the corpses littered around the castle were just a good-natured joke.

'Sashka! *Finally!*'

Gods have mercy.

But there was no turning back now, not unless she wished to face a demon's wrath *and* the mistrust of her own court; she cautiously ventured two steps into the hall, nudged the door as close to shut as the skewed frame allowed, and began unfolding her wings. The remaining floor looked beyond unreliable. If she could just fly to the other side—

'Oh, I wouldn't do that,' Naxi merrily said, her voice unnaturally loud in the ghastly, corpse-pink glow. 'A couple of fae tried to reach me by flying, and the Labyrinth took them all down as they crossed. Poor dear is still a little grumpy from all the time the Mother kept it locked away, you see, so best not to vex it.'

*Poor dear.*

What in the bloody world?

'It's sentient, of course,' Naxi added, cocking her head like a clever little bird – the tone of her voice suggesting they were discussing nothing more shocking than the care a particular houseplant required. 'Didn't Emelin tell you? Its emotions are slightly different from humanoid feelings, of course, so I can see why Creon didn't pick up on it right away – but once you know what to look for ...' She grinned, baring her sharp teeth, each of them a tiny, ivory weapon in its own right. 'It's unmistakable. Intriguing, isn't it?'

Thysandra stared at her.

*Intriguing*? She was supposed to accept that there was a sentient fucking mountain slumbering beneath her castle – a sentient mountain *murdering* people, if the rumours about the Labyrinth were true – and this was the first response this madwoman could come up with? To call the matter *intriguing*?

Who in hell had given a mountain consciousness in the first place?

More importantly, how in hell's name was she going to explain this insanity to the rest of her court? Had the Mother known? Most likely she'd at least had a suspicion, and the fact that *she* had never told anyone else suggested—

48

'You don't seem to be particularly enchanted by the magical mysteries of our world,' Naxi dryly added, swinging her legs back and forth so that her pink skirt billowed up around her knees. 'A shame. Let's talk about something else, then. I presume you had a good night? Your head is feeling much better.'

For fuck's sake.

She kicked herself into motion, damn the crumbling marble edges and the gaping cave below – because the hall may be ruined beyond recognition, but it was still *her* hall, and she wasn't going to stand here on the doorstep for however long this conversation would take. What did the little murderess think – that a steady string of pleasantries would somehow make her forget about the several dozen corpses sprinkled across her castle right now?

'We need to talk,' she bit out.

'Which is what I told you yesterday,' Naxi reminded her, her fluttering lashes and wide blue eyes somehow distracting from the blood stains on her dress and arms. How did she manage to look *harmless* in this light, like a fragile pink flower rather than the monster that lurked beneath her almost translucent skin? 'And then you forced me out of your rooms, if you recall.'

'Yes, of course I kicked you out!' Heat was stirring in her gut – anger, or at least *mostly* anger, hands itching with the feverish potential of violence. It took four centuries of self-control to slow her steps instead. 'I wasn't looking for your bloody company. I'm *still* not looking for your bloody company. If you hadn't killed half a regiment to get my attention, I wouldn't be here at—'

A scoff. 'You know that's not why I killed them.'

'No, but—'

'Although I'm happy to kill a few more of them, if it helps?' Her blinding smile returned, the blushing light from the Labyrinth below lending a disconcerting gleam to those pearly white teeth. 'A small sacrifice, if it means I get to tell you—'

'You're getting to tell me now!' Thysandra snapped, control slipping through her fingers with disconcerting ease. Gods help her. How in the world was she supposed to lead the entire bloody Crimson Court if she could barely handle a single infuriating demon on her own? 'I'm just asking you to stop beating around the bush, for hell's sake. What do you want?'

'I told you.' Naxi shrugged. 'You.'

Her heart stuttered.

Damn her body for betraying her so easily – for being so stupidly susceptible to the sound of that single treacherous word. She *knew* it was a lie. At least, that it could not possibly be the full story, and yet the eagerness of her own flesh and bones was making it far too hard to remember the lesson life had painstakingly taught her again and again, the lesson that should have been second nature to her by now—

That no one wanted *her*.

They wanted her magic, yes. Her loyalty. Her secrets and her skills. The Mother had been the one exception, until she hadn't – and if even that had been a lie, then how could she ever think a gods-damned *demon* would be any different?

'And what part of me do you need, this time?' she choked out, hating the way the words shook on her lips, the way her hands clenched and unclenched no matter how hard she tried to keep them still. 'My information? My helpful surrender in battle? Or perhaps—'

'I could name some parts, if you like?' Naxi humbly suggested.

'Fuck *off*.' And damn the flare of warmth sizzling down her stomach, her burning anger tangling up with some twisted, nauseating feeling she refused to name. 'I thought you might have something to say, but if we're not getting anything but coy innuendo ...'

'Oh, as you wish.' Naxi rolled her eyes as she swung up her legs and turned away from the hole in the floor, then crossed her ankles and planted her willowy elbows onto her knees. Her eyes were suddenly so blue they almost seemed to glow. 'I want to get to know you better. I want you to stop pretending you're not smitten with me. And most of all, I want to pull you out of this hellhole and make you come live with me on some nymph isle far away from here, but I'm willing to negotiate on—'

There was no helping the shrill laugh that burst from her lips. 'Oh, it's not *me* you need to negotiate with. Your fucking friends are the ones who just chained me to this island, in case you forgot.'

'They did,' Naxi slowly admitted, flicking the tip of her tongue across her upper lip. 'And I'll confess I was thoroughly unhappy with them when they first told me. But then Emelin said you'd be free to leave once you'd restored order here – so now my plan is to help you restore order first and *then* convince you to come to some superior island with me.'

Wait.

*Free to leave?*

There was an end date to her obligation here? A caveat to the threats Agenor's daughter had made, and no one had even *told* her?

'But ...' Her thoughts were reeling. 'Look, what if I don't *want* to go anywhere with you? Have you considered—'

'Oh, yes, yes, of course you'd say that.' The point was discarded with a quick, flitting gesture, as if it was nothing but a stubborn fly to be chased away. 'We'll work on that. Just let me help you for now, alright? As I was trying to tell you yesterday, you can clearly trust me, given that it *is* in my own interests to help you succeed as soon as possible.'

'Have you considered that I may not *want* to work with you?' What little remained of the marble floor stayed unmoving beneath her feet, and yet she felt as though the ground was shifting beneath her, crumbling towards her at an alarming speed. 'I could just say no. I could just refuse to tell you anything, and you—'

'Hmm,' Naxi interrupted, thoughtfully pursing her lips. 'You could. I could also kill a few more people, of course.'

Thysandra gaped at her.

Her small, blood-stained opponent sent a smile dripping with honey up at her, eyes gleaming guilelessly, fingertip tapping a gentle rhythm against a plump bottom lip. As if she hadn't just uttered that ice-cold threat. As if she didn't *mean* it, this creature without a heart or a conscience – as if she wouldn't truly commit twelve more grisly massacres, and do it cheerfully, for nothing but access to the inner workings of the Crimson Court.

Tonight's corpses were still lying in their beds and rooms outside this hall, screaming in eternal soundless agony.

'Yes,' Naxi murmured, such impossible *sympathy* in her unblinking gaze. 'That would be rather unpleasant, wouldn't it? All the more so because we both know you don't even want me to stay away in the first place. Wouldn't it be a shame, if all those lives were to go to waste just because you didn't get over your own denial in a timely manner?'

Fuck.

Did she ... *did* she want this?

The rational answer was clear – the answer given by the part of her mind that knew the rules of the game and played it to perfection, that wouldn't let her take so much as a nap without a lock on the door and three knives beneath her pillow. The part of her mind, most of all, that had suffered the sting of betrayal before, and knew that a fickle ally could do much more damage than even the most vicious of enemies.

And yet ...

And *yet*.

Gods, how could anyone *not* be tempted by promises of such loyalty – by the unimaginable luxury of even a single person one could safely fall asleep around?

'Does it matter what I want if I'm unable to trust you?' she rasped, barely hearing her own numb voice.

Naxi scoffed. 'Why wouldn't you trust me? I hate this place and everyone in it. Do you really think I'm sticking around at a court itching to kill me for the sole purpose of betraying you to people I don't care about?'

Did she think so?

Hell, how did that argument sound so bloody sensible – how did *everything* the little vixen was saying sound so bloody reasonable, when the words couldn't be fuelled by anything other than treacherous, violent insanity?

Cold sweat prickled down between her wings as her thoughts spun in all the wrong directions. Was she overlooking anything? But there was no denying Naxi could simply have left with the rest of the Alliance. She *should* have left, if her wellbeing meant anything to her – and since she was a demon, egoistic by nature, her own wellbeing *had* to be at the heart of her decisions. Which meant there was something at the Crimson Court she wanted more than her safety. More than her friends, more than the home she was dreaming of – some goal, whatever it might be, for which Thysandra was in whatever way necessary.

And if that was the case ...

Couldn't she, if not be trusted, at least be relied upon?

Looking at the sharp-toothed, blood-soaked demon sitting before her – the same creature responsible for the tortured corpses in the hallways, for the demise of the Mother's empire and the treason Thysandra had committed – it was an utterly laughable thought. And yet ...

Yet she was thinking it.

Eagerly, even.

'There's no way I can let you stay at the court after your murders this night,' she hoarsely said – as close to a confession of her wishes as she dared to come, falling back on those of the rest of the world instead. 'Every single fae in this castle will be dying to take revenge, and I don't have the authority to make them leave you alone. They'll riot if I try.'

Naxi shrugged, a gesture that was all willowy limbs and wicked glee. 'Just tell them I'm here on behalf of the Alliance to keep an eye on things.'

'That will only make them want to kill you *more!*'

A devilish grin. 'Wishing them the best of luck, then.'

'It's not funny,' Thysandra snapped – more vexed, admittedly, by the needless stutter of her heart than by the reckless flippancy itself. What in the world was *wrong* with her, to get all hot and bothered by threats and murderous smiles? 'Do you realise they might come for my head next, once they figure out you're not the easiest target?'

'Oh, they might,' Naxi admitted, her dazzling smile dimpling her cheeks. 'I suppose they are like that. I'm here to protect you, though.'

There really was no reason for that sentence to knock the air from her lungs.

She knew better. She could do better. This was not how the world worked, and this cunning, scheming creature had to know it as well as anyone else – relying on anyone else to shield your back was a glaring weakness, and a sign of stupidity, too. Because one day you'd lose your use to the people you'd thought your friends and allies and just like that, they would be gone – leaving you twice as vulnerable as you'd ever been before, and twice as attractive a mark.

She *knew*. She'd learned the lesson too many times to ever forget it again ... so why, *why* did her heart still shrivel in her chest when good sense kicked in?

'I'm afraid I must disappoint you.' Her voice came out too harsh, too sharp, to compensate for the strange, weak mushiness creeping up on her. 'I don't need anyone's protection, yours least of—'

'Oh, I know you don't *need* me,' Naxi sweetly interrupted – looking the epitome of radiant innocence in the rosy light, a girlish pout on her lips, her round face framed by the pink and pale blonde of her curls. Her eyes were so large they seemed to swallow the entire hall. 'You're far too strong and capable to ever need me, of course. But I could help you all the same.'

Gods help her. This had to be a trap, hadn't it?

She was being played like a puppet. Thysandra *knew* she was, and yet no matter how hard she tried, she couldn't escape the strings – couldn't stop dancing to this irresistible tune. No one ever helped her. Why would they? Life was not a charity, and the stakes at the court were too high to play nice; why waste time and energy on someone else's victory?

Then again ... the demon before her wasn't in the game at all.

She didn't have anything to lose. She didn't have anything to win. Which meant—

'Don't try to tell me you're not tempted,' Naxi murmured before that thought could fully fall into place, her unblinking gaze trained on Thysandra's face with what felt like physical weight. 'I can read your heart, Sashka. I know you need safety more than you need anything else in this hell of a place.'

Safety, yes. Not building her reign on the quicksand foundations of a demon's loyalty, and yet, what *if* ...

What if she was just very, very careful?

What if she kept the most important cards close to her chest?

She'd have to make sure nothing Naxi did was indispensable. That her maybe-ally was never the very last failsafe between herself and death. But if she kept that in mind – and surely she would be able to keep that in mind? – then a demon by her side *could* make all the difference in a court where not a single warrior owed her their allegiance …

'I'm going to need a bargain for this,' she heard herself say.

Naxi jumped to her feet in a flutter of curls and blood-stained skirts, the movement so swift and explosive Thysandra feared for a fraction of a moment she'd lose her balance and tumble into the silent Labyrinth beneath. 'Of course! Bargains! What do you need me to promise – that I won't kill you?'

'Amongst other things, yes.' She glanced down at the slender nymph hand reaching out to her – soft, slender, and coated in a thick layer of dried blood. 'I can't have you disobeying me in public, either. People will think—'

Naxi scoffed. 'I'm not going to bargain for *obedience*, Sashka. Won't willingly harm you, and that's as far as I'm prepared to go.'

Not *willingly* – a dangerous clause to add to any bargain. The more foolish a person, the more likely they would accidentally breach the contract. Then again …

This little demon was no fool.

And if Naxi's magic senses could offer helpful information in cases of emergency, it would admittedly be unhelpful if she had to wait for permission to act.

'Fine.' Deep breaths. It wouldn't help anyone if she were to pass out from nothing but sheer nerves. 'Do we have a deal, then?'

'Oh, I would like your guarantee that you won't quietly sacrifice me to the court either,' Naxi dryly said, beaming up at her. 'Not that I could imagine you ever being tempted, of course! But it can't hurt to be sure. And we need to include an end date – I would like for the bargain to be voided if you ever send me away.'

'If you decide to leave the Crimson Court for whatever reason,' Thysandra amended, her throat dry. Demons got bored. There was no use in pretending this one wouldn't. 'I'm not going to go on protecting you if you get sick of me tomorrow.'

Naxi rolled her eyes, then extended her blood-crusted hand again, ignoring the alarming red flickers of the Labyrinth beneath them. 'Deal?'

It took an effort not to recoil as their fingers twined together. The blood was still a fraction sticky in places.

'Deal,' Thysandra said hoarsely.

The bargain magic flared between their palms. Blinding light, stinging pain – she barely saw and felt it anymore. It was over in mere seconds, leaving nothing but the bargain mark on the inside of her wrist: a pale shade of pink, like a small shard of rose quartz embedded in the umber of her skin.

The last bargain between them had been white. It was hard to ignore, suddenly, what that one had led to.

'How *lovely*,' Naxi purred, pulling back her hand to study the identical mark in her own forearm. Against her tender, unmarred skin, the sharp edges of the crystal looked oddly out of place – a violation of something far too sweet to be damaged like this. 'So where do we start, Sashka? I could murder a few more people for you?'

She thought of the glaring eyes outside. Of Nicanor, stiff with justified disgust. Of Bereas and Orthea, looking for traitors, for people to blame.

Her ribcage squeezed her lungs a little tighter.

'Perhaps you should take a bath before you start thinking of murdering anyone else,' she ground out.

'That's not a bad idea,' Naxi blithely admitted, looking down at her blood-stained feet. 'Not sure where I could safely take a bath in this castle, though. Would you mind if I borrowed your quarters for a bit?'

# CHAPTER 6

THEY BARELY SAW A single living soul on their way up through the castle. All that moved was the occasional flash of wings around a corner as yet another fae managed to get out of the way just in time; other than those lucky survivors, there were just the corpses on the marble floors, curled up in their never-ending agony.

Naxi's cheerful humming didn't falter as she passed them by.

It felt like a terrible idea, giving this ruthless creature access to her only safe haven at the court ... but by the time they'd reached the familiar redwood door, Thysandra still hadn't come up with any better solutions. So she opened the locks and gestured for her unwelcome visitor to go first, wincing at the sight of Naxi's bloodied feet against her spotless wooden floor.

A temporary solution, she reminded herself. A few days, maybe, and she'd have her home to herself again – she could handle that, couldn't she?

'Just to be clear,' she said nonetheless, waiting by the doorstep, 'you *will* harm me by destroying anything in my rooms. I'm fond of this place.'

There. That should at least keep the bargain active.

Naxi whirled around, eyes narrowing. 'You're not saying you'll let me roam around on my own here, are you?'

'Did you think I was planning to join you in that bath?' Thysandra sharply retorted, realising a moment too late that that had been *entirely* the wrong thing to say. It conjured up mental images she truly should not be thinking about – that lithe body in her bathtub, willowy limbs and small, foam-covered breasts, wet skin gleaming like mother-of-pearl in the faelights ... She hastily pushed the vision away with a panicked stutter of her heart and added, voice choked, 'I still have a bloody court to rule. Which won't have gotten any easier after your antics of last night, either.'

'Oh, it probably hasn't,' Naxi admitted in that breezy, careless way of hers. Her smile grew broader, then more wicked. 'You'll manage, though. And of course, if you need a reward for your hard work—'

'I'm good, thank you,' Thysandra interrupted tightly. 'Enjoy your bath.'

No matter how swiftly she slammed the door shut, it didn't block out the subsequent melodious peal of laughter, or the way it sent her heart jumping alarmingly in her chest.

Fuck.

A hundred-and-thirty years and a series of betrayals should have been more than enough to purge this madness from her veins ... yet here she stood, High Lady of the Crimson Court itself, battling the urge to yank the door open again and kiss the gods-damned little menace on those gods-damned silky lips until she was no longer capable of laughing at anything.

'I can still feel you!' Naxi yelled from within the room, sounding delighted.

*Fuck.*

She forced herself into motion with a shuddering jerk – down the winding stairs, away from those demon senses picking up on every spark of senseless lust burning inside her. Perhaps she would be more rational with a few more walls between them. Perhaps she would manage to stop thinking of all that delicate prettiness, of that bloodstained fragility so very different from the swaggering and the posturing of—

'Well, well,' a male voice drawled, far too close. 'No more demons with you, I see?'

She swept around so fast her left wing slammed into the balustrade.

He'd taken up position in a shallow alcove a few steps back – Bereas of Bereon's house, prize-fighter and sixty-something-time champion of the yearly wing-racing tournament. With his flaming red hair and wings to match, he'd inspired more than a few joking comparisons to the phoenixes living on the east side of the archipelago ... except the phoenixes were known for their poise and prudence, of course, and the male slouching smugly on that marble seat didn't possess a crumb of either quality.

How in the world had she overlooked him? If he'd snuck up on her with malicious intent, she'd already be dead.

'Is anything the matter?' she bit out, all the more coldly to cover up the shock.

'The demon.' He crossed his ankle over his knee as he leaned back, his wings filling almost all of the alcove. 'She's no longer with you. Do I understand correctly that you put her in your *bedroom*, of all places?'

The smirk on his face was alarming. Admittedly, this was Bereas, who could turn even a brutal battle into a vulgar joke ... but on the other hand, if he continued to do so often enough, someone with a little more cunning would sooner or later start asking questions.

Best to nip it in the bud as soon as possible. She folded her arms, chin raised a fraction, and flatly said, 'Would you rather have me put her in yours?'

'I'd rather see her dead,' Bereas retorted, thrusting out his chest like a bird puffing itself up for a fight. 'Why the hell isn't she yet?'

*None of your fucking business*, she wanted to inform him. Or alternatively, *Because I still need her to kill you if you make a fuss*, which was not even that far from the truth. But the bastard was popular at the court, and among the ranks of the army in particular. Pissing him off in such an unnecessary way was just asking for trouble.

'The demon alleges she's here on behalf of the Alliance,' she said instead, aiming for just the right note of disapproval – that tone that would hopefully tell the male before her that she was just as unhappy about the meddling as he would be. 'I need to look into that claim before I make any further decisions. I'm not itching to anger Emelin to the point where she returns to destroy the castle after all.'

'Emelin?' His cocky grin showed his unnaturally white teeth. 'Oh, don't you worry about *her*, Thys. We've spent all night feeding traitors to the hounds and preparing for the next battle, so if the little mongrel thinks she can—'

'Beg your pardon?' Thysandra sharply cut in, and it took the greatest of efforts to keep her voice from soaring as the memories flashed by. Father. Hounds. Agonised screams. 'The *next* battle? What next battle are we talking about, exactly?'

'The one to take back our islands?' He leaned forward so that his sleeveless shirt fell open at the collar – that shirt she was quite sure he wore for the sole purpose of displaying his bulky, tanned shoulders to as many eyes as possible. 'What else would we be doing?'

Gods help her.

It was reckless, overconfident madness, of course – the brash strategy of a male so used to winning that the notion of defeat didn't even occur to him. Which didn't need to be her problem, technically speaking. Had it been only him and his circle of equally brazen friends, she might have happily let them fly to their death.

The problem, though ...

Emelin would take note of the attack. And possibly, quite possibly, she would find it enough of a reason to spread those damning secrets among the court, the traitor's daughter following in her traitor father's footsteps – as close to murder as simple words could come.

*Fed to the hounds ...*

Her pulse was quickening.

Her mouth had suddenly gone dry.

'And who gave you permission to do any of that, may I ask?' she bit out. 'I don't recall saying anything about—'

'Why the hell should I care about your permission, Thys?' Another blinding white grin. 'If you're afraid of a bunch of rebels, I don't see why I ought to be afraid of you. Just because some bratty child handed you a title for no fucking reason at all?'

'That bunch of rebels,' she said through gritted teeth, 'are the same people who defeated you in battle three days ago. Who are currently wielding godsworn magic. Who are no longer held back by the Mother's bindings, either. I'm not afraid of them, but I sure as hell know what we're up against, and it isn't pretty – so whatever our plans are, don't you think we ought to be going about them with a *little* more circumspection?'

Bereas emphatically yawned, planting his feet back onto the ground. 'Lovely speech, Thys. Are you going to let us into your bedroom to slit the demon's throat, then?'

'What? *No.*' The bargain mark on her wrist likely wouldn't even let her – and surely *that* was the reason her stomach knotted so abruptly at the idea, wasn't it? 'You wouldn't survive the attempt in the first place, and even if—'

'Alright.' He shrugged and rose, raking a hand through his wine-red locks as he smirked at her one last time. 'I'll go find some friends to break down the walls, then. Enjoy that title as long as you manage to keep it, love.'

And with two slaps of those famous, prize-winning wings, he elbowed past her as if she was no more than a powerless inconvenience.
\*\*\*
Her flight to the north-west tower was, objectively speaking, more of a free fall.

Her heart thrummed frantically in her chest – a panic that *had* to be bargain-born, the pink mark on her chest reminding her that she'd taken on a life-and-death obligation to protect the little demon currently taking a bath in her chambers. Even though Naxi surely would be able to handle a handful of musclehead fae. Even though walls could be repaired and doors could be replaced. Reassurances she could repeat to herself as often as she wanted ...

And yet.

What if she returned to her tower to find the bathroom stained with blood and strewn with pink hairs, some leftover shreds of a flowery dress, and not even a body to be found?

*Fed to the hounds.*

She slammed down onto the wrought-iron balcony she'd aimed for, all but yanking open the door that gave access to the room beyond. To her surprise, it was unlocked. Which seemed too good to be true, on this hell of a morning ... but as she staggered to a halt in the familiar office-turned-laboratory, looking around wildly for attackers in wait for her, Nicanor's voice emerged from the adjoining room as if he'd been expecting visitors.

'Thysandra?' He sounded so unhurried she wanted to shake something. 'Is that you?'

'How'd you fucking guess?' she snapped, out of breath, as she slammed the door behind her and wilted against the glass and wood.

A soft laugh, and he ambled into the room – having changed out of his bloodstained clothes and into a pale lilac ensemble with lacy sleeves and intricate silver embroidery. She should have known that would be his first priority after alerting her to the murders of the night: restoring his usual faultless appearance.

'I figured you might be in need of some assistance,' he said, which told her all she needed to know about the state of *her* appearance. 'A drink?'

She glared at the wall-filling brass-and-glass construction to her right, where a plethora of crystal flasks and beakers stood gleaming in the morning sunlight – some of them bubbling, some of them steaming slightly, most of them corked and waiting patiently for their contents to be used. There was always a certain risk involved with accepting this particular male's drinks. Even if the large table at the heart of the room was mostly empty at the present moment, the lack of notes and formulas was all but a guarantee he wasn't looking to test any revolutionary new potions on unsuspecting suspects.

'Don't worry,' Nicanor dryly added, following her gaze. 'We're in the middle of a war. I've paused my experiments for the moment.'

That made enough sense for her to believe him. 'Could use a drink, in that case.'

He poured her a glass of elderflower juice. Their fingers didn't touch as he pressed the crystal into her hand – no attempts at seduction, then, or at least not yet. Thank the gods. She didn't want to know what Naxi would do if he made an earnest attempt.

Would Bereas have gathered his friends yet?

Hell, should she have returned to her bedroom to warn Naxi first, before running off to look for allies?

'Handled matters with the demon?' Nicanor said, interrupting her frantic thoughts.

'More or less.' She sank onto one of the high stools at his table and gulped down a swig of juice – winning time to think rather than quenching her thirst. How much information was enough to answer his questions, but too little for him to draw any dangerous conclusions? 'I had a word with her. She isn't going to kill anyone else for now, assuming no one attacks her.'

He seated himself on the other side of the table, lips pursed, his own glass hanging askew between his long fingers. 'Made a bargain on it, I see.'

'You and those eyes of yours,' she muttered.

Another of those faint laughs. 'Why isn't she dead yet?'

'Because killing a demon isn't what one would call a pleasant af-fair,' Thysandra said tightly, trying to make herself believe it. Sure-ly gods-damned Bereas wouldn't manage so easily, either? 'Also, she claims she's here with the Alliance's approval, which suggests there's some risk involved in killing her. And I've been thinking ...'

She hesitated, unsure if the next thought was too close to treason, close enough to make him wonder what other disloyal ideas she might be hiding. Nicanor smiled before she could come to a decision, though.

'And she might be useful, under certain circumstances?' he suggest-ed.

Thank the gods for his particular brand of ruthless pragmatism. 'Yes. That too.'

'Hmm.' He sipped from his drink. 'Bold.'

'I once heard you argue that safe decisions don't lead to victory,' she shot back, and he granted her that point with a small grin and a swift lift of his glass. 'Look, the trouble is I currently don't have any military force to back my decisions. As unpleasant as Naxi's magic may be ...'

'She certainly does have an advantage in battle, yes,' he dryly admitted. 'The lack of military support might be solvable, though.'

Her heart skipped a beat. 'Might it?'

'The third is technically still under my command.' He tilted his head, two snow-white locks of hair falling out from behind a pointed ear. 'I'm quite sure most of them will still follow me even without the Mother to back me. And several other regiments have lost their commander – we could likely convince some of their members to join us as well. In either case, there wouldn't be any organised opposition for at least a while.'

All the words she hadn't even dared to hope he'd speak.

The hairs were rising on her neck.

This was too easy. Much, much too easy. She had expected to argue, barter, plead – and here he was, offering her exactly what she needed on a shining silver plate? Which didn't make sense. Life was not a charity, and Nicanor *certainly* wasn't one to hand out favours for nothing ... so if he wasn't going to point out what he wanted from her in return right from the start, what game was he playing?

Was he hoping to make her dependent on his support so that he would be able to demand some outrageous price later, when she was no longer capable of refusing at all?

She kept her face carefully expressionless, her fingers loose around her glass, as she slowly, deliberately said, 'Why?'

He raised a white-blond eyebrow. 'Why what?'

'Why would you risk your head like that, when you don't even know what plans and strategies I'm thinking of? Whether we stand any chance of surviving?' She grimaced. 'Or whether you'll even agree with my decisions, for that matter?'

Even his shrugs were oddly elegant. 'We're old friends, aren't we?'

She rolled her eyes. 'Nicanor.'

He gave her one of his sardonic half-grins. 'Yes?'

'I'm well aware we're old friends.' A little more than that, even – she could have done without the reminder. 'I'm also well aware you poisoned another old friend of yours two summers ago, so forgive me for not being terribly impressed with that particular argument. You don't like me enough to choose the losing side for me.'

'I do like you more than most people,' he countered, looking wryly amused at worst by the entire conversation.

'So you'd pick a painless poison for me. I'm glad to hear that.' She raised an unimpressed eyebrow at him. 'Don't offend me by pretending I might fall for this nonsense, Commander. I'm happy to work with you, but you can't expect me to trust you if I don't have the faintest clue of what you want in the first place.'

He considered her for a moment, then smiled and nodded – a small gesture, but the way his wings relaxed a fraction was a clear sign she'd won. 'Fair enough, Your Majesty.'

She glared at him.

'Here's the thing,' he said, putting down his glass and planting his palms flat on the table as he shifted straighter on his stool. Gone was the mocking tone, the silver-tongued flattery. They were talking business now. 'I've spent the last few centuries playing mid-level commander to the Mother. Useful enough to be trusted with a regiment, not useful enough to have any hopes of promotion. What I want is a decent position, and so far, my estimate is that you might be willing to give it to me. I have no reason to assume the same of anyone else.'

There. That was more like it.

And if it was true – which was not unlikely, at least – then that meant she would be able to trust him as long as no one else offered him an easier path to fulfil his ambitions. That seemed doable. She could make things pretty damn easy for him, if she wanted.

'And you want that position badly enough to get involved with this madness?' she said, keeping her expression pointedly blank. 'Enough to risk losing a potential civil war for it?'

His grin returned, more genuine now. 'Safe decisions don't lead to victory, I've been told.'

Damn him – but she couldn't help but laugh, his unabashed oppor-
tunism far more tolerable than Naxi's fickle claims of almost-altruism.
This might still be quicksand, but it was quicksand she knew like the
back of her hand. It felt more reliable, somehow, than the notion of safe
ground beneath her feet.

'So what exactly does victory look like to you?' she inquired.

He didn't hesitate for even a moment. 'Did you already have anyone
in mind for the post of Lord Protector?'

Bold start. One of the most powerful offices at the court, the Lord
Protector was responsible for managing both internal threats and ex-
ternal defences; it was a position that came not just with great influence but with great risk, too. Agenor had held the title as long as she
could remember under the Mother's rule, and now that he was gone,
she had trouble even imagining anyone else in his place.

Then again ...

She *would* need someone to oversee the military on her behalf, and
she did not have anyone else in mind.

'Would you agree to a trial period?' she said slowly.

Nicanor's smile was full of sharp angles. 'Depends on how long you
wish to make it.'

'A year?' If she was still alive after a year, he would most certainly
deserve some credit for the achievement. 'I'm willing to make a bargain
for that duration. Once it expires, we can reconsider and tweak the
agreement if necessary.'

He held out a slender hand without further commentary.

'Wonderful.' She grasped his fingers without hesitation, the motion
so familiar it made even this hurried decision feel like a reassurance.
'I'm guaranteeing you the position of Lord Protector of the Crimson
Court for exactly one year, in exchange for ...'

'... my loyalty to the crown and the best of my abilities to get this court
under control,' he filled her expectant silence. 'Do we have a bargain?'

She drew in a deep breath. 'We have a bargain.'

The surge of magic was blindingly bright, blazing whiter and whiter
between their palms until she could see the outlines of bones through
the skin and flesh of their fingers. Hours seemed to pass before finally,

*finally*, the familiar sting of pain shot through her wrist. The light receded in the same moment, as if swallowed by her skin.

The bargain mark it left behind was a dark purple. *Red for destruction, blue for healing* – she could see the sense of it.

'Congratulations to me,' Nicanor said, face deadpan, as he swung his legs to the ground and finished his drink in a single gulp. 'To you, too, for that matter. Time to get to work, then, Your Majesty?'

'First order,' she said, throwing him a death glare, 'is to stop calling me Your Majesty. Second order ...' She rose as well. The unmistakable relief was so strong she feared for a moment her knees would buckle. 'Make sure someone finds Bereas and stops him from breaking into my rooms. If you need to chop off his head to calm him down, so be it. Everything else can wait until the afternoon.'

# CHAPTER 7

WHATEVER COMPLAINTS ONE MIGHT have about Nicanor of Myron's house, he was undeniably brutally efficient.

By the time Thysandra had scarfed down a quick breakfast of bread and goat's cheese, Bereas had been given a stern enough talking to that he had relinquished the notion of glorious revenge for the foreseeable future. A handful of fae had taken up position around the entrance of the ruined bone hall to prevent anyone from entering the Labyrinth. Some of Nicanor's most trusted people had been appointed to replace the slain commanders of other regiments, and orders had gone out to pause all unauthorised activity among the military, especially battle preparations of any kind.

Perhaps most important of all, the news of the new Lord Protector's appointment had spread through the court like wildfire. Which meant that everyone Thysandra encountered on her way through the wine- and perfume-scented corridors, every envious courtier and grudge-bearing rival, knew she was no longer a lone ruler with a target between her wings.

It wasn't enough to feel safe. It was never enough to feel safe. But it took an edge of urgency off her fear, and that was already more than she'd dared to hope for.

The archives were her next destination, she'd decided once she'd left Nicanor's chambers and taken stock of her plans. All the demon murders in the world hadn't changed anything about the precarious food situation the court would soon find itself in, and as long as she didn't know how bad it was, she could hardly expect to solve it. The archivists could get her numbers. Once she had those ...

Well. She'd see.

*I could kill a few more people?* she could already hear Naxi suggesting, the voice in the back of her mind accompanied by a vision of guileless blue eyes. *Fewer mouths to feed means your provisions will last longer. That's simple mathematics.*

An annoyingly stubborn smile tugged at the corners of her lips as she descended the next flight of stairs.

Not that she should be thinking of Naxi, of course. Naxi was wholly irrelevant to the daily reality of this court. Soon she might not even need any demon assistance anymore, if it turned out she could keep herself alive perfectly well without it, and—

'Thysandra?' a voice yelled behind her.

Her hand already lay against the dark red of her dress.

Miraculously, though, the curly-haired male jogging towards her from a lush courtyard did not seem about to murder her in cold blood; if anything, he gave the impression he was about to complain about a hair in his soup. Symeon, she recalled after a moment, or at least she *thought* that was his name. In any case, there were so many Symeons at the court that it was a reasonable guess.

'Yes?' she said tartly, wondering if she should be making a point of using the proper titles of people who weren't close allies. 'Is it urgent?'

'Quite, yes.' The young male rubbed his forehead with the back of his hand. His skin was so dark she only then noticed the bloodstains on his fingers; his black leather trousers and velvety, half-buttoned shirt of the same colour made it hard to estimate just how bad the situation was. 'It's about that gory mess the Alliance's demon left behind. Usually we'd send the servants to clean it up, but ... well, you know ...'

No more humans.

No more servants.

For the bloody gods' sakes. She wasn't sure if she wanted to curse Emelin and her meddling or shake this fool and his utter lack of problem-solving capacities until some bright ideas miraculously fell out of his mind.

'I suppose you know what a mop is?' she said.

He blinked at her, apparently stupefied. 'Beg your pardon?'

'A mop,' she repeated, more of a bite to her voice than intended. 'And a bucket of hot water with some soap. No human assistance necessary. It's not exactly a fun job, I'll grant you that, but it's significantly better than living with the stench of rotting blood. Anything else with which you need my help?'

His hollow expression suggested he was far from done. 'You ... you're suggesting *I* clean it?'

'Or anyone else you persuade to do it in your place,' she added, sending him a forced smile in a belated attempt to soften the blow of her irritation. Behind her, someone was unmistakably sniggering. 'Now if you don't mind, I have some other matters to take care of. Thanks in advance for your efforts.'

He was still stammering half-hearted objections behind her as she strode off. Around her, small groups of fae hastily made way, conversations quieting as she passed – all of them sharing the worry, no doubt, that she might appoint them to the cleaning force as well if they made the mistake of catching her eye.

Perhaps she should. She'd consider it if the bloodstains weren't gone by the end of the day.

She made it two stairs down before the next interruption, a flock of fae demanding to know what burial arrangements would be made for those who had fallen in battle at the White City. Unwilling to admit she hadn't spent that much thought on the hundreds, if not thousands of dead warriors yet, she promised them a plan would be announced the next morning – enough to send them on their way again, except that they were replaced within minutes by an even more unwelcome arrival.

Orthea of Orontes' house.

The Mother's Master of Ceremony was dressed in a lavish golden dress, its skirt so voluminous it seemed to fill half the hallway – the sort of dress that pointedly ignored the fact that any sort of battle had taken place in recent days, let alone a *defeat*. Her smile was honey-sweet as she gave the most minimal curtsy in the history of faekind. Her green eyes, on the other hand, glared daggers.

'How *fortunate* to find you here, Thysandra.' It didn't sound as though the meeting was at all coincidental; knowing Orthea, she'd lain in wait ever since she'd heard the demon threat had been taken care of. 'I was just wondering about the upcoming Hunter's Moon festival, as it happens. Do you have any instructions for the celebration, perhaps?'

Gods damn it. The casual cruelty of Hunter's Moon was the *last* thing she wanted to think about.

'Let's keep things small this year,' she said, not slowing down so that the other female was forced to hurry along with her, skirts whooshing dramatically. 'No big banquets. Just the hunt itself, I'd say, followed by a relatively simple meal.'

It came out a little curter than she'd aimed for.

Once, she'd believed them friends, herself and Orthea. Once they'd roamed the academy halls together, studied together, giggled their way through feasts together; Thysandra had pilfered the other girl's wardrobe and returned the favour by writing in a larger hand at tests. Then Creon had been born, the Mother had no longer graced her with a seat at the royal table – and all of a sudden, she'd sat alone during meals.

She'd stopped caring long ago. She *thought* she had, at least – but the power felt unnervingly good in her hands all of a sudden, and she couldn't help a twinge of spiteful satisfaction at the twist of the other female's face.

'*Small*.' There was an unequivocal glint of contempt in Orthea's scowl. 'Because of the gods-damned Alliance starving us?'

'No,' Thysandra impatiently said, although that was in fact exactly why she'd suggested the approach. 'Because our High Lady died three days ago, a thousand of our people aren't even laid in their graves yet, most of us have lost family and friends, and maybe a night of lavish feasting and fucking is not *entirely* appropriate right now, don't you think?'

'Oh – oh yes, of *course*.' Orthea might be an opportunistic viper, but she'd never been slow to adapt. 'I was absolutely planning to include a memorial theme this year – I thought that would go without saying. But to keep things so small ...' An affected peal of laughter. 'Do you really think the Mother would want us to neglect ourselves and our sacred days in her name?'

A hysterical laugh burst free from Thysandra's chest with such speed that it was all she could do to disguise it as a muffled cough.

*Have you gone mad?* she wanted to shriek. *The Mother drove me to neglect myself even while she was still alive. I promise you she never cared about your wellbeing either. Actually, it turns out she never cared about anything other than keeping herself on that throne of hers – so now that she's failed to do that, do you really think she'd give a shit about the size of your bloody Hunter's Moon festival?*

But Orthea had never been called a traitor's daughter. Orthea wouldn't know the meaning of sacrifice if it hit her in the pretty green-eyed face.

And Thysandra really shouldn't be making any new enemies if she could at all avoid it. Her former friend might have grown into one of those bone-idle courtiers whose job had only ever been to provide the Mother with endless entertainment, but even if her ties with the army were weak, she held far too much sway with the others of her kind.

'Regardless of what the Mother would have wanted,' she said, quickening her strides, '*I* am not in the mood to celebrate her violent death, nor am I planning to give the impression that I'm doing so. I imagine I might not be alone in that.'

Not a threat. A reminder, though, that those who *had* been at the White City might feel more inclined to mourn their High Lady and the many others fallen in battle, and that not all of them would be kindly disposed to the notion of feasting their grief away.

A warning, too, that Thysandra would be the last to soothe those inevitable misgivings.

'Ah,' Orthea said curtly – more displeased, presumably, by the fact she had been outmanoeuvred than by the outcome of the discussion itself. 'I see. I'll make some appropriately modest plans, then, *Your Majesty*.'

The title was an unmistakable sneer.

Thysandra smiled as if it had been a genuine token of respect and continued her walk to the archives without pause, shedding her conversation partner within seconds. Perhaps a glimpse of centuries-old fury did still show on her face, though, because no one else approached her on the last staircase to her destination; she reached the fireproof steel doors of the archives unbothered by anyone, although observed by at least fifty pairs of ogling eyes.

She slipped into the parchment-filled halls beyond so swiftly her wings almost caught between the doors.

The archives were strangely unchanged, her first reflexive scan of the hall told her, although they were quieter than the last time she'd visited them – rows of towering cabinets, equipped with slender ladders to prevent wingbeats from disturbing the perfectly organised piles and folders. Usually, a small army of human scribes would be flitting around the aisles. Now only dusty silence answered her as she cautiously strode into the hall, her hand once again on her dress just in case someone tried to exploit the lack of witnesses.

'Hello?' she called when nothing happened.

A dull thud sounded from an adjoining room.

Then the rhythm of irregular footsteps, limping closer at surprising speed. She whirled around just in time to see a ruffled fae male appear from behind the cabinets, his brown hair bound into a messy queue, his hands stained with ink. The blocky shape of his left boot suggested a clubfoot or some similar disability. His russet-brown wings propelled him forward with measured slaps, though, betraying hidden strength and agility.

His white and grey clothes seemed harmless. She let go of her dress with some hesitation, the silence around them a threat rather than a reassurance.

'Hello?' she warily repeated.

The clerk – or at least she assumed that must be his function – came to a standstill, looking her up and down twice before he met her gaze again. 'Yes?'

He sounded, if anything, a fraction impatient.

Hardly the welcome she had expected. It was nonsensical to feel miffed about the lack of proper regard – all the more so because she had done exactly nothing to deserve it – and yet she couldn't help the crackle of ice in her voice as she said, 'I'm looking for Anysia.'

'Ah.' He clasped his hands behind his back, clearing his throat. 'That is unfortunate. I'm afraid she died in the battle.'

'She— Oh.' For some reason, Thysandra hadn't expected the head of the court archives to have been on the battlefield of the White City at all ... but then again, it stood to reason that a mage of her capacities would not stay at home waiting for the war to pass. Without doubt, the Mother had enlisted many of her civilians to temporarily join the army when the threat posed by the Alliance had grown. 'I'm sorry to hear that. Could I see the second archivist, then?'

The brown-haired male cleared his throat once again. 'Also dead, regrettably.'

A slow, deeply worrying suspicion rose. 'Is Iphis—'

'Dead as well.' The clerk's grimace showed a hint of nervousness now. 'Sorry to be the bearer of bad news.'

She should feel more, presumably. These were people she'd known well, people she'd worked with for decades or longer, people she had liked and respected. But through the worries and the whizzing of her mind, there was just the hollow in her chest – the sense of too many emotions to feel at once, and the sinking realisation of even more trouble than anticipated.

'So ...' Her glance around the deserted hall was reflexive, a last spark of desperate optimism hoping a familiar face would magically materialise in the aisles. 'Who is head of the archives now, exactly?'

'Ah.' A sheepish cough. 'I suppose that would be, um, me.'

She blinked at him.

'I'm officially the supervisor of the education department,' he clarified, pointing a half-hearted thumb at the section in question. 'Which appears to be the highest position left. Of course, if you'd prefer to appoint someone else to the post, I fully understand. Your Majesty.'

The title wasn't a jab from his lips. Rather, it sounded as though he simply realised half a second too late that he was probably supposed to attach it to his sentences.

'Right,' Thysandra said blankly, which was about the most insightful response she was able to come up with on the spot. She'd vaguely assumed she'd solved the worst of her problems by dealing with the army ... but at least she was familiar with the military. The already minimal numbers of archivists she knew well enough to trust them had now officially shrunk to zero. 'And your name is?'

'Oh. Gadyon. Galynthias's house.' He cleared his throat again. 'If I'd known you'd be here ...'

'Never mind about that,' she interrupted. She hadn't known *he'd* be here either, after all. 'We'll make do. How many other clerks do we have left, roughly?'

'About fifty,' he said, looking cautious. 'More than half of the fae died, and well, most of the humans left, of course. I sent the remaining fae archivists we home for the day. Most of them had family members to mourn. I figured we'd make a start at updating the population registers tomorrow, but of course, if you—'

'No, no. That's all fine.' She briefly closed her eyes, suppressing the urge to rub her temples – headaches were weakness, and she couldn't afford that right now. 'I would like to take a look at the administration of our food supplies. Production within the fae isles, tribute amounts of the past decade, storage at the court – all the details. Where do I find those files?'

'That's Rhodia's department,' Gadyon said, even more nervously now. 'Or well, she's officially sub-sub-supervisor of the department, but there's no one else left. I could go ask her for an overview, if you need—'

'Don't bother.' How was she to predict the unknown Rhodia's political preferences? She might be Bereas's niece, for all Thysandra knew, and even if she wasn't, it was best not to owe anyone too many favours. 'I'll take a look myself for now. Where do I find the information?'

Gadyon looked sceptical, but nodded and quickly muttered, 'Third room through that doorway, then recent years will be on your left and historical summaries on your right. And um, if you don't mind me asking, does that mean—'

'Please keep the position for now,' Thysandra curtly said, already turning for the door he'd indicated. 'I don't have anyone else for it at the moment. And see if you can find a bunch of new clerks, considering all the administrative changes we have coming up.'

From the corner of her eye, she could see him give a half-bow, half-salute, uneasy like a male who's never set foot on a battlefield. The irregular tap-*thump* of his limping gait died away behind her as she hurried into the next room, jolting at every shadow that moved on the edge of her sight.

The third room was much, much bigger than she'd hoped – twenty-five aisles on either side of the main corridor, endless walls of drawers and shelves and leather folders, organised according to some arcane system that likely only made sense to a handful of people in the world. Still ... if she applied some patience and common sense to the task, how hard could it be to find the lists and overviews she was looking for?

Unfortunately, it soon turned out the task was significantly larger than her patience.

She'd never paid much attention to the archives; information was generally provided to her whenever she needed it, sent her way by the tireless army of mages working in this realm of parchment. Now, surrounded by looming shelves and unintelligible labels, she found herself wishing for the first time in her life that she'd spent a few more hours with these dusty tomes in her hands – because surely this would have been much, much easier if at least she'd known what to make of cryptic drawer labels such as *4225 gr. c. 56b* ...

Perhaps it would be a better idea to find the unknown Rhodia, dangers be damned. If they made a bargain to guarantee the accuracy of the information, at least she could stop wasting time on—

'Oh, *here* you are,' a brisk female voice said.

Thysandra whipped around, grabbing instinctively for the nearest dark leather surface.

A distinctively wingless, suspiciously human-looking silhouette had appeared at the end of the aisle, drawn sharply against the frosted-glass windows. For a single heart-stopping moment, Thysandra thought it might be Naxi, having escaped her locked rooms in gods-knew-what unholy way ... and then the reality of her observations came punching through, shattering that hope-like fear with something that felt worryingly like disappointment.

The silhouette was too tall. Her hair too sleek and blonde. Her voice hadn't sounded remotely like Naxi's, either, too blunt and too bitter.

She didn't look *young*, exactly, this unknown human woman; she stepped closer with a tired determination that suggested several decades of disillusionment. All the same, there was no trace of old age to be found in her appearance. No wrinkles. Not a glimpse of grey in her long, pale hair. Really, she wore that sense of agelessness that Thysandra only ever saw on immortals ... but that didn't quite make sense, did it?

Then again, neither did that greeting. *Here you are* – as if Thysandra was some disobedient child caught sneaking off into forbidden places.

'Beg your pardon?' she cautiously said, trying to figure out whether there was any danger she could be overlooking before she got rid of the unwelcome interruption.

'I've been looking for you.' The human woman slowed her steps, then leaned sideways against the cabinets, crossing her arms. She was almost as tall as most fae. 'Your demon friend said you'd be around here, but it's a nightmare finding anyone in this maze. This is not the right aisle if you're looking for grain stores, by the way.'

Thysandra barely even heard that last sentence.

*Your demon friend.*

Naxi. What game was she playing this time, sending humans for … well, for what? It didn't seem likely that this willowy girl – or woman, whatever she was – was standing here with the intent to violently usurp her. Then again, it seemed highly unlikely any humans would still be roaming the island in the first place; hadn't Emelin announced that she'd send all of them back home immediately?

'Who the hell are you?' Thysandra blurted out, realising a moment too late that High Ladies should probably ask for their information in more dignified ways.

'Inga.' As if that were the only answer she needed. 'I'm one of your former slaves, in case that helps.'

Her manners weren't those of a former servant. If anything, they were the manners of a woman who couldn't wait to take up a sledge-hammer and smash the walls to pieces – a vaguely alarming thought even if she looked entirely unarmed.

Thysandra slowly stepped away from the drawers and straightened to her full height, deciding that perhaps this matter did deserve her undivided attention for the few minutes it took her to get the other woman out of here. 'And what exactly are you doing here, when all humans should have long since left the island by now?'

'Not all of them,' Inga said curtly. 'There's a few hundred exceptions, as a matter of fact. Some of us don't have anywhere else to go, you see.'

What in the world?

But before she could so much as ask a single question, the servant – no, *former* servant – gave a scowl and tucked a handful of blonde hair aside, revealing …

Fae ears.

That explained a number of things.

'They don't take kindly to half fae on the human isles,' Inga said, her voice flat. 'Honestly, they don't even take kindly to half fae on *this* bloody island, but at least I know people here. There's others like me, too. Half fae. Quarter fae. Full humans whose families have lived here for so many generations they have no clear place of origin to return to. We're not cattle, you know. We have a community you can't just tear apart.'

Thysandra realised a moment too late her mouth was still hanging open; the retort she'd hoped would emerge had not, in fact, done so.

'So.' Inga shrugged. 'I'm here to tell you to do something about us. Happy to offer some suggestions, if you need them.'

*Suggestions?*

It took all she had to restrain her voice. 'What exactly do you—'

'We'd like full citizen's rights, first of all.' A blistering glower. 'Meaning that it would become legally punishable to murder or assault us, just to name one thing. And that you'd have to pay us if you'd like for us to keep working. A more decent place to live than the hovels in which you've been housing us would be appreciated – shouldn't be a problem, honestly, now that gods-know-how-many of you have fought themselves to death for the glorious sake of tyranny. Figure you should at least have some castle rooms available.'

So much for the servant's manners. 'Do you have the faintest idea of the uproar it would cause if I were to—'

'Oh, yes.' Inga shrugged, long hair tumbling down over her shoulders. 'Wishing you much wisdom in dealing with that. I do suggest you deal with it, though.'

'Who do you think you *are?*' Thysandra snapped, anger and bewilderment finally getting the best of her. 'You can't come stomping in here and make demands just because you're no longer working here. I'll make my decisions however I see fit, and—'

'Ah, yes.' The other woman sighed. 'Emelin already mentioned you might be a little stubborn about the matter.'

Thysandra's mind went blank.

'*Emelin?*' It came out infuriatingly breathless. 'What in the world does *Emelin* have to do with this?'

'Oh, she's more or less my niece,' Inga said dryly. 'I'm Allie's sister – you know Allie, don't you? Very moving family reunion, I can tell you. Very useful, too. Emelin told me some immensely interesting things about your time with the Alliance.'

Fuck.

*Fuck.*

79

'So I strongly suggest you make a good attempt at securing a decent future for the humans living under your rule.' Inga finally pushed herself off the shelves she'd been leaning against and straightened, still unsmiling as she stuck her hands into the pockets of her servant's frock. 'Would be a shame if someone got carried away by vengeful feelings and slit your traitorous throat. Let me know if there's anything I can do to help, though – I can usually be found in Rustvale.'

Thysandra barely even heard that last sentence, standing paralysed between the looming bookcases as the weight of yet another complication came crashing onto her shoulders. Funerals and festivals. Miles and miles of archives she couldn't for the life of her make sense of. And now the bloody humans wanted *rights*, as if saving a court full of bloodthirsty fae wasn't enough of a burden already?

There was absolutely no way she was going to explain to the likes of Bereas and his friends why they would be sharing the court's scarce resources with a huddle of former servants. Worse, she might not even be able to explain it to Nicanor.

And then they would wonder ...

*Fed to the hounds.*

'Anything else I need to clarify?' Inga added, her impassive voice coming from miles away. 'It's my first free day in months. I'd prefer not to spend all of it at work anyway.'

Lightning struck.

*This is not the right aisle if you're looking for grain stores ...*

'Wait.' Too loud, too abrupt – her voice was a thunderclap in the eerie silence of the archives. 'Wait a moment, please. You're saying you work here?'

Inga's eyes narrowed. 'Worked.'

'Yes, yes,' Thysandra hastily agreed, because damn it all, verb tenses were not what she was concerned about right now, 'but you know your way around the place? You've been here for a while?'

'The last twenty years.' A snort. 'Agenor got me this job to keep me safe after Al was banished from the island. Pretty decent of him, considering that I refused to talk to him at the time, but I suppose he isn't the worst in general.'

Hardly high praise – for the male Thysandra had respected more than perhaps anyone else at the court – but she decided to let that point go. 'So if I need someone reliable to dig into some numbers for me, could you do it? I'll look into the human issue in the meantime. We could make a simple bargain—'

'Oh, no,' Inga interrupted, visibly inching backwards. Her face twisted into a disgusted scowl. 'You'll keep your foul magic away from my body, Your Majesty. I can look into the registers if it helps you, but you can trust me on my word or don't trust me at all – I'm not going to bind myself to you.'

Oh, come *on*.

'Not even if it means you can hold me to my promises too?' Thysandra tried, fearing the worst and seeing her suspicions confirmed as that almost-human face darkened even further. 'If I bargain to do something about the human position ...'

'I don't need a bargain for that,' Inga said, huffing. 'If you fail us, I'll just let your people know that you sold them out by blathering about the bindings to the Alliance. Should kill you faster than any bargain would.'

Hell take her; it would.

Thysandra closed her eyes. The last of those hard-won illusions of security were rapidly dissolving.

'Alright.' Deep breaths. Swift thoughts. She had to keep herself together now; crumbling on the cold floor of the archives wouldn't keep her alive. 'Let's try another approach. What can you tell me about Gadyon?'

'He's mostly alright,' Inga said, sounding unwilling to admit it. 'Has been sneaking us extra food whenever the village supervisors put us on rations.'

Which suggested some moral compass from the brand new head of the archives. A certain defiance towards the Mother, too, and a willingness to do the sensible thing rather than making decisions based on nothing but pride and glory – not much to go on, but at least it was *something*.

'Good,' she said, giving herself no more time to think. 'I'll make that bargain with him, then. He can help you and any other volunteers with your work, and I'll leave it to him to double-check the numbers once you've gathered all the relevant information. You can join us when we discuss the results. Does that work?'

'If it makes you feel safer to never trust a single soul around you,' Inga said, and the glimpse of mockery in her grey eyes suddenly made her resemble a particularly caustic Naxi, 'I suppose that works, yes. Anything else?'

'Just be careful.' The words slipped out before she could think twice about them – hell, why bother warning this woman when *she* was the one flinging threats around? 'People aren't going to be happy about any of those changes you're looking for. Worst case, they'll attack you outright, and—'

'Of course they will,' Inga said with a snort. 'So? I'm a human-looking half fae at the Crimson Court. Your lovely subjects haven't done anything *besides* attack me as long as I've been alive.'

That knocked the words straight from Thysandra's brain again.

'Let me know what you need from the archives.' For the first time, Inga smiled – a hard, steel-edged smile, not a glimpse of joy in it. 'And when we're getting together for that discussion. If no one kills me before then, I'll be there.'

# CHAPTER 8

By sundown, Thysandra was too tired to fly.

But no one had killed her yet, and no one had declared war on anyone; the world had begun to pull itself together after the earth-shattering changes of the last few days. The clerks at the population department were updating the registers. The first letters had arrived from other fae isles pledging fealty to the Crimson Court. Her last quick meeting with Nicanor hadn't presented any new challenges, and even better, she'd succeeded in informing him of the humans' demands without rousing any suspicions about her motives for humouring them.

Which meant she was as much in control as she'd ever be while she dragged herself back to her rooms, a stoic expression plastered on her face even as her legs threatened to give way beneath her.

Which meant she was in control all by *herself*, no demon assistance needed.

She still hadn't figured out how she should inform Naxi of that fact by the time she reached her own floor. Two fae corpses lay sprawled over the upper steps of the stairs, knives in their chests and hands around the hilts – having disregarded her command to leave their demon guest alone, clearly. The door showed some faint traces of blades and crowbars. None of them had gotten through; the Mother's protective magic held, even now.

*A traitor's daughter.*

How ironic, that the favours that had once bought Thysandra's unwavering loyalty were still the ones protecting her now.

She sparked her red magic at the right spot, and the locks clicked open. Without granting the dead fae on her doorstep another glance, she turned the handle and slipped inside, bracing herself for anger or tears or whatever else would be Naxi's reaction to the news that her help and loyalty were no longer needed ...

She made it half a step into the room.

Then froze again.

Whatever she had expected to find upon her return, an explosive invasion of houseplants had not been on the list. Yet there was no other way to describe the sight that welcomed her in the golden evening light – not the familiar, meticulous row of pots in the windows and corners of the room but a tangle of greenery that seemed to have taken over every surface in its vicinity. Heartleaf vines framed the balcony doors, winding elegantly around the bookshelves on the wall. The monstera had grown to nightmarish proportions, leaves shrouding half of the sitting area in shadows. Blood-red begonia flowers pulsated like living hearts in their pots, having swollen up to twice their size like sponges soaked in deep red wine.

The room smelled of forest, suddenly. Of moist earth and sweet blooms, a heady mix that made her head swim even in the moment she stood paralysed in the doorway.

Then Naxi's elated voice exclaimed, 'Oh, Sashka!'

Naxi.

*Nymph magic.*

The realisation was still in the process of landing when the culprit came dancing into view, blushing and beaming like the sun itself. Her blonde-and-pink curls had been bound up in a messy braid that seemed equal parts ribbon and hair. Her cheeks were rosy; her bare feet were spotlessly clean.

Most baffling of all, she was wearing one of Thysandra's own bathrobes – a black, lacy thing that flowed around her slight form like water, the sleeves flopping just past her small hands, the hem trailing over the floorboards behind her.

She looked utterly, radiantly joyful.

Worse ...

Much, *much* worse, the first word that popped into Thysandra's mind at the sight was an unforgivable *delicious*.

'You're back!' her tormentor triumphantly declared, rushing past her, tugging the door shut, then twirling around to bounce about the overgrown room. The elegant black silk suited her like midnight suited a bright-coloured butterfly – not at all – and yet there was something strangely enticing about the contrast, the smooth darkness brushing over those slim, pale legs. 'How was your day? Are they listening to you? Did you murder anyone, or have I been the only one amusing myself?'

'I ... I did not.' The answer slipped mechanically past her lips, her stunned mind grasping the lifeline of those questions as she staggered into the room. Vines had crept over the mirror, too, and a monstrous clematis now covered half of the small kitchen counter. 'And they're accepting me for now, more or less. What in the world have you—'

'Oh, just cheered the place up a little,' Naxi brightly interrupted, shooing heartleaf vines aside as she cleared a seat on the couch. 'Poor things were miserable, being confined to those grisly pots. You should sit down, you know. You're absolutely exhausted. Would you like some cheese pastries?'

What?

Too many developments. Too many surprises. Her mind wasn't even done processing the first one, and it took a moment too long to blink and stammer, 'Where the hell did you get *cheese pastries*?'

'Oh, I opened the window and scared a passing fae male into getting them for me.' Naxi sent her a wide, sharp-toothed grin. 'Turns out they believe I can curse them at a distance if they're not fast enough. Very useful – we should keep that in mind. He also brought us some cinnamon rolls, if you're in the mood for something sweeter. And won't you sit down? You're feeling a little overwhelmed.'

Thysandra fell down onto the couch. Her wobbly knees didn't leave her much of a choice.

'That's better,' Naxi cooed, dragging a blanket from the nearest chair and draping it clumsily around her wings and shoulders, like a fussy but inexperienced nurse. Her delicate hands were all movement, all vivacity, never pausing for the shortest moment. 'Don't move. I'll get you food and tea, and then you can tell me all about your day, alright?'

Food?

*Tea?*

No. No, this was not at all how this was supposed to go, some twisted imitation of cosy intimacy between them – because the little menace was going to *leave*, the sooner the better, and what was the sense of going along with this charade if that simple fact would be looming over every second of their meal? It wouldn't be fair, would it, to toy with those fickle demon feelings like that?

Not that she should care about Naxi's feelings in the first place, of course, but all the same …

'We need to have a word,' she said weakly, unable to tear her eyes away as her self-declared caretaker bustled around the room and pulled plates and mugs from cupboards. 'I've had some time to think about that help you offered, and—'

'Oh, hush,' Naxi interrupted, swatting at her. 'No talk of politics on an empty stomach, Sashka.'

'But—'

Naxi sent her a glare and flicked back the clean white cloth hiding the pastries.

It was only then – at the sight of that flaky, golden-brown goodness – that Thysandra abruptly realised she was starving.

She hadn't even noticed it. She'd worked much longer stretches of time on an empty stomach before, had trained herself not to pay attention to the rumbling and the hollow aches … but now, with the salty scent of melted butter and grilled goat's cheese filling the room, there was no avoiding the sudden, keen awareness that she hadn't eaten since her hasty breakfast of that morning. Which was no excuse, of course. All the plants and pastries in the world couldn't change anything about the necessity of the conversation they were about to have, that conversation she really didn't feel any nervous dread about ...

But when had anyone last prepared dinner for her?

And when had anyone last placed a plate of food in her lap with such excessive, meticulous care, the way Naxi did now? People didn't *serve* her at this court. She was the one who answered to others, who took care of their every wish and whim without complaints; the role of the spoiled one was strange to the point of discomfort, the urge to stand and get her own damn cutlery so overwhelming she might have obeyed it if not for her buckling knees.

Instead, she watched as Naxi fussed around for a few more minutes, pouring two mugs of piping hot tea, finding a jar of mildly crystallised honey, pulling knives and forks and napkins from drawers. By the time the demon curled up in the large green armchair with her own meal, it had become a challenge not to burst out crying on the spot.

Weakness. She ought to know better.

She averted her eyes and started eating instead.

The pastries were delicious – crisp on the outside, creamy on the inside, the flavours of briny cheese and thyme mingling to create something altogether divine on her tongue. She ate two, then a cinnamon roll, then another pastry. It felt unbearably *decadent*, to sit here with her blanket and her tea and just allow herself to drown in these treats ... but hell, what was she to do about it if Naxi wouldn't allow her to talk before she was fully satisfied?

She ate another cinnamon roll.

Only when her stomach felt full to the point of bursting did she manage to shove her plate aside and sag back into the cushions. In the armchair, Naxi was nibbling on a roll of her own, one round cheek bulging with food.

'There.' Her smile was smug, in an oddly endearing way. 'That's better, isn't it?'

It wasn't better at all.

Quite the opposite – it was much, much worse.

Was this some clever trick? Some cruel demon's game? Had Naxi known what she was about to say, and was this how she tried to avoid the hard, simple facts – by making Thysandra feel so stupidly peaceful, so ridiculously comfortable, that it became almost impossible to speak those damning words?

*You need to leave.*

But she had to speak them. She *had* to. She didn't need the assistance anymore, and the very presence of a demon at her court was a tinderbox about to ignite in the deadliest of ways – it was simple pragmatism, basic politics, and what was she thinking, letting something as silly as cosiness get in the way of her own survival?

Naxi's long, melodramatic sigh interrupted her thoughts. '*Fine*, Sashka. Out with it, then.'

Gods-damned demon senses.

'You offered your help.' Keeping her voice level, almost curt, was the only way she could get the words past her lips at all. 'And I accepted it because I needed it. Now I've spent a day building a reliable group of allies around me, and I'm no longer in need of outside assistance. Which means you should ... well ... you know ...'

*Leave.*

This wasn't hard. This couldn't be hard.

Her lips faltered all the same.

'Ah,' Naxi said cheerfully, stretching out in the armchair like a content cat. Black silk cascaded like a shadow around her in the deepening twilight. 'You're telling me to get out of here, aren't you?'

Thysandra blinked.

'You're so predictable, Sashka.' A fond, radiant smile. 'But don't worry, I'll leave you alone if that's what you really want. I'm not a monster, you see.'

That last sentence was definitely a lie.

Which didn't inspire much confidence in the one that had preceded it, either – because good gods, this was much, much too easy again. Where was the shock? Where were the pleas? This was the same female who'd snuck into that bloody underground cell over and over again, no matter how hard Thysandra had shouted at her to stay away ... so what were the chances that she would just give up now, not even a word of discussion before accepting the inevitable?

'What is the catch?' Thysandra said slowly.

'Catch? What catch?' Naxi's smile grew even more disarming. 'You're telling me to leave, so I'll leave first thing in the morning. There doesn't have to be anything else to it, does there?'

*First thing in the morning.*

There it was.

'You think I'll let you spend the night here?' Her voice cracked. 'When you know I'm going to make you leave? What's stopping you from strangling me in my sleep if—'

Naxi rolled her eyes. 'Don't be dramatic, Sashka. Of course I won't strangle you. And what else were you planning to do – kick me out onto the streets in the middle of the night? You know as well as I do that I'm not going to find a ship or an alf to get me out of here at this time of day.'

That was an annoyingly good point.

She really hadn't thought that far ahead, but at the same time ... 'You'd survive perfectly well for a single night. Just cosy up to the Labyrinth again if you need to.'

'I made the *bed* for us,' Naxi complained, draping herself dramatically over the padded armrest, blinking up at Thysandra with moist blue eyes. 'Do you really want to make me sleep on hard stone after I—'

'You made the fucking *bed*?'

'Yes?' A sullen, alarmingly tempting pout. 'I thought I'd take care of you, and also, I didn't have anything else to do except scare the living daylights out of passing fae. Why are you looking so surprised, exactly?'

'You ... you thought ...' She was running out of words and sense at the same time. 'You thought I'd crawl into bed with you? Just like that? With *you*? After ... after ...'

'I'm proposing we *sleep*, Sashka.' In a flutter of movement, Naxi sat upright again, nimble fingers toying with the sash of the black gown. It had fallen open a few inches, revealing a thin shoulder, the ridge of a fragile collarbone, and absolutely nothing else beneath. 'You know it's possible to lie in the same bed without fucking, don't you?'

Did she?

That was to say ... of course she knew. She'd spent plenty of nights sharing narrow tents with fellow soldiers, male or female, and not had contact with anything except the occasional inconvenient elbow flying around – the sort of sleeping that was just business, just pragmatic necessity. But none of those tentmates had been tiny, silk-clad demons with lively little hands and pouty lips that just begged to—

No.

No, she was *not* going to think about kissing anyone.

'I'm not sleeping in a bed with you,' she said through gritted teeth, averting her eyes. It felt like a surrender to look away – but hell, if she just kept repeating that simple sentence, she couldn't be talked into anything, could she? She didn't owe the little terror any explanation. Explanations would just lead to discussions she could lose. 'That's all I have to say about it. Leave now or leave tomorrow, but—'

'Well, you'll have to take the couch, then,' Naxi said dreamily. 'You're not banishing me from the bed I made myself. That's just unfair.'

'I'm not sleeping on my own fucking couch! I—'

'Excellent.' Naxi beamed at her. 'Then I'll just crawl into the bed with you and we'll both sleep like roses. Was that so hard?'

For the bloody gods' sakes.

'Leave my rooms,' she ground out, because the alternative was thinking for even a moment about that image – lithe limbs tangled with her blankets – and she'd be damned if she let those demon games get the better of her once again. 'Leave my rooms right *now*. Sleep in fucking Faewood for all I care, but—'

'Pity I didn't bargain to obey you,' Naxi interrupted, glancing appreciatively at the pink bargain mark on her wrist. 'And since I'm not feeling any pain, I'm going to assume my disobedience isn't a breach of my promise not to harm you either – funny, isn't it?'

'I don't care what the bargain thinks!' Thysandra sputtered, her voice growing shrill. 'I'm telling you *I* don't want—'

'Oh, of course you want it.' An eyeroll, visible even in the deepening twilight. 'But fine, let's make a deal. I'll take the couch, on one simple condition.'

Simple conditions were *never* simple. She felt like a wide-eyed fawn ambling straight into a hunter's snare as she braced herself and snapped, 'Yes?'

'You kiss me first,' Naxi said brightly.

Her heart stuttered.

'What?' She must have misheard. She *must* have – because that was not a suggestion anyone, sane or insane, would reasonably come up with, right? 'Did you say—'

Naxi leaned forward in the armchair, pink hair spilling over the black silk of her robe, lips curving into a mesmerising little rosebud smile. 'Kiss me?'

No.

*No.*

Her heart was a fluttering mess, and the worst of it was that it wasn't all repugnance – that she couldn't possibly deny the little spark of anticipation, *eagerness*, flaring to life in her chest. Even though they weren't going to kiss. Of *course* they weren't going to kiss. Kissing would only lead to emotions, and emotions were the last thing either of them needed – and anyway, she didn't even *want* it, not really. Surely this was just … just …

Just curiosity?

Just memories. Just the day of the Last Battle returning to her, white hills and dying screams and soft, soft lips on every inch of her body—

Naxi giggled.

*Fuck.*

'No!' Thysandra sputtered, realising only then she should have objected at least five stunned heartbeats ago.

'No?' The sound of that one word was so infuriatingly knowing it barely counted as a question. 'Are you really quite sure of that, Sashka?'

'Of course I am sure!' The frantic beat of her heart said otherwise. She sucked in a cool breath and hurriedly added, 'And didn't I tell you to leave my rooms? We're done with this conversation. We're *done*. I have absolutely zero intention of kissing you or—'

'You're such a liar,' Naxi said fondly, rising from her chair.

'And stay away from me!' She scrambled back over the couch, then to her feet, away from those all-seeing blue eyes. Away from every inch of smooth, vulnerable skin whispering at her to come closer instead. 'Stay where you are. I—'

'And what if I don't?' Naxi's tiptoeing steps didn't slow, her movements so light they seemed almost otherworldly, her head tilted at a taunting angle. 'What if I already know exactly what you want? I could give it to you, you know. All the little bits of indulgence you deny yourself, and—'

Thysandra almost stumbled over her own feet in her hurry to move back. '*Stop* it!'

'Why?' A soft, melodious laugh. 'Because you won't stop yourself?'

'No,' Thysandra gasped, her wings bumping against the overgrown bookshelves. No way to retreat farther unless she were to fling herself out of the window. 'No, because ... because ...'

'Because you can't stop me, then?' Naxi was close enough to touch, and yet she didn't reach out. A head shorter than Thysandra, half as broad, and still her half-whispering voice was the only weapon she needed. 'That's why you refuse to sleep in your own bed with me, isn't it, Sashka? Because I could kiss you, and you'd happily give me those pretty lips of yours. I could slip my fingers—'

'Shut *up*.' It was almost a moan.

Naxi chuckled. 'Why?'

She made her decision in the blink of an eye.

A desperate reflex rather than a well-defined plan, but who cared so long as it worked? Who cared so long as it saved her from a stupid mistake she was guaranteed to regret? Her hand flew to the shelves behind her back, grabbling for the knife she'd hidden between the books – yes, *there* was the smooth leather hilt—

A glint of light broke through the dusk as she swung her right hand up. The edge of the blade slid against Naxi's pale throat the next moment – crude steel against vulnerable skin, and yet Thysandra's fingers didn't tremble.

'Happy now?' Her voice had gone rough. 'If the word *no* doesn't mean a damn thing to you, perhaps this makes my point. Get away from me, and—'

The corners of Naxi's lips were trembling.

Oh no. Oh no, no, no. 'What the hell are you laughing about?'

'You're *adorable*, Sashka.' The grin growing on that round, blushing face was nothing less than alarming – all shark's teeth and sparkling villainy. 'Did you really think I'd fall for that trick a second time, darling?'

'What—' she started, and then something slithered around her neck.

Around her shoulder.

Around her wrists.

A cold, leathery touch, not coarse like rope but smooth in the most alarming of ways, skimming across her heated skin and tightening on her arms, her chest ...

Vines.

Those fucking *vines* were creeping over her wall with snake-like speed, slipping around her ankles, her thighs ... They yanked back her knife hand, away from Naxi's throat. The dagger clattered uselessly against the floorboards. And still the plants weren't done, curling tighter and tighter around her limbs – pinning her against the bookshelves no matter how hard she tried to pull away from her bonds.

'Oh, I really don't recommend fighting them so much,' Naxi muttered, stepping back to lean against the armrest of the couch. Her eyes gleamed with unholy delight. 'They'll only hold you more securely if you try to escape. For your own safety, of course – I really don't want to have to fight you.'

The words barely registered.

Vines still skimmed across Thysandra's bare skin, almost *tenderly* now – a thousand maddening touches at once, caressing the hollow of her throat, the insides of her wrists. She tried to draw in a deep breath and found the plants had wrapped around her chest as well. Leaves brushed like lover's fingers over the inside of her thighs, and before she could pull herself together, her body clenched around a sting of heat ...

It was all she could do to swallow her moan.

'Oh, dear,' Naxi murmured, cocking her head. 'Surely you're not enjoying this, are you, Sashka?'

'Of course I'm not,' she ground out, despite knowing better, despite her own body betraying her with every ragged breath. Squeezing her eyes shut for a moment only made her feel every sensation *more* intensely, leaves stroking across her scarred wings, her nape, the sensitive spot behind her ear. 'Why would I enjoy—'

The vines tightened like clawing fingers on her thighs.

Her hips bucked forward, a shameful, inadvertent confession – every fibre in her body straining closer to Naxi's distant, delicate silhouette no matter how well she knew to stay away. Naxi laughed again, moving closer. It was dark enough now to see nothing but the glint of her eyes, the ravenous intensity in that gaze.

And then it was her *finger*, not another bit of murderous greenery, that came sliding down Thysandra's cheek, chin, throat ... such a gossamer touch, incomprehensibly sweet against the relentless control of her nymph magic.

'You can't lie to me.' That melodious sing-song voice, coming from miles away through the roar in Thysandra's head. 'You really should know that by now, Sashka. Do you like it, being all at my mercy?'

*Yes.*

'No,' she gasped.

'And still you're trying to deceive me.' More fingers. Slipping across her collarbone, swirling idly over the swell of her heaving breasts. 'Good thing I know better than to listen to your silly words, when that delicious body of yours is telling me all I need to know – you want my lips, don't you, Sashka? Care to tell me *where* you need them?'

Her body was a filthy traitor.

A slide of hot, slick arousal burned through her, down and down and down, blooming into a maddening ache at the apex of her thighs – and the vines responded instantly, tugging at her ankles, her knees, forcing her legs apart even as she cursed and wrestled against their inhuman hold.

She needed this. Needed it *desperately*, and yet she could never, *never* afford to have it – not if she wanted to survive another month, another *day* in this world. It was weakness, the shameless lust soaking her underlinen. Utter humiliation, to lose all that control of herself. And weakness had nearly killed her once before, her pathetic pining for a love that never came; the hole it had left behind was still a gaping hollow in her chest, too bottomless to survive another fall into its shadows ...

She could barely even think anymore.

She only knew, down to the marrow of her bones, that she couldn't, *couldn't* let herself reveal the unforgivable depths of her need.

'Stop.' It was barely more than a wheeze, the sound of her voice. '*Stop.*'

The vines slowed.

No time to think. No time to reconsider. The words spilled from her lips in a garbled, desperate mess. 'Fine. *Fine.* I give up. You win. I'll sleep on that gods-damned couch. I'll—'

Naxi stiffened for the shortest moment, then burst out laughing.

'Please.' Thysandra almost sobbed the word, wilting against the shelves. It was too light, that laughter. For a moment, it chased away every lingering shadow. 'That ... that was the deal. Leave me alone and I'll let you take the bed – *please*. I ... I can't ...'

'Oh, as you wish, Sashka.' At once the sultry temptation was gone, that tightly wound predator focus. Naxi bounced to the bedroom as the vines slithered away like snakes into their dens – a spring in her step that was almost more horrifying than the ruthless seduction of a moment before. 'Make yourself comfortable here, then. You're always welcome to join me if you change your mind.'

The next moment, the bedroom door fell shut behind her.

As if nothing of note had happened at all.

Thysandra staggered back to the couch, burning shame and burning arousal warring in her gut – the memory of those inhuman caresses lingering long after the vines themselves had retreated. The closed door seemed to be laughing at her. How easy, how incomprehensibly easy, would it be to turn that handle and—

*A traitor's daughter.*

Fuck.

Was this all she'd be doing for the rest of her life, then – sacrificing her principles to pleasure over and over again?

The velvet cushions enveloped her as she let herself fall into the softness of the couch, eyes shut, skin aching with emptiness. Just like all those years ago, after the Last Battle. Just like all those nights she'd spent curled up in her windowsill, unable to face the praise and the victory waiting for her at court ... Because that was what happened when you gave yourself even the smallest taste of what you wanted, wasn't it?

You couldn't stop craving it anymore.

One crack in your armour, and weakness would never stop pouring out again.

*Just one night* – she repeated the words to herself again and again as she wrapped her wings around her body, hiding her face between her arms so as not to see the bedroom door. Just a few more hours. Then Naxi would be gone from the Crimson Court, never to return, and she'd be free of these maddening desires, this constant pull to give in and hand herself over to yet another illusion of love ...

One night.

Then she would be strong again.

# CHAPTER 9

SHE WOKE TO THE banging of fists on her door.

For a moment she barely knew where she was as she rolled off the couch and staggered to her feet, the riot of leaves and vines around her so different from her familiar living room that her sleep-fogged mind refused to recognise it. Then she hit her knee against the low table, and pain and memory bloomed together.

Right. Couch.

Naxi.

And a shrill, urgent voice on her doorstep, shouting her name.

Changing course, she raked a hurried hand through her tangled hair and snatched last night's dagger from the floor. Could it be a trap? It could be a trap. Perhaps she should demand they bring in Nicanor first, to vouch for their peaceful intentions. Then again, that would put her further in Nicanor's debt *and* show the court that she didn't dare rely on herself, which—

The bedroom door swept open, and Naxi darted into the room as if she was about to leave for a summer picnic.

She was wearing her own flower dress again, although without the bloodstains; she must have washed it the previous day. Her hair hung loose over her shoulders. From the smile on her face, one could have thought she'd lived in these quarters for *years* – a suspiciously oblivious cheer, as if she had forgotten that she'd be out of here before she could move another vine.

Or ... well, as soon as this more urgent disturbance had been dealt with, at least.

'Morning, Sashka!' she sunnily greeted, hiding a little yawn behind her hand. 'They're genuinely panicking outside, if you want to know. No murderous feelings waiting for you.'

Right.

That shouldn't have been a reassurance.

Really, *nothing* this treacherous little creature said or did should make her feel any safer ... and yet she couldn't help her loosening shoulders as she took two steps towards the door and swung it open. Damn the caution, then. If anyone attacked her, at least she'd have a demon watching her back.

The black-haired female who came tumbling over the doorstep looked like attacking anyone was the last thing on her mind, though.

'Thysandra.' She gasped the name, falling to her knees in a rush of violet wings. 'Your Majesty, I mean. My son, Your Majesty – my son was taken by the Labyrinth! He's nowhere to be found, and the others aren't either, and—'

Thysandra stiffened.

Her mind needed half a second to shift – an almost physically painful adjustment from the simple court quarrels she'd expected to something with the potential to be much worse. The bloody *Labyrinth*? But she'd given orders that no one was to enter that cursed place yesterday, hadn't she? She'd posted fae around the bone hall to keep curious idiots out?

Vaguely, she was aware of Naxi's muffled giggle behind her.

'Could you repeat that,' she slowly said, bracing herself against the carved doorframe, 'and then start from the beginning, please?'

'It … it started last night,' the kneeling female stammered, her purple wings quivering. She was wearing a particularly flimsy chemise and nothing else, Thysandra only noticed then; most of the company around her was similarly dressed, or rather, barely dressed. 'There were strange lights coming from the bone hall. Which didn't seem much to worry about at first, but now people have started going in, and—'

'Tell me more about that,' Thysandra interrupted sharply. 'Who? Why? I seem to remember I gave explicit commands yesterday that no one was to go anywhere near the place under any circumstances.'

The female at her feet let out a shuddering wail. 'It wasn't *voluntarily*, Your Majesty!'

A disconcerted silence fell.

'Not … voluntarily?' Thysandra repeated, lifting her gaze to the rest of the company standing huddled in the corridor – hoping, against her wiser expectations, that one of them would step forward and turn this madness into sanity. 'Could you elaborate? Is anyone *forcing* people to go into the Labyrinth?'

A lanky male wearing only a lacy dressing gown cleared his throat, nervously glancing back and forth between Thysandra and the female on the floor. 'The … the Labyrinth itself, it seems.'

Centuries of keeping a straight face were barely enough to keep her expression in check. 'Come again?'

'It seems to be … enchanting people?' He swallowed visibly. 'Their eyes go all glazed and they wander off towards its entrances. I saw three or four people flounder into the bone hall before I got the hell out of there, but some others—'

'My son,' the violet-winged female sobbed. 'My son was lured into the gate near the west cove, Your Majesty!'

'But that gate is *sealed*,' Thysandra sputtered, knowing damn well it was hardly the most important point about this situation but unable to ignore it all the same. 'The Mother closed it centuries ago. How could anyone—'

'That little halfblood opened it!' the desperate mother burst out. '*Emelin!*'

Oh.

Oh *gods.*

*It took them all down,* Naxi had said about the fae who tried to reach her in the bone hall – but that had been only the bone hall, and only the people unwise enough to actively fly within the Labyrinth's reach. Why in the world had no one told her the other entrances to the caves had been opened as well? She was the fucking High Lady of this court, for the bloody gods' sakes – how in hell was she supposed to protect its people if no one even informed her of the dangers in the first place?

'Alright,' she said, gritting her teeth to keep down the scream welling up in her throat. *Show no confusion,* her thoughts droned. *Show no weakness.* 'You there – get me a list of the opened gates within an hour. The two of you – I need names of the people who disappeared into the mountain. In the meantime—'

'I could go take a look?' Naxi's bright voice interrupted.

Thysandra hadn't thought anything could further startle the gathered fae around the doorway, but it turned out the presence of a broadly smiling demon in an adorable pink dress was enough to stun even the wailing female at her feet into silence.

'*You?*' she heard herself blurt, and there was far too much shock in her voice. 'But—'

*But you were going to leave.* She almost let those pathetic words fall from her lips for half the court to hear – *but I no longer needed you. You agreed so easily that you should finally leave me alone ...*

Far, far too easily.

The floor was sinking away beneath her feet.

'Well, the Labyrinth is a natural phenomenon. With feelings.' Naxi beamed at her, as if her magic wasn't picking up on every tendril of escalating panic. 'Nymph and demon magic seem rather well-suited to the task, wouldn't you say, Your Majesty?'

*Your Majesty.*

Not *Sashka,* at least. She was almost grateful.

'Do you have anything to do with this?' she bit out, her tight voice the only shield between the outside world and the utter collapse of her composure. That little giggle, a moment before. Those knowing smiles

– as if the demon had *known*, last night, that they'd wake up to this particular alarm. 'Did you expect—'

'I didn't *expect* anything,' Naxi protested, that plump bottom lip falling into a pout again. A few of the other fae shuffled hastily backwards. 'But it was clear enough that the poor thing was still rather grumpy yesterday, wasn't it? So I'm not entirely *surprised* it's acting up. Honestly, I would be lashing out too if someone locked me down for eight centuries – it might just be getting started, for all we know.'

The disconcerted glances among the gathered fae were unmistakable now.

'Alright,' Thysandra said, making her decision in a heartbeat – because *she* sure as hell wasn't descending into the eerie-lit bowels of the mountain beneath the castle, and she doubted many other volunteers for rescue missions would be available. There would be plenty of time to kick the bloody menace off the island after this had been resolved. 'Do what you can, but if even a single fae dies on your way through the castle, you'll feel the consequences. Clear?'

For a single moment she thought Naxi would object.

Worse, that the demon might laugh in her face and remind her she was in no position to make demands, not unless she wished for some particularly interesting rumours to spread – traitor's daughter, counterfeit queen, and who was she to think she could make the rules after a handful of vines had been enough to reduce her to a pleading mess?

But Naxi merely considered her for three thundering heartbeats. Her smile dwindled. Her blue eyes grew thoughtful – no, *calculating*.

Then she nodded, so deeply it was almost a bow, and said, 'As you wish.'

She flitted off before Thysandra could recover from the shock. The ranks of fae parted wide around her slight form, then turned to gape at Thysandra again – not in outrage, as she'd feared, but rather with something like ... baffled respect?

*Awe?*

Only then did she realise what the exchange must have looked like to the rest of the world – to those who had not witnessed the events in her rooms last night. Thysandra Demonbane, valiantly threatening the monster who'd single-handedly slaughtered all surviving members of a regiment the day before. More unexpectedly, the same uncontrollable demon *bowing* to that authority.

Reinforcing, deliberately or accidentally, Thysandra's illusion of power over the court.

Gods have mercy. Who'd have thought any political savvy was hiding behind that carefree façade?

'Anything else?' she said out loud, using the silence to her advantage while it lasted. 'Because if that was all, I suggest you spread the warning to stay away from the entrances and wait until our demon guest returns with news.'

She expected more objections, pleas, lamenting over children and lovers lost to the wiles of the mountain. But the purple-winged female at her feet scrambled up without another word. The rest of the company was already turning around, gathering robes and skirts, casting cautious glances at the stairs Naxi had just descended. Within a minute they were gone, murmuring quietly among themselves as they hurried out of her reach.

Were they too stunned to cause trouble, or were they too *afraid* of her to do so?

Perhaps it was a coincidence that no one accosted her on her way to the archives this morning, but Thysandra didn't think it was.

The narrow aisles of the archive hall were no longer so hauntingly quiet as they had been the previous day, fae and a handful of humans hurrying between the cabinets against a background of constant murmurs. Somewhere in a far corner of the first hall, someone was slowly reading a list of names out loud. Elsewhere, the dull thuds of books against tables rhythmically broke through the hushed atmosphere. If the news of the Labyrinth's antics had reached these dusky rooms already, no one seemed to be terribly bothered by it; more likely, the clerks had simply been too busy to hear about it.

Thysandra sure as hell wasn't going to be the one to tell them.

She returned all greetings she received on her way to Gadyon's new office, but never paused to engage in any further conversation. The lack of familiar faces was disconcerting. Even though she *knew*, rationally, about the slaughter at the White City, her heart still clung to the odd illusion that all absent fae were simply off on a lengthy vacation; that any moment Anysia could sweep from behind the bookcases and crack some deadpan joke about illiteracy and the army.

Perhaps it would have been easier to wrap her head around it if she'd *been* there. If she'd seen the blood soaking the grass, heard the screams of the dying.

Perhaps she would have felt less like a traitor, too.

She pressed that thought away as she finally reached the office that had been Anysia's, the nameplate that had adorned the door for over a century gone.

The head of the archives worked from a spacious, octagonal room, sparsely decorated but for the broad desk and the carved bookcases along the walls. A single arched window looked out over the olive-covered hills and the azure sea beyond. At first, scanning the office for would-be murderers, she thought the place was empty; only as she stepped inside did she notice the small shape huddled in the corner behind the desk, a messy grey blanket from which only a blonde head and an arm emerged.

The pointy tip of a fae ear unmistakably stuck out from between those pale blonde locks.

Frowning, Thysandra came to a standstill in the middle of the room, throwing another quick glance around to make sure she hadn't somehow overlooked Gadyon as well. But the brown-haired fae really was nowhere to be seen, and here was a half human clerk taking a nap in his office – did he have any idea?

Why hadn't the bloody woman just gone home to sleep?

She considered her options for a moment, then closed the door, cleared her throat, and cautiously said, 'Inga?'

Allie's sister shot up from her makeshift bed with a speed that could rival the most vigilant of soldiers.

'I have permission to— Oh. It's you.' She slumped back against the side of the bookcase, voice lowering a little as she grabbed an old waterbag off the floor and took a swig. 'Apologies. I was expecting Gadyon to wake me before you arrived.'

Which suggested her supervisor knew about the clerk in his room. Thysandra considered that for a moment, then suggested, 'Long night?'

'Yes. Stayed up until sunrise to get all the paperwork in order.' Inga took a few more sips of water, then rubbed her eyes and rose to her feet, folding the blanket with efficient ease. 'And then I couldn't go home anymore, of course.'

She did not sound annoyed. She sounded, if anything, wearily resigned to whatever had made her tuck herself in on this hard wooden floor instead.

'Ah,' Thysandra said, with more confidence than she felt. 'Yes. Why, exactly?'

A frown. 'Why what?'

'Why couldn't you go home anymore? Sunrise was hours ago – you'd have had plenty of time to—'

'Oh. Too many fae around.' Inga shrugged, dropping into one of the chairs at the desk without waiting for an invitation. 'To avoid getting caught by anyone with unsavoury intentions, it's generally best to sneak in before sunrise and out during dinnertime. If one of your mages could accompany me back to Rustvale after we're done with this meeting, I would greatly appreciate it.'

Thysandra blinked.

To avoid getting *caught*?

A line of reasoning presented with such bland indifference. Was this something humans did all the time? Something *all* humans did?

She was still figuring out how to ask without sounding like a fool when Nicanor slid into the room – his silvery hair braided, his damask coat a sensible black today. His smooth steps faltered only for the briefest moment as he caught sight of Inga by the desk; then, as if nothing had happened, he closed the door behind him, nodded at

Thysandra by way of greeting, and wryly said, 'Another morning of bold choices?'

He must already have heard about Naxi and the Labyrinth, then. Better not to discuss that right before Inga's wary grey eyes.

Instead, she said, 'This is Inga, Nicanor. Inga, meet my Lord Protector.'

Nicanor gave a small, nondescript smile as he sat down. Inga's response was a long, scathing look from behind loose strands of her long blonde hair.

Promising start.

Thankfully, the door creaked open before the silence could stretch to the point of awkwardness, and a pile of parchment stumbled into the room, followed by the tall male carrying it. Gadyon's face and messy brown hair were barely visible behind the fruits of his labour. His unmistakable limp was enough evidence of his identity, though; there weren't *that* many fae with a clubfoot at the Crimson Court.

Really, he might be the only one. The education system of the court was hardly gentle on those with a disadvantage on the battlefield.

Inga darted from her chair to help the head of the archives unload his burden onto his desk, sorting the books and scrolls into piles with a swiftness that proved she hadn't held her job *only* because of Agenor's interference. Gadyon muttered a word of thanks, and another one as Nicanor rose to close the door once again; he fell into the chair beside Thysandra as if it was the first time he was sitting down in twenty-four hours.

'Busy night,' he clarified with a nervous nod at the piles of parchment. 'Think we should have all the information you asked for, though.'

Nicanor plucked a sheet from the nearest pile on his way back to his chair, frost-blue eyes shooting over the lines as he sat down. 'Ah, the food again?'

'Unfortunately,' Thysandra said sourly, 'twenty ships full of grain have failed to materialise in our harbours overnight. So yes, the food again.'

He granted her that point with a quick grin. 'Where do we stand, then?'

'It's rather bad,' Gadyon muttered, rubbing his temple. 'I had the numbers calculated by three people independently, as the High Lady asked, and all three clerks ended up with the same estimates: we have about two months of food left in the stores at the moment. Perhaps two and a half, if we limit the feasting. After that ...'

'We're left without provisions in the middle of winter?' Thysandra finished.

He grimaced. 'Yes.'

'How about the other fae isles?' Nicanor asked, pursing his lips at the document in his hand. 'Their harvests—'

'—are far from sufficient,' Gadyon interrupted bluntly. 'Although, well, the main issue is that I'm not entirely sure which islands will end up pledging loyalty to the Crimson Court at all. The head of the department for tributes and taxation is dead, so administration is severely delayed on that side, and many houses seem to be biding their time before making a decision.'

Until they knew how successfully the three new courts would be ruled. Until they could be sure Thysandra would not lead this one into flaming disaster. No one spoke the words out loud, but she could read them in every pair of eyes in the room.

She cleared her throat. 'But say we assume that roughly a third of them will choose to stay allied to our court ...'

'We never produce much in the winter,' Gadyon said, shaking his head. 'A few carts of cabbages aren't going to keep this castle fed. So even if we can double domestic production for next year's spring and summer – for which we should start taking measures soon, if that's what we need – we're still left with a gap of a few months between our provisions running out and the new harvests arriving.'

A few months.

Thysandra had *known* it would be the likely outcome of his research, and all the same, a stone sank in her stomach at the confirmation.

'Thank you,' she forced herself to say, calm and stoic, fighting to keep the dread from her voice. She did not want to know what the likes of Bereas would say if they heard about these numbers – something about armed raids and conquests, in all likeliness. 'It's good to know what we can expect, at least. In that case, it seems to me that our only reasonable option is to swallow our pride and reach out to the other magical communities, isn't it?'

'Good luck with that,' Inga muttered under her breath.

Nicanor threw her a quick glance, then raised a silvery eyebrow at Thysandra. 'I agree, but speaking as your Lord Protector, be careful with how you spread that news. Plenty of people would rather take that food by force.'

Inga's muffled cough sounded suspiciously like a scoff.

'Yes, thank you,' Thysandra hurriedly said, before Nicanor could do worse than narrow his eyes in annoyance. 'That was going to be my next question, as a matter of fact. What approach would you recommend to communicate the decision?'

'We should probably keep the matter quiet for now,' he said, rubbing his fingers over his sharp jaw – visibly making an effort to rein in any biting remarks in Inga's direction. 'At least until we have some idea what price the rest of the archipelago will demand. If the court finds out about the plan before that time, the scaremongering and speculation will run wild, and I can't guarantee that I'll be able to keep that in check entirely.'

Sensible. She looked at Gadyon and Inga, who both nodded – the first more eagerly, the second with a scowl that suggested she'd have loved to disagree.

'Alright,' Thysandra said, straightening her wings and spine. 'I'll start reaching out to some of the other peoples, in that case – I think it's best I do that in person. Gadyon, could you get me an estimate of the minimum we need until spring and an overview of the tribute volumes we've received per island in the past decade?'

He nodded again, then added a slightly redundant, 'Of course.'

'Good. Other than that, please continue the work on the list of fallen warriors I asked for and have it sent to Nicanor once you're done. Nicanor, could you reach out to Orthea and come up with some fitting memorial ceremony together? Please remind her that not *every* occasion requires wine and orgies.'

His sour grin broke through, sharp as a dagger but seemingly genuine. 'Will do.'

'Excellent.' She braced herself, then added as calmly as possible, 'That leaves only the matter of the humans for now.'

All eyes shot to the slender figure perched on her chair by the desk.

'Oh, well done,' Inga said testily – the bite in her voice not enough to hide the tension beneath. 'You've all successfully identified the human in the room. As I informed Her Majesty yesterday, I'm here to ask for full citizen's rights, legal protection, and decent wages and housing. I don't need to elaborate on that, do I?'

What had she said, a few minutes ago? *It's best to sneak in before sunrise and out during dinnertime ...*

'No,' Thysandra said, suppressing the confusing twinge of her heart. 'No, you don't need to elaborate, thank you.'

Inga clenched her jaw, waiting. Gadyon was nodding again. Nicanor sat leaning forward, his blue wings splaying out ever so slightly behind his shoulders ... but like last night, when she'd summarised the matter to him, he did not object.

Did he have the faintest idea of *why* she was going along with this, of the threats haunting her every decision?

'I intend to honour the requests,' she added, almost blurting out the words. 'And I will do so as soon as possible. That said, we may need a little time to figure out how to best go about it. We can introduce wages rather easily, but as for housing, we'll have to decide on a suitable location that doesn't force us to relocate too many fae.'

'Ah, yes,' Inga said bitterly. 'Imagine that, relocating people against their wishes.'

There was nothing Thysandra could say in response to that.

She *tried* – she opened her mouth in the hopes that some counterargument would come to her all by itself – but none of the words welling up in her held water in the slightest. *That's different*, she wanted to say. *That's not at all the same thing as recruiting servants from human isles ...* but it was, wasn't it?

If anything, the fae would only be made to move across the same island. The humans had been taken from all over the archipelago.

And that difference hardly strengthened her position.

'Yes,' she said numbly, a full five seconds too late. 'Yes, good point.'

Inga's expression didn't soften.

'All the same,' Nicanor said, graciously breaking the painful silence, 'it may be safer for the humans to move slowly. There are plenty of fae around who might take out their anger on you if they disagree with these changes.'

'Ah.' Inga scoffed. 'How very convenient.'

'I made a bargain to keep this court under control,' Nicanor sharply retorted, his upper lip curling into an alarming sneer. 'Convenient or inconvenient, I have no choice but to do my best for us all. If you prefer to spread the news before we have solidified our hold on the island, by all means, go ahead, but—'

'I think you've each made your point,' Thysandra interrupted, throwing Inga a warning glance. 'Thank you. We'll move as fast as we can, and in the meantime, we'll keep these plans quiet outside this room. Does anyone have any objections to that?'

Nicanor sagged back in his chair, folding his arms. 'Do you think it might be wise to make a bargain on our collective silence?'

'I'm not making any bargains,' Inga snapped.

'I think we'll be alright,' Thysandra said, hoping this wasn't a mistake, or at least no more than a small, easily fixed mistake. 'None of us profits from leaking the information. Gadyon, please find a new head for the staff department and then instruct them to get wages for human employees set up. Nicanor, let your commanders know I'll treat attacks on humans as punishable crimes from now on, and discuss enforcement with them. Is that enough for now, Inga, or is there anything else we need to talk about?'

It seemed for a moment that Allie's sister would say something, but in the end she merely rose from her chair and snatched her blanket and bottle from the floor, her movements brusque and impatient. 'If that's all for today, would one of you be so gallant as to accompany me home?' She turned, glared at Nicanor, and sharply added, 'Not you.'

A biting smile curled his lips. 'Don't worry. I had no intention of volunteering for the task.'

'I'll come with you, Inga,' Gadyon hastily offered, throwing uneasy glances between the other two. 'Now that the preparations for this meeting are done, I have a few minutes to spare.'

'That works.' Her nod at Thysandra was strained, as if it took all she had not to throw a punch instead. 'Thank you, I suppose. I'll take that back if you disappoint me, though.'

'I'll try not to, then,' Thysandra said wryly.

The next moment, the two archivists were gone – their footsteps echoing through the quiet archives as they removed themselves, hers brisk and impatient, his irregular and accompanied by the supporting slaps of his wings.

She fully expected Nicanor to say something, or worse, to *ask* something. Surely this was the moment to inquire why she was going along with Inga's demands despite the woman's outrageous manners. Why she wouldn't so much as consider the far more popular option of food raids over costly treaties. Why Naxi was still at the court and what in the world she'd been doing with a demon in her rooms all night ...

But all her newly minted Lord Protector said, rising from his chair and sauntering to the door with effortless grace, was, 'Let's have a word about the Labyrinth.'

# CHAPTER 10

THE CRIMSON COURT WAS drenched in fear.

It was a sensation not unlike the warmest summer days on Mirova, when the air had been so heavy with humidity that drawing in a breath felt like drowning ... except that the weight existed only to Naxi's demon senses here, and except, of course, that it would be blasphemy to compare Mirova in any way to this hell of a place.

She loathingly bounced down the stairs, glaring at every wall and window she encountered: stupid violent frescos, stupid pompous marble, stupid flashy gold. There was not an inch of this castle that *wasn't* stained with that hallmark fae pomposity. Hoarding treasures here, building this grand and glittering façade for the rotten core of the empire, while the world was left to starve around it – a game the Mother had played better than anyone else, but it surely hadn't ended with her.

It wasn't the disregard for life that bothered Naxi. She wasn't much bothered with anyone else's life herself, after all.

Rather, it was the arrogance of believing only *fae* had the right to kill without consequences. The way they'd left thousands dead in their wake, yet razed Mirova and murdered everyone on it after some islands took up arms against them and returned the favour.

It wasn't unwelcome to her, the fear permeating every insufferable nook and cranny of this place.

But Thysandra wanted it sorted out, and she wanted Thysandra – so down the quiet corridors she dashed, scanning her surroundings for those telltale flickers of emotion that indicated fae were nearby. Unsurprisingly, the few of them she found were all moving rapidly away from her. The only exception was a presence in one of the bedrooms she passed, who was exuding more pain than fear; a moment of focus told her someone had cut out the poor sod's tongue and broken their legs, then presumably left them to die in their bed.

Just another night of fun and games at the Crimson Court. Naxi shrugged to herself, skipping past.

No one else came near on her way down. No fae warriors stood guard at the ruined entrance of what had been the Mother's bone hall. Either the magic had lured them into the caves, or they'd fled; whatever fate had befallen them, their absence was rather convenient.

The hall beyond still looked much like it had done the day before. Naxi tiptoed to the edge of the crater in the marble floor and peeked into the depths below – the glorious, deadly hollow Emelin had uncovered with a few offhand blasts of red.

The heart of the Labyrinth was as large as the hall itself, a gaping cavern shaped by rocks darker than ink. It might have looked bleak and ominous if not for the hundreds, *thousands*, of glowing gemstones embedded in those same rocks. Sparkling in all the colours of the rainbow and then some, they lit up the space like stars in a midnight sky.

*It's very friendly as long as you're nice to it*, Emelin had said.

So Naxi crouched down on that marble edge, smiled her sunniest smile at the flickering gems below, and cooed, 'Hello, sweetheart.'

The lights blazed brighter for a moment, then began sizzling out one by one – dimming the green, the purple, the yellow, until only a sprinkle of pink remained, shrouding the enormous cave in a blushing glow.

'Oh, you remember my favourite colour!' Naxi clapped her hands, beaming at the dusk below. 'That is so very lovely of you. Do you think it would be possible for me to come down somehow even though I don't have wings? We only had time for a short chat yesterday, and I'm so excited to get to know you a little better.'

There was a moment of silence.

Then the mountain rumbled.

A deep, unearthly thrum, echoing back from the ruined walls and arches of the bone hall ... and beneath her, in the shadowy depths, the smooth rock rippled, then billowed. Rising like a wave from the floor of the cave, shaping ...

*Stairs.*

A peal of laughter tumbled from her lips as the upper step bumped into the crumbling marble edge of the floor; she hopped onto the dark stone, hurrying down into the depths. Behind her, the staircase sank back into the smooth surface of the cave. Which meant she'd have to ask the Labyrinth for permission to leave again ... but then, if it wanted to keep her prisoner, it would probably stop her before she returned to this part anyway.

She wasn't too worried. The mountain's emotions were subtly different to those of more conventional sentient beings, but they were emotions all the same, in the same way an unknown language still sounded like *language*. She'd studied its reactions and responses for an hour or so the previous day, while waiting for Thysandra to show up. Unless she was terribly mistaken, the main feeling surrounding her now was one of a slightly grumpy satisfaction, like a sulky housecat who's finally found someone to rub its belly.

'They've been neglecting you terribly, haven't they?' she said, rolling her eyes at the castle above.

The light turned from pink to something that was closer to red – a light red, but red all the same.

'Yes, I know.' She skittered to the nearest wall to sympathetically pat the dark stone. It was surprisingly warm to the touch. 'I too would prefer to burn the whole place down, if you want the truth. But my friends are trying to make it better rather than destroying it, and it seems polite to at least give them a chance, don't you think?'

The Labyrinth felt doubtful.

'We'll see,' Naxi said philosophically, making her way to the nearest tunnel. The floor was smooth like slippery ice beneath her bare feet, but much warmer, like stones that had basked in the sunlight all day. 'For now, let's just have a chat. You're probably rather bored, aren't you?'

All the colours slowly flickered back to life around her, but they remained muted. Even the pink and red were no longer so bright now, a dullness that seemed almost ... sad?

'Oh, dear.' She sighed, glancing into the winding dark of the caves ahead. 'Is that why you started pulling people in, now that Emelin's opened the gates? So you would have some company again?'

The stone went a little cooler beneath her feet. Not anger – the wave of emotion that rolled in around her was nothing like that scalding sensation of true fury. Instead, the mountain seemed to be withdrawing in a way Naxi could only call ...

Yes, *defensive.*

Like that same housecat, caught stealing bites of meat from the kitchen counter.

'Oh, don't worry,' she said, an entirely genuine giggle catching her by surprise. 'It's not as if I *care* about the fools. You can crush all their toes and fingers, as far as I'm concerned. I'm just wondering if we can't find you some better entertainment, because I imagine a bunch of frightened fae aren't really doing the trick. Could you show me where you're keeping them?'

For two endless heartbeats, nothing happened.

Then veins lit up in the floor beneath her feet.

Not gems, this time. Rather, it looked like a trickle of some sparkly pink fluid running just below the surface, drawing an almost-straight line towards the low tunnel to her left. Naxi turned and whirled after it, following the glowing trail deeper into the maze. Right, right, and left again. Past a gem-studded forest of stalactites, through a passage so narrow she only fit sideways and holding her breath ...

It was then, just a faint tickle of emotion in the distance, that she caught her first glimpse of the Labyrinth's fae captives.

Unsurprisingly, the sensation was mainly one of fear.

Good news for them, in a way. If they were still experiencing fear, that suggested there was something left of them to save.

The screaming came soon after, a bend or two past the place where she'd first become aware of the fools. Sobbing, too. Hoarse cries for help. If Lyn were here, she would no doubt remind Naxi that these were natural reactions to the shock of being held captive by a mountain and that it would be rather callous to roll your eyes at desperate people in need ... but natural reactions or no, how the hell was anyone supposed to think clearly with all that useless whining in the background?

Naxi rolled her eyes anyway. Lyn wasn't here to see, and she suspected that the Labyrinth quite probably agreed with her.

The gust of warm air brushing past her suggested it did indeed.

On she walked, more slowly now. She'd thought matters through until roughly this moment, but confronted with the unexpected fact that the Labyrinth's guests were still alive, she had to admit she wasn't quite sure how to save the fools. Convince them to be better entertainment from now on? Explain to them that all they needed to do was stop crying and start complimenting the caves around them, preferably with genuine excitement?

The waves of suffocating panic rolling over her demon senses suggested most of them might be well past that point.

Bloody unhelpful. She rolled her eyes again.

The pink veins in the floor ran around the last bend, and a small cavern opened up before her. No colours here, not even that ominous red. The only gems still glowing were white, shrouding the dark walls and low ceiling in a sickly pale glow; between them, the slumped, writhing fae figures were little more than silhouettes.

They were also stuck.

It took her a few blinks to realise it: that the Labyrinth hadn't chopped off their feet but rather *buried* them. Each of the captives were sunken ankle-deep into the ink-black stone floor. Some had lost use of their hands in a similar way, and one or two wings had been caught into the walls – pretty secure, unless they tried to chop off their limbs and crawl out of the caves on the bleeding stumps.

Not that the Labyrinth would allow that, of course.

For now, it didn't seem any of the captives had grown *that* desperate yet. Mostly, they were crying. In the back of the cave, a tall male was desperately flinging red magic into the floor, to no avail; every chunk of stone crumbling away beneath that destructive force grew back in place before the next blow struck.

'Have you considered,' Naxi said, as patiently as she could bring herself to be, 'that you might not win its good favour by *hurting* it, you dummy?'

A fae female close to her shrieked, louder than anyone else.

And then at once they were all silent, gawking at her as if they'd swallowed their tongues – quite the improvement on the earlier cacophony, but not terribly productive all the same.

Time for a good chat, then. Naxi plopped down onto the floor, carefully rearranged her skirt around her knees, then looked up and beamed at the gathered company. *Be considerate*, Lyn would have said, so she swallowed the urge to rush straight into plans she didn't yet have and instead started with a bright, 'Looks like you haven't had the greatest of mornings so far?'

They inched away from her as far as their trapped feet would let them.

Their fear turned denser, *sharper*, at the same moment – no longer aimed at the general deadly circumstances they couldn't make sense of, but rather at her personal appearance. Which always made emotions hit her demon senses harder, and here were twenty-five souls or so feeling the exact same thing; the wave hit her with unpleasant strength in the fraction of a second before she yanked her shields up.

Bloody hell.

Never mind about the consideration, then.

'Yes, yes, I'm a demon,' she said, casting a disgruntled look at the ceiling. Unfair, admittedly. The ceiling couldn't help the situation. But this was so stupidly *tiresome*, to always be the scary one even when she was there to *help*, and glaring angrily at the captives would only make them fear her more. 'And yes, sometimes I kill people. No, I'm not going to kill you. I'm not *even* going to torture you. Well, just a little bit, maybe, if you say something particularly annoying. But probably not at all.'

That did not seem to have reassured them much when she lowered her gaze to the group before her. A quick peek around her shields told her their fear continued to burn at blistering intensity.

'Did you ... did you lock us in here?' a young male whispered from the left side of the cave.

'Of course I didn't.' *I'm here to save you* – but then again, that would possibly not go over well with the Labyrinth itself. She didn't need the mountain to think her friendliness so far had been mere trickery. 'Look, you're getting on the poor Labyrinth's nerves, and we need to do something about that. So can we talk about this with our big fae words, please? None of that wailing and whining?'

They gaped at her so blankly she feared for a moment the Labyrinth was spelling them all over again. But their emotions had changed when she quickly sampled them once more – still fear, but the sensation had mellowed and mingled with that woolly, fuzzy feeling of confusion.

'The Labyrinth's ... nerves?' someone repeated, sounding choked.

'Very good. Words.' She smiled at them encouragingly, only to be rewarded with another flare of immediate fright. Damn it. 'See, the poor Labyrinth just wants some civilised company, and your screaming and fighting are *really* not going to do anyone any good. Alright? So let's try again. Give it a little wave' – she demonstrated the gesture, just in case it would help – 'and greet it politely. "Good morning, Labyrinth." I promise it's not hard.'

The group of fae continued to blink at her motionless. In the back of the cave, one of them burst out sobbing again – shrill, grating sounds.

No waves.

No polite greetings.

All visible signs suggested this was not going to work.

Under any other circumstances, Naxi would have shrugged and gone on her way again. Not her problem if a bunch of snivelling fae didn't feel like being saved; perhaps they would feel more inclined to listen to her after they'd spent twenty-four hours below the earth without food or water. If not ...

Well, she wouldn't miss them, would she?

But Thysandra would. Thysandra wanted the idiots saved, for some unimaginable reason, and that meant Naxi couldn't just run off now and leave them here to die. Which was bloody vexing, but then again ...

Thysandra wasn't scared of her.

She could smile at Thysandra without getting that poisonous sting of fright reflected right back at her – anger and frustration and unwilling arousal, of course, but never *fear*, and she would be damned if she let this group of blockheads stand between her and that unimaginable relief. So she was going to suffer their company a few minutes longer. She was going to save them and take them back home, and then she would delay the next time Thysandra tried to send her away for as long as—

Oh.

*Oh.*

Inspiration struck like a tidal wave.

'I'm afraid it's hopeless,' she said, taking her eyes off the paralysed fae and aiming her words at the ceiling again. She didn't turn away entirely, though. The captives had to hear her in order to spread the word later. 'It seems they're too stupid to comprehend how pretty you are. Or too blind. Maybe both, actually.'

The air around her warmed in agreement.

Naxi snuggled up against the smooth wall, grinning at the pink gems sparking back to life around her. 'I have a suggestion for you. How about you let these boring idiots go, and I'll keep visiting you instead? I'll make sure to come say hello every day. Maybe I'll persuade some others to come with me after a while – I don't think they'll agree to do that if you kill their friends now, though.'

There was a flicker of uncertainty in the mountain's strange, all-encompassing emotional landscape. Not exactly doubt, but definitely a crack in the simmering anger and disappointment ... creating room for Naxi to slip her hands around those inhuman feelings and knead them into the shape she needed.

'Every single day,' she repeated, enunciating clearly to make sure the fae heard her as well. 'I promise. If I stop coming, you can start dragging them into your caves again, as far as I'm concerned.'

A collective shiver ran through the group of fae; a few muffled whimpers broke free. But the Labyrinth ...

The Labyrinth moved again.

With a rumble not unlike the echo of distant thunder, the stone began to shift – melting like ink-black ice as it slowly pulled away from locked arms and feet and wings. Fae gasped and staggered forward. Coloured gemstones lit up again. A warm, almost *cheerful* kaleidoscope of a thousand different hues – as if this promise was exactly what the mountain had hoped to claim.

If that was the case, Naxi was not ungrateful for its assistance.

'Let's go, then!' she said, turning away from the cave to pat the smooth black walls. 'Would you kindly show us the way to the nearest exit, sweetheart?'

The pink veins returned, lighting up even brighter this time.

She shepherded the group of stumbling fae into the indicated tunnel, pretending not to notice the way they kept a few inches away from her. One or two of them had the presence of mind to mutter something about the place being very pretty, actually. The others just clung to each other as they hurried through the maze, heads bowed, voices muted if they dared to exchange any words.

The path sloped down and farther down – not back to the remains of the bone hall, then, but to one of the other exits Emelin had opened during her brief stint of court reforms. Naxi didn't keep track of their direction. She was too busy petting and complimenting the Labyrinth at every turn, and besides, who cared where they ended up?

Every part of this island was as ugly as the next, after all.

The walk seemed much longer than her original path to the prisoners, now that she was stuck with a horde of hysterical fae clamouring against her demon senses. She barely suppressed a loud cheer of relief when finally the first whiff of fresh sea air reached her through the underground tunnels. Nearly there, then. Now all she had to do was shoo her accidental protegees out the Labyrinth and into the world outside, and they could—

The path turned its final bend.

Naxi froze.

Not because of the open gate before her, or the sound of crashing waves in the distance. Nor did she give a rat's arse about the cries of relief as the fae captives stormed outside, smelling their freedom; she didn't even care, not *really*, that none of them bothered to throw her the briefest parting glance as they swept out their wings and soared out of view, their voices rapidly dying away in the distance.

Rather ...

It was the vision waiting for her outside.

The *trees* waiting for her outside.

So, so many of them, their presence digging into her nymph magic like roots digging into fertile earth ... making her heart squeeze with some emotion she hadn't felt in centuries, something she didn't dare examine too closely as she staggered towards the looming exit. Gnarled trunks filled the world before her. Knotted vines. A mottled canopy of leaves that seemed to swallow every ray of sunlight, shadows curling through the undergrowth in decidedly unnatural ways.

It was *alive*, this wood.

Not in the way she was used to, lush and joyful like the forests on Mirova had been before the Mother's armies had burned them, down to the last sapling. These trees were all crooked and twisted. There was something dark, something savage, in their veins that made a mockery of all nymph principles of peace and loving compassion ... but hell, what did it matter if they didn't sing to her, if they growled and snarled and hissed instead?

She wasn't all sweetness and sunshine either.

She'd never been that good at playing nymph in the first place.

The Labyrinth warmed around her as she stumbled her last breathless steps forward, its fond feelings washing over her almost like a hug. Only then did she understand – that the second part of her walk *had* been much longer than the first.

The mountain's guidance hadn't led her to the nearest exit at all.

'You knew,' she whispered, feeling her bottom lip wobble danger-ously. 'You *knew* that I would understand this place.'

A last whisper of balmy air followed her, as if to nudge her into the wood. She tiptoed out, the breeze catching her hair and skirt even as the leaves and branches around her remained eerily still – waiting for her to act, perhaps, or simply not caring about mundane matters like little demons wandering into their domain. There were no birdsongs to be heard. No chirping crickets or small animals rummaging through the undergrowth. Just the perpetual rush of the sea close-by, and ...

Distant but unmistakable, a howl.

The Mother hadn't brought *all* her hounds to the battlefield, then.

Naxi grimaced and started walking, finding her way through the grey-green tangle of roots and thorny vines with feather-light steps. To her right, the mountain rose high and steep. Beyond its jagged edges, towering over the wood, she caught glimpses of the castle's red marble walls. Somehow, she'd have to get back up there eventually ... but in this thrilling place, surrounded by these mirthless but living trees, she didn't mind if it took her a while.

Really, perhaps it was best if she wasn't anywhere near when Thysandra heard about the deal she'd made with the Labyrinth.

A giggle escaped her, all by itself.

The forest didn't respond, remaining grim and aloof around her. Had it always been like this? Was that why the Mother had chosen this place to build her red court, the urge for death and destruction already present in the very soil of the island? Or—

She stumbled.

Not over a root or vine – she *never* stumbled over plants, her nymph heart too aware of them to ever be caught by surprise. Instead ...

A bone.

A rib, by the look of it, long and curved, sticking from the grey earth as if its dead owner was reaching for her ankles from the grave. The rest of the skeleton was nowhere to be seen. Naxi was hardly an expert on these matters, but it seemed unlikely it had walked elsewhere by itself – which suggested that *someone* had—

Another howl went up behind her, like the whistle of wind on a stormy night.

Right.

The bloody hounds.

Who were the Mother's favourite way to dispose of her enemies ... and if she'd done so *here*, in this forest, that would explain a thing or two about the trees as well. All that blood and despair soaking the soil would mess up every living thing.

Trust the old bitch to ruin the best part of her court with her blood-lust.

Naxi scurried on, keeping her eyes on the earth this time. Now that she knew what to look for, the traces were everywhere: a shard of a skull lying in the moss, two weathered knucklebones beneath the drooping ferns ... *Myriskeia*, she knew the fae called this place. Deathwood. Bit of a melodramatic name, she'd always thought when Lyn or Tared mentioned their clandestine trips to the island, but now it was starting to sound like a euphemism; really, calling it a graveyard would have been more appropriate.

Another clearing opened up before her ... and with it, carnage.

The other bones had been old, traces of fae who'd died decades or even centuries ago in this wood. This butchery, on the other hand, was recent. *Very* recent. Recent enough for the blood to remain clinging to the tree bark around the clearing; recent enough for the hounds not to have eaten all of their victims yet. Naxi didn't care much about the unfortunate souls who had been reduced to the tattered bits and pieces spread out before her, but the smell was unpleasant, and she'd have turned away immediately if not for a single detail catching her attention a few trees away.

Half a blue-grey wing.

Marred by what seemed like an unusual pattern.

The edges had been torn by teeth or claws or both; that in itself wasn't so strange. But across the rumpled velvety surface, crude lines had been carved – *letters*, likely cut into that sensitive membrane while the owner of that wing was still alive.

Only three letters remained now, the rest of the wing shredded beyond recognition. With some effort, Naxi could make them out: ... *tor.*

*Traitor.*

A prickle of discomfort ran up her spine.

Because this was not the Mother's doing. The Mother had already been dead by the time this butchery had occurred. Which meant others had fed these unlucky fae to the hounds roaming this forest – people still at the court, people still looking for vengeance.

As she'd *known* they would, of course. Emelin had made her threats for a reason. And yet it was a different thing entirely to stand here and *see* those pitiful remains of what had once been living, breathing individuals ... A messy heap of bowels. A dark-haired scalp. Two hands bound together, neither of them still attached to wrists.

And that torn wing.

*Traitor.*

Naxi's stomach rolled with a sudden premonition ... and then she was running, to hell with the living trees and the treasures of the Labyrinth waiting for her.

She should not have left Thysandra alone today.

She should *not* have left Thysandra alone today.

# Chapter 11

'EVERY SINGLE *DAY*?' THYSANDRA repeated, her soaring voice echoing along the alabaster corridor. 'You can't possibly mean—'

The fae male before her winced but didn't retreat, even as his gaze cautiously shot back and forth between her and Nicanor by her side. 'I ... I'm just reporting what she said, Your Majesty. I don't mean to endorse anything, of course.'

Gods help her.

'Yes, of course,' she managed through gritted teeth. There were too many people listening for her to lose control of herself, even if a significant part of her felt like crumbling to dust and never getting up again. Dust at least wouldn't have to deal with sharp-toothed seductresses. 'I'll have a word with the demon herself about this. Please continue the report.'

The story came out with much hemming and hawing, none of it particularly relevant but for the confirmation of the Labyrinth's sentient nature. Somehow, over the course of twenty-four hours, the fact had almost begun to seem like some trivial detail to Thysandra; she needed the sagging jaws and widening eyes of her audience to remind her it would be the very opposite to all other members of her court.

It might just be for the best. This way, at least they were all too occupied with the news of the Labyrinth to realise they were now stuck with a murderous demon for gods-knew-how-long – until their High Lady found some other way to handle the equally murderous mountain beneath the castle, and unfortunately, the High Lady in question had no idea where to even *start*.

So much for ending this madness.

So much for sleeping in her own bed again.

'Thank you,' she cut in as soon as the story had reached its sort-of-end; she wasn't going to give the gathered flock of fae around her any chance to subside into hysterics again. 'Glad you've all returned home safely. If anyone runs into Anaxia, tell her I want a word with her – and please stay the hell away from her otherwise, will you?'

By the looks on the faces around her, nobody had needed that re-minder.

'Off you go, then,' she told them.

Off they went.

It was getting easier surprisingly quickly, giving commands as if she deserved to – and odder still, more and more people were actually *listening*. Even with Naxi's presence hanging over her head, it was hard not to feel a sting of satisfaction as the corridor quieted within seconds. Perhaps it wouldn't be *that* bad to have a demon hovering around. At least now the rest of the world knew there were clear, objective reasons for it that had absolutely *nothing* to do with Thysandra's personal pref-erences, and—

'Thysandra?' Nicanor said, holding open the door of the map room for which they'd been headed, politely gesturing for her to go first. 'Time to get back to work, then?'

It was the hope that did it.

It was the stupid, dewy-eyed notion of things possibly going *well* that had her stepping through that doorway and into the room without her habitual glances to each side, those checks she *always* ran through be-fore entering any new environment – and it was because of that stupid, dewy-eyed negligence that she did not notice the attacker before the first flash of red magic exploded towards her face.

She dodged before she thought.

Battle reflexes took over, dulling everything in the world but the immediate presence of danger, the simple facts of defence and survival. A winged shape lunged from between the cabinets. A knife flashed. She spun around, wing hitting wood, narrowly missing the blade diving for her throat; her own hand fell to her red dress even as her mind whirled to identify those black wings, that dark head of curls. Where the hell had she seen this male before?

Not the time to think. He was already turning back around. Bright crimson shot from her fingertips as she drew the colour from her dress, and destruction slashed her attacker's wrist, sending his knife clattering to the floor. One more blow and he'd be done for. She aimed, barely hearing Nicanor's cry of alarm as her focus zoned in on nothing but a vulnerable, dark-skinned throat ...

'*Traitor!*' the male before her screeched.

She stiffened.

He leapt forward again.

Red filled her vision in the same moment, and pain splintered through her left shoulder, inches away from her heart. Blood spurted from the wound. Which meant she had to act. She had to act *now* and save herself, but—

'Just like your gods-damned father!' that half-familiar voice spat.

Father.

*Father.*

And at once she was no longer there, bleeding and staggering back in some nameless map room at the heart of the Crimson Court. Instead she stood on the precipice above Faewood, the Mother's hand on her shoulder as beneath her a hound's jaws closed around her father's leg. As bone snapped. As he cried her name again and again and she couldn't move, couldn't—

Her head was slammed back against a wall.

She barely felt it.

*Traitor. Traitor. Traitor.* What was the use of fighting, if that was where she'd end up after all – cast out and torn apart by the court she'd tried to serve? Hands bound, wings bound. Running from her death the way Father had tried to run, not away from the hounds but towards her—

'Thysandra!' someone shouted in the distance.

Not Father's voice.

The red magic dulled, then sizzled out around her.

Nicanor – that was *Nicanor* who was dragging her accuser away from her, his pale face flushed with shock and effort. Only then did she recognise the young fae thrashing and writhing in his grip. Symeon. The same male she'd told to grab a mop and take care of the bloodstains yesterday – but surely that wasn't why he'd attacked her, was it? That would be ridiculous, wouldn't it?

Although it was better than—

*Traitor.*

She couldn't make herself move, thrown wing-first against the wall like a discarded ragdoll. Mere feet away, Nicanor dragged Symeon against the nearest cabinet, drawing a long dagger from his belt with the ease of a male who took lives like he took breaths.

*No*, she wanted to shout. *Wait.*

Nothing but a strangled sound escaped her. Neither male seemed to hear her.

'No!' Symeon choked, his eyes widening with terror as he caught sight of the blade. 'Wait, no, Nicanor! I was just—'

Just joking?

Just messing around?

She'd never know. Sharp steel ripped through his bobbing throat before he could finish that wafer-thin excuse, and he collapsed with nothing but a last wet gurgle. Blood spattered the floor, Nicanor's pristine black coat, as the twitching body sank to the ground and went utterly, lifelessly still.

For a moment, the room was so silent she could hear the blood dripping onto the floorboards.

Then Nicanor hoarsely said, '*Fuck.*'

She didn't manage to respond to that. She barely even managed to move as he strode towards her and pulled her back to her feet, his left hand straying to his coat as his right pressed against her wound. *Blue for healing.* The black lace turned a tawny brown as he drew, and the stinging pain in her shoulder softened until nothing but the aching memory remained. That and—

*Traitor.*

It still seemed to echo around the room.

'Fuck,' Nicanor repeated, out of breath as he retreated and glanced back and forth between Symeon and her. His fingers twitched around the hilt of his knife. 'You're alright? Or, well ...'

She was not alright.

She was farther from alright than she'd been in days.

'He ... he called me ...' Her hands clung to the wall behind her, as if her knees would buckle again without that minimal support. 'He ...'

'Yes. Fuck.' Nicanor drew in a deep breath, his eyes a little too wide as he threw yet another wary glance at Symeon's corpse. 'I was hoping— But clearly that was ...'

He faltered. Panicked, perhaps, and still tense from the fight – but not, she realised with a sinking, sickening sensation in her guts, surprised.

She could barely breathe. In the back of her mind, the hounds were howling, snarling, louder than her own stifled voice.

'What were you hoping?' she rasped, dark blots crowding the edges of her sight.

'Look, there've been ... rumours.' He threw a hurried glance into the corridor, then slammed the door with nothing of his usual icy composure and turned to lean against it. The hand he rubbed over his temple was bloodied, leaving bright red smears behind on his pale skin. 'I'm not sure who started it – Bereas has been talking a lot, but I don't think he's the only one saying ... well, you know?'

'No!' Her voice cracked. 'No, I *don't* know, Nicanor.'

'Saying that you sold us out,' he hastily clarified, his blue eyes cautious as he kept his gaze trained on her. As if she might lash out at any moment. As if she might just *be* that traitorous bitch the court was whispering about. 'That you helped the Alliance win the battle in return for this court. They've been mentioning Echion.'

*Echion.*

Her gods-damned traitor father.

Worst of all ... were they even wrong?

'But ...' she stammered without knowing what she would say – knowing only that she had to say *something*. 'But ...'

'I know.' He closed his eyes for half a heartbeat, then looked up again, visibly steeling himself. 'Thys, I'm really, really sorry I'm even asking this at all, but *did* you betray anything? Even just the smallest bit of information? I'm not saying—'

'No!' she shrieked again – too fast, too shrill, sounding like a liar. Her heartbeat was a blur in the tips of her fingers. 'No, of course I didn't! You've known me for hundreds of years, for hell's sake – you know me better than that, don't you?'

His wings and shoulders sagged simultaneously. 'Yes. Yes, of course I do, but ...'

A small, dripping silence stretched between them.

But it was his life on the line as well, she realised belatedly – his reputation, at least, which boiled down to the same thing. If the accusation spread, he would be the Lord Protector who'd bound himself to a treasonous High Lady. Perhaps he'd be spared the hounds, but he'd be dead all the same.

Guilt sunk its teeth into her heart, speeding her already frantic pulse.

'I told Bereas the same,' Nicanor finally said, his thin lips twisting into a familiar sneer at the mention of the name. She clung to it with all of her being – more reassuring to see him venomous and calculating than to deal with his uncharacteristic panic and its implications. 'That you'd be the last person in the world to betray anyone. I just ... I just wanted to be sure the Alliance won't be releasing any damaging information while we're trying to keep you alive.'

Her throat squeezed shut without warning.

Emelin. Fucking *Emelin*.

'If they do, they're liars,' she choked out – a pathetic defence against that attack that would be coming sooner or later. 'Gods know what game they're playing with us, but—'

'I know,' he interrupted, rubbing blood over his forehead, his pale brows. 'But people will believe them, won't they?'

They would.

Fuck. She wanted to close her eyes. She wanted to sink onto the floor and curl her wings around herself, wanted to pretend he and his words and Symeon's bleeding corpse did not exist – fuck, fuck, *fuck*.

'What do I do?' she said instead, voice small like a child's.

'I'm not sure.' He was quiet for a moment but for his pacing footsteps, brisk and restrained. 'We should probably be careful not to fan the flames right now. Perhaps don't make any decisions that could be seen as going against the court's interest for a while. Even if we both know things are more nuanced than that, I doubt Bereas will care much about nuance.'

Oh, yes, she knew what Bereas would have to say about food treaties and human rights – but if she *didn't* do either of those things ...

*Emelin told me some immensely interesting things about your time with the Alliance*, Inga had said.

Traitor if she helped them. Traitor if she didn't.

There was no escaping the net as it slowly, mercilessly closed around her.

'I ... I'll try to keep it in mind.' Feeble, meaningless words. She barely had a mind left in the first place. 'I'll be careful. I'll ...'

She ran out of words again.

Nicanor's sharp features softened into something she might have called concern if she'd thought him capable of an emotion that altruistic. 'Do I need to get you back to your rooms?'

'No need. I'll fly there.' The last she needed was for the court to see him haul her up the stairs; it wouldn't just be a sign of weakness, but a source of unwelcome gossip, too. 'Get Symeon's corpse out of here and make someone clean the room. And ... and investigate whether he was working with anyone, will you?'

'He wasn't the brightest,' Nicanor said wryly, throwing the young male's body an icy look. 'Might have come up with a senseless plan like this all on his own. I'll check, though.'

'Thank you.' Her body seemed to have grown five times heavier as she pushed herself away from the wall, glancing down at the blood soaking her dress and staining her skin. 'For pulling him off me, too.'

'Made a bargain.' He turned his wrist with an elegant flick of his hand, demonstrating the purple mark in his skin – almost back to his usual polished, calculating demeanour, and yet the threads of tension remained there in his every movement. For a moment, she dared to believe he would have saved her even without his magical obligation of loyalty. 'And I told you I like you more than most people.'

*For now.*

If he ever found out – her treason, her lies …

'Thank you,' she breathed again, staggering to the window.

He didn't stop her as she swung open the frame and let herself fall out, into the blissful emptiness of the open air.

Her wings swept out to catch her mid-fall, and for a single moment she was weightless and free – as if she could just abandon this mess any moment she wanted, as if she wasn't chained to the court behind her by her own guilty secrets and Emelin's vicious scheming. Then her gaze swept over the grounds below, the mountain slopes and the grey-green forest beyond.

Faewood.

Where traitors went to die.

The memory of her father's death seized her again, crashing over her with such force she nearly lost control of her wingbeats. Why, *why* was that cursed execution still haunting her? She hadn't thought of it in years – in *decades* – before this hell of a week. Yet here he was, the backstabbing Echion Thenes, rising from the grave to wreck her life all over again …

Although he'd certainly had help this time.

A brand new fury sparked in her veins. She veered off-course just moments before she reached the high, vine-framed windows of her rooms.

What was it she expected to achieve? She wasn't even sure. But the new rage bubbling from her fear and despair wouldn't let her do *nothing*, and if she was to find the object of her wrath anywhere, it surely wouldn't be in the hermetically locked safe haven of her quarters ... So into the stairwell of her tower she swept instead, covered in blood and trembling with terrified anger. Up the last dozen steps to her own floor, to find—

'Sashka!'

Naxi.

Waiting for her.

There was a single glimpse of shining blue eyes and a smile as bright as the midday sun before that blushing face darkened abruptly, demon senses catching up with the storm of emotions that came roaring in. Thysandra didn't slow. Didn't take note of the shrill questions and demands for an explanation as she unlocked her door and shoved the both of them inside, away from the prying eyes and ears of the court.

'There's blood on your dress!' Naxi shrieked, struggling against her hold as Thysandra slammed the door shut behind her. 'Who hurt you? *Who hurt—*'

'Shut. *Up*.' The rush in her ears was deafening. She dragged the wrestling demon in her arms to the couch, not caring for once about the heated sensation of their bodies pressed together – not when the flames were all anger, all violent fear. Their faces were far too close as she threw Naxi into the cushions, and she couldn't be bothered about that, either. All that mattered was the rage boiling within her – at her father, yes, but her father was dead, and here before her sat the one other culprit to blame for this predicament that would kill her ...

'Why?' she heard herself gasp, chest heaving, hands clawing into thin, pale shoulders. 'Why did you have to turn *me* against the Mother, you fucking blight?'

132

# CHAPTER 12

BENEATH HER, NAXI'S EYES widened abruptly, the bright blue of her irises darkening with what might be shock or understanding or hurt.

Thysandra did not fucking care.

'You *knew*.' The words spilled from her lips like burning acid. 'You knew where I was coming from – you knew what I'd survived at this court – and you still decided to hook your cursed little claws into me? Could have captured fucking *anyone* and tortured them until they talked, and instead you had to pick—'

'Oh,' Naxi said breathlessly. 'Oh, but that's not true. We needed someone who knew about the bindings.'

'—the traitor's daughter, of all people?' she seethed, unwilling or unable to deal with such unwelcome reason right now. 'They didn't trust me already! Not really! And then you and your fucking friends had to mess with my head until I caved, and then you threw this fucking court into my lap to make everything *worse*. Of course they'll think I'm just like him! Of course they'll think it's just history repeating itself, just—'

'Thysandra,' Naxi muttered.

Nothing else.

No arguments, no *Sashka* ... and yet her tirade faltered, tongue and lips stifled by nothing but a wordless look.

That definitely *was* understanding in those blue demon eyes – understanding and an odd, resigned calm, the very opposite of the guilt-ridden despair that should have appeared in their place. And Naxi didn't cower in the cushions. Didn't send her tangled vines to attack. She just sat there, small and unyielding, and ...

And far too close, now that Thysandra had a moment of silence to fully notice the distance between them. Close enough to distinguish every lash and freckle. Close enough that the tips of her own dark hair brushed the thin shoulders she was still clutching with such desperate force.

She hastily loosened her fingers a fraction and snapped, 'What?'

'You're upset,' Naxi informed her.

'Oh, really?' Her voice soared again. 'How very fucking useful to have a demon around! I hadn't noticed yet! Listen, someone just tried to fucking *kill* me – of course I'm—'

'Haven't people tried to kill you for centuries?' Naxi interrupted, brows drawing into a slight frown. The small tilt of her head brought their faces even closer together – five inches at most between their noses. 'I thought that was just life at the Crimson Court. Were you in such a state over every single one of those attempts?'

'No,' she said through gritted teeth, 'because most of them didn't accuse me of becoming like my gods-damned *father*.'

Naxi blinked.

Just a single blink, but a clear-enough sign that even those all-seeing demon eyes could be surprised. 'And that's all?'

Thysandra bit out a cutting laugh. 'Is it not enough?'

'Nobody died? No one else was terribly wounded?' Naxi's gaze shot down to the blood on her dress. 'You weren't harmed beyond repair? It's just—'

'Who cares about my wounds?' she exploded, yanking back her hands for the sole purpose of flinging them towards the ceiling. 'Do you understand this might *kill* me if it spreads? Getting this court would have been a bad enough look for someone without a treasonous family history! But with them knowing what my father did ...'

She fell silent, not daring to finish that sentence – to make the consequences real by speaking them aloud.

Naxi didn't move. She just sat there in the golden sunlight, staring up with that small furrow between her brows and something in those cornflower eyes that was nowhere near penance and guilt, and far, far too close to thoughtful interest.

'So what exactly *did* he do?' she finally asked, unusually slowly.

Thysandra stiffened. 'Beg your pardon?'

'Your father.' Naxi shoved forward on the couch so that she was able to perch on the edge of the seat, her feet touching the ground for the first time. Her thin elbows settled on her thighs. 'I know he was executed, but—'

'He betrayed the Mother.' Too brusque. Too sharp. She couldn't help it – not as the sight of those snarling hounds rose in her memory again. 'As they'll all accuse me of doing, if that wasn't abundantly clear.'

'Yes, yes, very dangerous, very troublesome – but how did he betray her, exactly?' That dangerous little head-tilt was a sure sign of trouble. 'We all heard about his death on the other side of the archipelago, but the details never reached me. What did his treason entail?'

The silence lasted just a heartbeat too long.

The space on Thysandra's parted lips felt just a little too hollow.

'He ...' she stammered, because surely it would come to her if she gave herself a moment, wouldn't it? Surely this was just another of those things she'd buried deep, deep in her memory, another little fact she'd rather never look at again? 'He ... well ...'

'You don't *know*?' Naxi said, eyes narrowing to slits.

Again that treacherous silence.

It still didn't come to her.

It *should* have. Everything in her memory felt like there ought to be something in the place of that odd blank spot – a lack of knowledge that wasn't a *gap*, exactly. She would have noticed a gap. She would have wondered, asked questions. This ... this was rather as though an existing memory had been blotted out, leaving everything else in her mind unaffected.

Was this what trauma did, shielding off the parts of her that were too painful to remember? But then, she'd never forgotten those snarling hounds ...

'I was very young when it happened,' she said weakly. 'I never asked for details.'

The suspicion on Naxi's face didn't soften. 'How old were you?'

'Ten summers or so.' She hesitated, then staggered to the overstuffed armchair and allowed herself to sink into it – not sure when her right-eous rage had morphed into this bone-deep confusion, but unable to revert to her earlier shouting now. At least she could think a little better with her face buried in her hands. 'No, wait. It was a few months after I'd started my formal education in magic, so I must have been twelve or thirteen.'

'Hmm.' Even without seeing the demon's face, the dissatisfaction was clearly audible in that short, hummed sound. 'And then as you grew older, no one told you?'

'I ... I suppose they may have wanted to spare me the unpleasant-ness?' Thysandra muttered.

A snorted huff. '*Spare* people? At the bloody Crimson Court?'

'I know it may sound a little unlikely,' she desperately said, jerking up her head again, 'but the fact is no one even bothered me with the specifics. So ...'

'So the reasonable conclusion is they don't know either,' Naxi fin-ished, shaking her pink and blonde curls over her shoulders with the air of someone winning a debate. 'There's no way they wouldn't have used it against you otherwise.'

'But ...' Fuck, what *was* it, that elusive memory slithering from her grip no matter how hard she tried to pin it down? 'But that doesn't make *sense*. Why in the world wouldn't the Mother have told the court? She *always* did. As a little warning not to follow the example, you know?'

Naxi shrugged, a sharp-toothed grin spreading over her face out of nowhere. 'Maybe there wasn't any treason?'

'What?' Thysandra snapped.

Naxi only spread her hands, looking smug.

'No. No, that's ridiculous.' When the Mother framed innocents, at least she always came up with a decent story to tell the world, and besides ... 'Why would she execute him if he hadn't done anything terribly wrong? He was one of her most powerful mages! He was far too useful to her to just do away with him like that – even Ophion admitted once or twice that it was annoying not to have—'

'And yet *something* here is off, isn't it?' Naxi merrily interrupted.

The silence was a useless one, a proud, stubborn refusal to agree. The lack of disagreement said all there was to be said – that something was very, very off indeed. Something so glaringly obvious that it was hard to imagine it had never stood out to her before ... Why in the world had she never asked these perfectly simple questions?

Had she been *that* desperate to forget her father ever even existed?

'What happened to your mother?' Naxi cut through her thoughts, leaning forward on the couch, the gleam in her eyes reminiscent of a predator smelling its prey. 'Do you know?'

'She ... she's dead.' As little as she tried to think about her father, somehow she'd spent even fewer thoughts on the memory of her mother – nebulous glimpses from a time when the world had seemed simple and happy. 'I think she died a while before my father did?'

More narrowing of eyes. 'How?'

'What?'

'How did she die?'

'I ...' She faltered, a horrible hollowness to her thoughts once again. 'I ... I think ...'

'You don't know,' Naxi dryly concluded.

'Don't make it sound like I'm some sort of idiot!' she burst out, her voice cracking with sudden frustration. 'Fine, I could have asked! And I didn't! But whatever my father did, it nearly killed me too, and it's only by the grace of the Mother's mercy that I survived – so of *course* I haven't gone digging in that history!'

'Sashka.' A deep sigh. 'I'm not calling you an idiot.'

She blinked. 'But—'

'But you feel like an idiot? That's an entirely different thing.' Naxi's grin was smug and strangely soft at once. 'It's all very interesting, don't you think? These lapses in your memory? I'll have to look into it.'

'Into *what?*' she croaked.

'Oh, no matter. You need to calm down first. You feel—'

'Calm down? You're telling me to fucking calm *down?*' All at once the anger was back, flaring from her confusion like a rekindled flame – stronger now, even, with the weight of those blotted-out memories behind it. 'When the court is about to come for my head? When the Alliance could sweep in any moment to deal the finishing blow? How the fuck am I supposed to—'

Naxi fell back into the couch, her expression a hair's breadth removed from an eyeroll. 'They won't.'

She scoffed. 'How would you know—'

'Oh, I told you.' A shrug. 'I'll protect you.'

'You *can't.*' Her voice went shrill again. 'There'll be hundreds of mages hunting me down! And even if you could stop them, why the hell would you? You're a demon! You don't feel loyalty! You'll get bored and leave, and—'

Something clanked against glass behind her.

She shot to her feet.

*There they are,* her thoughts screamed, *the first fae pounding against the windows, cutting off your last escape* – and then she turned, and there was not a single pair of wings to be seen outside. All that moved were the monstrous plants, their vines and leaves braiding together faster than her eyes could follow ...

Shaping a wall over the glass.

She whirled around, heart leaping into her throat. They were moving over the door, too, a tangle of greenery sealing the only exit from her rooms. The deafening rustle from the bedroom suggested those windows were receiving the same treatment. Around her, leaves and flowers were changing shapes, growing sharp and elongated – petals like razorblades curling from the clivias and begonias as if searching for skin to slice open.

Naxi hadn't even moved yet, a sprawled-out vision of pink and ivory against the couch cushions.

'What are you *doing?*' Thysandra sputtered.

'Protecting you.' A heart-stopping, blood-curdling smile turned that rosy face into a riveting mask of shadows in the darkening room. 'Want to see what happens when those mages of yours try to reach you? I'm sure we can persuade a few of them to try, just by way of experimenting.'

'I ... *No!*' She staggered back, away from the overgrown windows. 'And you still haven't given me a single good reason why you wouldn't abandon—'

'Because you're mine,' Naxi said, blue eyes wide as if it was the most obvious thing in the world. 'And I hate, hate, *hate* it when people ruin what's mine.'

Thysandra stared at her.

Around her the vines continued to slide over the windows, shutting out all but the last rays of sunlight. The begonias continued to sharpen their petals. Still her eyes wouldn't focus on anything but that small demon figure on the couch, pink and soft and gorgeous and utterly, stunningly lethal ...

Her heart slowed as if by command.

Her shoulders cautiously unclenched.

And then she noticed – catching up with her body's unthinking re-flexes a moment too late – and her heart leapt back into a dizzying rattle all at once, because what in the world was she *doing?* Allowing herself to be lured into some twisted parody of safety by the very creature that had already used and discarded her twice before? Lies, all of it. Pretty, deadly lies. She should know so, so much better.

'I'm not *yours,*' she choked out. 'I've never—'

'Oh, that's irrelevant,' Naxi brightly informed her, jumping from the couch with swift, dainty grace. The flowers turned as she moved, following her path as though she were the sun itself. 'Just go along with it for now, Sashka. We'll talk about the details later.'

'These aren't *details!*' She couldn't inch away fast enough, the room a blur to her eyes as her heartbeat soared out of control. *Just go along with it.* And then what would happen when she wouldn't? When even Naxi finally had to admit there was nothing here for her to gain? 'If you're helping me for the sake of my non-existent feelings—'

'Oh, no,' Naxi dryly said. 'Existing feelings only.'

Fuck.

What even *was* she feeling?

Panic – that was the brunt of it – pure, undiluted fright buzzing through her veins. Because Naxi *was* going to abandon her. Like the Mother had. Like Orthea had, and all those others she'd naively called her friends before she learned the ways of the world. Everyone left in the end, and demons most of all; it was a simple fact of life that no amount of pretty promises could ever change.

But if it was that inevitable prospect that was paralysing her with such utter dread ...

Gods help her. Did that mean she wanted the little menace to *stay*?

That couldn't be right – that couldn't possibly be right – and yet her spinning, spiralling mind could no longer figure out just *why* it was such an impossible conclusion. The court would tear her to shreds over fraternising with demons ... but the court had been fed a perfectly acceptable reason for this particular demon's presence now. She didn't even *like* Naxi ... but then again, she'd been perfectly, stupidly comfortable eating pastries and rolls yesterday. And those damningly pretty lips ...

She could not stop looking.

She could not stop wanting.

The vines were swaying on the edge of her sight.

'You could make this so much easier for yourself, you know,' Naxi murmured from the other side of the room, a flawless sympathetic sadness to her melodious voice. 'You could simply be honest, for a start. Just because you're a warrior doesn't mean you need to fight yourself all the time.'

*Honest.*

Honesty was weakness, too.

'I can't,' she heard herself breathe, feeling dizzy, light-headed. 'I ... I don't know how.'

'Oh, I'm well aware.' Swift steps padded forward, and at once Naxi stood before her – eyes glinting in the dim light, two or three blood-red petals caught in her rebellious curls. 'Do you need my help?'

*No*, she ought to say, *no, of course I don't need anyone, and you least of all.* Needing help was dangerous, for the gods' sakes. And giving in to a demon's temptation was exactly what had landed her in this spot in the first place, a captive at her own court, a traitor about to be discovered; she'd be mad to make the same mistake again. She'd be—

'Yes,' she whispered.

All of a sudden, she was so fucking tired of fighting.

'Oh, very good.' Naxi's voice was little more than a content purr – but her *finger*, good gods, her finger came up and found Thysandra's cheek, drawing an agonisingly slow line down her jaw, her chin. 'What do you need from me, Sashka?'

That touch.

That blissful, impossible touch.

She tried to part her lips and couldn't – tried to draw in a breath and found her lungs equally paralysed. Soft, feathery fingertips moved down the skin of her throat. A pleasure she didn't deserve, couldn't afford. Even if that gossamer caress was the last thing left in the world, her very own body wouldn't allow her to admit it.

'Can't stop, can you?' Naxi whispered, the words mingling like a spring breeze with the rustling leaves around them. 'Can't lay down the armour for even a minute?'

Because people were trying to kill her. Because outside this room, the court was plotting her imminent demise, and how, *how* was she supposed to lose herself in mindless lust when—

Something nudged her shoulder.

She hadn't realised her eyes had fluttered shut until they flew open.

It took about the time of a single gasp for the first vines to sweep around her upper arms – those same sinewy bonds again, crawling from the walls and ceiling to slither around her limbs, yanking at her legs until she had no choice but to stumble back. Her wings and spine thudded against the green quartz surface. Plants crept over her stomach, her chest, her throat the next moment, almost eagerly so, plastering her flush against the wall.

They slid around her wrists last, smooth yet rope-like against her skin as they swiftly pulled her arms to her sides.

Naxi was still smiling innocently.

'What are you *doing*?' Too numb to struggle, she'd thought a moment before, but her limbs struggled all the same now, straining against the unflinching bonds. 'Stop this! Why are you—'

'I'm just helping, Sashka.' That sweet, sing-song voice was much, much too amused for the panic flooding her veins again. 'I'm just ... taking the fight away from you.'

Sweat was breaking out on her lower back, between her wings. 'What the hell?'

'It's really very simple,' Naxi announced, stepping closer – two small, gingerly steps, as if she was balancing on some invisible tightrope. Against the background of vine-covered windows, she looked slight and fragile, more nymph than Thysandra had seen her in a long time. 'You can't feel guilty this way, can you? You can't feel like you ought to know better. If some evil demon is forcing you, it's really not your fault you're getting what you want.'

Oh.

*Oh.*

She forgot to fight, just for a moment, forgot to be furious or frightened as billowing relief swept over her. Only her lips moved, out of habit rather than driven by any conscious thought. 'But—'

'Hush, Sashka.' A slender finger settled over her lips, the touch searing through her like a brand. 'I feel what you feel, remember?'

Her gods-damned relief.

Worse, her skin waking up in the embrace of her bonds, aching and craving, begging for more ... Plump, pouty lips, far too close to her own. Willowy limbs, nimble hands, fingertips she'd felt in her feverish daydreams for decades upon decades. A sight that smouldered all the way down, anticipation sinking like molten fire beneath her navel ... and Naxi would know about it.

Naxi would *always* know.

'I ... I told you to stop,' she whispered, slumping against the wall. Only the vines kept her knees from buckling. Her breath came in shallow gasps. 'I really did.'

'Oh, yes,' Naxi agreed, coming up on her toes, her finger sliding to the edge of Thysandra's jaw. 'You told me. Very convincingly. Multiple times.'

She parted her lips to say, *Good.*

Naxi's mouth was already on hers.

Wet and warm and sweet like honey – a kiss smothering all words of objection, tasting of stolen moments and deadly secrets. She melted into it before she could stop herself. Shameful surrender, but there was no resisting the lure of those demon lips kissing her as if they *knew* her, taking possession of her as if they'd done so a hundred times before ...

And perhaps they had.

In dreams, they just might have.

Naxi kissed like she smiled – unrestrained, unapologetic, a slight thrill of danger just beneath the surface. One of her small hands fisted in Thysandra's hair. The other roamed down across her body, brushing and pinching in all the right places, drawing a tantalising line over her throat, her chest, her stomach ... There was no resisting that touch. Even without the vines tying her against the wall, she would have been unable to pull away now, to stop this cresting wave.

*Traitor's daughter.*

But how could she help it when treason tasted so, so good?

A mewl escaped her, swallowed by their kiss.

Naxi's fingers in her hair drew tighter. A perfect sting of pain, accompanying the perfect sting of pleasure as those clever little fingers slid beneath Thysandra's dress and – gods have mercy – up over the inside of her thigh. Every muscle in her body tensed as she arched into that forbidden caress, pride and shame forgotten. Vines dug into her skin, and she barely felt them anymore – felt nothing but those delicate fingertips, skimming closer and closer to where she so desperately needed them.

'Please,' she heard herself moan. '*Please ...*'

Naxi abruptly broke their kiss – lips flushed and wet, something frenzied in her large blue eyes. Her fingers continued their frantic circling, up, down, and never close enough as she whispered, 'Did you miss me, Sashka?'

Fuck.

'No,' she gasped. 'Of course I didn't—'

'*Don't* lie to me.' That sweet voice turned to razor-edged steel in an instant. Naxi's cornflower irises seemed almost aglow in the darkened room, piercing and ravenous, nymph eyes gleaming with a demon's hunger. 'I'm done with playing games. Did you miss me?'

Thysandra hesitated, just for a moment.

Fingers pinched the flesh of her inner thigh, hard and vicious.

'*Fuck.*' It was half gasp, half shriek as her back came away from the wall again, limbs straining towards that merciless touch. 'I didn't miss you torturing me, damn you!'

A ruthless, breathless giggle. 'Are you saying you did miss the rest?'

She knew the truth she wasn't speaking out loud. Any other truth was safer. 'I once let Emelin escape just to pass you a message, for fuck's sake – wasn't that enough?'

'To let me know you should have killed me when you had the chance, yes.' The unholy glee in Naxi's voice should have scared her, should have chilled her to the bone. Instead, it merely sent another feverish shiver down her spine, towards the heat gathering at her core. 'So I did haunt you, then?'

Thysandra could no longer think.

She just wanted to be *free* of this.

'Haunting is too gentle a word,' she ground out, slumping against the wall, her fists clenching in their fetters. 'You're a gods-damned plague, if you want the truth. A ... a grievous affliction. You turned my greatest triumph into a fucking nightmare – is that what you want to hear, then? That I spent a century wishing I'd never laid eyes on you in the first place?'

Naxi laughed, the sound sensual and spine-chillingly harsh in equal measure. 'Because you couldn't stop missing me?'

She was beyond lying.

'*Yes*,' she snarled. 'And go to hell, you—'

A finger flicked up between her legs.

Stars exploded behind her eyelids as finally, *finally* that taunting caress found the heart of her pleasure, relief and torment at once. There was no cautious exploration, no fumbling to learn the shape of her body. Naxi's first strike was a ruthlessly perfect one, as if she, too, had spent that same century committing every detail to memory – a single slide of finger against flesh, igniting a thousand brand new hungers.

Thysandra cried out.

Another bruising kiss smothered the sound of her pleasure.

A second fingertip joined the first, slipped beneath the drenched linen of her underwear. She closed her eyes and allowed her knees to buckle at last, surrendering her body to the vines that bound her; she barely felt the bonds anymore, biting into skin and muscle. Not as Naxi plunged two digits inside her at once. Not as those fingers began to *move*, a maddening rhythm both slow and relentless – reducing her to a gasping, writhing mess, pulling her closer and closer to the edge.

'Look at you,' Naxi murmured, her breath a heated whisper. The words barely even registered through the storm of sensations. 'So pretty. So needy. Do you want more, Sashka?'

'*Please*,' she whimpered, trying in vain to tilt her hips towards that breathtaking friction. The last of her pride had become a distant memory. 'I'll do anything – *anything*—'

'Oh, there's no need for that.' Sharp teeth nipped her bottom lip, making her gasp again. 'I'll happily fuck you for free every day of the week. Consider it my humble tribute to the crown, if you will.'

The crown.

Oh, gods, the *crown*.

For half a moment, she jolted out of her pleasure-drunk haze ... and then Naxi pressed a third finger into her without warning, and every thought of dignity and court intrigue shattered like glass against rocks. She bent away from the wall, wings flaring helplessly against the merciless vines. Deeper and deeper they filled her, those clever nymph fingers, pistoning back and forth, stretching her open wide ...

And then they *curled*.

In the same moment, Naxi's thumb slid beneath her linens, swirling over the little bud between her lips – and Thysandra broke.

*Fractured.*

A thousand little pieces, each of them another shard of heartbreak, fright, bitterness ... and for a single blissful moment she was no longer any of them, the little girl hiding beneath her blankets, the false queen glancing over her shoulder at every step. For a single instant, she was nothing but this raw, bare, empty vessel. No shields left to hide behind. No secrets left to keep. Just pleasure pulsing through her veins and vines lowering her gently to the floor as she trembled and shuddered, soft hands running tenderly through her tangled hair ...

'Oh, sweetheart,' Naxi muttered, and for once, Thysandra could do nothing but lean stupidly, hopefully, into that perfectly convincing note of tenderness. 'You needed that, didn't you?'

She had.

She'd needed it for decades.

The feeling stealing over her was a strange one, so rare its name only dawned on her after what felt like minutes – quiet, boneless *peace*. As if the court had ceased to exist entirely and taken all its murders and schemers with it. Which it hadn't – she *knew* it hadn't – and yet sitting here on the floor of her overgrown living room, her muscles unclenched, her thighs slick with pleasure ... she had trouble remembering why it had ever been such a problem.

'There,' Naxi murmured, disentangling the last vines from her slumping wings. 'Now let's get you something to eat, alright?'

That shook her awake with almost dizzying abruptness. 'Don't you want—'

'Oh, don't you worry about me, Sashka.' There was nothing but wicked knowing in that shark's grin. 'I'm not going to let you think I'm doing this for my own pleasure. By the time you're begging for it, there'll be plenty of opportunities for me to sit on your face.'

Thysandra managed to scrape a hoarse scoff from the bottom of her heart. 'Assuming no one kills me in the meantime.'

An obligatory jab, lacking the bite of true fear. Judging by Naxi's blithe shrug, she'd noticed it, too. 'No one's going to kill you, silly.'

For once, it was strangely easy to believe it.

'Here's how we'll keep you alive,' Naxi merrily continued as she straightened and made for the kitchen corner, flitting through the room like a little sunbeam in the flesh. Around her, plants slid away from the windows, letting the light back in. 'You're going to continue your preparations for treaties and legal changes – we just won't tell anyone about it yet. We're going to figure out what happened to your father, too. And in the meantime, you're going to blather about the grandness of the court whenever you need to show your face in public, alright? No one needs to know you're not planning to start another war next week.'

Thysandra gave a feeble laugh. 'You make it sound easy.'

'Perhaps it is?' Another grin, dazzling as spring mornings. 'Oh, and one more thing, Sashka. You're going to sleep in your own bed again.'

She stiffened.

'No, we won't tell anyone,' Naxi added, pulling a face as she swatted the unspoken objection aside. 'I promise I'll complain about my sore spine and those horrible couch cushions to Nicanor whenever he shows his face. But you need your night's rest, and what's the worst that could happen? You get to come screaming a few more times?'

It didn't matter how hard Thysandra tried to keep her face straight; her lips insisted on trembling all the same. 'Some evil demon might sit on my face.'

'Oh, that wouldn't be too bad,' Naxi airily informed her, whirling around to reach for the linen-wrapped rolls on the top shelf. 'I'm delicious.'

There probably wasn't much use in feigning disagreement.

But this was madness – reckless, foolish madness. Already she was surrendering much too easily. Already she was inching much too close to *liking* the little terror, her eyes clinging to those swift, dainty feet rushing around her living room. The months after the Last Battle had been bad, so very bad, and this ...

This had the potential to be a thousand times worse.

It was weakness to even admit it. She would end up twice as weak if she ignored the fact, though.

'I'm serious,' she ground out, wishing it sounded more convincing. Wishing she was more convinced. It would be the beginning of the end, she knew, letting this grow into more than mere ill-advised infatuation ... but staring at the small creature spinning through her room, dancing on that thin line between charm and threat, the end seemed a glorious destination. 'Just sleeping. No fucking. I'll agree under those conditions.'

'Oh, sure, Sashka. Tell yourself that.' Naxi rolled her eyes at her, then turned away and fluttered towards the kitchen counter, all blushing innocence again. 'Anyway, lunch?'

# CHAPTER 13

THE DOCUMENT IN HER hand was a nightmare.

Thysandra had been staring at it for a good ten minutes already, until the ink had begun to blur before her eyes, and still the numbers and letters refused to arrange themselves into something slightly more palatable. She wasn't even hoping for it to turn into something *good*. It didn't even need to be *acceptable*. All she wanted was for it to be ...

Well. Not *this*.

*Mortal deaths in the year 3215*, the heading at the top of the page said, and below that was a list as stark as it was horrifying:

*Accidents (farm, construction, etc.) – 46*
*Infections – 39*
*Childbed – 21*
*Various diseases – 61*
*Starvation – 53*
*Execution – 7*
*Fae encounters – 48*

And at the very bottom of the list, almost an afterthought ...

*Old age – 2*

For what had to be the fiftieth time this morning, her eyes flew back to the start of the list, scanning down the same unchanged words again.

It did not make sense. Nothing about it made the smallest lick of sense. Infections and diseases weren't supposed to *kill* people, for bloody hell's sake; a bit of blue magic could heal all but the most extreme cases. And *childbed*? About a hundred human children had been born on the island in that particular year, another administrative document had informed her ... which meant that, good gods, a *fifth* of the human mothers had died giving birth?

What was the statistic for fae? One in a thousand?

And somehow, impossibly, the rest was even worse. How in hell did anyone starve at a court where lavish banquets were a weekly occurrence? What in Korok's flaming hell was *fae encounters* supposed to mean?

*Best to sneak in before sunrise and out during dinnertime,* Inga had said, and a hollow feeling in Thysandra's stomach suggested these were exactly the sort of *encounters* the girl had been talking about. Forty-eight casualties. And unless all involved fae had proudly confessed to their actions, that might not even be the full extent of it. How many human bodies lay buried in Faewood, unseen and unregistered? How many murders had coyly been classified as *accidents* instead?

A vicious headache was sharpening behind her eyes.

It had been five days since Symeon had made his attempt on her life. Four since Nicanor had gathered his commanders and informed them that, since humans were now a scarce resource at the court, their High Lady would be most displeased to lose even more of them. Which was the safest way to put it, of course, a way that didn't sound like she was conspiring with the Alliance, and so far it had technically *worked* ...

But staring at this list – at the world of suffering that hid behind these blunt numbers, year after year after year – she was overcome by the reckless, foolish urge to slam her fist onto the table and tell them they would be following her orders for the sake of fucking *decency* first.

Had the Mother known about this?

Knowing how she had ruled her court, it seemed thoroughly unlikely that she hadn't.

Thysandra dropped the cursed sheet of parchment onto the low table, sagged in her chair, and closed her eyes. The room was far too quiet around her – a disconcerting thought, and yet there was no denying that she could really, *really* have used Naxi's ever-cheerful commentary on the situation right now. Not enough to *need* it, of course. She was not going to need anyone, cheerful commentary or no. But it would have helped to have someone to talk to. Someone who wouldn't accuse her or glower at her, someone who—

A knock echoed through the room.

She shot to her feet.

Had Naxi returned from the Labyrinth already? That would be early but not impossible – a thought accompanied by another disconcerting skip of her heart. Just as likely, though, it would be another aspirant murderer. No need to throw her doors wide open just yet.

She cleared her throat. 'Hello?'

'Oh good, you're here,' an unexpected voice said on the other side of the door – so unexpected that for a moment, she couldn't for the life of her remember who it belonged to. Male. Northern accent. Calm, wryly amused tone. Then, just as it dawned on her, he added, 'It's your favourite alf here to deliver a message. Purely peaceful intentions.'

Tared fucking Thorgedson.

She hastily flipped the list of human casualties upside down, just in case those bloody alf eyes could read it from a distance, and strode to the door. It was unlikely he was here to conspire with fae assassins, wasn't it? And there were no unusual sounds to be heard from the corridor, either, which was somewhat reassuring; if an entire horde of alves had stormed into the castle, it was unlikely the place would still be so peacefully quiet.

Indeed, he turned out to be alone as she cautiously opened the door – tall, blond, sword on his back as always. His only greeting was a mirthless half-smile – an expression that said, *I haven't forgotten, I haven't forgiven, but don't worry, I'll be civil for the sake of diplomacy this time.*

She returned an equally forced twist of her lips. 'Morning.'

'Same to you.' He pointed a thumb at the stairwell, one eyebrow crooked up a fraction. 'And just out of curiosity, are you aware there's a corpse lying practically on your doorstep?'

Good gods.

'Oh.' She shrugged, resisting the temptation to step out and take a look. She'd be damned if she allowed any alves to sneak into her sanctuary; as soon as Tared set foot inside for the first time, he would be able to fade back whenever he wanted. 'I suppose they tried to stop Naxi on her way down to the Labyrinth.'

'Ah,' he said, his smile still wry but looking significantly more genuine now. 'Glad to hear she's feeling right at home already. I don't suppose you'll be inviting me in for cake and a cup of tea on this lovely morning?'

'You guessed correctly,' she said tartly, realising in the same moment that there was one small problem with that resolution. 'I do actually have a few letters you might be able to deliver on my behalf, though, seeing as you're here anyway. So if you could—'

'Go get them,' he interrupted, resting his weight against the outside of the doorframe and sticking his hands into his pockets like a male prepared to wait for a week. 'I'm not moving.'

That seemed ridiculously charitable of him, but no matter how many times she glanced over her shoulder on her way to her desk, he appeared to be keeping his word. Perhaps he knew she might well get violent if he made the mistake of crossing that threshold. No one was ruining her last safe refuge at court, peace and Emelin's threats be damned.

The letters to the other magical rulers lay on the edge of the desk, where she could easily grab them – a small mercy. And as little as she liked to admit it, the alf's presence *was* a convenient surprise. She'd written the messages two days ago and spent the time since figuring out how she was going to send them without any risk of their contents leaking – a series of humble apologies followed by a cautious invitation to discuss the possibility of treaties. Even Nicanor hadn't been informed about the plan. There was little use in letting him know at this stage; they could discuss the opinions of the court once they knew whether other magical rulers would even be willing to talk.

Only Naxi had inevitably been around to see her agonise over every turn of phrase, offering unhelpful suggestions that had somehow made the process easier all the same.

'Here you go,' she told Tared as she returned, holding out the five sealed sheets of parchment. 'Let me know if there's anyone among them you won't be able to reach.'

He pursed his lips, browsing through the missives. 'The White City won't be a problem. Nymph isles are fine, too. I'll leave it to friends to visit the phoenixes and vampires, but we should be able to arrange that pretty swiftly, and ...' He paused on the last letter, which she had addressed to *Whoever is in charge of the alves these days*. His grimace was almost apologetic. 'I'll be keeping this one for myself, I suppose.'

It was twistedly gratifying to know she was not the only one unhappy with the title bestowed upon them. 'So why is the apparent leader of the alf isles playing messenger boy today, if I may ask?'

'Matter of efficiency,' he said with a shrug, pulling another letter from his pocket. 'I was visiting Agenor to talk about some other important but supremely tiresome matters. He asked if I could pass this on to you.'

Her heart stood still.

*Agenor.*

At once, the food treaties faded to the back of her mind. Even the damning list of human deaths on her table no longer seemed nearly so urgent anymore, a problem that could perfectly well wait until tomorrow; all that mattered for a shamefully eager moment was the folded parchment in that alf hand, coming with ... Oh, *please* let it come with information ...

She all but snatched it from Tared's fingers.

His chuckle barely made it through to her conscious mind, as did the words that followed. 'An anticipated message, I understand?'

'Yes, please,' she mumbled vaguely. No, wait. Was that a coherent answer? 'I mean, thank you for delivering it, and um, let me know if—'

'I know when to make myself scarce,' he said, stepping back. 'Give Naxi a pat on the head from me.'

The next moment, he was gone without a trace, faded back to wherever he and the rest of the Alliance were living these days. She couldn't be bothered to consider that half-relevant question.

Agenor's letter burned in her hand as she flung the door shut, broke the wax seal, and unfolded the parchment before she'd even reached her desk. She dropped into the chair, rushing her gaze along his familiar, messy handwriting.

*Thys,*

*Very glad to hear from you. I hope you're doing well, or as well as can be expected; from Inga's letters, it sounds like matters are at least under control at the moment. Please let me know if you need my thoughts or advice on anything. I'll be happy to help.*

*Then, because I'm sure you can do without more elaborate well-wishes, let me get straight to your questions—*

*No, I was never informed about the details of Echion's treason, either. I have wondered about it in the past, and my best explanation is that his actions must have somehow reflected poorly on Achlys and Melinoë in an embarrassing way. They did not deal well with humiliation. If your father made them appear weak, ignorant, or otherwise imperfect, their silence would not be unexpected.*

*As to your second question, I'm not sure if anyone would know more. The usual sources – Ophion and Deiras in particular – are dead. The only exception I can think of is Silas; last time I checked, those who bargained with him still had their marks, which suggests he's alive. His disappearance just before Echion's death suggests he was involved in the situation, too. That said, finding him might be a challenge after all this time.*

*If you'd like for me to ask around, let me know. There have been theories about him hiding with other magical peoples; if that's the case, the Alliance might know more.*

*I'm sorry I can't be of more assistance at the moment. I'll keep an eye out as I'm working through the paperwork I took from the Crimson Court last week and write if I find anything of relevance.*

*All the best,*
*A.*

She stared at the words until her eyes began to ache, trying to make sense of the feeling stirring inside her – that feeling that should have been disappointment, and yet ...

Yet it wasn't.

Thoughts were unfolding in her mind, prodded back to life by *something* Agenor had written. Shreds of memories. Words, sights, events that she had buried deep and forgotten, clawing their way back to the surface now with sudden vehemence.

*Thys, darling, there will be some changes soon ...*

Her father's voice.

That deep, soothing timbre.

She fell back into the couch. The letter dropped from her hand and swirled to the floor; her paralysed fingers barely noticed.

She'd forgotten what he even sounded like, her father, the memory of his voice drowned out by the dying screams that had followed her in her dreams for years. But now he was back, and with him came flashes of a conversation so old that even remembering it made her feel small again ... *I need you to keep a secret for me. Can you do that, Thys?*

She'd been holding a doll when he'd pulled her aside. How was it possible that she still remembered, that she could still feel the soft, worn fabric against her fingers?

*You and your mother are going on a little trip tomorrow,* he'd said, the memory clear as day all of a sudden – his hands on her frail shoulders, tired lines around his eyes which she only now understood must have meant something. *Don't tell anyone. It's ... a surprise. But if anything happens – if you get lost, or if you run into someone you don't trust – I need you to go to Ilithia and find——*

'Uncle Silas,' she whispered, finishing the sentence, and sunlight flooded back into her mind.

Silas.

Good gods, *Silas*.

Her mother's ... cousin, wasn't he? Out of nowhere, images of glistening bargain marks shot by before her mind's eye, of a laugh as loud as bursting fireworks, of large hands lifting her off her feet and tossing her up and up into the air until she cried with joy. Silas, who had vanished – yes, now she remembered, even though no one had mentioned it to her much those days ...

To Ilithia?

The island had once been inhabited by the now-extinct line of Castor Thenes, its soil so barren that no one else had bothered to claim it after the death of the last thenessa. Barely an hour's flight away from the court – she could have managed that distance even on her half-grown wings at twelve summers old, couldn't she?

Why hadn't she?

*I'm so sorry, Thysandra*, the Mother had tutted as she sobbed and snivelled in those thin, pale arms. *He made some terrible choices, your father. I don't think he ever had your best interests at heart – really, he could easily have killed you with his foolishness ...*

And she'd believed it. She'd shoved the memory of her father's instructions far, far away with every other useless shard that was left of her childhood, and eventually she'd forgotten about it – not a white blob in her memory like her mother's fate, but simply a time she had never wanted to think about again.

At once she was standing, tripping over her own feet in her hurry.

Boots. Coat. What more did she need to get out of here for a few short hours? The humans ... well, surely the humans would survive for another day with Nicanor's orders in place, and if Tared returned with replies to her letters, surely he wouldn't do so before sunset. Naxi ...

She faltered, one arm already in her coat-sleeve.

Naxi wouldn't be able to enter these rooms in her absence.

But then again, the last four days had been blissfully quiet. What were the chances anyone would take up demon-hunting again this afternoon? And even if they did, the Labyrinth made for a perfectly suitable hiding place – so surely Naxi would do just fine on her own, and *surely* there was absolutely no reason to feel guilty if she left here without warning.

They weren't *lovers*. Just ... accidental roommates. Temporary allies. Naxi would be leaving too, one day.

And she absolutely did *not* feel any dread at the prospect.

Biting out a curse, she unlocked the window, flung it open, and threw herself outside, careful not to make the mistake of looking back. The breeze carried her up before a single wingbeat. She swerved to the east easily, soaring past pointed towers and spires she could have navigated with her eyes closed; within moments she'd left the court behind, nothing but the wide-open sea stretching out before her.

Every slap of her wings took her farther away from the hornet's nest below. Closer to a goal that was all her own, a quest that had not been bestowed upon her through threats and blackmail – and perhaps that made her a traitor, sneaking away from the people she was supposed to rule and protect ...

But if she just flew fast enough, surely the guilt and responsibility wouldn't catch up with her for a while.

Soon there were no sounds to be heard but the whistling wind, no movement to be seen but the gulls ahead. Small islets slid by beneath her, allowing her to orient herself as she flew; after decades of passing by these same craggy rocks and half-flooded reefs with every errand she ran, she knew their positions like the back of her hand.

She could have done this for the rest of her life, just flying and feeling the wind in her hair.

It was almost a disappointment to see the rugged shore of Ilithia loom up on the horizon – a brusque reminder that there *would* be an end to this blissful escape. Slowing down didn't save her from arriving. Mere minutes later, she was circling above the dry landscape; every inch of it still looked as dead and uninhabited as she remembered from her last and only visit, several centuries ago.

The island stretched barely a mile in every direction. At its heart stood what had once been the grand seat of its inhabitants, now fallen prey to the passage of time – a sprawling country home that the legendary Castor Thenes was said to have built with his own hands.

The house formed a large square around a shaded courtyard, in which nothing but a few hardy succulents had survived until the present day. Pillar galleries stretched out along walls that had once been white and now blended perfectly with the dusty beige of the surrounding soil; cracked windows and shattered roofing tiles evoked images of spring rains and autumn storms. A few birds had made their nests in empty niches and basins. Apart from their agitated squaws and flutters, nothing moved when she landed by the front gate of the house and carefully folded her wings against her shoulders.

It seemed thoroughly unlikely anyone had lived here for even a week, let alone decades.

All the same, Silas must have spent time here at *some* point, and he might have left traces. A letter, perhaps, just in case she showed up later? A map? A handkerchief with phoenix embroidery, cleverly demonstrating his intention to hide himself on the isle of Phurys for the rest of his life?

She ignored her twinge of doubt as she nudged open the creaking wooden doors, glanced left and right through the sandy atrium, then slipped into the building. Doubt wasn't useful to her right now. As hopeless as matters might seem, leaving without looking at all would just be a waste of time.

And as long as she was looking, at least she didn't have to be at the court, wrangling human rights and foreign rulers.

She pushed open the next door, breathing in the smell of dust and stale neglect as she tiptoed through the empty corridors. Faded mosaics on the walls. Serene statues, covered in cobwebs. Hardly any trace of fae habitation at all. The family hadn't moved out of here in a hurry, in fear of some attack or natural catastrophe. Their last lady must have cleaned up the place when she fell sick and realised she wouldn't have an heir.

At first, she searched the house methodically, combing through even the smallest linen closet. In a handful of rooms, names had been scribbled on walls – fae youths probably, the result of bets and challenges at the court. One room showed traces of a party, the soot-stained floor used as a fireplace, the centuries-old bottles strewn around a clear sign there had been plenty of drink involved.

No Silas. No secret messages hidden beneath rugs or behind curtains. She couldn't help but mutter a curse at herself as she left the large and disappointingly empty dining room behind – what had she expected, some cipher of the sort one only found in unlikely tales of adventure?

*Thysandra, follow the northern sun and find me. The password is "blue tiger".*

Ridiculous. Silas would have been more sensible than that, and she should know better than to hope for impossible things.

By the time she'd worked through three quarters of the house, her search had grown sloppier and sloppier, the lack of results no longer worth the effort of meticulous precision. Another door, another empty bedroom. Another door, another bird-infested bathroom. Another—

She blinked, coming to a halt with the doorknob in her hand.

It was locked.

Or was it just stuck, perhaps? But even as she shouldered into it with all her weight, it didn't yield an inch – a lock, then, and a decent one, too. Which was odd, wasn't it? Nothing in the house had been locked so far. If the old thenessa had wanted to store her jewels somewhere, surely she would have chosen a safer place, and either way, what were the chances she would have left anything of value behind?

Thysandra took a step back and considered the layout of the house as she'd seen it so far. In all likelihood, the room behind that door was a reasonably large one – perhaps another bedroom with adjoining bathroom. In that case, it would probably have windows. She could step outside and try to catch a glimpse of—

The slap of a wingbeat sounded behind her.

A footstep echoed through the lifeless hall.

She reacted too slowly, turned too late. Before the alarm could spread from her senses to her muscles, a ruthless arm had already hooked around her throat and yanked her backwards; in the same moment, a knife swept into view, settling against the soft underside of her jaw before she could so much as cry out.

She stiffened from head to toe.

Ragged breath rasped against her ear.

'One move,' a voice she knew and didn't know growled, arms tightening around her throat as the tip of the knife dug into her skin. 'One wrong move, and you're dead.'

# Chapter 14

It wasn't the blade that paralysed her.

She'd felt and dealt with daggers to the throat before. As unpleasant as they might be, they were rarely the end of a fight; if it had been only the knife, she would have raised her hands in surrender, talked her way out of things, then taken down her assailant in a swift and efficient storm of magic as soon as she'd been released from his hold.

But the sight of the arm *holding* the weapon ...

She could feel the blood draw from her face just looking at it.

Every visible inch of it was covered in bargain marks. Dozens upon dozens of gem shards in every colour of the rainbow, scattered across a skin as dark as her own – the resulting pattern strangely reminiscent of the Labyrinth's gem-studded walls. And again, age-old, long-buried memories stirred in dusty, spider-webbed corners of her mind ...

She hadn't even *known*, back then, how dangerous it was to stack bargains. How great the risk of incompatible obligations and inevitable death. She'd just sat in that familiar lap and counted marks. Picked a new favourite colour every single time. Asked for the stories behind them and giggled at the more and more ridiculous fabrications.

*The Bargainer*, they'd called him.

Now she remembered.

'Uncle Silas?' she whispered, voice choked. 'Is ... is that you?'

He froze behind her.

'Oh, gods.' She almost forgot about the knife against her throat, remembering only at the last moment not to whip around. 'It's me. Thysandra. I—'

The hand on her throat loosened. '*Thys?*'

'Oh gods.' Now she fully recognised his voice, the sound hitting her like the scent of an old home one hadn't visited in decades. 'Oh, *gods*. You actually *are*—'

He let go of her, and she spun around so fast her wing missed him by inches, her heart a drum against her ribs. There he stood, the male she only remembered as a giant towering over her, now suddenly a mere half head taller. Black hair shorn short. Golden wings drawn tense. And those bargain marks, gleaming like the world's most menacing jewellery beneath the collar of his off-white shirt ...

'Oh,' she breathed again, staggering backward to find the support of the wall.

'How in hell—' he started, then abruptly interrupted himself, gaze shooting to the nearest entrance with the vigilance of a hunting falcon. Gone was the moment of dazed bewilderment, the mutual paralysis; his voice went tight, urgent in the blink of an eye. 'Never mind. Who else is with you? Who else knows you're here?'

'I— No. No one.' The words fell from her lips like mindless babble. 'I'm alone. I—'

His golden eyes narrowed – distrust and disbelief thick as storm clouds. 'Really? Did she send you here?'

*She.*

It took a moment to figure out who he was talking about.

'No!' she blurted, breathless and rushed. 'No, you don't under-stand— She's *dead*. The Mother is *dead*. I'm the only one—'

He stiffened. 'What?'

'There was a battle.' Gods, where was she even supposed to start? 'Almost two weeks ago now. She challenged the other magical peoples. At the White City. Then she lost, and ... and they killed her.'

The words echoed through the deserted corridor, quiet and hollow.

Silas didn't sheathe his knife as he slowly turned the full bulk of his body back towards her, a small muscle working in his broad jaw. It was the only outward sign of his agitation. The rest of him was still, almost ominously so, as he looked her up and down twice as if he might be able to read the truth from the scars on her wings and her sandy boots.

When he finally jerked forward, it was almost a relief. His hand came up and extended towards her, a simple, wordless gesture that required no further explanation.

She placed her hand in his. Even the back of his fingers showed the occasional bargain mark; gleaming, colourful reminders that she didn't stand a chance trying to trick this particular male into any half-truths or false promises.

'You'll answer the first three questions I ask you after we close this bargain,' he said, his voice as tight as his grip. 'Honest answers, full truth and nothing but the truth, and no attempts to goad me into misinterpreting your words. I'll answer your first three questions in turn, under the same conditions.'

She swallowed. 'We have a deal.'

The magic blazed and died away swiftly. By the time the small, ocean-green gemstone had appeared next to Naxi's, Nicanor's, and Gadyon's marks on the inside of her wrist, she still hadn't figured out what would be the best way to use her three guaranteed answers.

Silas clearly had no such trouble. She'd barely let go of his hand before he sharply said, 'Is the Mother dead?'

'Yes,' she blurted out, the magical obligation moving her lips before she could decide to herself. 'She is, and I'm certain of it, too.'

He stared at her for another moment, then cursed and turned away, rubbing his palm over his face once and a second time as if he might press the fact into his mind with sheer physical force. She waited in the desolate silence until finally he gave a sharp shake of his head, glanced at his own forearm, and muttered, 'I *did* wonder what happened to all of them.'

'Oh,' she said numbly. 'The battle.'

'Yes. Lost a few dozen marks over the course of a couple of hours – Arion, Thyestes, Anysia ...' His left finger thoughtlessly pointed out the spots where the marks had been, nothing but smooth dark skin to be seen now. 'Was planning to ask about it at the next food delivery. I'd like to hear who killed her.'

Emphatically not a question. Which meant there was no magic forcing her to answer, let alone to answer truthfully ... but then again, there was little reason to lie about this.

'Emelin,' she said flatly. 'Agenor's daughter.'

Silas blinked. 'I wasn't aware Agenor had a daughter.'

'Neither was anyone else, until recently.' She couldn't keep the bitterness from her voice. 'She's half human. Unbound. Agenor left the court and joined the Alliance a while ago.'

'Smart fucking bastard,' Silas muttered, moving back until he bumped wing-first into the opposite wall. There he sank into a crouch, elbows on his thighs, and stayed quiet for a moment, blinking into nothingness. 'More sense than I'd given him credit for, honestly.'

'Creon also deserted. Turned out he'd been working against her for decades.' Again the note of spite in her voice was painfully obvious. 'Ophion was found charred from the wrist up, I've been told – death by bargain. Seems to have been Emelin's work, again.'

'Girl's been busy,' Silas mumbled, casting a last glance down the corridor before groaning, rising to his feet, and grabbing a key from his pocket. A mirthless laugh slipped from his lips as he met her gaze. 'Let's have a cup of tea, then.'

For a single moment, she faltered.

Was this a bad idea? She didn't actually *know* him. He was family, yes. Her parents seemed to have trusted him. But that had been a lifetime ago, and no one had seen any sign of him in the meantime; gods knew what he might have been up to in the meantime, what unholy ideas might have festered after four centuries in this desolate place.

Then again ...

He might just have all the answers she was looking for.

She cautiously followed him as he unlocked the room she'd tried to break into minutes ago, unsure where to start, and settled for, 'You mentioned food deliveries.'

'Oh, yes.' He shrugged and held the door for her. 'Couple of people who were unwise enough to bargain with me for unnamed favours. Made them repay me with secrecy and supplies. Come in.'

The space beyond was an old bedroom as she'd expected, looking only slightly more inhabitable than the rest of the house she'd just explored – cracked tiles on the floor, the curtains little more than old, sun-bleached blankets tied between pillars. The bed was narrow and austere. A makeshift stove had been installed by the wall; bags of flour, root vegetables, cheese, and eggs lay piled up beside it.

The room of a male who'd spent four centuries doing nothing but surviving ... but then there was the desk.

Handwritten notes covered most of the wide wooden surface. Colour guides, the sort used by dressmakers, had been thrown haphazardly in between, and small stacks of leather-bound books balanced precariously on the edges. At the centre of the chaos, a single notebook lay open to show two meticulously ordered pages: tables and lists, in a far neater hand than the surrounding writing.

'Only upside of the whole cursed business,' Silas's low voice said behind her before she could ask. 'I finally have time for my research. Take the chair – it only wobbles a little.'

It was the only chair in the room, but she did not have the composure left to politely protest. He shut the door behind them, then strode to the hearth without looking at her; she didn't speak as he lifted his kettle from the glowing embers and filled two antique mugs with a dark brown brew that smelled grassy and bitter. Acacia, perhaps? It seemed like a shrub that might grow even on this dead, desolate island.

She sat in silence until he pushed a mug into her hand and sank down on the edge of his bed. His expression had gone from dazed to grim, a look that said he definitely hadn't invited her to cosily muse on the good old days together.

'So,' he finally said, savouring that one word, his eyes trained on the floor between them. 'Why are you here, if the Mother didn't send you?'

Again there was that tug of a force that wasn't her own, a pull her lips and tongue couldn't help but obey. 'I'm trying to figure out what happened to my parents.'

He crooked up an eyebrow. 'After all this time.'

'What?' she blurted, realising only a fraction of a second later that that might just count as a question ... but her uncle took a sip of piping hot tea without showing any hurry to answer, so she dared to believe she hadn't wasted one of her three precious truths. 'I mean, I'm not sure what you mean.'

'They've been dead for a while.' The sharp set of his jaw didn't fit the cold bluntness of the words. 'So one wonders what has happened to suddenly rouse your curiosity, after four full centuries without them.'

He didn't trust her.

The realisation should not have been such a slap in the face, and yet she almost winced at the impact – because of *course* he didn't. She was the one who'd remained loyally at the Mother's side for all those centuries, wasn't she? The one who'd fought and killed for the sake of her tyranny? While he had hidden in this ghastly place and feared for his life – feared that people like *her* might discover him ...

'She cast me out,' she said quietly. 'The Mother.'

He remained motionless, head tilted – eyes demanding better.

What more was there to say? *I'm a fucking mess* – that was the simple truth. *I no longer know who or what to believe in.* The court she'd thought she'd loved, the people she'd thought she knew, they'd all abandoned her – moved over for a brand new world in which she lacked all the security of known danger, in which she was a little fledgling all over again.

And who was to take her by the hand and teach her to navigate it, now the Mother was no longer there to do so?

If he'd spoken the question out loud, she'd have been forced to tell him. She could only be grateful that – knowingly or unknowingly – he'd at least spared her that humiliation.

'I'm starting to realise I've been lied to for most of my life,' she muttered instead – still a confession that reeked of weakness, but at least one she could restrain, regulate. 'About … almost everything, it seems. It's making me doubt everything else I took as a given while the Mother was still alive.'

His face was hard, stony, in the dusty light. 'I see.'

'So I would very much like to know …' No, wait. This was not the moment for noncommittal requests – not when she had far better means at hand to make sure she received the answer she needed. 'What did my father do, exactly, that got him killed?'

For a single suspended moment, her uncle sat motionless.

Then, averting his face, he said, 'I don't know.'

'What?' It burst from her lips with too much force. 'What do you mean, you—'

'I only ever heard bits and pieces.' He drew in a slow breath, mug balancing in one gem-covered hand as he ran the other through the half-inch of his dark hair. 'What Echion told me was, "I did something entirely ill-advised, it may well be the end of me, and I won't regret it for a moment." He wouldn't give me any details. Said I'd insist on butting in and making things worse if I knew the rest.'

'He knew he was going to die,' Thysandra said breathlessly.

'He was prepared for the possibility, at least. He was also determined to get Cy and you out before he took you down with him.' Again that hand through his shorn hair – jerky, agitated motions. 'That was the plan, you see. I was to wait here for the two of you. You were supposed to join me in the middle of the night, and Cy would explain everything as we got the hell away from the court.'

*You and your mother are going on a little trip tomorrow …*

Her throat clenched suddenly and violently. 'So she *was* alive at that point. My mother.'

'Oh, yes,' Silas said grimly. 'Up until the night before Echion died, she most certainly was alive.'

'And … and then …'

'Then I don't know what happened.' His breath was strained. 'She never showed up here at the time she was supposed to. Neither did you, for that matter. There was no mention of her in any of the accounts I've ever heard of the day that followed, so I can only assume she somehow died during the course of that night. And Echion—'

Something glass-like shattered within her. 'Yes. I … I know.'

'Yes,' he said tightly, returning his mug to his nightstand with a thud that was almost a bang. 'I don't suppose you forgot.'

And for a moment the silence had a different quality to it, not sharp and distrustful as before, but almost like a truce – because he might still be a stranger, but she knew that darkness on his face. She knew who his heart was bleeding for. No matter the years between them, they had lost the same male – friend, father – and there was something strangely comforting about grieving the *same* person for once in her life ...

No one had ever mourned her father with her.

Even if they'd cared, she'd never known it.

'And then you stayed here,' she finally whispered, cautious, all too aware a single wrong word may just shatter that fragile understanding between them. 'All this time, while they were looking for you.'

'Oh, not immediately.' Again that tightening of his lips. 'I tried to get you out of that place in those first days. Figured the alves or the vampires might at least be willing to take in a child, even if they slit my throat the next moment. Didn't manage to get through to you, though.'

She blinked. 'What?'

'She kept a bloody sharp eye on you. The Mother.' His knuckles tightened at the mention of the title; the marks on the backs of his hands glittered dangerously. 'You shouldn't underestimate what an asset you've been to her from the very start. Cy and Echion were two of the strongest mages of their generation – of course the old bitch wasn't going to let such a promising young talent slip away.'

She had never thought of herself as an asset.

Or perhaps the reality was rather that she'd never been *treated* as one, as some valuable treasure to be cherished and won over. She'd just been ... there. No one had even doubted that. *She* had never doubted it. Assets were people like Creon, who had been fussed over and flaunted for all the world to see.

And yet ...

*You'll be guarded well*, the Mother had said, smile sweet as honey. *There's no need to be afraid anymore, sweetheart. We'll make sure our most trusted people stay close to you for as long as you want.*

Not to protect her.

To *contain* her.

'I had no idea,' she whispered – hollow, woefully inadequate words for the memories tilting upside down inside her mind. 'I ...'

'You were a child,' Silas said, his tone bitter. 'Of course you believed what you were told. It's what children do.'

A biting laugh slipped past her lips. 'I haven't been a child for a while.'

'Trust me.' He rose from the bed to pour himself another cup of tea. 'I'm well aware.'

Four centuries of unquestioning loyalty. Four centuries of obeying the Mother's every wish and whim – the High Lady who'd *spared* her from the hounds, perhaps, but why had she never in all those years realised that her saviour had also been the one to put her in danger in the first place?

*But I did take her down in the end*, she almost blurted, a strange, desperate plea for that tightness in her uncle's jaw to soften. *I helped, at least. I told them how to break the bindings.* But she should know better than to angle so eagerly for anyone's approval, and this very secret was the *last* thing she should share with anyone ...

*A traitor's daughter.*

Far, far too many people knew already.

'And then after those first days ...' she forced herself to say instead, trying to hold back the confusion, the shame, the weakness cracking through her shields. 'Some people thought you'd sought refuge with the other magical peoples.'

'I never even tried.' The shadows deepened on his face. 'Made myself a little too useful during the wars the Mother waged against them. They had no reason to risk her wrath for the sake of my sorry neck.'

She could see that.

'And I didn't have many other options.' He sank down on the foot of the bed again, golden wings splaying out behind his broad shoulders. 'Your father was the best friend I ever had. Cy was like a little sister to me. The Mother damn well knew I wouldn't sit back quietly after the way she destroyed them, and half the court owed me favours at the time – I was far too influential for her to risk any public defiance from my side.'

'You didn't try to ...' She hesitated, hearing the hollow naivety in her own words but unable to stop all the same. 'You didn't try to *change* the place.'

He gave a short, sharp laugh. 'There is no changing the Crimson Court.'

'But you had all your bargains! You said so yourself!' Her voice had no business sounding so shrill all of a sudden – the past bleeding into the future, into the viper's nest she'd left behind a mere hour ago. 'If the Mother tried to stop you, that means she thought there *was* something to stop, so—'

'The Mother was only half of the problem, Thys.' He leaned forward, elbows on his thighs, mug loosely clasped between his hands as his gaze narrowed on her. 'No one spoke a word of protest as she fed one of her most loyal followers to the fucking hounds. No one even asked a single bloody question. They happily went on feasting and fucking to their heart's content, as if nothing had ever happened. So you can change rulers, you can put a new face at the top of it all, but you won't change what's festering beneath. The rot is in every fibre of that place.'

'No,' she said, breathlessly – not even sure what she was denying anymore but unable to do anything else, to accept the perfect sense he was making. 'No, that can't be right. There *has* to be a way. There always is. I ...'

*Fae encounters.*

Her breath hitched.

And the people she'd thought her enemies ... Tared, waiting patiently outside her door. Agenor, offering his help. Naxi ...

Naxi.

All of a sudden she was fighting the urge to hunch over, hide her face in her arms. Her voice was almost pleading, now – 'There has to be something we can do.'

'*We?*' His broad jaw twitched. 'I'm not going to be the one trying, thank you very much. If you like impossible tasks, maybe settle for something slightly more manageable? Try draining the ocean with a teaspoon, or—'

'They named me High Lady of it,' she muttered.

He stiffened with his teacup halfway to his lips.

'So ... so I don't particularly have a choice.' Her chest constricted. 'I just need to—'

'Wait,' he brusquely cut in, wings tensing as he rose half an inch from the thin mattress. 'Wait a moment, Thys, I'm going to need a little more context here. What in the fucking world? Who named you anything?'

His third question, and he did not even seem to realise it even as her lips burst into motion. 'Emelin, again.'

'She didn't take the place for herself?'

'No,' Thysandra said, putting her untouched tea aside so she could bend over and hide her face in her hands. 'She split the empire in three, ran off with Creon to the Cobalt Court, and left the mess to me.'

Silas cursed under his breath. 'Who took the Golden Court?'

'Agenor.'

'Ah. Of course.' He dragged in an audible breath. 'Well, that ... explains a couple of things. And that's your plan for the place, then? Fixing it? Turning it into a pleasant, peaceful environment where no one ever stabs their friends in the back for a small promotion?'

Was that her plan?

It was then, in the wordless silence that followed, that she realised not a single other person had asked her that question since the Mother's death – not *really*, at least. What was her plan? Much had been assumed about her intentions, certainly. Forced upon her. She had feigned opinions too, had talked around them for diplomatic reasons, had pushed her thoughts aside for the sake of peace, law, and order ...

But at the heart of her, everything felt weak and unsettled, nothing like the safe, hard shell of her old convictions. Like wet clay that just wouldn't harden, shaped by everyone's fingerprints but her own.

And wasn't that true of *everything* about her?

Save the court. Protect the court. Those were her duties, she *knew* they were – so why did they suddenly seem so gods-damned nebulous, so jarringly unlike herself? That list of mortal deaths shouldn't matter. The army's thirst for war, Symeon's knife diving at her, even the mystery of her parents' deaths ... none of that should change a damn thing about the responsibility that had been placed upon her shoulders, the responsibility she'd chosen to accept.

And yet ...

'Yes,' she said tersely, because the alternative was to let herself follow that train of thought, and she couldn't, *couldn't* give in to these treacherous doubts. Her life depended on this, for the gods' sakes. Emelin's threats were still hanging over her, and weakness would kill her, fixed court or not. 'Yes, that is my plan. Bind the right people to me and make sure everyone else behaves.'

He was silent for so long that she almost asked her second question just to make him *talk* – sitting on the edge of that unhospitable bed, watching her with narrowed eyes and lips set in hard, straight lines. The bargain marks on his neck and corded forearms glinted in the dusty light. Dozens upon dozens of them, many-coloured relics of a past she could barely remember.

It seemed like half a century passed by before he finally drew in a deep breath and said, 'Alright.'

His tone suggested some sort of conclusion had been reached. She blinked and began, 'What—'

'Time to go, then.' He downed the rest of his tea in a single gulp, thumped his cup onto the bedside table, and rose with the air of a male bracing himself for war. 'Give me a few minutes to pack the most important stuff. We can send someone over for the rest later.'

'We— What?' She gaped at him. 'Are you *joking*?'

A question; she realised it only as he stiffened for a fraction of a moment. 'Not at all.'

'But you said— I thought you never wanted—'

'Of course I don't want to return.' He crouched by the bed, pulled a worn bag from beneath it, and flicked a spark of blue at the canvas to heal a tattered hole in the bottom. 'The damn place eats souls for breakfast and spits them out again by lunchtime. But I promised Cy and Echion I'd keep an eye on you, and it does sound like you could use a hand over there.'

Fuck. 'I'm doing *fine*.'

He threw her a look, eyebrows arched up.

'I don't need help,' she weakly added – because she *didn't*, did she? She was strong. If she wasn't strong, at least she had to *seem* strong. And how was she to know he was even joining her with good intentions, this male who'd spent an entire lifetime studying bargains? Even if she made him vouch for his loyalty, he'd know all the tricks to render his word effectively meaningless, and then—

'Ask me,' he said, not even looking up as he chucked two books into his bag.

Oh.

One question left.

'Are you ...' She cleared her throat, feeling infuriatingly young on his wobbling desk chair. 'Are you planning to harm me or cause me trouble in any possible way?'

'I'd rather tear off my own wings,' he said, voice flat.

She parted her lips.

No words came out.

Out of nowhere, she felt shamefully close to crying.

# CHAPTER 15

AN HOUR WAS NOT nearly enough to get her thoughts back in line.

Which was a problem, because her thoughts *had* to be in line – there was no facing the Crimson Court with a spinning mind and a stutter in her voice, not if she wanted to make it to the next sunrise. But Silas's resolute wingbeats beside her did not help. Nor did the knowledge of what was waiting for her upon her return, the court she'd somehow have to protect from itself even as it clamoured for war and killed its own ...

*So that's your plan for the place?*

It itched, that question. It chafed.

Far too soon, the familiar maze of pointy spires rose on the horizon; minutes later, they were descending to the court itself, sprawled beneath them in red marble and gleaming gold. Silas's expression never changed beside her, his hard-set jaw the only evidence of old memories returning – a whole life he'd led in the place until it all collapsed from one day to the next. She didn't doubt he'd see the echoes of it in every hall and doorway.

'Where did you use to have your rooms?' she shouted against the wind, belatedly realising she should probably house him somewhere.

He scoffed. 'Put me in the stables for all I care, as long as you don't make me return to my old rooms.'

Fair enough.

'My own tower, then.' She swerved left, over the training grounds below – which were strangely empty, she noted with half a glance. Something to ask Nicanor about. 'It has quite a few empty floors at the moment. I'm sure we can—'

Shouts reached her from the castle.

Or rather ... a *chorus* of shouting.

It was too far away to make out individual words, that faint racket in the distance. She could distinguish that unmistakable rhythmic cadence of a clamouring mob, though. The layered sound of dozens, if not hundreds of voices.

What in the world?

Some impromptu duel happening somewhere? But fights usually took place on the training fields, yet the courtyards below them were still suspiciously deserted. And at once, that odd but innocent fact took on an entirely different meaning – because if her warriors weren't *there*, training where they usually were ...

Then what were the bastards doing?

'Anything wrong?' Silas asked sharply as she swivelled around mid-air.

'Possibly.' Hell take her. Three hours she'd been gone, after five days of blissful peace, and *this* was the moment the court decided to start stirring trouble again? 'Don't worry about it. I'll look into it. See you in the eastern cliff tower in a bit – fifth floor.'

She shot away before he could object and try to follow her. Bad enough if the court was collapsing around her – he didn't need to know just how badly it was doing so. He'd probably turn back around and run for his life if he found out.

The yelling voices grew louder and louder as she flew over the bone hall at breakneck speed, past the symmetrical towers to its right, past the dining halls and the bathhouses. It seemed the noise was coming from the direction of the academy galleries – no, from the *archives* – which didn't make sense. Gadyon was about the last person to cause trouble, and why for the gods' sakes would anyone feel tempted to attack a hall full of paperwork?

And yet it was before the steel entrance doors that she finally found the source of the uproar.

A crowd of a hundred, maybe a hundred and fifty fae had gathered in a corridor far too narrow to hold them, carrying weapons, ropes, torches. Fists were raised. Red flashes burst from the throng. Chanting voices reverberated off the high marble ceiling, rendering the hollered words themselves unintelligible – but more than a few of the assailants had donned the grisly skull masks that were only ever worn at Korok's festivals, and she didn't need words to know the meaning of those.

Gods help her.

What had they *done*?

Only as she landed in a high, open window did she catch a glimpse of the dead fae near the doors, their blood smeared across the corridor in hundreds of bright red footprints. The first two she could make out seemed to have died from a simple blow of magic to the throat, but the third ...

Hands around the knife in her chest. Face contorted in that tell-tale agony of demon magic.

Naxi.

For a single moment, she forgot to be cautious.

'What in hell is going on here?' she snapped, and although her voice didn't rise above the clamour, the first few fae who whisked around to see her alerted their neighbours well enough. Within seconds a sudden silence spread through the corridor. Eyes turned towards her; fists ceased their furious pumping. Just a moment of stalemate, and then—

'Oh, there you are,' a familiar voice sneered.

Bereas came elbowing through the mob, his long red hair swept across his brow in a particularly dramatic fashion; a trail of blood, as red as his wings, trickled down his biceps and his sleeveless shirt. He was grinning, though, a wild, violent grin – the look of a tiger finally released from its cage.

Where the hell was Nicanor?

Where was the rest of her army, for that matter?

'As moving as it is that you missed me,' she bit out, 'what is the meaning of this bloody—'

'When were you going to tell us?' Bereas interrupted with a broad, theatrical swing of his hand – a gesture that was no doubt intended for his audience rather than her. Cheers went up behind him. 'While you were kicking us out of our houses, perhaps? Or were you at least planning to give us a warning a few minutes beforehand?'

She blinked at him.

Weakness, to let herself be stunned into silence for the whole world to see – but what in the gods' names was he talking about? Kicking him *out*? Why would she kick anyone out of—

'The *humans*,' Bereas snarled. 'Did you really think we wouldn't find out? Your plans to force us out of our homes to let the fucking *servants* live there instead?'

A chorus of hissed curses and yelled agreements rose from the crowd behind him. Someone flung a blistering ray of red at the archive doors, merely to make a point, it seemed; the steel grew back in place a moment later.

Mages on the other side. Was that where Nicanor had gone?

'My ... my plans?' She forced her attention back to the broad-chested, beefy-necked male before her, wrestling to stitch the clues together. Was this about the promise she'd made to Inga, decent living quarters for the remaining humans at the court? But she had *said* in that meeting she wouldn't be relocating any fae, hadn't she? 'There are no plans to—'

He scoffed. 'Well, then, tell your pet demon to step aside and let us remind the servants of their proper place at the court, because *they* sure as hell seem to think there are.'

*Remind them.*

*Fae encounters.*

'You'll do no such thing.' Her voice cracked. Damn it. 'You'll get the hell out of here and—'

Bereas shrugged, turning his back on her without another word and swinging up his butcher's knife. 'Let's get on with it, friends!'

More loud cheering rose as the crowd returned its attention to the archive doors. Torches flickered. Red magic crackled through the air, shooting from a dozen hands at once; the thick steel splintered to nothingness, and she caught a single glimpse of Nicanor's people behind it before a storm of blue restored the entrance again.

A couple of yards away, a smaller group was starting to break through the walls, where no such defences would be present.

Gods have mercy.

What could she do? She threw a glance over her shoulder – no army, no reinforcements. Just a court keeping very, very quiet as a hundred of its strongest members set out to torture the weakest of them in the name of pride. Greed. Cruelty. The Mother would have been able to stop this, would have been frightening enough to send even these savages fleeing to cower beneath their beds ... but Thysandra wasn't frightening.

Just frightened.

If she stepped into the fray, if she tried to stop them, what would they do? Call her a traitor and kill her too? Sweat was breaking out between her wings – no, she couldn't take that risk, couldn't waste her last little bit of authority by turning actively *against* her subjects. She'd have to find another way to stop this. Fly to the archive windows and evacuate the humans before the walls were broken down? A better plan, surely, than—

'Don't let her get away!' Bereas yelled from the middle of the crowd.

Before she could wonder who he was talking about, rays of red splintered the window-frame inches away from her unfurling wings.

No. *No.* She ducked just in time to avoid another barrage – but they couldn't in all seriousness be planning to attack *her*, could they? She was the High Lady of this court, for fuck's sake! She had a bloody army! Except that same army was nowhere to be seen right now, and more and more members of the crowd were turning towards her, knives drawn from sheaths wherever she looked ...

*Fuck.*

Could she flee? But fighting mid-air would just give them more dimensions to attack from, and if they were truly looking for blood—

Red magic shot past her face, ripping through the rim of her ear.

Her reflexes took over.

Even as her stomach clenched in shock, battlefield habits were stronger. They'd expect her to retreat, and so she made a desperate dive forward – into the lines of shouting fae, taking down three of them with a first wild swing of red before she'd even landed on her feet. A sting of pain exploded in her left shoulder. She swivelled around, instinctively putting her attacker's wing between herself and his companions; her dagger lay in her hand before she'd decided to draw it. Neck, swing, gurgle of blood. The male before her collapsed.

She barely dodged the next burst of red exploding towards her.

*Traitor's daughter.* The world was spinning around her. Even as her body went through the motions, none of it seemed truly, fully real, a nightmare from which she could wake at any moment. Five calm days, and what had she done to deserve—

'*To her left!*' Bereas was shouting on the other side of the corridor, and she blindly spun in the opposite direction, having heard these tricks before. Her dagger sank below the ribcage of the female sneaking up on her just in time.

Magic bit the back of her knees, vicious enough to nearly send her to the ground.

She staggered, the rush of panic sharpening her focus as her remaining opponents closed in on her. A swift volley of red took down perhaps five of them. There were several dozen left around her, teeth bared and daggers drawn. Far too many to shield herself from. She barely avoided another crackle of magic at her face, then dodged the knife thrown at her wing so that it only tore through the outer edge of the vulnerable membrane; the pain blinded her for a moment and a half, and she only just managed to take down the two males who lunged towards her in that instant of weakness.

No help to be seen. No army sweeping in to save her.

Gods have mercy. Was she going to *die* here?

Fury kept her going through the haze of crippling pain, red magic spilling from her hands like the blood spilling from her wounds. Fae collapsed before her. Magic hit her in the side, just below her liver. She bent over, suppressing a scream, and above her head, the wall exploded into fragments that peppered her neck, her shoulders.

This was the end.

She knew it as she staggered back, firing a last, hopeless charge at the horde of fae prowling closer. Her wings thudded into the wall. Nowhere left to go but down, and it was a matter of seconds now. So what would it be? A blade to the heart? A ray of red to the throat? Or would it be the hounds after all, the blood-soaked death in Faewood from which she'd been running all her life ...

And it was only then, grossly delayed by the fear pulsating through her veins, that she realised the storm of red had sizzled out.

That the crowd was no longer moving.

Odder still ... when she looked up, blinking away the humiliating tears, eyes were widening all around her, gaping at the window above her head. Lips were parting into gasps; feet were staggering back. It looked like a trap, some sly attempt to distract her – but she was way too far gone to require distraction, and a few yards away, even Bereas had gone white as a sheet.

She risked a glance over her shoulder – and froze.

Silas.

It was *Silas*.

Standing in the window through which she'd arrived. Golden wings spread wide behind his shoulders. Where he'd left his worn, dusty shirt, she hadn't the faintest clue – but he was now dressed in a magnificent blood-red, the colour a weapon and a warning at once. In the sunlight, his bargain marks glowed like many-coloured cat's eyes against his burnt-umber skin.

He did not look like he was about to run.

Rather, he looked about to bite someone's head clean off.

'It's the *Bargainer*,' someone breathed behind her, and the unmistakable shuffling of footsteps suggested that more than mere surprise had halted their attack.

Silas didn't move. Didn't attack. Just swept his gaze over the battle-field once, lingering briefly on the corpses strewn about, then calmly said, 'Bereas?'

Through the haze of agonising pain, Thysandra suddenly understood why the bastard had paled so abruptly.

'I'm calling in the first of the favours you owe me,' her uncle continued in that same flat, low voice. 'If anyone hasn't left this corridor before one minute is over, you will kill them. If anyone attacks my niece in the meantime, you will kill them. Thank you.'

There was a single moment of paralysed deadlock.

Then Bereas's voice, suddenly shrill, shouted, 'Get *out*, you fools!'

Footsteps thundered around her. She tried to turn her head and found her vision swimming so violently she almost collapsed where she half-stood, half-sagged against the wall. Fuck. *Blue for healing* – she needed to find a coloured surface, right now, before she bled out on the floor ...

A firm hand gripped her shoulder, and the pain in her left side softened.

'Steady, Thys.' This time she saw the flash of bright azure before it hit; the mind-numbing agony in her wing dulled to a faint, manageable ache. Silas didn't release her as he grimly added, 'Don't move. Keep breathing. You're not going anywhere until I have you stitched up.'

She would have made some retort if her tongue hadn't felt so impossibly heavy, and if a door hadn't slammed open in the same moment.

Naxi's voice cried, '*Sashka!*'

So much for the public illusion of respect.

But Bereas was no longer anywhere near, and none of the others spilling out of the archive doors seemed to care what anyone called her. Nicanor's face was as pale as his silver braid. A handful of other mages followed in his wake, all blue drawn from their wings and clothes. And Naxi – *Naxi* – who shouldn't care about anyone but herself, who shouldn't be involved in any fights but those for her own sake, came flitting towards her in an endless stream of questions – 'Where *were* you, what *happened*, what did you *do*—'

'Fuck's sake,' Nicanor muttered in the same moment, striding from the doorway with his hands still on his knife. '*Silas?*'

A curt nod was the only greeting he received in return. 'Commander.'

'Lord Protector, these days,' Nicanor wryly corrected, casting a glance at the twenty, thirty bodies of the fae Thysandra had taken down. 'Not that the current situation is a glowing recommendation of my skills, admittedly, but—'

'Where *were* you?' Naxi squealed again, her voice twice as high as usual.

'Finding some family,' Thysandra managed, making a valiant attempt to drag herself back to her feet. Silas's hand on her shoulder didn't loosen. 'Where the hell did any of these people get the idea we're planning to force fae out of their homes?'

'Not a bloody clue.' Nicanor threw a swift glance over his damask-covered shoulder. 'Need me to find a couple of them and have a word?'

She almost collapsed in relief. 'Yes, please.'

He gave half a salute, finger to temple, then snapped around on his heel and swept out in a flash of icy blue wings. The remaining fae seemed to doubt for a heartbeat, then hurriedly followed him through the open windows – looking, more than anything, relieved to have an excuse to get out of Naxi's vicinity.

Naxi herself had gone alarmingly quiet.

'Alright,' Thysandra ground out as she made another attempt to stand. This time she succeeded, even managing not to stumble over the nearest fae corpse as she took two cautious steps forward. 'Now would anyone care to tell me what in the world *happened?*'

\*\*\*

It turned out nobody else quite knew what in the world had happened, either.

The most recent events were clear enough. Someone had heard Bereas preach bloody revenge on the training fields. The archives, with their sizeable human staff, had presumably seemed a good first target. Nicanor had tried to dispel the mob, and when a considerable part of his army refused to come to the humans' aid, he had pivoted to defensive measures instead; Naxi, who had also run afoul of the group, had been left little choice but to join him.

But what no one could tell her was the most important part: how the so-called news had spread in the first place.

News that had only been discussed in an explicitly private meeting. News that had not just leaked to the worst possible ears but had leaked *incorrectly*, too – so much so that the source had to have known what the consequences would be. One of the humans? Bereas had mentioned that the servants seemed to think something was going to happen, and Inga had been the only one at that meeting who hadn't made a bargain ... but then, what did any of them have to gain by enflaming the fae populace against themselves?

Thysandra didn't want to think anymore.

She just wanted to hide, hide, hide.

But the court was still there, and so she had no choice. She somehow gathered the composure to send Silas and Nicanor's remaining people to escort the human archivists home. She ordered Gadyon to find them a safer place to stay. Then suddenly the hall was almost empty and only Inga and Naxi were left by the writing tables – the first looking even more furious than usual, the latter still oddly quiet.

A terrible moment to burst out crying, and yet Thysandra was sorely tempted.

She could have been dead.

She was ruling a court of murderers.

The game she'd played for four hundred years had turned itself against her, and all of a sudden, she was being trounced at every step. Which meant she had to make plans, that she had to be strong and stubborn and show the bastards ... and yet all she could do was sit in silence, aching and numb, until at long last the archive doors were thrown open again and Nicanor hauled the shackled, bloodied shape of a fae male into the hall.

Progress, in theory.

She couldn't force up the energy to be glad about it.

'Bereas is nowhere to be found,' her Lord Protector grimly reported as he dragged his cursing captive into the nearest chair. The male's hands were bound and wrapped in white cloth – a simple but effective measure to stop him from drawing magic. 'Most of his friends seem to have made themselves scarce, too. We found this one as he was packing his stuff to flee.'

'*Bitch*,' the fae male spat, wrestling with his chains. 'Filthy, traitorous—'

Then he gasped.

His face contorted.

An agonised howl emerged from his throat as he bent back against his chair, wings cramping to the point of shrivelling. His voice shot up an octave and a half as he let out another screech, then a garbled, 'No, no, please, *please*, I—'

'Naxi,' Thysandra said, rubbing her eyes. 'I think that's enough.'

The screaming died away at once, leaving only quiet sobs behind. Naxi huffed from her edge of the writing table, feet dangling a few inches above the floor as she glowered at the captive and grumbled, 'Manners, arsehole.'

The male let out a quiet whimper.

'Efficient,' Nicanor said, looking mildly disturbed yet deeply intrigued as he folded his arms and cast the slumping fae a contemplative look. 'More inclined to talk now, Lyron?'

Another pained moan.

'I'll take that as a yes.' He cast Thysandra a sideways glance. 'I'll leave the questions to you, Your Majesty.'

Asking questions was the last thing she wanted to do. They might lead to her discovering more, and she had already discovered far, far too much.

She drew in a deep breath all the same and said, 'Who told you that fae would have to move over for humans?'

Lyron's bloodshot gaze swerved towards Naxi, then towards Inga beside her. His lips moved soundlessly for a moment before he ground out, 'Bereas.'

'And who told Bereas?'

Again that moment of silence. Then, even more quietly, he mumbled 'Iaris.'

Nicanor let out an uncharacteristic string of curses.

'What?' Thysandra said sharply, snapping around in her chair. Unexpected news, perhaps, but not *that* unexpected, given the dressmaker's unfortunate tendency to blather endlessly about every crumb of gossip she caught. 'Could you tell one of your people to—'

'That's not the point,' Nicanor interrupted, upper lip twitching into a sneer she knew to be a sign of the greatest distress. His long fingers were fidgeting with the lace ends of his sleeves. 'We found Iaris with her throat slit a few hours ago.'

Thysandra gaped at him.

He grimaced, blue eyes apologetic. 'I know.'

'*Iaris?*' She didn't even care that her voice was breaking. 'Are you saying someone might have killed her—'

'So she couldn't tell us who her source was?' Nicanor finished tightly. 'You've got to admit it bloody well looks like it, don't you?'

Gods help her.

Lyron had gone very quiet in his chair, eyes darting back and forth between each member of the company as if looking for an escape. Inga was stiffly, furiously silent. Naxi sat with her chin in her palm, fingers tapping her chin, as if she was contemplating how much trouble it would cause her if she were to torture their witness for a few more minutes.

Thysandra didn't even care about torture anymore.

All she wanted was to get out of this ever-deepening nightmare.

'That'll be all,' she heard herself say. 'Unless anyone else has any questions for our guest ...'

'Now that you mention it,' Inga brusquely cut in, 'I do. I'd like to know what exactly you were planning to do with me and the others once you'd broken into the archives and found us, if you'd care to elaborate?'

Naxi was the only one in the room who didn't seem surprised. Even Nicanor gave a single blink that could almost be described as owlish before he pulled his face back into its usual sly, polished mask.

'Kill a few of you, probably?' Lyron sneered, his glare making a good effort to achieve the same effect now. 'The fucking nerve, to—'

Naxi rolled her eyes.

He let out another blood-curdling scream.

'Oh, don't bother,' Inga said testily, flicking her hand at Naxi without glancing at her. 'I need him able to answer my questions. Could you clarify *why* exactly you want us dead? Because we would prefer not to live in leaking hovels? Is that a crime worth killing for?'

Lyron slumped in his chair again, gasping for breath as the demon magic subsided. 'You mortals die anyway. Who cares about a few years more or less?'

Thysandra felt her mouth sag open.

Inga's nostrils flared, but somehow she didn't shout, didn't argue. All she said, curt and cold, was a simple, 'Thank you.'

And why was no one else looking even remotely shocked?

'Get him out of here,' Thysandra choked, her breath quickening. The red of her dress itched beneath her fingertips, begging for release. 'Take him away and make sure I never, *never* have to see his face again, will you?'

Nicanor nodded, hauling the chained male off his chair with elegant ease.

It was not enough, not *nearly* enough, to soothe the restless rage heating to explosion point under her skin. *You mortals die anyway.* And even if this particular bastard would soon breathe his last breath with a blade through his throat ... how many others like him were walking around at this cursed court? On the other fae isles?

Inga was looking tired and unsurprised. Naxi was looking furious and unsurprised.

Way too many of them, then.

How fucking blind had she been, if *this* was what she'd overlooked for the full four centuries of her life? And then she was still supposed to call the court hers – was supposed to serve and defend it even after it had tried to end her?

She couldn't save this place.

Not because she couldn't try, but because she no longer *wanted* to try.

The realisation felt distant like a dream, and yet it fell into place so very easily, no shock or surprise as it settled in her mind. It didn't seem to belong to the version of herself she'd known for all her life. Old, dutiful Thysandra, always at the world's beck and call, would have died before she let these thoughts see the light, would have tucked them far away in the deepest pits of her memory and never looked at them again.

New Thysandra had no one left to serve.

Decisions took shape as if they'd always existed.

'I'll be gone for a few more hours.' The words slipped from her lips as if spoken by someone else; her feet moved her to the window as if obeying some other mind entirely. 'Please let Silas and Nicanor know. And keep yourself safe until I'm back, will you?'

It was that easy to escape again.

Within minutes, the castle lay miles behind her. Just as soon, she was soaring over the open sea once more, the brightest azure as far as the eye could see – leaving nothing but time, wind, and water between her and her destination.

Emelin.

Creon.

The gods-damned Cobalt Court.

# CHAPTER 16

THE SIGHT OF THOSE crumbling walls and towers on the horizon came with a very particular flavour of bittersweet.

The Cobalt Court was where the Mother had stored her bindings – those little cornerstones of her reign, preventing all individuals under her rule from using magic against her. A secret that Thysandra, and only Thysandra, had been entrusted with. The only key to the magic shield of the ruins had been hers; the catalogue book of those thousands of trinkets had been written in her hand. Not too long ago, she'd believed it proof that her High Lady at least saw and valued *some* of her loyalty.

Then the Alliance had captured her in the very same spot.

And now, as she flew towards those razor-sharp cliffs in the gold and purple autumn sunset, she couldn't help but wonder whether the Mother had simply picked her because she'd been too blind, too clueless, to ever be a danger.

Very little had changed about the castle ruins in these last few weeks. The same overgrown gardens, the same pointed window arches with not a shard of glass left in them. The same lone, almost skeletal tower rising from the rocky earth. But at the heart of the castle, in the last few rooms that still had their roofs, the glow of a fire was lighting up the walls, and two or three figures moved in the rapidly lengthening shadows of the ruins.

She circled down, wary of defences or alarms. No one stopped her as she landed in a deserted courtyard, though; nothing but the sound of voices a few walls away disturbed the never-ending cadence of waves crashing against the cliffs below.

Cautiously, she began to walk.

As much of a mess as the Crimson Court might be, it was hard to believe anyone would choose to voluntarily live *here* instead, weeds and debris wherever she looked. It would take years to build something resembling a castle from this devastation. Decades, maybe. If one could claim every single fae isle in the archipelago, why—

A loud squeak interrupted her musings.

Something loud, white, and fluffy shot from an open doorway to her left, fast enough to almost hit her on the temple.

Thysandra staggered two steps backward, realising only then that she was fleeing a bird small enough to fit in the palm of her hand – a tiny, white-and-grey falcon, screeching and fluttering as it hovered in the air before her. The effect might have been somewhat like a swan protecting her young, except that this little monster rather lacked the necessary dimensions to back up the threat.

All the same, she hesitated to walk on. What if anyone thought she'd attacked the damn bird?

'Alyra?' a familiar voice yelled from close-by. 'What are you—'

Silence.

And then, with such sudden cheer it *had* to be feigned, 'Oh, Thysandra!'

The High Lady of the Cobalt Court herself emerged from the low doorway the next moment, dressed in slippers and a knee-length tunic so dusty it was hard to say what its original colour might have been. Her brown hair had been bound into a messy braid. In her hands lay what appeared to be a pile of maps and sketches, all bleached sheets of parchment, not a fleck of colour on them – an informality, a *vulnerabil-*

*ity*, that seemed utterly irreconcilable with the woman who'd featured in Thysandra's nightmares for weeks.

Which Emelin had to know or at least suspect, and yet all she said was, 'Would you like to come in? You must have been flying a while.'

She'd vanished into the half-collapsed room before Thysandra could gather the wits to inform her she would in fact prefer to stay as far away from the castle as possible.

Damn it. She could hardly start shouting about her important decisions with walls and an angry bird between them; she'd look even more ridiculous than she already felt. With a muffled curse, she shook her wings, folded them, and ducked under the low door jamb, bracing herself for whatever awaited in the dusky space beyond. Traps? Collapsing ceilings? Creon fucking Hytherion?

But the room looked disconcertingly harmless – almost like a command post of sorts. Large central table. A mismatched collection of mugs and glasses. Paperwork, most of all, *so* much paperwork, maps and sketches on the wall and the table and even the floor ...

'We're working out our exact building plans,' Emelin cheerfully clarified, rummaging through a pile of notebooks without looking up. The fact that she was in the company of a possible enemy didn't appear to be bothering her in the slightest. 'Seeing as you're here, would you say it's better to have a bedroom balcony on the east or the west? There's something to be said for waking up with the sunlight in your room, but—'

'I'm resigning,' Thysandra said.

It echoed a little in the silence that fell – a hollow, dusty sound.

Emelin blinked once. Nothing else, nothing more, as she let go of the notebooks and lifted her gaze, a look of mild concern crossing her dust-streaked face. There and gone again – her smile grew back in place almost immediately.

'Of course you aren't,' she said.

It didn't even sound like a threat. If anything, it had that amiable, ribbing undertone of friends who have gotten used to each other's nonsense after a few centuries in each other's company – *Don't be silly, Thys, you always say that and haven't meant it even once ...*

'What?' Thysandra said.

'It doesn't sound like you at all,' Emelin informed her, entirely unruffled, turning back to her sketches as if nothing had happened. 'Giving up so easily, I mean. Anyway, I'm just thinking ... if we put these windows on the east side ...'

'I'm *serious*!' Thysandra spat, staggering two steps forward, then thinking better of it as the little bird let out a shrill protest. 'And your blackmail isn't going to make a difference either, because they're trying to kill me anyway, so—'

'Oh, Thys?' an even more unwelcome voice interrupted behind her, and this time it *was* Creon, sauntering into the room in an equally dusty, slightly misshapen sweater. His leisurely grin at her looked only a fraction forced. 'To what do we owe the honour?'

'She says she's quitting,' Emelin said in her place.

Creon raised an eyebrow as he settled himself on the edge of the table, looking as undisturbed as his lover had. 'That sounds thoroughly unlikely to me, frankly.'

Emelin shrugged. 'Exactly what I said.'

'Well, then it must be true,' he dryly agreed, only then looking back at Thysandra again. 'Are you staying for dinner? Assuming you don't hate barley stew, that is.'

She gaped at the both of them.

'I don't think she hates barley stew,' Emelin said as she grabbed a coat from a chair and flung it over her shoulders. 'And even if she hates barley stew in general, I don't think anyone could hate *yours*.'

He threw her a grin. 'In that case, we should probably get moving, before the alves scarf down all of it. Coming, Thys?'

She really didn't have a choice.

Bluntly refusing to join them would make her look childish rather than principled. Demanding they stay and have a conversation with her would only make her look powerless, given that there wasn't a chance in the world they would actually obey. And so she found herself trudging after them like an unwilling youth at a family gathering, unable to keep the bewilderment from her voice as she stammered, 'Alves?'

'They're helping us figure out the building plans,' Creon said over his shoulder, one hand on the small of his High Lady's back. 'Very helpful, even if you factor in the cost of their breakfast. Watch the hole there – we still need to get it fixed.'

An alarmingly considerate warning: in the vine-covered corridor, nothing but a few last sunrays spilling in through the gaps in the wall, she wouldn't have seen the crack in the floor until she had already broken her ankle. Now she just managed to circumvent it before stepping into the next room. Here was the fire she had already spotted from above, burning beneath a ceiling that was half-gone – the resulting gap offering a stunning view of the darkening sky above, streaks of pink and purple in the west and the first stars appearing in the east.

Three alves were sitting around the fireplace, loud as all members of their kind, plates already in their lap. They glanced up briefly at her arrival, gave some half-hearted waves, then resumed their raucous yet cordial discussion on acceptable ways to win an argument without committing any murders. Emelin mentioned something about breaking noses as she plopped down next to them. This was, apparently, hilarious.

Creon pressed a plate into Thysandra's hands. The stew smelled annoyingly delicious.

She sat and ate in dazed silence, the chatter around her evolving from alvish argumentation theory to card strategies to something to do with Creon and numbers. One alf, who went by the name of Thorir, seemed to know a thing or two about architecture. The other two were clearly incapable of telling a door from a window, but seemed more than happy to fade chunks of stone back and forth all day. No one bothered with titles. No one threw wary glances at the flickering shadows even once. Towards the end of the meal, Thorir found an excuse to challenge Emelin to a duel, which she merrily accepted without any visible fear for her life.

It was utterly bewildering.

She still hadn't pulled herself together by the time everyone had emptied their plates and Emelin and the alves had bounced off in search of a more suitable location for recreational violence. Creon was quiet as he cleared the table and filled a kettle – an oddly snug, content silence, so different from his usual menacing stillness that Thysandra had trouble imagining it as belonging to the same person at all.

He wasn't even wearing black, she realised belatedly. She had *never* seen him in anything but black, and yet in the firelight, there was no denying his sweater was rather a peaceful dark green beneath the dust.

Perhaps New Thysandra wasn't the only innovation of the past few weeks.

By the time he'd finished his cleaning, the sky was inky black above them and the kettle was steaming. Which seemed about the moment he'd send her on her way home with a pat on the head and a few well-aimed threats ... but all he did was chuck his dish towel into a corner, pull two mugs from a wooden crate, and sink down onto the opposite bench, staring pensively into the sparkling fire.

For a moment, nothing could be heard but the waves crashing against the cliffs and a shred of alvish shouting in the background.

Then Creon dragged in a breath, eyes not lifting from the flickering flames, and said, 'Want to talk?'

She almost choked on her own tongue.

A joyless grin grew around his lips as he lowered his elbows to his thighs, wings folding in behind his shoulders. 'Didn't mean to startle you.'

'Since when do you *talk*?' she sputtered.

He gave a shrug. 'Since when do you quit?'

A fair point, and a bloody unpleasant one too, coming from *him* of all people. It came too close to all those centuries of gloating, that endless competition between them in which she'd never stood a chance. Even before the years he'd spent robbed of his voice, the beloved prince of the Crimson Court had never *talked* – just swaggered and blustered and relished the triumph of his own existence, at the cost of everything she'd ever held dear.

And here he was. Happy. Loved. At home.

Watching her lose yet again.

'Congratulating yourself?' she muttered, averting her eyes before he could see the sudden gleam in them. Useless defiance. It wouldn't shield her from his all-knowing demon senses. 'If you're here to tell me you'd have done everything better in my place, I'd rather you leave me alone.'

He sighed. 'I'm not.'

There was a tiredness in those two words. Old and dark and bone-deep, the sort of exhaustion *he* truly had no right to feel.

'Then what do you want?' she bit out, sharpness the only way to cover up the tremble in her voice.

Again he was silent for a moment. Between them, the fire danced quietly in the night breeze, the kettle forgotten amongst the embers. In the distance, the shriek of steel against steel suggested the alves had found their battlefield.

'I just wanted to say I know what it feels like,' Creon finally said, slowly, quietly, his gaze still trained on the flames. 'To wake up one day and realise the game is not the game you thought it was, your allies are not the people you thought they were, and the rest of the world has every right to see you as a villain. I've been there. So feel free to ignore that, but if you're looking for thoughts ...'

His voice died away again, melting into the quiet of the night.

She sat frozen on her bench.

*Danger*, her mind was screaming, an overwhelming, paralysing reflex. *Get out of here. This is a trap.* It had to be, because the alternative explanation was that Creon Hytherion himself was being *vulnerable*, and the gods would sooner return to life. Except ...

Except he *was* here, in this crumbling, rotting ruin.

Miles and miles away from the court and the game he'd once played to perfection. Miles away from the crown he could so easily have placed upon his own head, the ultimate victory in the scheme of backstabbing and strategic treason she'd vaguely assumed had been beyond every one of his decisions in the past few decades.

The Cobalt Court was a senselessly humble abode for the most powerful fae mage the world had ever known, and the Creon she knew would have agreed with her on that.

'Who are you?' she weakly said.

He gave a joyless laugh. 'An idiot.'

Which had to be even more devious trickery, because of course the Mother's son would never describe himself as anything less than the epitome of cunning and glory. But the look on his face was one she'd never seen before – a hollowness in his dark eyes far emptier than the black sky above.

If it was a lie, it was a strange one. She'd only ever seen him lie to make himself seem stronger, braver, fiercer.

'Did I have the right, then?' she tried, watching him closely, waiting for the mask to crack. 'To see you as a villain?'

He hesitated.

'Or does the penance end there?' Her voice grew thorns again. 'All well and good to accept the ire of the rest of the world, but not that of the one person sitting—'

'Thys.' He closed his eyes. 'I could ask you the same thing.'

A shrill laugh escaped her. 'What in the world have I ever done to become a villain in *your* eyes? Failed to prostrate myself at your feet whenever you entered a room? Offered insufficient praise for every fucking blink of your eyes?'

'You don't remember?' he said, and now he was the one to look away. 'That time you found me in the barracks where I was hiding? Trying not to get dragged back onto the training field for the fifteenth time that day?'

She faltered.

The memory arrived in shreds, rapidly stitching themselves together – wooden walls, narrow beds, the pungent stench of sweat and bile. He'd been young. Very young. A bleeding gash in his shoulder, a puddle of vomit on the floor – the Mother's ruthless training, that same training that had him fussed over and fawned over at every turn of his stupid little feet.

*Stop whining*, she'd snapped, hauling him from under the bed.

*You have no idea how many people would kill to be in your place*, she'd snapped, pushing him out of the door.

She stared at him now – fully grown, predator-sized, the inked scars of his training crude lines against the bronze of his skin – and felt the horror rise in her.

'You do remember,' he flatly concluded.

'I haven't thought about that day in decades,' she whispered. 'We ... we were both so very young, weren't we?'

'I was.' His smile was joyless as the grave. 'You a little less so.'

'I was nowhere near an adult!' Sickening heat stole over her, shame as much as anger. 'And it had barely been *years* since you—'

'Thys, I'm not attacking you.' He rubbed a hand over his face, then faltered, not meeting her gaze as he lowered his arm again. 'I'm trying to stop hating you. And to explain why it's taking somewhat of an effort, as rational or irrational as it may be.'

She stared at him, stunned.

He *hated* her?

It was clear enough that he'd never liked her, of course. She hadn't thought him capable of liking anyone in the first place, and she'd never made the slightest effort to form an exception to that rule. But disdain, disinterest, a careless delight in her suffering ... None of that came anywhere close to *hate*, did it?

She'd never thought herself powerful enough to hold that much sway over him.

'I was trying to justify it to Em,' he added, a wry, self-deprecating smile twitching the corners of his lips. 'My dislike of you, I mean. And she made the mindboggling point that this might be exactly what my darling mother aimed to achieve in the first place – us blaming each other for all that was wrong in our lives. Imagine two of the most powerful mages at her court realising she was fucking both of them over.'

Thysandra swallowed. 'Well, you *did*—'

'I was *born*, Thys.' She'd never heard anything so close to despair in his voice. 'I promise you I didn't ask for her to kick you into the dirt the next day.'

'No,' she said numbly. 'No, I suppose you didn't, but ...'

But what?

But he'd been an insufferable little shit for three and a half centuries since? Undeniably true, and then again ...

She too had been playing the game.

'Fuck,' she muttered.

'I know,' he said, throat bobbing, and then again, 'I know.'

'Is that why Emelin gave me that cursed court, then?' The crumbling walls and broken arches were tilting around her. 'Revenge on your behalf for the way I've been treating you?'

'No.' He paused, then slowly added, 'I think she mostly picked you because you offered her your help once. That night after the Mother took me captive.'

For a moment, Thysandra could do nothing but blink at him.

That strange, violent night when everything had shifted ... Creon, dangling from the ceiling of the bone hall with hooks through his wings. Emelin, small and human-looking and seeming so very lost on the pavilion's doorstep.

*Come see me if you need help.*

Mere hours before the girl had escaped. Mere hours before Thysandra had let her.

'That ...' She swallowed. 'That was stupid of me.'

'Maybe,' he said dryly, some of the usual careless arrogance returning to his expression as he stretched his legs towards the fire and tilted his head at her. 'But I wouldn't have invited you for dinner if you hadn't done it, so I would argue it won you at least *something*. Speaking of which – tea?'

'As long as you don't poison it,' she numbly said.

His grin held a faint edge of that familiar wickedness. 'Happy to switch cups.'

Which would have been an obvious double-bluff if they'd been at home – but they weren't at home, no one else was serving them the drinks, and she watched him retrieve the kettle from the fire and pour two mugs of tea without a single suspicious twitch of his fingers. It smelled a damn sight better than whatever brew Silas had served her this morning. Mint. Chamomile. Something like ... cinnamon?

By the time she wrapped her fingers around the warm, smooth earthenware, the conversation hadn't started making even a fraction more sense.

'So are you trying to imply ...' She paused, breathing in the fragrant steam. 'Are you suggesting this was supposed to be some sort of *reward*, then? Blackmailing me into taking on a role that would most likely kill me?'

Creon sank back onto the bench, raking his long hair out of his face before he slowly said, 'More of an ... opportunity, I'd say.'

'Oh, *that* sounds promising.' She gave a sharp chuckle. 'To see how I do without any High Ladies holding my hand?'

'No.' His face looked tired again in the flickering light. 'Just ... just to do better.'

It took several moments for that to land.

*Do better.*

Better than Old Thysandra, who hadn't asked questions, who had refused over and over to see what was right in front of her. Who had been so desperate to reach the top that she hadn't cared who she might be trampling on her way up – who had dragged a crying child back into the hands of his tormenters and felt like the sensible one in the situation, too.

*Better.*

The world fractured. Shifted. Glued itself together into a picture so different it was practically unrecognisable.

'Wait.' It came out breathless. 'You're saying ... you didn't put me there for the sake of the court at all? For the fae? You—'

His scarred eyebrow arched up. 'Oh, no. Not in the slightest.'

'It's ... it's the *humans* I'm supposed to protect?'

'And the rest of the world. Yes.' He took a sip of tea, then sent her a mirthless grin. 'Well done. I expected that to take you a few more months, to tell you the truth.'

'A few— You *bastard*!' Her voice hitched. 'You could have fucking told me that! You—'

'Could have,' he wryly admitted, 'but would you have understood?'

Before the attempt on her life.

Before Bereas's cocky cruelty. Before Inga's weary rage. Before the *fae encounters*, before the mystery of her father's death, before those unforgivable words – *they die anyway.*

'No,' she said, dazed.

Creon merely shrugged.

'All the same …' A desperate laugh fell from her lips. 'What if I don't *want* to save the world? Or the bloody humans? Did you even consider that possibility at all?'

'Well,' he said, face deadpan, 'you could quit, of course.'

'Except that your bloody threats—'

'Oh, those.' He threw her another joyless smile. 'Just a little nudge to motivate you. I suppose we could take them back if you really wanted out of there.'

'If I— Have you even been *listening*, Hytherion?' It was a feat of monumental self-restraint, really, that she managed not to fling her half-boiling tea into his smirking face. 'Of course I want out! I never wanted that crown in the first place! In how many different ways do I need to spell it out for you before you understand I don't wish to lay eyes on the entire cursed place for the rest of my life?'

He nodded slowly, looking suspiciously unaffected by the declaration. 'And then?'

'What?' she snapped.

'Then what will you do once you're out?' The look of guileless interest on his face was about as convincing as a bargain-less promise. 'Live a peaceful life on some backwater island and try to forget?'

She had already parted her lips for a retort before she realised she didn't have one.

*Forget.*

While the humans were still suffering and dying. While the rest of the court no doubt happily resumed the war that had cost so many lives already, throwing the rest of the archipelago back into years of carnage, spilling gallons of blood for nothing but the sake of pride and arrogance.

Old Thysandra wouldn't have cared. Wouldn't even have realised. But now that she knew, now that she'd opened her eyes …

What would be the sense of fleeing?

She could leave the court, yes – but would the court ever truly leave *her*?

'You *bastard*,' she whispered, the realisation locking around her heart like ice-cold chains. 'You ... you ...'

He just sighed.

No gloating. No mockery. Not a trace of that insufferable smug smirk he would have sent her any day of the past three-and-something centuries, and somehow that genuine sympathy made everything much, much worse.

'This is all pretty damn convenient for the two of you, isn't it?' she added, desperation lending an uncomfortable shrillness to her voice. Lashing out was easier. Safer. 'Is this just another way to keep me tied to the place, now that your threats are no longer working? Did Emelin tell you to—'

'Em didn't tell me a single thing,' he said, looking inexplicably amused by the suggestion. 'I was the one who asked if she could leave us alone for a bit. Why do you think she was needling Thorir so much during dinner?'

Thysandra was not aware the needling had been unusual. 'I ... I didn't see you exchange a single private word with her.'

He quirked up that gods-damned eyebrow again. 'Should have kept an eye on our hands.'

Oh.

Right.

She slumped on her bench, fighting the sudden urge to close her eyes and give up entirely on making sense of the male sitting before her. Cruelty and consideration. Scheming and sincerity. Threats, and then this advice that somehow seemed unusually genuine and perhaps even ... well-intentioned?

The very notion of thinking about the Mother's son as *well-intentioned* required the sort of mental strain that could knock a person out for a day.

'And why,' she muttered, eyes on the tea in her lap, 'did you want a word with me, exactly?'

'Told you.' He paused a moment. 'I've been there.'

Hero, villain. Winner of a game that suddenly was no longer a game at all. *And then?* he'd said, and only now did she fully understand the vicious weight behind that question – a question he must have asked himself a thousand times as well.

'Is that why you decided to come live here, of all places?' she managed, looking up at the mossy, time-worn walls around them. 'Because it would allow you to try and build things for once, rather than destroying them?'

There was no hesitation in his voice. 'Yes.'

That shapeless, dusty green sweater. The lack of knives on him. The strange calm in his eyes, no more deadly glowers, no more menacing darkness – as if by doing something else, the male she'd thought she knew had *become* someone else entirely.

'Does it help?' she whispered.

His hands cramped around his mug for a moment. 'More than I ever thought it would.'

And perhaps for the first time in their long, quarrelling lives, she trusted him.

# CHAPTER 17

SINCE THERE WAS NO one else left in the archives to do it, Naxi took it upon herself to walk Inga home.

It was not a pleasant walk. The Crimson Court was soaked in fear once again, and this time there was no triumph to the heated, humid sensation – not when Naxi had done nothing to cause it and was almost equally scared herself. Thysandra had almost *died*, for hell's sake. Right before her bloody nose! And now she'd vanished again, leaving the court and its leaked secrets in the hands of a bunch of potential traitors – while no one knew when she'd return from wherever she had gone to.

*If* she'd even return.

Accompanying Inga home wasn't an act of charity. More than anything, it was a most welcome excuse to get out of the gods-damned castle.

Neither of them spoke as they descended the path that zig-zagged down the slope of the mountain, into the valley that cut through the hills at the heart of the island. To their right, glittering fae abodes stretched along the azure-and-ivory coastline. The human village, in contrast, was dusty and colourless, nestled in a narrow crevice between two hills as if it had crept away from the eyes of the world.

It was also crawling with fae at the present moment.

'Welcome to Rustvale,' Inga muttered as they approached – the first words she'd spoken since leaving the castle behind. Her anger was so sharp Naxi could almost taste it. Sour and pungent, a flavour that had spent a lifetime brewing and fermenting. 'Where our winged masters like to keep the cattle.'

'I like most cattle better than most fae?' Naxi helpfully offered.

Inga snorted a laugh, the flash of bitter amusement not nearly enough to soften the fury she emanated. 'Oh, you and me both.'

A rare moment of agreement. It did not diminish the distrust wrapped around her heart in the slightest, Naxi couldn't help but observe.

They were noticed a moment later by two patrolling fae, familiar faces who had been there to defend the archive doors as well. Inga didn't return their greetings as she strode past them into the village. Naxi did, to be rewarded with two brand new stings of fear.

Damn it.

Not that she cared, of course.

A few dozen humans were standing on the sandy road, muffled cheers and cries of relief rising from their midst at Inga's arrival. Most of them appeared to be in the process of packing their belongings, bags and trunks standing by nearly every front door. A few babies whined unhappily. A human girl of around fifteen summers stood sobbing in her father's arms. None of them threw Naxi even the briefest glance as she slowed to a standstill on the edge of the village, unsure of what to do next.

Not that she cared about their glances either, of course.

Should she just leave them to their own devices, then? Turn back to the court, hide in the Labyrinth, and hope Thysandra would be back soon?

A few dozen feet away, the newly arrived, bargain-covered fae male named Silas landed next to Inga and exchanged a few quick words with her. Inga's look of revulsion at the hundreds of bargain marks spoke volumes, but all the same, they swiftly reached an agreement; Silas flew off again, while Inga returned to her fellow villagers and began handing out orders with determined gestures at houses and humans. Waves of relief rose from the crowd. Of ... fondness.

Perhaps, Naxi cautiously considered as she stood there and watched them scurry around with renewed frenzy, she could help out a little more?

She wasn't sure where the thought came from. Helping people was a waste of time unless they could help you too, and there was little that this huddle of drained, worn-out people would ever be able to do for her – nothing she couldn't do herself, at least. She didn't feel sorry for them either. She never felt sorry for anyone. She liked making things harder for the fae, of course, but she doubted packing an elderly human's bags would make life significantly more unpleasant for any winged citizen of the Crimson Court; if she wanted her revenge, she'd be better off just killing a few more of them.

And yet ...

Yet *something* drove her feet forward.

Closer and closer to where the humans stood comforting each other, hauling heavy trunks from dilapidated houses together, pulling each other's children away from passing fae. Stifling fear still permeated the air, but it was mingled with something softer – trust and camaraderie and the hard-won attachment of people who'd faced hell together.

A feeling as addictive as stolen sweets. Hell, perhaps she wouldn't even have to help anyone? Perhaps she could just stand here and bask in the mellow softness of that sensation, the sense of home, of *belonging—*

One of the younglings screeched out in alarm.

Fear slammed down like a summer storm as every fae and human in the village snapped around at once, all amity and kinship gone in the blink of an eye.

Throwing them her most harmless smile was an unthinking reflex. Only as the fear spiked in response did Naxi remember that mortals tended to get nervous about her teeth – immortals too, for that matter – and that perhaps she should have started by explaining herself. Belatedly, she tiptoed two quick steps back, gave them a sheepish little wave, and tried, 'Anything I can do to help?'

An infant started crying in its mother's arms.

From behind a group of broad-shouldered men, Inga's voice snapped, 'Oh, for fuck's *sake.*'

She came stomping into view the next moment, muttering something to the people around her before she made for the edge of the village in a straight and furious line. For a moment it seemed she would grab Naxi's arm and physically drag her away, but she held back at the last moment; instead, she settled for a sharp jerk of her blonde head to indicate Naxi should follow.

Objecting seemed to be of little use, so Naxi didn't.

'You should be getting out of here,' Inga said under her breath as they strode off the way they'd come. Her jaw was set in a grim line. 'They're jumpy enough already after that attack. Loitering demons is the *last* thing any of them need.'

'But ...' Naxi stammered, stumbling over her feet to keep up. 'But I'm just helping!'

'Not to be blunt,' Inga said, clearly intending to be blunt, 'but that sounds a little unlikely coming from a demon, doesn't it?'

'Well, yes, but—'

The girl finally stopped short in her tracks and whirled around, levelling Naxi with a cold grey glare. From that look alone, one couldn't have known just how frightened she was ... but of course the fear was still there, visible only to demon senses, hidden behind a lifetime of channelling every spark of panic into unbreakable resolve.

'But?' she sharply repeated.

Naxi hesitated, unsure what point to make.

*But I just want Thysandra to know I'm serious about staying* – which was a useless argument, as none of these humans would trust Thysandra any more than they trusted her. *But I have nowhere else to go* – a lie, even if she couldn't enter Thysandra's quarters until her return. *But I'm bored* – as if any human wanted to think that their life-or-death survival was nothing but an amusing pastime to her.

None of those reasons told the full story, anyway.

*Because sometimes, just sometimes, I wish I could be like you.*

Which wasn't a thought she could simply speak out loud.

'Look, I'm very grateful for the offer,' Inga added when Naxi remained silent, unnaturally patient like a mother about to present a hard truth to her child. 'And I'm sure you didn't have any intention of eating anyone's babies just now. But when we already have a few thousand fae to worry about, I'm not going to ask people to invite some fairytale monster into their homes as well, alright?'

But she was trying to *help*.

She was *really* trying to help.

'Yes,' Naxi said, desperately fighting her wobbling bottom lip. 'Yes, of course.'

'Good.' Inga gave a curt nod, then stepped around her, added a belated, 'Take care,' and strolled back to her waiting townspeople. Those same people who were now emanating waves of hopeful relief dispersed with pangs of expectant dread – as if Naxi would turn around any moment and start chomping on their children anyway.

*Some fairytale monster.*

She wiped her suddenly watery nose and started running.

It wasn't *fair*, damn it – it really, *really* wasn't. She'd risked her own life to defend them in the archives! She clearly hated the fae as much as they did! And babies didn't even taste *that* good, her father had said, so why would she make the bloody effort to snatch them from their cradles in the first place? They had no right to kick her out like this. They ... they ...

A blubbery sound escaped her.

She ran faster.

For the first time since she'd arrived at the court, she missed her friends. Not that she'd ever been fully at home with them, not *truly* – but at least they had made a heroic attempt to pretend she had been, even if it was always on the condition of her sticking to the rules. Don't kill. Don't maim. Don't gossip about feelings – instructions she'd followed religiously, and in turn, they'd hardly ever inched away from her.

She hadn't even *wanted* to kill or maim them. The downside of killing one's friends was that one no longer had any friends after the fact.

Like now.

Like here.

Her breath was squeaking through her throat, and still she could not stop running. Away from that cursed village. Away from the cursed castle. A doomed flight to some place that might not even exist anymore ...

*Home.*

If only her mother had still been alive, and her aunts and cousins and nieces ... and then she missed *them* too, a slumbering gap in the bottom of her heart that hadn't grown any smaller even with all of the sixth regiment in their graves. Not that she had belonged on Mirova, either, of course. Not when Mother had always happily called it her greatest mistake, letting some demon male seduce her; not when it had been so mind-numbingly boring, growing daisies and singing songs all the time. And then she'd flitted off with Father and his demon friends, and when she returned—

Ashes.

The salt of her tears was stinging her cheeks, raw and painful.

She wasn't *lonely*, she'd told Emelin weeks ago – demons shouldn't be capable of the emotion. Yet right now, that very fact seemed like half of the problem, not the solution: one more reason to feel different, one more reason she was always, inevitably, an outsider.

She'd just wanted to *help*.

For selfish reasons, perhaps, for reasons of belonging, but did that make the offer any less genuine?

A wall of grey and dark green loomed between the hills before her, and only then did she realise what call her feet had unthinkingly answered. She slowed as she reached the border of Faewood, sniffing tears away as she stumbled between the twisted trunks – feeling the faint but unmistakable heart of the forest settle over her like the world's most uncomfortable blanket. It was thorny and raw, the sensation. Threaded with nettles.

A blanket all the same, though.

She found a clearing without any bones or wing shreds in it, not too far from the beach, and sank down between the gnarled roots with a last bone-deep sob. Around her, the shadows rustled in menacing ways. Distant howls mingled with the crashing of the surf. But no one told her to leave, or to be sweeter and less violent, and no one, not even the smallest patch of moss beneath her bare feet, was scared of her.

She buried her face in her arms.

She let the misery wash over her.

By nightfall she was no longer feeling anything but numbness, an apathy that kept her rooted to the soil as if she'd joined the trees around her.

She ought to return to the castle at some point, presumably. See if Thysandra had returned from wherever she had gone. Make sure that Bereas and the arseholes he called his friends hadn't taken over the court yet. But if she returned, she might find the redwood door with its magical lock still closed – and then where would she go next, if she wasn't able to enter the only rooms that would truly keep her safe?

Around her, the forest was almost entirely dark. Only the thinnest drips of moonlight came seeping through the foliage, drawing silvery blots on bark and leaves; she watched them move over the clearing as the hours went by and the moon slowly crept across the firmament. Maybe she could just stay here. Slowly turn into a tree herself and stop bothering with such infuriating things as humans and their fears – or maybe ...

Something moved in the corner of her eye.

She froze.

But it wasn't a hound or a smirking fae warrior with a knife in hand, and it wasn't Thysandra either, having magically found her in this desolate spot. Instead ...

A ribbon of light.

The softest, sweetest shade of blushing pink, emerging from the moonlit shadows of the wood and looping between the gnarled trunks towards her.

It was pretty and delicate like the first flowers of spring, that ribbon, alluring like the singing voices by the Elderburg cliffs. Naxi stared at it as it floated closer and drew a slow, wide circle around the clearing – no doubt about it, the light was here for her somehow. Which she should have known from the start. It *was* her favourite colour, after all.

There weren't many people who'd ever asked her that, though.

Lyn, probably. A handful of nymphs, maybe. Apart from them ... the Labyrinth.

All of a sudden, it was no longer so hard to move.

She jumped to her feet, avoiding roots and tangled branches instinctively as she dashed after that twisting ribbon of glowing pink. Could the mountain even reach so far? But then, it had been able to enchant fae and lure them in as well, and that seemed significantly more complex than flinging some light around – so she rushed on, ignoring the distant howls and the sharp pebbles beneath the bare soles of her feet. There was the outline of the mountain's slope, drawn sharp against the starry sky. There was the entrance of the Labyrinth, a many-coloured glow lighting up the trunks around it. At long last, the foliage parted, the moonlight spilling in ...

And there she was.

Whetted blade in one hand, bunched-up coat in the other – Thysandra of Echion's house, in all her breathtaking glory.

She stood straight and tall in the arched doorway, eyes narrowed at the forest, the glow of a thousand colours playing over the rich umber of her skin. Her feelings came through a moment later, bewilderingly different from those with which she'd flung herself from the archive window mere hours ago: wariness, yes, *always* that same court-bred wariness, but mixed this time with a whiff of something Naxi could only describe as ... resolve?

*Confidence*, even?

And then Naxi staggered out from between the trees, and Thysandra's every other emotion was swept aside in a surge of vast, exquisite relief.

'*Naxi!*' There was a perplexing crack to the sound of her name – something that sounded close, really suspiciously close, to concern. 'Oh, thank the gods, it worked. What are you doing here, of all places? Inga said you were—'

*Some fairytale monster.*

Inga was the last person she wanted to think about.

'I was just resting,' she squeaked, making a brave yet doomed attempt not to sound like a whiny wreck. Not that she *wasn't* a whiny wreck, but there was no reason Thysandra needed to know that, was there? 'Taking a nap with the trees. Just ... just taking a break from people trying to kill me all the time.'

Thysandra's eyes narrowed. 'You look absolutely dreadful.'

'That's not a very nice thing to say,' Naxi tried, voice far too high-pitched for the humour to sound at all convincing. 'I was really just—'

The most unnerving thing about Thysandra's speed was that it didn't *look* like she was moving swiftly.

From her expression, her bearing, the casual way she sheathed her knife, one could have thought she was simply ... ambling forward. Barely getting into motion, even. Yet she crossed the clearing in less than the time it took to blink an eye, centuries of honed battle reflexes contained in three lightning-quick steps – reducing the distance between them to a foot at most, a twitch-forward-and-touch distance.

Her free hand grabbed the collar of Naxi's dress.

Her cedar scent turned every breath into perfumed agony.

'I never thought I'd hear myself say this,' she muttered, and hell have mercy, that *was* concern hiding behind the brave attempt at wry amusement in her voice, 'but am I the one supposed to torture you for the truth now?'

Naxi's mouth had abruptly gone dry.

She should answer the implied questions, probably. Honestly, this time. But Thysandra was close enough to feel the warmth of her, and then there was that stunningly beautiful face in the moonlight, close enough to kiss ... Strong cheekbones. The stubborn curve of wine-red lips. A jawline made to rule the world, begging for fingertips to trace along its smooth, chiselled edges ...

She was sad and tired and hurting, and how was anyone supposed to come up with *words* in the face of such magnificence?

Thysandra's worry was a chilly fog around them. Frustration, too, a pressure like stone about to crack. More than anything, though, there was an *absence* – of that chafing, abrading feeling that Naxi had known to follow her wherever she went, as constant as the rush of the sea and the caress of the island breeze.

'You're not scared of me,' she breathed.

A flicker of confusion stirred between them.

'What?' A blink. 'No, of course I'm not. Haven't we established that plenty of times by—'

'Why?' Naxi said feebly.

Thysandra stared at her. 'Beg your pardon?'

'Why aren't you?' Her bottom lip was trembling again. 'Everyone always is.'

There was a single beat of silence.

Then Thysandra said, 'Ah.'

It sounded tired, that one word. Resigned. The confusion between them had vanished at once, and so had the frustration, leaving nothing but that numbing, swirling coolness of concern behind.

It was getting harder and harder to keep her lip under control.

'It helps that I know how demons work,' Thysandra finally said, sounding as though she was choosing her words with the greatest circumspection. As though Naxi might shatter at a single unfortunate turn of phrase. 'Most people haven't spent their life studying your kind. Which means they think you're entirely unpredictable, which I suppose is rather more alarming than knowing you'll simply always choose the path of least inconvenience. Once there's a path, it can at least be influenced.'

'But ...' It made sense, and yet it didn't. 'But you still don't trust me, either.'

'No.' Thysandra grimaced. 'Because I know how demons work.'

Naxi swallowed. 'Oh.'

'All the same …' Before she realised what was happening, a coat swept around her shoulders, woolly and warm against her chilly skin. Strong arms scooped her off the forest ground the next moment, cradling her like a child to be coddled. 'All the same, I've decided I'm going to need your help.'

The night was getting more bewildering every minute.

'I told you that ages ago,' Naxi managed, unable to keep down her indignant little huff even though three quarters of her mind was not at all bothered with huffing, and much, much more concerned with the warm, muscular body carrying her into the glowing caves of the Labyrinth. Thysandra was so very *strong*. So perfectly *shapely*. Hard and soft in all the right places, and it was getting more and more challenging to think about being right when she could also be thinking about the fastest way to get her hands on every inch of those delectable curves. 'And then you told me to get out of your sight.'

'Yes,' Thysandra sourly admitted, making a smooth quarter turn to avoid a protruding mass of rock, 'because I didn't have the faintest clue of what I was actually trying to achieve. You've got to agree you aren't the most obvious ally when it comes to building up a fae court.'

Something really *had* changed about her. A frothy, foamy lightness bubbling from her heart, a feeling that was the opposite of weight – as if something had lifted or loosened or finally slotted into place. Naxi knew her cautious and dutiful. *Reactive*. Not like this, tight with the pressure of impatience, ready to burst into action like a kettle about to boil.

It was utterly intoxicating.

'So what *are* you trying to achieve, then?' She was growing a little breathless. Above them, the Labyrinth twinkled brighter than ever, like a constellation of dazzling colours. 'Are you planning to raze a fae court to the ground?'

Thysandra shrugged. 'If we don't have another choice.'

'If— Wait, what?' She tried to veer up, only to find that the strong arms holding her weren't at all inclined to let go. In a tangle of limbs and skirts, she wilted and protested, 'That was a *joke*, Sashka!'

'Not from me.' A wry grin. 'Let's get some food inside you before we talk about that.'

She lowered Naxi to the ground as she spoke those last words, onto the smooth, unexpectedly soft stone floor of the Labyrinth. The air was warmer here, two bends removed from the night outside. The black coat around Naxi's shoulders was so long it brushed the tunnel floor; its sleeves hung past her hands, making her feel snug and infuriatingly small at once.

She turned where she stood, following Thysandra's steps with her eyes. Only when the other female knelt to retrieve it did she notice the large wicker basket tucked away in a narrow corner of the cave.

'Oh,' she said with a little gasp. 'We're having a *picnic?*'

'Inga said she hadn't seen you since the early afternoon.' Thysandra didn't look up as she opened the basket and began extracting its contents: grilled peppers, small, boat-shaped pies stuffed with minced lamb, sticky honey cake. 'And the cooks said you hadn't visited the kitchens either, so I figured you might be hungry. Took some food with me before I went to ask the Labyrinth where to find you.'

Naxi only barely suppressed another sniffle as she glanced at the ceiling and whispered, 'Thank you, Labyrinth.'

Most colours dulled a little in response; only the pink gems flickered brighter.

She settled herself onto the tunnel floor, next to the steadily expanding pile of food, then tucked her bare feet beneath her coat and snatched a handful of sugared almonds from a small linen bag. A plate of stuffed dates and a bottle of rose lemonade emerged from the basket last. Out of nowhere, she felt utterly peaceful – warmth, food, safety ...

*Like home.*

She quickly shoved that thought away.

'So,' she said instead, munching on her nuts. 'Tell me about your plans to destroy the court. It sounds delightful.'

'It's not a plan, necessarily,' Thysandra admitted with a joyless grin as she leaned back against the opposite wall and crossed her long legs. 'Or rather, the plan is to stop trying to work *with* the bastards and start to work *against* them if they refuse to behave. We won't get to the destruction part unless it turns out they need some ... well, more forceful encouragement.'

Oh, that *smile* on her lips.

Naxi forgot to register the words she was speaking, forgot to chew – riveted, *mesmerised*, by the curve of that luscious mouth, the way the corners edged up and revealed two irresistible, almost mischievous dimples. A fleck of honey clung to Thysandra's bottom lip. Next to it, the smallest crumb of cake. Messy, inelegant, and *stunning* – she wanted nothing more than to lick those distractions away, then—

'Naxi?'

She saw the shape on that gorgeous, wine-red mouth more than she heard it.

'What?' she stuttered.

'I asked if you wanted something to drink.' Dark brown eyes narrowed on her face, and again the flimsy sensation of worry prickled in the air between them. 'Are you alright? Still cold?'

'No,' Naxi spluttered, as truthful as she'd ever been. Her cheeks were burning. So was every other part of her, really. 'No, not at all. I ... I was just wondering how you changed your mind so suddenly.'

'Oh.' Thysandra reached for the basket again, pulling out two glasses. As she filled them with lemonade, she added, 'I made a quick visit to the Cobalt Court.'

Creon and Emelin.

Some sense began to seep back into the whole situation.

'I was driving myself insane trying to keep up with everyone's threats and demands and expectations,' Thysandra sourly continued as she leaned over to press a glass into Naxi's hand, their fingers brushing against each other in a brief, stolen caress. 'Still trying to serve the whole world. I've never done anything else, you know? Turns out I don't have to. That I ... I might as well stop catering to every shouting voice around me and do what *I* think must be done.'

Blazing hell. It was unfair, really, for a person to be *so* shockingly beautiful – radiant eyes, flushed skin, the mouthwatering contours of muscular shoulders and flawless breasts ... Relief radiated off that dutiful fae heart in featherlight waves, potent enough to get drunk on it. Potent enough, too, to *almost* drown out the ever-present watchfulness below; enough to almost, *almost* pass for security.

This, then, was Thysandra Demonbane when she stopped trying so desperately to be strong: a gods-damned force of nature.

'Yes,' Naxi said, feeling a little lightheaded as she clutched her drink. 'Of course.'

Thysandra took a sip of lemonade. Licked a last drop off her lip. Leaned back against the wall, the glowing purple and orange gemstones behind shrouding her face in an otherworldly light, and closed her eyes as she said, 'I've been an idiot about you, too.'

Naxi stopped breathing.

'See, I was trying not to accept your offer to help because I assumed you would be leaving any moment.' Another flicker of a smile. 'But if I'm about to take on the court, I'm going to need you around here. And if I need you to stay while I'm making things right, if I need you to not betray me—'

Naxi scoffed. 'I wasn't going to—'

'—then I'm going to need a different approach,' Thysandra continued, as if she'd barely heard the interruption – giving the impression this was a monologue she had prepared well in advance, every sentence refined and memorised over the hours it must have taken her to fly back from the west. 'And you're a demon. You're inherently selfish. So if you help me, I'll give you anything you want in return, alright? If anyone promises you a better deal, you come back to me, and I'll double—'

'Will you come live somewhere else with me?' Naxi said.

Thysandra's mouth snapped shut.

For a single, gem-lit moment, they just stared at each other – sparkling glasses in their hands, a pile of food between them. Thoughts were visibly crashing into each other behind those dark eyes, wishes and promises, sensible politics and personal preferences ...

'*Almost* anything, then,' Thysandra finally said, her voice a little weaker now.

Not unexpected. Really, it had been an experiment rather than a genuine request in itself. Naxi was pretty damn sure she knew exactly what demand was expected from her, what demand Thysandra was *hoping* for her to make – four nights in the same bed with not even a chaste kiss between them, and finally the High Lady of the Crimson Court had found a way to justify what she wanted. No vines this time. No pretence of powerlessness. Instead ...

Loyalty. A simple, dirty bribe.

Fucking your enemy, the safe way.

Which Naxi should probably point out, ethically speaking. Clear as hell the trust wasn't there. She *wasn't* going to betray Thysandra, bribes or not, and accepting the bribe nonetheless would only undermine that simple fact – which could only cause plenty of problems along the way, she was perfectly aware of that.

Then again ...

She hadn't stopped dreaming of that warrior's body unravelling around her fingers. And damn it all, what was the fun of *ethics*?

'As you wish,' she said, smiling wide – revelling in the astounding lack of fear that followed, person-to-person rather than monster-to-victim. 'In that case, you could always just fuck me, of course.'

The relief echoing back at her almost made her laugh out loud.

But Thysandra merely hummed and sipped her drink – as if the flare of heat in her lower body wasn't so perfectly obvious even through the haze of Naxi's own. 'Suppose I could. As a purely political course of action, of course.'

Oh, yes. This was *much* more fun than ethics.

'Of course,' Naxi said with an innocent flutter of her lashes. 'Perfectly diplomatic. I never feel more loyal to you than when I have three fingers inside you, as a matter of fact.'

Thysandra half-choked on her drink.

'In fact,' Naxi added, setting her glass aside and scrambling to her knees to shed her coat, 'I feel like this is the *perfect* moment to fortify international relations, don't you agree? To, let's say, lay the ground-work for fruitful future collaborations?'

Her reward was another of those intoxicating, half-reluctant stings of both shock and arousal. 'What— *Here?*'

'Yes?' Damn it all. She needed to forget this mess of a day. She needed, most of all, to forget the slumbering questions it had so cruelly un-veiled, of home and belonging and a future she did not want to face. 'You didn't think you could present me with a picnic and expect it to stay purely platonic, did you?'

Again there was that war waging in Thysandra's expression – duty against want, good sense against the delightful madness slumber-ing beneath her skin. Half-heartedly, she stammered, 'The Labyrinth might be unhappy about that particular sort of diplomacy, don't you think?'

The air grew noticeably warmer around them, or at least Naxi was quite sure it wasn't just her own blood rushing to the surface.

'I think the Labyrinth might be quite excited about us,' she cheerfully countered, a little apologetic giggle escaping her. 'May or may not have spent several hours rhapsodising about your pretty pussy, so—'

No matter how dark Thysandra's skin might be, it turned out she *could* blush – explosively and feverishly. '*Naxi!*'

'What?' She grinned, crawling closer. 'I promised to entertain it. And it's not like I had anyone else to talk to.'

There was a sputter about something-something dignity and some-thing-something manners, which Naxi wholeheartedly ignored. Her fingers brushed along the length of Thysandra's toned shin, pausing at the knee – soaking up the exhilarating hunger reverberating back at her, every nerve burning with the urgency of a dying plea.

Thysandra didn't move. Her breath had gone shallow and strained, the swell of her bosom heaving temptingly against her red dress.

'You know what?' Naxi said, pulling back her hand and schooling her face into an expression of severity. 'I'm suddenly overcome by an urge to betray you in the most dastardly ways. To all of your enemies at once. Unless you give me a very good reason to—'

Hands fisted in the front of her dress.

Raw warrior's strength yanked her forward.

Their kiss was rough, almost *violent*, slamming the both of them against the glowing walls in a burst of sudden closeness. It was a pent-up kiss. A break-free kiss. A kiss that said *finally*, even if Thysandra's ravenous lips would never speak the word out loud, and Naxi did the only thing she could think of through the roar in her ears – reached up, clawed her hands into the flight-mussed mass of gold-black curls, and drew herself even closer.

Hands dug into her hips in turn, flipping her onto the smooth stone floor.

Thysandra's lips were greedy, hot and urgent, as if this one taste might be all she'd ever have. Her lust flared like a wildfire. Which was surely an invitation to do much, much worse ... so Naxi untangled one hand from her silky locks and brushed down a slender neck, a rock-hard shoulder, the plump, magnificent swell of a breast – finding the hard bud of a nipple, finally, beneath that blood-stained dress.

She pinched, sharply.

Thysandra's hiss was nothing to the spike of her pleasure. 'You little—'

Naxi bit down on her bottom lip.

'—*vixen*.' Hoarse, breathless, curse and compliment at once. 'Looking so sweet and pretty, while underneath—'

Naxi pulled away from their kiss, gasping for breath. 'You think I'm pretty?'

A rough laugh. 'Diplomatically.'

'Oh. Right.' It was hard to string whole sentences together with the weight of that tall body pinning her down, cold stone and burning heat turning her skin into a beggar for more – a need so urgent it felt like she was turning inside out with it. 'Diplomacy. Can I ... can I diplomatically sit on your face now?'

Thysandra's muscular thigh pressed between her knees, forcing her legs apart. 'I'm not going to offer you the best right from the start, of course. That's just sloppy negotiating.'

Naxi whimpered. 'But you said—'

'I *will* give you what you want. Eventually.' Full, hot lips brushed her jaw, her temple, the sensitive rim of her ear – turning the words into caresses, the sensuous promise into a torment of its own. Naxi tried to squirm closer. Tried to soothe the feverish craving at her core and failed, utterly and pathetically, as Thysandra breathed a laugh against her cheek and repeated, '*Eventually*, I said.'

'But then— *Oh.*' She flailed for grip against the smooth floor as that merciless thigh finally moved up the last few inches and dragged a single slide over her aching flesh. Slow, maddening friction, dulled only by the layer of underwear separating skin from skin; her hips bucked up as if they'd gained a will of their own. '*Sashka*—'

'Be a very good girl for me first.' Heated words, muttered against the skin of her neck. The colours of the Labyrinth swayed like dancing leaves above them, reflecting off gold-flecked wings swept wide. 'Kill a few people for me, little monster. Keep me safe for a while. You'll have to earn your rewards.'

'That's just cruel!' she gasped, rubbing herself against the little reprieve she was offered. Needy and humiliating, but she was drunk on lust, on oblivion, and fuck, she *needed* that release. 'And very unfair! *I'm* supposed to be the cruel one between us!'

Laughter brushed her skin again. 'Seems like you're an excellent teacher, then.'

It was too much. Too much and not nearly enough at the same time, the lips on her throat, the weight on her body, that hard thigh pressing her drenched linens into her equally drenched flesh. Most of all, the feeling of *want* that radiated from Thysandra's every touch and movement, no flinching, no cowering away.

As if Naxi was harmless.

As if she *belonged.*

'Please,' she moaned, no other words left in her mind. *Please let me drown. Please let me believe it.* 'I need ... I ...'

'I know,' Thysandra murmured. 'You'll get it, don't worry.'

With a sob, Naxi clawed her fingers into corded shoulders and thrust up her hips once more, seeking, begging, aching. There was nothing demonic about this anymore. Demons took, rather than waited to be given; demons demanded without caring what they deserved. But she was so very sick of taking, of demanding – of being a creature that didn't know how to do things in any other way.

She just wanted to *have*.

'Please,' she whimpered again, feeling the salt of tears on her cheeks again as she fought for that sweet release. Her mind was folding in on itself. The void within her spread like poison. But Thysandra was here, Thysandra was *hers*, and she clung to that lifeline – no home, no family, but the body she was rubbing herself against was devastatingly real, and she needed, *needed—*

Thysandra's leg vanished from between her thighs.

'No,' Naxi gasped, grabbing at empty air. The world was a blur of colours and tears. 'No, *please*! I'll be good! I'll do whatever you need! I—'

Strong hands dug into her inner thighs and spread her open in a single, ruthless yank.

And then – stars above, hell below – hot, hungry lips dragged over her desperate flesh, and her mind shattered like fragile glass dashed against unforgiving rocks.

There was no time to catch her breath. No time to brace herself before Thysandra's tongue slid inside her, drinking deep, voraciously – an urgency like a first sip of water after years and years of thirst. Naxi cried out, arching away from the smooth stone floor, and again that hot invasion filled her, lapping up every drop she had to give, feasting on her frenzied need.

She did not demand.

She just surrendered.

Fingers speared into her, laying her bare. Teeth scraped over her most sensitive spot, and already she was unravelling at the seams, her entire world contracting into a single savage point of ecstasy – because Thysandra did not relent, did not stop licking and sucking and thrusting, and fuck, that insatiable greed – *that* was what she needed, more than the pleasure itself.

'Please.' It had become a breathless, rhythmic chant. Her body sang, burned, trembled with unfulfilled need. 'Please, Sashka – *Sashka—*'

Fingers curled inside her. 'Come for me.'

'Can't,' Naxi babbled, too far gone to hear herself, let alone stop herself. 'Need to touch you – need to – please—'

'You can touch me later.' A hoarse laugh heated her soaked, swollen flesh. 'First, you're going to come for me. Screaming.'

She gasped. 'But—'

'Naxi.' The fingers thrusting inside her slowed for the first time, and she wanted to cry, wanted to *kill* something. 'You're so fucking wet. You're so fucking beautiful. You taste like honey and roses. Feel what you do to me.'

What she did.

To Thysandra.

And then a voracious tongue dragged all the way up between her thighs, from her slit to the throbbing bud of nerves above, and she *felt* it. An unmistakable burst of pleasure that wasn't her own at all, the undiluted delight of devouring the most delicious thing in the world ...

Just a glimpse, but it was enough – it was *better* than enough.

She crashed over the edge in a single blinding flash of pleasure, moaning garbled pleas as her body folded in on itself. Every convulsion of her muscles echoed back at her in gleeful triumph. Every breath was full of Thysandra, that perfect, sweaty, earthy scent. She let the sensations wash over her, wave after wave after wave, until at long last the shudders eased and she was just blissfully hollow, numb even to the sizzling emotions flaring around her.

Thysandra's arms wrapped around her, lifted her, cradled her. Smoothed her hair from her clammy forehead. Tucked her dress back around her sticky thighs.

Naxi breathed.

Just sat and breathed and felt ... home.

'Think you won the negotiations,' she heard herself mutter, strangely slurred words, as if she was dead drunk on pleasure. 'At least a day of loyalty, I think.'

Her reward was a low, husky laugh. 'Oh, trust me – you don't want to betray me tomorrow, either. I've got plenty more in store for you.'

Something was wrong with that assertion, Naxi vaguely, drowsily realised. Because the fucking had nothing to do with it, really. She wouldn't betray Thysandra even if they went back to being celibate for the rest of their lives, not as long as she still had a place to be harmless – was that something she ought to say out loud?

But talking was *hard*, and she was so very happy, and really, she did have better ways to put her lips to use …

'Can I tear that dress off you now?' she murmured into Thysandra's shoulder.

A matter of priorities.

Orgasms first. Food second. Surely they'd have time for talking later.

# CHAPTER 18

OLD THYSANDRA WOULD NEVER have asked for a tour of the servants' quarters.

Then again, Old Thysandra had been a wilfully blind fool.

And so New Thysandra found herself making for the castle's easternmost expansion in the early hours of morning, her skin tingling with an odd mixture of tension, determination, and the afterglow of half a night spent fucking a pretty little demon halfway to death. Her eyes were itchy with exhaustion. Her heartbeat refused to settle into its usual pace. Around her, the court was as deserted as a mausoleum, the arches and spires lifeless and stilted – which was not uncommon around this time of day but unnerving all the same. Every whisper of wind became a sign of alarm, every shifting shadow a dagger about to sink between her wings.

She strode on all the same.

*Do better.*

Next to her, Gadyon and Nicanor followed without questions – the first mildly dishevelled as always, the latter's night-blue attire twice as flawless to compensate. Neither of them gave the impression they'd seen the inside of their eyelids much over the course of the night, but both had jumped into action the moment she woke them and asked them to accompany her; she hadn't even needed to elaborate on the matter of her own spontaneous disappearance.

'Still no trace of Bereas and the others,' Nicanor summarised as they walked down the winding corridors – his casual efficiency unable to negate the fact he was wearing twice his usual number of daggers. 'Turns out he owes Silas two more favours. Funny, isn't it, how the fools claim to want war yet run off as soon as they get involved in anything truly resembling a fight?'

*Fools.*

Even tense and tired, Thysandra couldn't help but take note of that meaningful little word – a suggestion that he knew damn well it would be madness to resume the war against the rest of the archipelago. Which was a relief. She'd never explicitly asked for his opinion on the matter, and she hadn't been looking forward to testing just how much wiggle room the loyalty of their bargain allowed.

'Hilarious,' she wryly said.

He scoffed a laugh. 'Any orders?'

'Increase surveillance on the entire island for at least a few days.' She lowered her voice as she spoke; even if the castle remained dead quiet, there was no way to know if anyone was listening. The heavy velvet drapes on the walls seemed to smother the sound of her words. 'I'd prefer not to run into any more surprise mobs. Also, get me a list of the commanders who refused to come to your aid yesterday. I'm planning to have a word with them.'

Her Lord Protector nodded – his cold, efficient nod.

'The rest can wait.' Until she had this visit behind her. More importantly, until she'd gotten an answer to questions she could never ask him directly – answers for which she needed assistance that only Naxi's powers could provide. 'Gadyon, could you tell me a little more about this place you've found to house the humans?'

'Ah. Yes.' The tall male to her left cleared his throat, limping steps breaking their rhythm for a moment. 'We— Well, the short story is one of my people realised that only about half a dozen fae were still living in the ivy wing. It's never been too popular. Too remote. So we, um, told those last few inhabitants they could move into the villas by the north coast that were left vacant after the battle.'

Nicanor's swift grin suggested he might have been involved with that decision, but all he said was, 'Surprisingly, they were happy enough to oblige.'

'I hope you don't mind,' Gadyon hurriedly added. 'We wanted to proceed swiftly, and, well, with the uproar over exactly this sort of situation ...'

'No, that's excellent.' If she had minded, that would be her own fault for having disappeared so suddenly – and either way, it seemed a solution unlikely to enrage anyone but those waiting to be enraged. 'And there's an adjacent garden too, yes?'

She already knew there was a garden. She knew the wing in question as well as she knew any other part of the castle. What she needed to know was—

'There is,' Nicanor said in Gadyon's stead, long strides never faltering. 'Although it's heavily guarded at the moment, of course.'

Good.

She could work with that.

As if to illustrate the point, two fae guards stood waiting around the next corner, posted before the stairwell that led to the wing's main entrance. They veered up abruptly as they noticed her, saluting with a speed that suggested she hadn't lost *all* appearance of authority over the course of the previous day.

'Your Majesty, Lord Protector ...' The short but burly fae female speaking seemed unsure for a moment how to address Gadyon's ink-stained presence, then chose the path of least resistance by not addressing the head of the archives at all. 'Happy to report the night has been peaceful. No sign of any unusual activity, Your Majesty.'

'Excellent.' She nodded at Nicanor and Gadyon. 'Please wait for me here. There are a few other things I'd like to discuss once I'm done.'

Once again, they did not ask questions.

She ascended the broad stairs by herself, one hand hovering close to the mulberry purple of her dress, the other to the dagger hidden in the sheath beneath her split skirt. No one lunged at her from behind the pillars with their serpentine carvings. No arrows whizzed in through the high, narrow windows. She reached the next floor unharmed, unnoticed, and no less tense for the fact.

A broad, frescoed corridor stretched out before her. Whimsical forest scenery covered the plaster walls, and the dozens of wooden doors blending into that background as if they'd grown from the floorboards themselves. There was no living creature to be seen – but from the far side of the wing came the murmur of voices, the clatter of plates and cutlery.

Breakfast time for those used to waking early.

Thysandra suppressed the urge to retreat and come back at a more suitable moment. The wing's new inhabitants wouldn't welcome her with open arms no matter when she showed up.

Better to just get it over with.

She sucked in a deep breath and made herself walk on.

Here and there, doors stood half-open, offering glimpses into the disarrayed living rooms beyond – bags, suitcases, piles of meagre belongings. No one seemed to have brought many of their own possessions with them, and it took her a moment to realise it was because none of them *had* much to take along in the first place.

*Do better.*

When did inattentiveness cross into the realm of stupidity?

At the end of the corridor was a sizeable common area, windows on three sides offering a view over the gardens and the quiet beach behind – and it was there that she found them, the humans of Rustvale, sitting at the long tables and on the luxurious couches with bags under their eyes and breakfast in their laps.

For one moment, she watched them just ... be. A mother comforting the toddler in her lap. Two girls giggling by the window. A man inspecting a wobbling table with skilled, weathered hands. A single moment in which she might as well not have existed, and then—

'*Fae!*'

They jolted like hunted deer.

Within the blink of an eye, there was no more laughter, no more comfort. Children shot away behind their parents. Breakfast knives were snatched off the tables. A glass shattered against the floorboards, and Thysandra was the only one flinching at the sound – the only one who still had any alarm left to feel.

A hundred pairs of haunted eyes stared back at her in the sudden, deafening silence. Pale, gaunt faces. Ragged breaths. Trembling hands.

*See you as a villain.*

She didn't want to see it.

She had to, though.

The little boy by the nearest table, clutching his half-eaten apple to his thin chest as if it was the most precious thing he'd ever owned. The man behind him, face covered in grisly burn scars. The child cowering behind a woman's skirt, her downy white hair unable to hide the pointed fae ears – fae ears her mother did not have.

The fear, most of all, drawn sharply on every single one of their faces.

This was the world Thysandra had spent all her life building.

She *had* to feel it, the bile in her throat, the sickening understanding of who she had grown to be – because this was why she was about to declare war on her own damn court. This was why she'd need to face her opponents, finally, rather than try and slip around them for the rest of her life; this was why she could no longer be that young girl hiding beneath her blankets, wings tight around herself, trying to crawl away from the eyes of the world.

*Traitor's daughter.*

Had her father seen the same thing when he committed whatever ill-advised act that had cost both her parents their lives?

'Good morning,' she choked out – a laughable, pitiable start. There was nothing good about her morning. Little about theirs either, probably. 'I thought I'd walk by and see if you've all settled in properly. If there's anything else we can do for you while we deal with yesterday's events, too.'

They jerked back into motion as if it was a command.

Yes, yes, it was wonderful, hurried voices assured her – it was *better* than wonderful, this place to live in, more than what they'd ever expected. They'd been given plenty of food, and they were very grateful for that, too. Clothes? No, they really didn't need more than what they already had, they could easily patch up some of the old stuff they still had lying about, and—

'New clothes would be nice, actually,' Inga's gruff voice broke through the flustered lies. 'And we're in dire need of soap and other toiletries, if it's not too much trouble. Got a lifetime of filth to wash away, you see.'

Another shocked silence descended over the room.

The girl had appeared from behind Thysandra, still in her grey servant's frock, her long, pale hair swept into a bun that left her fae ears uncovered. Her fingers lay clenched tight around the apple in her hand. The look on her face suggested she might have used it as a projectile, had she not been so unwilling to waste a single bite of food.

*You see?* her scowl repeated.

Around them, humans and half humans sat motionless, breathless, as if Thysandra might chop off their friend's head for her impertinence the next moment.

Thysandra did not move.

'I see,' she said instead, because it was the only thing she *could* possibly say – the only thing that would be true, at least. 'I'll have soap and a few boxes of clothes sent to you all before the end of the day. Some sewing materials, too. If there's anything else you think of, please let me know and I'll see to that as well.'

The gathered humans did not relax on the edges of her sight – did not let out any breaths of relief, nor any murmurs of appreciation. As if this might just be a trap. As if even *acknowledging* her offer might be reason to send them straight to their deaths, proof of their disloyalty or lack of proper servants' manners.

Thysandra did not press. The least these people needed now, she figured, was *more* forceful fae demands.

'I'll leave you to your breakfast, then,' she said instead, stepping back with a last nod before turning to Inga and quietly adding, 'Would you mind having a quick word with me?'

Inga visibly contemplated refusing for a moment, then glanced at her friends and family and gave a curt shrug instead. 'If you wish.'

A hundred frightened gazes burned between Thysandra's shoulder blades as they made for the exit of the ivy wing together, and behind her, the conversation never returned to its previous volume.

'Let's go for a stroll in the garden,' she said when she reached the spot where Nicanor, Gadyon, and the two guards stood waiting. 'We need to discuss a few things, and I'd like to make sure we aren't accidentally overheard by anyone.'

By no one, that was, except the one person she *wanted* to overhear the conversation. No need to tell them that much, though – their ignorance was half the plan.

The guards stayed behind as the four of them made their way outside. Thysandra waited until they were out of earshot before adding, 'Oh, and Gadyon, could you find a few reliable members of your population department and make sure the humans get full citizen status? Effective ... well, today, I suppose. Or actually, make that the day I took the throne.'

Inga stiffened beside her.

'Understood,' Gadyon said, and she could have sworn he sounded almost ... *cheerful* about the matter. 'We'll take care of it as soon as possible.'

'Wouldn't it be wise to give that a little more time?' Nicanor cut in before Thysandra could say anything else, a hint of bewilderment to his gaze as he nudged the outside door open and held it for her. 'Making this change the very day after Bereas and his mob almost killed you ...'

She shrugged, stepping onto the meandering shell path outside. No one in sight behind the rose trees and the boxwood hedges. 'We already have payments and legal protection established. It's a largely symbolic change at this point.'

'Symbolism is all they care about,' he said, sounding desperate. 'I shouldn't have to explain this to *you*, Demonbane – this will be taken as a bloody clear message to everyone sympathising with them.'

Old Thysandra would have cowered at the thought. Old Thysandra would have believed she was failing her people, her throne, her sacred duty to the court.

New Thysandra just smiled and said, 'Good.'

'Gods help me,' Nicanor muttered, releasing the door as Gadyon stepped out last. The hand he raked through his silvery locks was tense with exasperation. 'No one benefits from more violence right now, Thys. Even if *you* manage to keep yourself alive—'

'Oh, don't bother pretending you're selflessly concerned about the wellbeing of the human population,' Inga grumbled, kicking a pebble. It splashed into the nearest pond. 'Your altruism is deeply unconvincing.'

'If the High Lady believed I was acting out of selfless concern, I would be significantly more concerned for her sanity,' Nicanor testily shot back. 'She ought to know damn well that I'm just trying to save my own hide here. Thysandra—'

'You know I have no intention of hurting your poor hide,' she said, in that *end of discussion* tone she'd only ever dared to use with those decidedly beneath her in the army ranks. To her pleasant surprise, it seemed to be just as effective now. 'But my decision is final. If you decide your current position comes with too much risk to your person, I will of course not hold it against you if you decide to resign.'

He glared at her – a look that carried as much unwilling admiration as annoyance. A gamble, of course, but she was almost certain of the path he would take. This was Nicanor of Myron's house, after all, ambitious to a fault, the male who maintained that safe decisions did not lead to victory, and she could not for the life of her imagine him stepping down from a position of power to go live a quiet life in the countryside.

Indeed, he gave a wry sigh and said, 'You know me better than that.'

Good.

This was the game she knew so well – the alliances she understood how to wield. She wasn't going to trust him, or anyone else for that matter; life was still not a charity, and no one with a lick of sense in their brain would voluntarily join her in pissing off some of the Crimson Court's most bloodthirsty inhabitants. But she *could* trust the simple rules of self-interest. She could figure out what people around her wanted and make sure she was the easiest path to achieve those goals. It was the safest way of building a network that she could rely upon.

She might be turning into a traitor, but she certainly wasn't going to be a fool about it.

They walked in silence to the spot she had in mind – a small, man-made pond in which a marble fountain in the shape of a dragon gurgled quietly. Three elegant benches stood around the water feature, looking out over the eastern beach of the island and the crystal-clear ocean beyond.

And there, behind a row of hedges ...

A glimpse of pink.

Something in her wings relaxed for the first time since she'd left her rooms that morning.

'This should do,' she said out loud, as if she hadn't been walking purposefully towards this spot since the moment she'd left the humans and their breakfast behind, as if she hadn't painstakingly described it to Naxi as they made their plans in the depth of the night. 'I'm sure Nicanor's guards have kept the place free of listening ears.'

More accurately, she was sure Naxi's demon senses would have picked up on any intruders in the vicinity of this little pond ... but the demon remained where she sat, hidden behind her shield of boxwood, and so Thysandra assumed the coast was clear.

It was an odd sensation, actively relying on the little menace in her plans. It made her feel uneasy. But she had decided on her flight back from the Cobalt Court that there wasn't *that* much of a difference be-tween fae selfishness and demon selfishness: the principles were the same, to know another's goals and be an asset rather than an obstacle.

Naxi's apparent selflessness had been dangerous. Unpredictable. Giving her what she wanted, on the other hand, was a perfectly sensible way to guarantee her loyalty.

Admittedly ... it had been a rather pleasurable way, too. Knowing that those bloody demon senses would pick up on the heat still smouldering in her lower belly only intensified the sensation.

'Take a seat,' she hastily made herself say, because weakness was death, and drowning in the image of Naxi shattering into yet another climax under her lips was about as close to the definition of weakness as one could come. 'This won't take long, but we need to have a chat about the events of yesterday. About the spread of information, more specifically.'

The silence was both abrupt and deafening.

She didn't even need to ask the question. It was visible in every stiffening pair of shoulders, in every narrowing pair of eyes and every gaze darting sideways – *Who of you talked?*

*Who of you leaked our plans?*

One of them must have. And no matter how many times she'd gone over the matter during hours and hours of flying, no matter how many times she'd lined up their wishes, their individual interests, their actions, she could not make sense of it.

'This is not an accusation,' she added when they remained silent, which was not entirely true but seemed a more productive way to go about the conversation than to threaten and blame. 'I'm the first to acknowledge that mistakes happen, and perhaps no one involved had malicious intentions. The most important thing is that we find out what—'

A shadow fell over her.

She had one moment to wonder what sort of idiot would voluntarily intrude on a High Lady's meeting, and another to wonder why Naxi hadn't yet intervened; then her eyes adjusted to the sunlight and she recognised the golden wings of the newcomer above, the dark skin, the glimmer of too many bargain marks to count.

Silas.

Gods help her – what was he doing *here*?

232

Her uncle landed with a grace that did not fit the sheer bulk of him, granting the company no more than a stoic nod as he folded his wings and tidied his plain white shirt. There was no sense of awkwardness in his bearing, no trace of apology in his expression. If Thysandra hadn't known any better, she might have thought he truly had no clue he was interfering with her plans ... but no, he'd survived at the Crimson Court for longer than a week in his heyday. That *had* to mean he understood the concept of private gatherings, didn't it?

'Morning?' she said, settling for a pointedly inquiring tone in the hope that he'd get the message and excuse himself.

He did not.

'Morning, Thys. Morning, everyone.' If anything, he settled himself more firmly in the grass as he crossed his arms over his broad chest and glanced around the circle – gaze lingering a moment too long on the boxwood hedge behind which Naxi was pretending to be an exceptionally large flower. 'Glad to happen across you all together. Would love to hear a little more about yesterday's events.'

What?

This was not the plan – this was not at *all* the plan – and it took all she had to keep her voice level as she coldly said, 'Why, exactly?'

There was no venom in his raised eyebrows. 'I might be able to help, for a start.'

Hell take her.

What game was he playing, this male who was still a stranger beneath the familiar surface? He wasn't here to hurt her, or at least that hadn't yet been his plan when they left Ilithia ... but that was a meagre reassurance when she had not the faintest clue why he *had* come with her to the court, or what his needs and wants might be. How was she supposed to deal with him if she had no idea of his goals and even less idea of how to be a necessary presence to him?

But before she could respond, Nicanor gave a soft, joyless laugh and sank down on the nearest bench, flicking his silvery hair over his shoulder. 'Who knows? A few more well-aimed bargains might be just what we need to clear up this unfortunate situation.'

And just like that, there was no opening left to send her uncle on his way again.

The deadlock broken, Gadyon plopped down next to Nicanor, muttering an apology as his wing almost hit the other male in the face. Inga seemed to vacillate between fleeing and screaming for a moment, then reached a compromise by settling herself in the grass by the path. Only Silas himself remained standing by Thysandra's side – a jarring, unmoving presence in the corner of her eye no matter how hard she tried to pull herself together.

Did she have to change anything about her plan? Was there anything she did not want to reach his ears – any risks she was overlooking?

'So what were you hoping to hear from us, Your Majesty?' Nicanor broke the silence – far, far too soon. As gracefully as he crossed his ankles and leaned back on his cast-iron bench, she was painfully sure his blue eyes looked straight through her crumbling mask. 'As much as I want your questions answered ... well, I'm sure I don't need to point out to you that both Gadyon and I have made bargains to explicitly prevent this sort of thing?'

Thysandra drew in a breath.

That, it turned out, was too much of a pause.

'Oh, of course,' Inga snapped, lip curled into a furious sneer, eyes blazing with spite when Thysandra jerked around to face her. The girl's gaze was making good attempts to draw blood from Nicanor's whetted features. 'We're back to blaming the humans, I see? How fucking convenient, for you to—'

'I'm not *blaming* anyone,' Thysandra sharply cut in, casting a quick glance around the gardens before aiming her glare back at her quarrelling allies. Avoiding eavesdroppers was a hell of a lot harder if the conversation evolved into a shouting contest. 'As I said before, I want to know what happened more than I want to punish anyone for the situation. I'm looking for information, not accusations.'

Inga scoffed. 'You'll have to ask someone else, then. I know as little as you do.'

Which did sound genuine, it really did – and hell, it wouldn't make *sense* for the girl to have betrayed the information, would it? Not when she would have known damn well that it would put her and her fellow humans in immediate danger. On the other hand ...

Who else?

Even without their bargains, Nicanor would never have brought such failure and humiliation upon himself, and it seemed unlikely Gadyon would deliberately have put the archives in danger. Could it have been an accident, then? But these were experienced fae, who had survived at the Crimson Court for centuries; surely they would know better than to accidentally leak anything?

Vicious circles. She'd spent half the night trying to find a way out of them.

'And you're very sure ...' It felt like prodding an open wound, to continue her line of questioning in the face of those frightened grey eyes. But words led to feelings, and feelings were her best way out of this ridiculous impasse – so Thysandra steeled herself, cleared her throat, and started again. 'You're very sure you didn't mention it to any of your family members, either? Even if they are family members you trust? It could have been as little as—'

'I did *not* talk,' Inga snapped, shoulders hunched up towards her pointed ears. Her gaze darted around the circle of fae like that of a rabbit caught between wolves. 'I'm half human, for fuck's sake, not half-witted. I know how rumours spread, Your Majesty.'

'There are arguments against the notion of human involvement as well,' Silas unexpectedly cut in, his voice too flat, too thoughtful, to make it sound like he was arguing. 'For example, it does seem unlikely that a human killed Iaris to cover up their involvement in any schemes.'

'Oh, I agree,' Nicanor said, throwing the Bargainer a look that came closer to gratitude than anything Thysandra had ever seen from him. 'It stands to reason that whoever killed Iaris was fae. My hypothesis would be that someone, *somehow*, caught a whiff of the story, told one of the most notorious gossips at court to make sure the news would spread fast, then ended her to protect their identity. That person might have heard humans talking about the matter, or they might have gained the information' – he grimaced, his glance at Inga a tangible risk assessment – 'well, in some other way. That I haven't quite been able to figure out yet, admittedly.'

Inga barked a mirthless laugh. 'Your lack of creative thinking is hardly proof of my guilt, is it?'

'They might not have heard it from any of us?' Gadyon suggested, his hasty words interrupting Nicanor's sharp inhale. 'We did not guard the office door during our meeting, and others were at work in the archives at that moment. Someone might have been listening.'

'Might have.' Nicanor rubbed his temple with spidery fingers, visibly bracing himself as he looked up again. 'The easiest way to remove all doubt would obviously be—'

'I am *not* making any bargains,' Inga spat.

Her voice echoed between the gurgling fountain and the rustling rose trees for a moment, then died away into yet another stretch of silence.

Even without looking at the pink, Naxi-shaped fleck hiding amidst the shrubbery, Thysandra knew exactly what quick, razor-sharp grin would be lying on the demon's face right now.

'Well, that's bloody unfortunate,' Nicanor was muttering on the bench, 'because as long as we don't clear this up ...'

'Don't pretend you'll stop suspecting me of foul play even if I bargain for this particular truth,' Inga bit out, her hands balled into trembling fists. 'It's all you fae do, isn't it? Lies and trickery, and so you assume everyone else must be doing the same. I—'

'Inga?' Silas said in his low voice.

She sucked in a shuddering breath. '*What?*'

He considered her for a moment, still unmoving, looking not unlike a male confronted with a feral, hissing cat he wasn't sure what to do with. And for the first time, the very first time since their meeting on Ilithia, Thysandra heard a fraction of uncertainty in his voice as he slowly said, 'Would you care to have lunch with me?'

Inga stared at him blankly, shock trumping even her anger for a moment.

'I'd like to show you some of my research,' he added, spreading his hands a few inches – almost as if to apologise for the suggestion. 'You might find it ... interesting.'

She parted and closed her lips, then let out a high, joyless laugh as she slumped in the grass. Her gaze wandered down to his bargain-covered collarbones, his bargain-covered arms, then back up to his face – all the usual distrust in her eyes, and yet the blunt refusal did not come.

The faintest sound of a giggle emerged from behind the boxwood hedge.

Inga's breath made an audible escape.

'Alright.' She sprung to her feet like a soldier called in for duty, her jaw clenched tight, her pale hair escaping its pins and swaying after her like a hip-length cloak. A last glower at the rest of the group was her only goodbye before she snapped around and marched towards the garden's exit, not even waiting for Silas to join her. 'Good fucking luck with your scheming, everyone!'

Silas gave Thysandra half a grimace – a look she interpreted as *we'll talk later, if I survive for long enough to see you again* – and swept out his wings, catching up with his lunch partner halfway to the castle. Neither of them spoke as they walked the rest of the distance side by side; Inga slammed the door behind her as if she wished someone's neck were caught between it.

Nicanor let out a low, meaningful whistle.

Gadyon looked visibly concerned for the Bargainer's sanity.

'I think,' Thysandra said, in her best, most decisive High Lady's voice, 'that that was enough for today's meeting. I'll let you know when we'll next come together.'

# Chapter 19

'Nothing odd about anyone's emotions,' Naxi merrily reported as they returned to the heart of the castle with a detour through the empty, and therefore safer, academy galleries. Lessons had been paused in the early days of the war, and with more than a few teachers dead and equally as many children left orphaned, they had only been partially resumed. 'Would have been helpful if one of them had been evilly pleased with themselves! But alas, no such luck.'

Thysandra gave a joyless laugh. 'So what *did* you find?'

'Oh, I'm pretty sure Inga isn't our leak.' Naxi gave a wistful sigh. 'She's mostly frightened. And—'

'She might be frightened she'll be found out,' Thysandra pointed out.

'But if it was her, she'd feel guilty, wouldn't she? She really loves her human friends.' Naxi rolled her eyes, then shook her curls down her back without slowing down her springy steps. 'So if she made a mistake and accidentally blathered about the plans to the wrong person, I would expect her to be brimming with self-reproach, which is very much not the case.'

Right.

That was a disconcertingly good point.

'But the others ...'

'Nothing suspicious there, either.' Naxi shrugged. 'Gadyon is incredibly worried. So at least we know he's sensible, but I don't think it's reason to suspect him of anything. Silas is barely holding himself together – not that he was even around to leak anything, of course, so I suppose it doesn't really matter how miserable he's feeling.'

*Miserable.*

Good gods. Perhaps she should have known, given his obvious reluctance to return to the court at all ... but at the same time, what in the world was he doing, getting himself tied up in more and more complex politics if he hated every minute of it?

*I might be able to help* – but that couldn't possibly be all of it, could it? Not if it was making him *miserable*?

Through her confusion, it took a moment too long before she realised a pointed silence had fallen after Naxi's last words. A little *too* pointed. As innocently as the demon was bouncing along by her side, they both knew one name had been very much omitted from that list.

'And Nicanor?' Thysandra ventured, feeling like she was ambling straight into a trap.

'Oh, *Nicanor*.' A blinding smile was her reward. 'Nicanor is *very* interesting. He's watchful, of course. Frustrated when he doesn't fully understand what is going on around him. And then he's also feeling a tad ... *hungry* whenever he looks at you.'

There it was.

'Right,' Thysandra said, as evenly as she could manage.

Naxi's smile was all sharp little teeth now. 'Did you fuck him?'

Gods have mercy. 'Before I answer any further questions, let me quickly remind you that you made a bargain to not willingly harm me and that you *would* very much harm me by killing or torturing the Lord Protector of—'

'That's a yes,' Naxi blithely concluded. 'Before or after you met me?'

It took a monumental effort not to lie. 'Does it matter?'

'After, then.' Naxi huffed as she darted onwards through the corridor, her bare-footed steps twice as quick as Thysandra's to keep up.

Sunlight fell in through red stained windows, casting blood-coloured pools of light across the pale floor. 'But you were still pining for me, so he can't have been a great lay. I suppose that's acceptable. Unless he tries something again, of course, in which case I'll sadly have to pour every single one of his own poisons down his sorry throat.'

Thysandra knew she shouldn't laugh. She really shouldn't. They weren't *partners*, for hell's sake! They shared nothing but a history of betrayals and ill-advised mutual obsession, and she should know so, so much better than to let a circumstantial bribe and some fluttering lashes fool her into illusions of loyalty and love. Yet all the same ...

When had anyone ever gone to battle just to keep her?

'Pretty mild of you,' she said, fighting to keep her face straight. 'I've been told most of his creations kill swiftly.'

Naxi's eyes narrowed dangerously. 'Good point. I could poison a bunch of other fae one by one and transfer all of their pain to him?'

An unwanted, unstoppable burst of laughter escaped, too swift to catch. A sound of weakness, of stupid sentimentality, yet for one reckless moment she couldn't give a damn – because it was so bloody *easy*, this game. Easy enough that it didn't feel like surviving. Easy enough that every now and then, in these unguarded, unthinking moments, she could almost forget it was a game in the first place.

'Anyway,' Naxi cheerfully added, as if they had been discussing dinner and evening plans rather than ruthless torture, 'the end of the matter is that we still don't know anything about that stupid leak. Maybe Gadyon was right and someone really has been listening in on your meeting?'

'Maybe?' It took an almost physical effort to drag her mind back to the topic of scheming and intrigue. 'Alternatively, someone made up a rumour to discredit me and accidentally came up with something close to the truth?'

Naxi snorted a laugh. 'Welcome to the Crimson Court.'

'It's not *impossible*,' Thysandra said wryly. 'Worrisome thought, though. If it happened once, it might happen again.'

'Oh, yes,' Naxi said vaguely, head tilting a fraction. 'Absolutely terrible. You're lucky to have me and my legendary devotion on your side.'

That sounded like yet another trap.

'Am I?' Thysandra said cautiously.

'Absolutely blessed.' The flutter of those pink lashes was alarming. 'Didn't you see how loyal I was? I kept myself hidden like you said, even though I was frightfully bored! And I didn't even bite Nicanor's fingers off while he was ogling you! Not to mention—'

'Alright, *alright*.' Another unwilling laugh broke free. 'You were immaculately loyal, and I'm beyond overjoyed to have you on my side – happy, now?'

Naxi beamed at her. 'Can I sit on your face, then?'

Gods have mercy.

'It is definitely not enough loyalty for face-sitting yet,' Thysandra said, making desperate attempts to keep her expression under control and managing very poorly. She was supposed to be gathering allies, damn it. She needed to have a stern chat with her army commanders, worry about island defences, figure out what to do with a rogue uncle making bargains all over the place ... but then there were the memories of last night, freedom and pleasure and pretty pink lips on hers, and suddenly courtly matters no longer seemed so urgent at all. 'Honestly, I would say this earns you a single finger at best.'

The outrage in Naxi's scoff was a work of art. 'Oh, I deserve at *least* three fingers, Sashka. Do you have any idea how delicious Silas's inner turmoil was? It took an *effort* not to say anything about it!'

'Two?' Thysandra suggested, struggling to maintain her businesslike voice as last night's fire reignited at her core.

'Hmm.' A narrow-eyed glance. 'If I'm supposed to stay loyal for two mere fingers, you'd better make sure I get them inside me at your earliest convenience.'

She had a busy day.

She was still surviving.

'We have a deal, then,' she heard herself say, stepping back from the stained-glass windows, away from any passing eyes. Her fingers tested the nearest doorhandle and found it unlocked. 'And – entirely unrelated – don't you agree this is an excellent moment to inspect these very private, very deserted classrooms?'

A dirty bribe, yes ... but as long as it lasted, would it be so bad if she enjoyed it, too?

'Look, it was a *misunderstanding*,' Imbros of Imbrias's house repeated for the fourth time, pacing back and forth across the soldiers' barracks where Thysandra had found him. 'Nicanor told us that the humans needed protection, alright? So we took a look at Rustvale and Greyside and a few other villages, didn't see any trouble, and went back home. Of course, if we'd *known* what was truly going on at the archives ...'

He plucked his glass of wine off the table, took a swig, and shook his head in silence like a male filled to the brim with regrets.

'If you'd known?' Thysandra prompted, unmoved by this dramatic show of remorse.

'Well.' He plopped down his wine again and turned towards her with guileless eyes, as if it was a joke to even ask the question. 'Orders are orders, aren't they?'

'And I expect my commanders to show *some* common sense when interpreting said orders,' she sharply retorted, keeping her eyes trained on his hands and the menacing cherry red of his shirt. He might attack. She had no doubt she would be faster, though. 'If you'd rather return to your boozing than spend five minutes finding out what's expected of you, I don't—'

Two walls away, a door slammed.

Outside the room, Naxi's voice erupted in vehement objections.

Thysandra spun around without thinking, a knife already in her hand. The barracks door burst open before she'd even completed the movement, and Nicanor swept inside in a storm of icy blue and black damask – out of breath, wings flaring wide, ignoring Naxi's shrill protests behind him with almost suicidal disregard.

'Thysandra!'

Only then did she realise his hands were covered in fresh, red blood.

'What's going on?' She threw a wild look at the door, Imbros and his wine forgotten at once. 'Did anyone attack the court? Are you—'

'Not the court.' He bent over, gasping for air. His trousers were bloodied too, she realised only then – his shirt as well, and yet he didn't seem hurt himself. 'It's the ships. Fishermen. Think ... think you'll want to take a look.'

Her feet were already moving.

It was disconcerting how instinctively her hand wrapped around Naxi's wrist in passing, how little thought it took for her to yank that lithe nymph-like body into her arms as her wings swept out. Naxi's shocked cry barely reached her ears. A dive at the window and they were out and flying. To their left, the deserted training fields shot by; to their right, the gleaming red walls of the castle rose over them like a tidal wave about to crash down.

'Entrance hall!' Nicanor hollered behind them.

She slammed her wings against the breeze, climbing higher.

'*Sashka!*' Naxi squeaked in her arms, little hands digging like claws into her forearm. Only then did Thysandra realise they'd never flown together before. Hell, that a demon without wings or a large number of winged friends may very well never have flown at all. 'Sashka, if you *drop* me—'

'I'm not dropping you,' she said through gritted teeth, quickening her wingbeats as they soared past the first row of towers.

'It *feels* like you're dropping me!'

'That's called gravity.' She scanned the blue horizon before them – where the hell were those ships Nicanor had mentioned? – then had to abruptly move her focus back to the warm weight in her arms when Naxi shifted without warning. 'And *don't* move. If you start wiggling, I actually might drop you, alright?'

Naxi wailed, squeezed her eyes shut, and wiggled harder.

'For fuck's sake.' She barely managed to grab a thin knee before both the demon's legs slid from her right arm's grip. Yards and yards beneath them, the castle's roofs slid by at dizzying speed. 'Calm *down*. Think happy thoughts if you need to. Like poisoning Nicanor, or killing—'

Naxi's fingers clawed into her shoulder.

Their lips slammed together.

This time Thysandra almost *did* plummet to the ground – her body too occupied, for just one moment, with the urgent press of that sweet mouth against hers to think of trivialities like moving her wings. Air rushed past them. Her stomach slammed into her throat, and still Naxi did not let go; with a small whimper, those soft pink lips parted, and somehow Thysandra's did the same ...

With desperate effort, her wings swept out.

Feet away from the roof beneath them, their freefall slowed.

And still Naxi was kissing her, both small hands clutching Thysandra's neck, all of her soft, small body pressed perfectly against Thysandra's hips, breasts, stomach. Her lips tasted of roses. They tasted like the sweet, wine-drenched figs she'd pilfered from the kitchens at lunchtime, hot and wet and utterly intoxicating, and gods have mercy, what was all this air doing around them? Why in the world weren't they in a bed yet?

Something to do with emergencies. Something to do with ships.

Nicanor.

Oh, fuck. *Nicanor.*

Thysandra yanked back her head, gasping for air and sense.

The terrace of the court's main gate stretched out beneath them, maybe two dozen yards below. A small crowd had gathered on the weathered granite, a bloodied fae shape at the centre, and thankfully that attraction appeared to receive more attention than anything happening overhead ... but Nicanor had been just behind them. If he'd *seen* – if he'd caught even the slightest glimpse of this madness—

No, there he was.

Already far beneath them, descending to the terrace in a long, graceful slide.

'Fuck,' Thysandra breathed, voice shivery, limbs shivery, the full force of her panic hooking its claws into her chest only now. '*Fuck*. Don't you *ever*—'

'Oh,' Naxi feebly said, glancing at the ground below. 'We're almost there already?'

The worst part was that it sounded genuine.

'Keep your hands off me when we've landed,' Thysandra forced herself to say in an even voice, because roaring out loud in frustration *would* draw attention from below, and she did not need a larger audience to see her clutching a frightened demon to her chest. 'Don't giggle at me, and don't you *dare* call me anything but Your Majesty with anyone around to hear, do you understand?'

Another whimper. 'Are you angry with me?'

Yes.

No.

Damn it all – what was she thinking? This was an alliance. Not a relationship. Which meant she only needed Naxi around as long as it advanced her goals. Which meant there was no reason, no reason at *all*, to make light of this situation or call that kiss anything else than an unforgivably stupid idea.

Wide blue eyes blinked up at her, filled with pleas and almost-tears.

'We'll talk later,' Thysandra ground out as she swept into her final descent.

At least the gathered fae below only noticed her moments before she landed on the granite tiles. At least she managed to shove Naxi from her arms swiftly, and at least she could pretend her mussed hair was a result of her hurried flight rather than any more scandalous activities; she impatiently raked the black-and-gold curls into place as she marched towards the circle and loudly said, 'Can anyone tell me what's going on here?'

Better to fake authority than to still feel that kiss on her lips.

The crowd parted instantly around her, whispers and murmurs stilling at once. At the heart of the group, only a blood-stained fae male remained behind on the tiles – the worst of his injuries healed but healed poorly, the gleaming pink scars and tatters of his wings silent witnesses of whatever had befallen him. Nicanor stood mere feet away, knife in his hand, eyes glittering dangerously.

'What happened?' she repeated, more sharply now.

'Your Majesty,' the wounded fae groaned. 'Your Majesty, I'm a sailor of the Zephyr – part of your fishing fleet, Your Majesty. We were ambushed this morning. Ship's sunk. Half ... half of the crew is dead. They attacked without warning, Your Majesty – clear blue skies one moment, and the next they were showering us in red—'

*They.*

Her thoughts stuttered.

Only one group he could be talking about ... but that did not make sense, did it? Why would Bereas ever bother to harm the court's fishing fleet, of all things? Even at the height of the Mother's war preparations, those vessels had never been enlisted to assist the empire's navy – small ships that had never been built to inflict or withstand any violence at all. They didn't fight. They just—

They brought in food.

Cold dread rose in her.

'Do you ...' She already knew the answer, and yet she *had* to ask – as if feigning ignorance might still change the inevitable facts. 'Do you know who they were, exactly?'

Everyone knew, and yet the pulse of silence was heavy with anticipation.

'Bereas,' the wounded sailor rasped, hoarse and furious. 'My daughter is obsessed with wing-racers, Your Majesty. I would recognise those fucking wings anywhere.'

So it was true.

Her foremost enemy, reappearing not to attack the heavily defended Crimson Court itself, but rather the vulnerable resources on which her peace depended.

It was clever. It was vicious. Most of all, it was an indication of more long-term thinking than she'd thought the bastard capable of – hell, had she been underestimating him? Was there an actual *plan* behind the seemingly random outbursts of violence she'd seen from him so far, a strategy she'd simply overlooked?

Then what was she to do now?

That age-old voice was still there in the back of her head – that voice that said, *hide, hide, hide,* that knew no words but the safe, stifling darkness of the world beneath her blankets. She knew what Old Thysandra would have done. Diplomacy. Compromise. Already she could see herself sitting at a table with Bereas, trying desperately to find some middle ground – *fine, but you can kill no more than ten humans a year ...*

She'd probably have thought it a fairly reasonable deal, too.

Eyes, so many eyes watching her as she stood there on the smooth black tiles and tried to keep thinking straight ... Hell, how many of these people were secretly glad for the attack? How many of them would support all violence as long as it did not harm their own skin? How many of them couldn't wait for the rebels to return and take control of the court?

And if she didn't let them ... how long would she survive?

She swallowed and tasted roses.

And just like that the world was clear again, the lingering flavour on her tongue like a whack to the head – because she *still* wasn't a fool, and damn it all, she still had her hard-won allies and her thought-out plans, didn't she? She didn't need to *tell* her audience that she was choosing the side of the rest of the world over theirs. There was no need to out herself as a traitor just yet.

She simply needed to act.

'Nicanor?' she said.

Her Lord Protector merely tilted his head.

'It appears that our friend Bereas has forgotten it's bad form to attack one's own people.' She stepped back, sending the flocks of fae a joyless, reassuring smile she was quite sure they did not need. 'Please scale up the court's defences to their highest level of alertness. We will need to stop him if he intends to make that same mistake again.'

# CHAPTER 20

'Sash— Your Majesty. Your *Majesty*.' Naxi's voice, quiet but shrill, caught up with her before she'd even reached the castle gates through the steadily thickening throng of fae pouring out. 'Your— Oh, come on, slow *down*! I have short legs!'

Short legs *and* stupidly delicious lips. Thysandra smoothly circumvented a group of armed fae jogging towards Nicanor, then finally crossed the castle's doorstep and into the magnificent hall beyond without looking back. There were even more eyes here. On the other hand, more walls and doors within reach, too, and she'd prefer to have at least a few of those around before daring to meet her pursuer's gaze again.

'*Thysandra!*'

She walked even faster.

Around her, feverish whispers rose from the crowd, the news moving swifter than even the fastest pair of wings. No one accosted her directly, though – not yet. Whether it was due to the little demon trailing behind her or her general dubious reputation, she wasn't sure; either way, it wasn't inconvenient.

It took a minute or two before she finally spotted an open door be-tween the flutters of wings, coats, and dresses. Another minute before she managed to reach it in a manner that did not give the impression of a flight. The small powder room was mercifully deserted, at least, just a circle of velvety chairs, two walls of gilded mirrors, and an imposing assortment of hair brushes, perfumes, and wing powders on the tables. She slipped in, unable to hold back a sigh of relief, and rested the back of her head against the brocade-covered walls as she waited for Naxi to join her.

Ten counts of rest were all she was granted. Then the door clicked shut, the noise abruptly quieted, and Naxi's high, breathless voice squeaked, '*Sashka!*'

She closed her eyes.

The wall was blissfully cool and stable.

'*Stop him if he makes the same mistake?*' Naxi blabbered on without waiting for a response. '*Scale up the defences?* Is that fae code for "we're at war with him now"?'

'It's fae code for "we're at war with him but he's the one in the wrong",' Thysandra sourly corrected. 'Otherwise, yes.'

The scoff she expected didn't come. 'So you're in danger now?'

'I was in danger already.' She rubbed her face, then warily looked up. Naxi's eyes were almost painfully blue, staring at her from three mirrors at once. 'There's no such thing as safety at this court.'

'But you're in *more* danger now,' Naxi shrilly insisted.

Gods have mercy – what in the world was this about? It wasn't new, was it, the notion of deadly risks in this place? Nobody came to the Crimson Court to experience a peaceful vacation, and either way, she'd been clear enough about her intentions when she returned from the Cobalt Court – no more sitting back, and no more accepting the unac-ceptable.

Really, wasn't that the entire reason she'd started making deals with demons in the first place?

'I suppose I am?' She came away from the wall and ruffled her wings into a more comfortable position, unsure how to proceed in the face of this unexpected protest. 'Good thing I have you and your legendary loyalty on my side, then.'

Naxi's face darkened. 'I'm not *joking*, Sashka.'

'Then what are you trying to say, exactly? Because I was under the impression we both came here rather prepared for—'

'You don't need to do this!' Naxi burst out, small fists trembling.

Thysandra stared at her.

'You could just ... leave. Couldn't you?' There was nothing melodious left in that singsong voice – nothing but shrieking misery. 'The bastards are making everything worse! You tried very hard already! So why not let them figure out their own mess and get out of here?'

And just like that, it made sense.

*Come live somewhere else with me.*

'And move to that idyllic island with you instead?' she said slowly, hearing the warning in her own voice.

'Well.' Naxi's bottom lip quivered, but she did not back down, did not move from where she stood stiff as a rod by the door. 'We're having fun, aren't we?'

Fun.

Hell take her.

It shouldn't be painful, the realisation – it shouldn't be new or surprising or even something that required a reminder at all. Demons chased their fun. Thysandra did not. As easy as it was to work together, as much as Naxi kept her safe for now, there would be no common destination in the end. They *would* go their separate ways one day.

Sweet lips and clever fingers be damned.

'The problem is,' she said, sucking in a breath as she turned away and paced to the circle of chairs, 'that I want to do this.'

'No, you don't.' Naxi sounded almost indignant behind her. 'You hate it. You're frightened every single minute in this place. You—'

'Alright, *fine*. I don't want to *not* do it – is that better?' It took an otherworldly restraint to keep her voice from soaring into a shout. 'I have a lifetime of mistakes to fix. I promise you I'm not going to feel any happier lying on a beach while I know innocent people are dying all over the archipelago again.'

Naxi was quiet for so long Thysandra almost started thinking she might have fainted. But when the demon finally spoke, she did so softly, feebly – almost *sadly*.

'So we're staying?'

'Well, I'm staying.' She turned back around, seeing the movement reflected in the mirrors on either side of her – a sweep of gold-black wings, a sway of purple. Naxi still hadn't moved, blue eyes trained on Thysandra's face as if to pin her in place. 'You're free to leave whenever you decide there's nothing for you at this court anymore, of course. I would just appreciate a warning so I can account for your absence.'

Cold. Pragmatic. And fine, she *would* regret losing an ally this powerful ... but then again, better to have no alliance than to have a former ally working against her. This, too, had no business making her heart twinge so painfully.

That kiss had proven all too well what a hazard demon hearts could be.

'Alright,' Naxi said, voice a little choked, and Thysandra's heart skipped a beat all over again.

'Do you ... do you mean you're leaving?'

'No.' A sniffle. 'Just that I'm an idiot.'

A befuddled silence fell. In the distance, loud enough to be heard through the closed window, Nicanor was bellowing orders at flocks of fae.

'What?' Thysandra said, feeling like she had somehow missed half a minute of the conversation.

'I should have seen that coming.' Naxi's joyless little laugh was bitter as unripe berries. 'I mean, I *did* see it coming, which—'

Something smacked against the outside of the door.

Not a fist. The sound was too dull, to unfocused for a knock. Rather, it sounded like an entire limp body had crashed into the wood; a roar of pain followed a moment later, the shriek of steel against steel, a flash of red visible through the chink above the threshold.

Someone shouted, '*Your Majesty!*'

Oh, hell.

'You know what?' she snapped, reflexively checking her knives as she made for the exit and all but shoved Naxi aside in passing. Soldier's instincts took over – fights before feelings. 'Let's have a word later, alright? Need to survive the day first.'

She was out just in time to see the first corpse being dragged away.

The trouble with war preparations was they left painfully little time for talking.

By the time all army commanders had been grilled thoroughly on their loyalties, all surveillance schedules had been implemented, and all scouts had been sent out to survey the surrounding islands for hiding spots, it was hours past midnight and Thysandra was tired enough to almost fall asleep before she'd dragged herself back to her rooms. Naxi was quiet and subdued beside her. Whether the reason was exhaustion or whatever emotion had overcome her in that powder room, Thysandra couldn't tell; she did not have the brainpower left to ask, either.

Checking her defences for the night was all she managed to do. She didn't bother to undress and fell asleep the moment her head hit the pillow.

Dawn woke her after what felt like mere minutes – an unusually noisy dawn, the shouts and clamour of armour outside signalling a change of guards around the castle. Beside her, the bed was empty. For a single, bloodcurdling moment, she thought Naxi might have slipped away in the night; then she heard the quiet humming from the living room, the padding of bare feet, and a watering can tapping against plant pots, and her heart abruptly settled back into its usual rhythm.

Just a matter of strategy, of course.

She would be a fool for it to be anything else.

All the same, it took her more effort than it should have to drag herself out of bed, get out of yesterday's rumpled dress, and make herself presentable again. *We're having fun.* The words still echoed, a demon's goals and dreams – dreams so utterly incompatible with Thysandra's that it was hard to imagine those uncanny demon senses had not picked up on it before.

Perhaps she had not been clear enough herself? Perhaps Naxi assumed that the loss of her loyalty to the Mother, to the empire of old, meant she had lost all sense of loyalty entirely – that she was no longer still the same fundamentally dutiful person beneath with that thin veneer of obligation scrubbed off. Perhaps demons just couldn't grasp the notion that there was so much more worth bleeding for: home, principles, love.

If so, it might be a kindness to them both to point that out as quickly as possible.

But when she finally gathered the courage to leave her bedroom, Naxi was already standing by the locked door, dressed in buttery yellow, a fuzzy pink shawl around her shoulders. And all she said – no greetings, no questions – was, 'I forgot to visit the Labyrinth yesterday!'

So Thysandra unlocked the door and then ate breakfast alone, with only the monstrous plants for company, reminding herself with every bite that it was nonsensical, truly nonsensical, to feel envious of a mountain.

'Your Majesty?'

She couldn't walk halfway down a corridor this morning without being waylaid by yet another fae with questions, warnings, demands. This girl was young, too young to be allowed at court at all, really, and yet she came striding from a small salon with the air of an accomplished courtier, all fawn-eyed shrewdness and glittering confidence.

She was holding a folded letter in her hand; on the inside of her wrist, green against brown skin, gleamed a single bargain mark.

'Yes?' Thysandra said, not bothering to force a smile.

'The name's Calaria, Your Majesty. Maleon's house.' A swift, artful bow; the girl's long blonde ponytail swept down and up with the motion. She smiled brightly as she straightened. 'My sister is one of the people who left with Bereas. I found a letter from her on my table this morning and thought it might be of interest to you.'

She held out the parchment as she spoke. A tempting offer, but *too* tempting – people did not betray their own kin without wanting favours in return.

'And what would you require for your service to the crown?' Thysandra said, not moving to accept the gift.

'Nothing at all, Your Majesty.' Calaria's sunny smile grew even wider as she turned her wrist up. 'I have already made arrangements with the Bargainer, as a part of which I am obliged to present you with this information.'

Silas?

Her spine went cold with either shock or dread.

But she took the letter, because it *might* just contain useful information, and smiled as if this wasn't a surprise at all, as if she'd always known of whatever game her uncle was playing behind her back. Confusion was weakness. Weakness was death. And so she kept her voice perfectly level, perfectly matter-of-fact, as she said, 'Thank you for your assistance, in that case – and do you happen to know where I can find the Bargainer at the moment?'

'Last I heard, he was having breakfast at the harbour master's place, Your Majesty.' The girl bent into yet another easy bow, then floated off without another word, long hair swishing against her moss green wings.

The harbour master.

Gods-damned Rhias – a relic from the Mother's time she'd thought she didn't need to bother with yet.

With a curse, she slipped the letter into her pocket and made for the nearest exit of the castle.

But of course she wasn't escaping so easily – not the very day after an effective declaration of war. A tall male demanded to know how the court would guarantee the safety of allied houses on other fae isles. A female soldier complained that only Bereas was being punished for killing fae, whereas the Alliance had yet to face any consequences for their violence against the empire. A father begged for mercy for his two rebellious sons, then turned to threats when Thysandra wouldn't make any promises regarding their fate.

She'd just disposed of that last conversation partner – the gaping gash she'd left in his wing a helpful reminder of all the reasons not to threaten one's High Lady – when a flash of glittering black and piled auburn curls came hurrying from the nearest garden entrance. 'Oh, Your Majesty!'

Gods-damned Orthea.

The Master of Ceremony swept towards Thysandra as if she owned the bloody castle, shooing a handful of nearby fae away so half-heartedly it was clear she'd be delighted to have an audience. 'There you are,' she drawled, louder than usual in another obvious bid for witnesses. 'I'm *so* glad to finally happen upon you.'

Her honey-sweet tone made it obvious that the meeting was neither accidental nor a pleasure to her. As it had been at least five minutes since Calaria's interruption and Thysandra still hadn't reached so much as an advantageously positioned window, the temptation to end the conversation with a blast of red and walk on was close to unbearable.

'Yes?' she said instead, so curt it straddled the edge of snapping.

'There's a question I've been meaning to ask you about the Hunter's Moon festival,' Orthea purred, looking delighted about her coldness. At times, Thysandra wondered whether the damn shrew felt a need to compensate for the illusion of a friendship they'd once shared. 'With all the recent ... *uproar* ... I imagined the list of guests might require some revisions, but of course I did not want to act without your thoughts on the matter. Do you feel like we should still send invites to those who were involved with the ... irregularities of the last few days?'

For fuck's sake.

The game was clear, of course. Orthea knew damn well what the answer would be; she'd never needed to ask. Which meant there could only be one reason she stood here nonetheless: that she sympathised with Bereas's cause, that she didn't want to catch flack for banning him and his allies from the festivities, and that this way, a dozen witnesses could confirm that it had been Thysandra's order, not her own, to rescind those invitations.

Throwing a former friend to the wolves all over again.

How bad would it be to just cancel the entire festival outright?

Bad, probably. Angering the Mother's loyalists was one thing; pissing off the additional part of the population that didn't care about politics but definitely fancied a party was perhaps a little too much. She'd have to discuss security with Nicanor, then. And speaking of Nicanor ...

'As a matter of fact,' she said, making her decision in a single spiteful heartbeat, 'I would just *love* to invite Bereas and his friends. Please make sure the message reaches them as soon as possible. Our Lord Protector has been most eager to have a word with them.'

Orthea's smile stiffened.

'Was that all?' A terse nod at the other side of the corridor. 'I have a busy programme for the day, unfortunately, so if we don't have anything else to discuss ...'

It was then, as she moved her gaze back to the Master of Ceremony, that she saw the bargain mark on the other female's bejewelled wrist.

A mark that hadn't been there last time they'd seen each other.

Fuck.

Had she visibly stiffened? She couldn't even tell. Orthea's obligatory parting words went straight past her, and so did the demand-disguised-as-question another passing fae flung at her – because this was Silas's work again, wasn't it? It *had* to be. Orthea was by no means in the habit of making bargains with anyone she ran into; who else would be able to offer her something worth the effort and the risk?

Had she been sent here as part of that bargain?

How many of the two dozen people who'd approached Thysandra in the past half hour had been playing someone else's game entirely?

She barely even saw them anymore, the faces lining up to speak with her. Their questions could bloody well wait. She should have known so, *so* much better than to let her uncle roam the court without a single question about his intentions, and she wasn't speaking to a single soul until she had remedied that mistake – until she knew exactly what web the Bargainer was spinning around her.

'Go see Nicanor for anything urgent,' she heard herself bite out as she shouldered past a pair of midnight blue wings, straight towards the nearest window.

Rhias lived in one of the comfortable villas along the north coast of the island, a marvel in white plaster and gold with a lush garden that bordered the beach beyond. A handful of young fae were working in that garden as Thysandra flew over; clearly, the harbour master hadn't wasted any time solving the issue of his human servants leaving.

Knowing him, she should probably have someone check whether his new fae gardeners were in fact working for him voluntarily.

She heard Silas's voice the moment she landed on the beechwood porch – his timbre low and guarded, a marked contrast to Rhias's ostentatious joviality. Her knock on the front door was little more than symbolic. She walked in before anyone had shown up to let her in, following the sounds of voices and clattering plates to the patio at the heart of the house – closer and closer to where Rhias was contently regaling his visitor with a story of some mutiny he'd ended by flogging the wings of the fae involved.

Bastard.

Was this the sort of ally Silas thought he needed? The sort of ally he thought *she* needed?

She tugged a last beaded curtain aside and stepped into the sunlight, where the two males were sitting around a table loaded with enough cream buns, strawberry tarts, and salmon sandwiches to feed an orphanage. As if the grain stores weren't running out at an alarming rate. As if the same gods-damned fishing fleet Rhias was responsible for hadn't suffered a devastating blow fewer than twenty-four hours ago.

It took every ounce of willpower she possessed not to smother the harbour master in his own fucking cream buns when he turned to her, barely rising from the seat in which he lounged, and gave her a lazy grin with not a shred of surprise in it.

'Your Majesty!' An expansive gesture at the table accompanied the greeting. 'What an honour to have you appearing at my humble morning meal. Will you be joining us, by any chance?'

*I'd rather share a dinner with a dozen alves out for my blood*, she wanted to say.

Instead, she turned to Silas, whose only greeting was a fleeting smile that did not reach his eyes. His simple white shirt didn't fit in with the extravagance of this home, the lack of colour almost a challenge – a reminder that he did not need any of that gaudy red as long as he had the powers that lay embedded in his very own skin.

Was she imagining things, or had the scattering of marks on his right arm become visibly denser already?

Alarming.

She schooled her face into stony indifference all the same. Alarm was weakness. Weakness was death.

'I was looking for my uncle,' she said, choosing not to respond to the invitation at all. 'Apologies for interrupting your breakfast, Silas, but could we have a word?'

From his nod, she couldn't tell if he was annoyed or glad to be out of Rhias's company; the gesture was as calm, as unemotional, as any other of his movements. He rose from the deep velvet seat with the stark composure of a mountain getting to its feet – the sort of composure that made one wonder if there even *was* any inner turmoil beyond.

*Miserable*, Naxi had said.

She shouldn't be thinking of Naxi now.

'Of course,' he said only when he was already standing, sending Rhias a look Thysandra couldn't easily decipher. 'Enjoy the remainder of your breakfast, Captain. We'll continue our conversation soon.'

The harbour master raised his glass of fizzy white wine in response, that same grin sliding across his face again. 'I look forward to it.'

Oh, yes. *Definitely* alarming.

Neither of them spoke as they made their way out through the maze of silk-lined walls and elaborately carved doorframes. Two of the gardeners had moved to the front of the house, it turned out when they stepped into the sunlight – better not to say anything on the porch, then, either.

'Beach?' she suggested.

Silas muttered an agreement as he swept out his golden wings.

They flew past that row of villas, up to the next small bay, where the houses were smaller and had been built farther from the surf. There Thysandra landed, her uncle following close behind. The sand was white and powdery here, the sea so crystal clear that it didn't even look blue for the first ten yards or so.

Gulls screeched overhead. As good a cover for their conversation as anything.

'Alright,' she tartly said, raking her hair back in place as she flattened her wings against her shoulders and turned to the male by her side. Frustration sizzled in her veins, dangerous and utterly useless. Being frustrated at that still, stoic face of his was like shouting at a piece of rock. 'First of all, *Rhias*?'

Silas shrugged. 'I'd rather have him restricted and in my debt than free to cause us whatever trouble he'd very much like to cause us.'

'Is that why you're going around making bargains with everyone and their mothers – to try and *restrict* them?'

'Yes.' He stuck his thumbs in the pockets of his trousers as he began walking, edges of his wings fluttering in the breeze. 'What else did you expect me to be doing, Thys? I'm a creature of habit, and my number of useful skills is, frankly, quite limited.'

What else had she expected him to do?

Perhaps the problem was she didn't even know.

'I'd have liked a *little* more information before you threw yourself back in the game,' she stiffly said, following him along the surf line. Flecks of white foam clung to her boots, to the hem of her tangerine dress. 'How am I supposed to work with you if I don't have a clue what you're doing in the first place?'

He raised his eyebrows a fraction. 'You can just tell me you don't trust me. I won't shatter on the spot.'

'That's not the point!' Even though, admittedly, it quite *was* the point. 'But I need to know what you're working towards. I need to know what you're trying to achieve. If I have to guess about your motivations while more and more of my own people show up with your bargains on their arms ...'

*Then how am I supposed to rely on you?*

*How do I know you aren't quietly working against me after all?*

She didn't finish the sentence out loud, although she wasn't sure why. He *wouldn't* crumble at the implied accusation, would he? She'd be nothing but sensible to point it out, either. Even if he hadn't been *planning* to hurt her, she had no idea how much he'd care if that turned out to be an accidental side effect of his activities.

But with the silence between them, the salty sea breeze in her hair, and the wet spray of the waves against her wings, it felt almost like a betrayal to speak the words.

'The main thing I'm trying to achieve,' he said finally, in that calm, low voice that made it so damnably tempting to believe him, 'is to keep you alive. It appears you could use the assistance.'

She winced as if he'd slapped her in the face.

*Weakness.* The shock of it made the words come out sharper than intended – 'I'm not twelve years old anymore, Silas.'

'No,' he said, eyes on the horizon. 'I'm well aware.'

'Then what makes you think I need—'

'A handful of soldiers,' he mildly interrupted, 'have been making plans to smuggle Bereas and his consorts back into the castle through a delivery of food crates. Their arrival was supposed to coincide with the Hunter's Moon festival, and their primary target would have been you. Did you know?'

From anyone else, that last question would have been a taunt. From him, it was just ... a question.

'Where did you hear of this?' she said, voice too feeble.

'A letter sent to a girl named Calaria. I've sent her your way – in return, I'll have to try and save her sister from the hounds, although banishment would be acceptable.' He paused, his golden eyes narrowed against the sun. 'And then someone was caught tinkering with the water pipes leading to your rooms – we found a bag of arsenic in her possessions. I'm also still working out who started the circulation of a letter that was allegedly sent to you by members of the Alliance, thanking you for your invaluable assistance in winning the battle at the White City.'

Thysandra swivelled around, almost losing her balance in the loose sand. '*What?*'

He merely shrugged, never slowing down.

*Traitor's daughter. Traitor's daughter.* Her voice went shrill as she hurried after him and started, 'I didn't—'

'Oh, I know,' he interrupted, swatting her protest away with a twitch of his wing. 'Two or three people have already admitted under bargain that the document is falsified, and we'll get to the root of it soon enough. What I'm trying to say ...'

He paused for a moment, as if to gather his thoughts. She barely managed to keep moving her feet in the silence that fell, her heart pounding its deafening rhythm of *hide, hide, hide* – because they could call her a tyrant for all she cared, they could call her a bitch and a murderer and a spoilsport intent on ruining everyone's parties ...

*Traitor's daughter*, the waves whispered to her left.

The hounds howled in her memories.

'I know you're bloody capable, Thys,' Silas finally said, his voice so unbelievably flat. 'I know you'd likely have survived most of these attempts by yourself, if not all of them. But you're also surrounded by a few thousand people all clamouring for their own gain, and for more than a few of them, you're standing between them and their victory. You only need to be unlucky once.'

'It's not a matter of luck.' Too quick. Too brusque. Her heartbeat wouldn't slow down. 'I have people working for me. Protecting me. Anyone who wishes to kill me needs to get through my allies before they can reach me at all.'

'Hmm.' He nodded on the edge of her sight, still no feelings or opinions breaking through the broad mask of his features. 'And do you trust them? Your allies?'

*More than I trust you.*

It seemed unkind to make that point out loud, though, so instead she went with a more or less composed, 'I offer them a path to achieve their goals.'

He glanced at her beside him, eyes boring into her face. 'That's not what I asked.'

Wasn't it?

She couldn't help an owlish blink or two. 'But you said ...'

'Yes,' he admitted, and there was a touch of grimness to the set of his jaw as he averted his gaze again and ran a gem-studded hand through his short black hair. 'Yes, I suppose I did. Gods help me – she trained you well, didn't she?'

What?

This whole conversation was making less and less sense. *She* was the one who'd had justified questions, for hell's sake, and somehow he'd pried those out of her fingers and punched them straight back into her face – sending *her* teetering, while he was still sauntering along without so much as a blink of confusion. How could he claim he was just keeping her safe when he was tugging at the very pillars that *had* always kept her alive in this world?

'I don't see where you're going with this,' she sputtered.

'Never mind.' He rubbed his brow, then stuck his hands back into his pockets. 'Tell me about your allies.'

Was he trying to destroy her trust in them, too?

'Look,' she said, voice rising above the crashing waves in a sudden burst of agitation, 'do you have any actual reason to think I should *not* be working with them? Any concrete accusations? If Inga confessed anything when you spoke with her yesterday—'

'Oh, no,' he interrupted – steady and without hesitation, yet all the same, she couldn't help but sense an unexpected sliver of ... was it defensiveness in his voice? 'The conclusion of that conversation was that Inga definitely did not leak your plans.'

Thysandra snapped back around to him. 'You managed to get a bargain out of her?'

His shrug showed neither pride nor false modesty at the accomplishment. 'We had a good chat.'

'Good gods.' That *was* helpful, admittedly – but then, it made his insistence that she distrust the people around her all the more ridiculous. 'Fine, so we can trust Inga. Whose loyalties are you doubting, then?'

'Everyone else's?' His wry grin came as close to an apology as anything she'd ever seen from him. 'What exactly made you decide to start working with a *demon*, of all creatures? To the point where you trust her to sample the emotions of others for you?'

So he had noticed Naxi behind that hedge yesterday. What could she say? *Don't worry, I bribed the little menace by feeding her honey cakes and fucking her into the ground several times over* – not a great way to improve his faith in her sanity, and in any case, with the odd way Naxi had been behaving yesterday, their agreement may not even last that much longer.

'Bargains constrain demons as well as anyone else,' she said instead, aiming her gaze at the motions of her feet, the small clouds of sand she was kicking up at every step.

'True,' Silas said, his voice neither sceptical nor impressed. 'Then again, poorly worded bargains constrain demons as little as they constrain everyone else.'

'I'm not a fool,' Thysandra said, looking up to glare at him. 'Anaxia bargained not to willingly harm me, and she's bright enough that I doubt she'll do it unintentionally.'

He canted his head. 'A demon's idea of harm may not be identical to yours, of course.'

'Of course,' she said, unable to keep the frost from her voice entirely. 'Your concerns have been noted.'

'Excellent.' Another joyless grin crossed his face. 'How about Nicanor, then?'

'Nicanor gets what he wants from me. Also ...' *We're old friends. He'd pick the painless poison for me* – sentimental arguments that she should surely ignore if she ever wanted to convince her uncle that she'd picked her allies well. 'If he wanted me out of the way, he could just have stood by and waited when I was attacked a while ago. Considering that he single-handedly saved my life on that occasion, I see no reason to distrust him now.'

'Beyond him being a self-serving bastard,' Silas dryly added.

She huffed an unwilling laugh. 'Yes, and that's been accounted for in the plans.'

'Alright. Gadyon?'

'Would Gadyon ever harm anyone except those leaving dog ears in his books?' she countered, starting to feel a little steadier on her feet. This was familiar ground. Better than the utter dread of that falsified letter still pulsing in the back of her mind – *traitor's daughter*. 'He doesn't strike me as the kind to stage violent uprisings.'

Silas pursed his lips. 'He survived at the Crimson Court despite the disadvantage of a physical impediment, though. I doubt he's as harmless as he seems.'

'Are you trying to make me feel like a fool for placing even the most minimal, well-considered amount of trust in *anyone* else?' Her voice soared. 'Then what should I do – never exchange a word with anyone for the rest of my life? Or is the suggestion that I rely only on you and your assistance, perhaps?'

His steps did not falter.

He did not even blink.

'What I want you to do,' he said, slowly and meticulously, every word punctuated as if it set the conditions for a life-or-death bargain, 'is to not take any assumptions for granted at this court. You're living in a tinderbox, Thys.' A mirthless laugh. 'One spark and it'll burn us all alive.'

# CHAPTER 21

THE SPARK CAME EVEN sooner than expected.

Not during her inspection of the forces Nicanor had posted along most of the coast of the island – her soldiers were grim but calm as they waited for the inevitable confrontation to come. Not even during the hours she spent hurrying around the court afterwards, answering questions, fielding thinly veiled attacks, bracing herself for accusations of treason that never came. But when she returned to her rooms for lunch halfway through the afternoon – overwhelmed, exhausted, and ready to commit bloody murder if a single person mentioned Bereas's name ever again – Naxi sat waiting before the redwood door, two dead fae by her feet, and a sealed and folded piece of parchment in her hands.

'Sashka!'

It would have been sensible, presumably, to ask some questions about the corpses first.

But the poor sods were dead anyway – they had probably done plenty to deserve it – and even the grisliest corpse couldn't have been as shocking as the dazzling brightness of Naxi's smile, an almost aggressive cheer that suggested the previous day's gloominess had never even existed. It was that surprise that had Thysandra jerking to a standstill on the stairs, the world stuttering and rearranging itself around her – because the little menace would be *leaving* soon, wouldn't she?

That smile didn't look like she was leaving.

It looked like she was about to burrow into Thysandra's skin and live there.

'I've got news!' Her voice was merry like a midwinter celebration – forced brightness, anxiously ignoring the looming dark on the edges. 'Tared just visited and left a letter for you, Sashka!'

A single letter.

For the five she'd sent out.

Which should be a crushing disappointment, and yet she barely felt that emotion beneath the far more urgent, far more ominous suspicion swelling in her. What in the world was going on? Naxi's grin was too broad. Her eyes too wide. There was something she wasn't saying, and few things were as utterly terrifying as a demon with secrets – had Tared given her any new information? Hell, had the *Labyrinth*?

'Sashka?' Naxi repeated, a flicker of uncertainty in her eyes.

'Right,' Thysandra managed, forcing herself to move, to step forward. Her thoughts swam, and so did the sound of her voice in her own ears. 'Yes, very good. Is there ... is there anything else we should talk about?'

Blue eyes blinked back at her, guilelessly. 'Talk?'

'Yes.' It felt surreal, the entire conversation, and the dead fae lying between them did not help matters in the slightest, their bodies grotesque props on the stage of some bittersweet comedy. 'You— Yesterday, you said—'

'Oh!' Naxi's peal of laughter was like bells, sharp and bright. 'I was just tired. I said things I didn't mean. Don't you want to read Tared's letter?'

Gods help her.

She didn't care about gods-damned Tared's letter. She wanted to know what the hell was going on, with an urgency that felt like a hand around her throat. This wasn't *Naxi*, the stilted, artificial little creature sitting against that door before her. This was some unnerving parody of the demon she knew, and how was she supposed to think about politics when something was obviously, mysteriously wrong with ... well, her foremost ally?

It made sense, didn't it, to be worried about the person who presented such an exceptional strategic advantage for your cause?

'Sashka.' A flutter of slightly bloodstained, buttery yellow and then Naxi was standing, the strained smile gone from her face at last. Her impatient glower was a relief, somehow. At least it looked like *hers*. 'I really am fine. Let us into your rooms and read the stupid letter. Tared said you should probably sit down before you look at it.'

That did not soothe her worries in the slightest. It *did* kick her back into motion, though, so abruptly that even her own mind was surprised to find her walking again, past the fae who'd slit their own throat, to the door with its secret lock. Only after she'd sparked red magic at the right spot did she remember she should have asked Naxi to look away.

Damn it all. It wasn't like a demon without fae magic could do much to open the door by herself.

She let herself collapse onto the couch, unthinkingly wiping vines off the cushions as she held out a hand for Tared's letter. Naxi passed it on, then hopped on to the heartleaf-covered kitchen counter to make tea – her humming close enough to her usual quiet sounds that Thysandra almost, *almost* managed to loosen her shoulders as she unfolded the parchment.

*Thysandra,* it began.

*After lengthy deliberation, we have concluded it is to our own benefit not to drive the Crimson Court to violence again. We are therefore open to discussing trade agreements. Prices would conform to market, although we would appreciate your assistance repairing some of the material damage the war has done.*
*There is one additional condition:*
*Crimes have been committed against our peoples for the century and a half we were ruled by the empire. Some of these were the direct consequences of*

the Mother's orders, and with her death, we consider justice done. However, others were committed by individual fae, of their own volition, and we do not want to see their actions go unpunished.

Attached, you will find a provisional list. We ask that you deliver these individuals to the Alliance so they can be tried and, if found guilty, penalised.

With regards,

Delwin of Khonna, interim senator of the White City
Helenka of Tolya, on behalf of all nymph queens
Bakaru Sefistrim, King of Kings
Yndrusillitha, acting Eldest of Phurys
Tared Thorgedson, hersir of Skeire, on behalf of all alves

Four sheets of parchment followed, every single inch of them covered in names.

For a full minute, all she could think was *no*.

*No.*

*No.*

An impossibility. An unthinkability. Not in the way a spectacular, heroic feat was impossible, like facing a demon in battle and walking out of the encounter alive – rather, impossible in the way of flying without wings. They couldn't ask this of her. They were *mad* to ask this of her. Didn't they realise what the response would be – that most fae would rather fight a losing war for another decade than allow themselves to be handed over so easily? A downfall devoid of all glory, and surely she couldn't—

*Do better.*

Her mind went still.

These ... these were Old Thysandra's thoughts again, weren't they?

This was her thinking about *fae* again, most of all, about the court's wishes and opinions – hell, this was her thinking like the Mother's loyal servant again. She didn't need to do that. She needed to *not* do that. If she wanted to make things right ... what would she do?

She read the letter again.

Closed her eyes for a few heartbeats, then unfolded the name lists attached to the message, and scanned them, too.

Names she knew, belonging to warriors she knew. *Allies*, part of her still whispered. *Your own damn people.* And then she thought again, and the sight of those ink-scribbled lines shifted – because gods, of course the Alliance wanted Lycaon after the fortune he'd amassed embezzling tribute payments. Aethra was undeniably guilty of flogging those rebelling phoenixes to death a few decades ago. And she'd had heard whispers about Chimalon before, suggesting he made a habit of stealing human girls away from their homes; why in the world would she let him get away with such crimes? Hell, why hadn't she throttled the bastard herself long before she'd even received this letter?

Her head spun.

She forced herself to keep reading.

The more names she recognised, the more reasonable the Alliance's conditions became. They didn't even demand a punishment of *all* fae, the way the Mother would have entire villages wiped out for an individual's rebellion. They asked only for the ones who did harm. Even better, only the ones who went out of their way to do harm – and really, what justification could she present for the fae who had stolen, maimed, and killed for nothing but their own pleasure and gain?

She did not serve them anymore. She didn't owe them any fucking protection against the consequences of their own fucking actions.

She'd just have to be very, very careful.

One last time, she read the letter accompanying the lists. Then she firmly folded it in four, slipped it into the hidden sheath in her skirt, and looked up to find Naxi by the stove, a bunch of verbena in one hand and two mugs in the other. The demon's rosy, knowing smile was entirely her own again.

'Glad you sat down first?' she asked brightly.

'Yes.' Thysandra straightened her dress, then rose, absently ruffling her tense wings. It was baffling, truly, how easy matters became when she was doing what she *wanted* to do. With caution, of course. She was a traitor. Not a fool. But all the same ...

'Never mind about the tea for now,' she added, making for the door. 'Let's go see Nicanor.'

'Ah,' her Lord Protector airily said as he opened the door for her mere minutes later, dressed this afternoon in a midnight-blue ensemble that was outrageously decadent even by his own, already fairly outrageous standards. The silver embroidery on his coat alone must have taken a handful of seamstresses months to complete. 'Even more guests? Do come in – I suppose we could all use a party these days.'

'A ... party?' And only then did she hear the voices emerging from the other side of the door – voices so unexpected that it took her a moment to convince herself she'd identified the timbres correctly.

Silas?

*Inga?*

After her uncle's almost-accusations of that same morning? After ... good gods, after every furious glare Inga had levelled at the Lord Protector over the course of their meetings?

Ridiculous, and yet the two of them were sitting at the worktable in Nicanor's living room-turned-laboratory as if they felt perfectly at home between the bubbling fluids and ominously coloured vials – sipping glasses of cold white wine as if the room wasn't stocked to the ceiling with every poison known to history and then some. Silas's arms rested loosely on the wooden tabletop, his wings relaxed. Inga, more bewilderingly, wasn't even glowering at anyone, her timid half-grin and fidgety hands suggesting she was no longer quite sure what to do with herself when she wasn't hiding behind the shield of her fury.

What in the world was going on?

What had changed so abruptly? *Had* anything even changed abruptly? Had the three of them been cosily getting along behind her back all this time, and had she fallen for some crafty performance for her eyes only, for—

'Oh!' Naxi exclaimed beside her, rushing into the room. 'So many friends!'

*Friends.*

Was that a hint? A subtle signal that this wasn't some malicious conspiracy coming together? Not that she should *need* any subtle signals, of course, because Nicanor's bargain was still in place and Silas must have spoken the truth when he said he didn't want to hurt her ... Besides, what did they have to gain by getting rid of her? Truly, she—

'Thysandra?' Nicanor dryly interrupted her thoughts, gesturing at the table with an elegant flourish. 'Were you planning on coming in?'

Right.

'Yes,' she said, forcing something akin to a smile as she followed Naxi inside. 'Yes, of course. Thank you.'

Inga was already helping Naxi climb up onto the high stools; Naxi was all fluttering gratitude and hiccups of laughter, her most disarming act. Silas turned towards Thysandra – and no matter how leisurely his faint smile, no matter how casually he'd rolled up his sleeves over his bargain-covered arms, something subdued in his golden eyes told her that carefree relaxation was the last thing on his mind.

Not cosily getting along, then.

Which made everything even odder.

'Afternoon, Thys,' he said, sending her a quick nod. She couldn't tell if it was intended to be a reassurance. 'Just catching up on a few centuries of courtly matters. If there's anything you and Nicanor need to discuss in private, we can get out of here, of course.'

*We.*

He was speaking for Inga, then? What for the gods' sakes had he told the girl during that mysterious conversation of theirs – how had he persuaded her to suddenly start *smiling*?

It would be wise to make them leave, presumably. The letter burned in her pocket, making her all jittery with an odd mixture of nervousness and determination; every extra pair of eyes on it only increased the chance of trouble. On the other hand ...

Sooner or later, the news would reach them anyway. Silas knew the court. Inga knew the court's opponents. They might be able to assist her in dealing with the backlash; if they were sitting here anyway, perhaps it wasn't too bad an idea to hear their thoughts before things came to pass.

'Don't worry about it,' she said, and Nicanor quietly shut the door behind her. 'Might be good to discuss this together.'

'Excellent.' Her uncle reached for the bottle of wine on the table. 'A glass, then, if I'm allowed to hand out Nicanor's supply on his behalf?'

She grimaced. 'I take it you've been drinking it without side effects?'

'As a matter of fact,' Nicanor said, feigning indignation, 'I have already been asked on a bargain of truth whether there is anything harmful in that bottle. Which there isn't. Nothing but the usual sort of harm a bottle of wine can do, that is, but I take it you're not planning to guzzle down a gallon of it?'

She did admittedly feel tempted but said, 'A glass should do, thank you.'

Silas poured two glasses. Around them, poison ingredients soaked, simmered, and steamed on the shelves; a faint smell of sulphur lingered in the room, although the sweeter, fresher scent of lily perfume was far more prominent.

The windows were closed, Thysandra noted. No chance of accidental eavesdroppers here, then.

'Alright,' Nicanor said, easily taking a seat at Silas's side. He picked up his own glass without taking his gaze off the company, swirling the crystal back and forth in his long fingers. 'Let us get down to business, then. To what do we owe this pleasant surprise, Your Majesty?'

She braced herself.

*Do better.*

'I've been corresponding with the Alliance,' she said. 'About the possibility of setting up new trade agreements.'

Had she pulled a maimed corpse from beneath the table, she could not have ruined the amiable atmosphere more thoroughly.

Nicanor stiffened in his seat, wine halfway to his lips. Inga's eyes went wide like saucers. Even Silas – who could not have heard of the topic before – didn't need more than a blink to grasp the implications of what she was saying; his fingers went tight enough to pale the skin around his gleaming bargain marks.

*You're living in a tinderbox ...*

Only Naxi was snickering soundlessly on the other side of the table, slender hands pressed over her mouth.

'What?' Nicanor said after a beat of silence.

'I reached out to them a while ago. Figured there was no use discussing it with you when they might ignore us entirely.' Thysandra drew in a breath and pulled the folded letter from her skirt, not yet opening it before she tossed it onto the table. 'But here we are.'

Three pairs of eyes watched the parchment as if it was a snake about to uncoil.

'And?' Nicanor said tightly.

'They are willing to trade with us for grain and other necessities. At standard market prices, even.' She managed a smile. 'Seems they aren't too eager to deal with the consequences of starving the court.'

He sagged a fraction on his stool, lowering his glass to the table. 'Good gods.'

That was shock, *genuine* shock in his eyes. What had he thought, all this time – that she was planning to let the court starve in a few months? Or was it rather her secrecy itself that had unnerved him so?

'What's the catch?' Inga demanded, her glower returning as she leaned over the table and frowned at the folded letter.

'What catch?' Nicanor asked, sounding bewildered.

'To their offer.' Inga glared at him as if he had personally insulted her. 'You all stole their food for centuries. Did you really think they'd just continue to hand it over, no questions asked?'

He blinked, then turned. 'Thysandra?'

'There is a catch,' she admitted, closing her eyes for the briefest of moments. 'They're asking for extradition of ... well, a number of fae.'

Outside her eyelids, the word remained alarmingly quiet for an alarmingly long moment.

Then Nicanor slowly, pointedly said, 'A ... number.'

She drew in a deep breath, looking up despite every instinct in her body screaming at her to try and make herself invisible. 'Yes.'

'And ...' His frost-coloured eyes were piercingly sharp on her face; on the edge of her sight, even Silas was watching her closely, his frown growing deeper and deeper. 'And what sort of *number* are we talking about exactly, Your Majesty?'

Thysandra was sure of herself.

She was really, very sure of herself. She really, truly knew what she was doing. And yet it took way too much effort to hold his burrowing gaze, to keep her shoulders straight and her wings in place as they ached to curl protectively around her – way too much effort, too, to part her lips and get the words out. 'A ... a few hundred.'

Nicanor blinked.

Next to him, Silas let out the quietest curse beneath his breath.

'That's hardly unreasonable, is it?' Inga brusquely said, glancing back and forth between the two of them so fiercely that blonde strands of hair fluttered around her fae ears. 'Gods know the empire has killed rather more than a few hundred of *their* people, and—'

Nicanor groaned. 'Thysandra.'

'I *know*,' she said, voice too loud, pulse quickening. Fuck. He was the one who needed to act on her decision, the one who could whip the army into obedience if necessary, and she really, *really* did not want to know what would happen if he bluntly refused to follow her orders. 'I know, but the alternative—'

'The alternative can hardly be worse than this!' He plunked his silk-clad elbows onto the table, buried his face in his hands, then desperately added from between his fingers, 'You're proposing to actively abandon our own people for the Alliance's benefit? To not just stop fighting them but to start *helping* them? You know damn well that not a single inhabitant of this court will accept—'

'Not a single inhabitant?' Inga coldly interrupted.

Nicanor froze, then cursed and hauled himself straight again, rubbing his temple. 'Fine. Not a single *fae* inhabitant.'

'Even then.' The girl scoffed, glancing at Silas as if to look for support. 'I don't know much about the bastards in the army, but from what I've seen of my archivist colleagues, I doubt any of them will care if a bunch of murderers get their just desserts. They'll be happy to avoid another war, if anything.'

Would they be?

Thysandra had to admit, in the slightly baffled silence that fell, that she'd never thought *that* much about the thousands of court members who weren't either in the army or part of the Mother's inner circle of courtiers. They had never been a danger to her, and so they had never been worth considering. But of course they were here all the same: the cooks, the teachers, the traders and craftspeople ...

Did they care?

*Their* names surely weren't on the Alliance's list.

'The problem,' Nicanor said, fingers digging into the poison-stained table surface, 'is that the archivists aren't going to be the ones feeding Thysandra to the hounds, alright?'

Every other thought fell away.

For a single, night-black moment, there was nothing in her mind but snarling.

'*Nicanor,*' Silas snapped somewhere far, far away, his voice sharper than she'd ever heard it. Her Lord Protector's answer, unwillingly apologetic, barely reached her conscious mind. Not trying to dredge up bad memories ... just making sure the stakes are clear ...

*Thysandra!* her father had screamed as jaws sank into his chest, snapping his ribs like dry twigs.

And only then did it hit her – that the Mother had *lied* all those years ago, claiming Echion had never had her best interests in mind. That her father *had* tried to save her. That he had done everything he could not to drag her down with him, and then he'd died his torturous death while watching her stand on that precipice, the Mother's hand a heavy claim on her shoulder – then he'd died *knowing*—

A vicious twinge of pain shot through her arm.

She jolted from the pits of her memories with almost physical effort, barely suppressing a yelp of shock. Had someone pinched her? But no one was even looking at her, the attention focused instead on the fervent discussion before her, and the pain had vanished far too soon for physical touch ...

Her eyes met Naxi's across the table.

The demon gave a small, cunning wink.

'All I'm trying to say,' Nicanor was saying to her left, sounding like he was repeating himself for the fifth time, 'is that we're not going to make friends by handing fae over to the same Alliance that caused our trouble in the first place. That—'

Inga snorted. 'I'd argue the court mostly caused its own trouble.'

'Yes, but that's not how *they* will take it, is it?' Nicanor shot back. 'All they're going to see is—'

A traitor.

Thysandra knew what he'd been about to say even as he snapped his mouth shut just in time, casting a wary look at Silas's widening nostrils.

'So ...' Her voice was too hoarse. 'What do you propose we do, then?'

'Tell the Alliance you can't do this,' Nicanor said in exasperation, before either of the others could speak up. 'Ask them for another way to pay for that food.'

'Oh, that's not going to work,' Naxi piped up. 'Tared told me when he delivered the letter that they wouldn't negotiate on their proposal.'

*Traitor. Traitor. Traitor.*

'So let me get this straight,' Thysandra managed to grind out. Her chest was constricting, her sight blurring a little on the edges. 'Our choices are to either start raiding islands for food, start another war, likely lose it after wasting a few thousand lives on both sides, and be punished even more severely ... *or* to let a few hundred people suffer the consequences of their own cruelty and allow the rest of the court to prosper. Do I have that right?'

Nicanor groaned. 'Yes, assuming that for the second option the rest of the court doesn't unite against you and cause you to die a senseless death.'

*By hound.*

They were still snarling in the back of her mind.

It would be so very easy to retreat. To try and find compromise, to let herself be cowed into supporting the goals of others ... but she was New Thysandra now, and New Thysandra did better than that. She *knew* what the right decision was, didn't she?

So if she didn't want to die ...

She could still be a traitor. She just had to do it quietly.

'Let's not tell them, then,' she said, making her decision in a single, brilliant heartbeat.

Even Silas blinked in surprise. 'Beg your pardon?'

'Let's arrest them and not tell the court why.' Relief came rushing in as she spoke – a fresh breeze filling her chest, driving back the stifling dark. 'Just ... just say they're suspected of conspiring against the crown. Everyone and their mother is conspiring against the crown these days, so that's a perfectly believable explanation. And then we can quietly hand them over to the Alliance after all and be done with it.'

Four pairs of eyes were staring at her now.

'The alves can take them from here without a whisper,' she added, a fraction more defensively. 'And I'm sure the Alliance will agree not to make too much noise about the trials themselves if we ask them. Then when that's all over—'

'Thys,' Silas interrupted, rubbing his temple as if to soothe a headache. 'You do realise that the truth *will* come out sooner or later, don't you?'

Sooner would be bad.

Later ... she could survive later.

'All I know is that it shouldn't come out *now*.' She gave a joyless laugh. 'The tinderbox can do without this particular spark. If it spreads by the time we have trade figured out – well, this is the bloody Crimson Court, yes? As long as there's food and wine, does anyone really care about their fellow fae enough to make a fuss?'

'They do care about pride,' Nicanor murmured below his breath.

Silas quietly grimaced beside him. Inga showed her unwilling agreement by not disagreeing at all. Even *Naxi* was looking a touch doubtful as she toyed absently with her own pink curls – but then, of course Naxi was doubtful about this development if it meant she wouldn't have any fae to kill soon ...

And damn it all, it was easy for them to doubt, wasn't it? None of them were the one whose head was on the line here.

'We're keeping it quiet,' Thysandra repeated, more firmly now, or at least she hoped firmness was the impression she managed to convey. 'That's my final decision, and you can take it as an order. Do we need bargains to ensure secrecy, or—'

'Already got mine,' Nicanor wryly interrupted, raising his wrist to show the pale purple mark. For a single moment she was sure he would object again, that he would argue or even refuse to obey ... and then the moment was over, and his blue wings slackened abruptly as he dropped his hand back to the table. All he said was, 'As you wish, Your Majesty. Can I see the list?'

'We're going to need copies,' Inga muttered as she shoved the letter towards him. Not a word of protest from her, either. 'Should I make a start on those, then?'

Should she?

Without a bargain to keep her in check?

But then again ... this was *Inga*, who had plenty of reason to wish a gruesome death upon every single fae mentioned on these sheets. She wouldn't be warning the bastards, would she? She wouldn't be causing trouble – trouble which would surely impact the humans, too – by spreading the explosive news?

'Please do,' Thysandra said, taking the leap. 'One for Nicanor, please, and one for Gadyon as well. We need to know how many individuals on the list are already dead and which of the survivors are living on other fae isles at the moment.'

Inga nodded and picked up one of the pages. On the other side of the table, Nicanor was already reading through another, eyebrow climbing higher and higher up his forehead even though he did not speak a word.

'Well,' Silas said on a long exhale, shoving back his stool to rise to his feet. 'I'll just go make a few more bargains, then, shall I?'

# CHAPTER 22

FOR THREE WHOLE DAYS, no one tried to throw Thysandra to the hounds.

Nicanor's people worked quietly and efficiently, dragging fae from their beds at night or intercepting them on lone flights, avoiding witnesses at every arrest. Per Silas's suggestion, the captives weren't locked up at the Crimson Court itself, but on Ilithia. The deserted villa of Castor Thenes had swiftly been equipped with alf steel chains and locks to contain around a hundred magic users – fewer than the full two hundred and fifty names on the Alliance's list, as it turned out over half of them had already died in battle, by the Mother's orders, or even due to simple courtly scheming.

For three whole days, Bereas did not show his face, either. The fishing fleet was left alone. The island's shores remained blissfully quiet. Only the whispers at court never calmed – but then, the mysterious disappearance of a few dozen prominent members did nothing to soothe the already feverish anticipation that hang over the halls and galleries. Perhaps, it was speculated, they had gone off and joined the Mother's loyalists, wherever the hell those were hiding now?

Thysandra did nothing to dispel the theory. It was a rather convenient one, and not unlikely either; about two dozen fae on the list could not be arrested because they had indeed vanished with Bereas's rebels.

For three whole days, the moon continued to wax.

On the fourth day, it had reached its fullest.

The morning of Hunter's Moon was a cold one, and from her balcony, Thysandra watched the members of the court gather before the castle gate in coats and fur-lined boots. Jokes and tense laughter misted the air around them. Orthea paraded around in their midst, dressed for the occasion in a useless but most decorative hunter's costume of slender leather trousers and a blood-red coat to complement her russet brown wings – she would, of course, not be participating in the competition herself.

'Don't they expect you to be there?' Naxi asked. She had reluctantly joined Thysandra on the balcony but stubbornly refused to go anywhere near the edge; instead, she sat propped up in the doorway, her chin in her small hands, her fuzzy shawl around her shoulders. 'Being their High Lady and everything?'

Far, far below, Orthea was loudly listing names. Hands rose from the crowd at each of them, accompanied by energetic shouts.

'No,' Thysandra said, eyes resting on the spectacle below.

'No what?'

'They don't expect me.' She sighed and straightened away from the cast iron balustrade, stretching her wings to shake off the chill. 'I've never joined the hunt in my lifetime. They know.'

Naxi was quiet for a few moments. The company of contestants began moving in the meantime, bows and swords slung over their shoulders as they made their way along the winding path down the slope of the mountain. Quite possibly, this was the only time in the year the trail was used by fae. The rules of the game forbade explorations of Faewood prior to the event, and flying over or even towards it was generally considered a breach of those rules.

'Is it the hounds?' Naxi said.

It was the hounds.

No magic, the rules said. Just wits and physical weapons. The first to draw blood from one of the monsters won a place at the High Lady's table for the feast; the first to kill one of them won a favour of their choosing. Usually, a few contestants died along the way. This was considered part of the festival's appeal.

'I understand if you're scared of them,' Naxi added when no answer came, leaning forward in the doorway. Her tone was thoughtful. Almost *earnest*. 'I was scared of fire for a while after they burned Mirova. Almost bit Lyn when she showed me her wings for the first time.'

To her own surprise, Thysandra chuckled – a hollow chuckle, but a chuckle all the same. 'It's not really a matter of fear.'

A scoff. 'You *are* frightened of them, Sashka.'

She considered that for a moment as she watched the troupe of hunters disappear behind the edge of the castle's cliff, the misty hills beyond still echoing with their ribald laughter and cries of excitement. Hundreds of others, she knew, would now be gathering on the south side of the castle, standing on tower balconies or on that same precipice where she'd watched her father's execution all those years ago, to keep an eye on the forest below and wait for the victor to emerge.

'I don't suppose I'm frightened of the *hounds*,' she said, finally. 'Just of the people who use them.'

Naxi hummed a little, non-committal note in response.

'Do you know why the festival exists in its current form?' Thysandra continued, her fingers wrapping tight around the edge of the balustrade. In the distance, the voices were quieting. 'It wasn't always like this, you know. It used to be a contest between the different fae peoples, when the Mother had not yet united us – they picked a different island every year, went after whatever magical creature was living there, and held the festival in the winner's name. The Mother only changed it after the Conquest.'

'Couldn't let a good thing exist without ruining it, of course,' Naxi said dreamily. 'Why did she change it?'

Thysandra closed her eyes. 'Because the hounds are not so dangerous at all.'

In the small pause between that sentence and the next, a horn blared in the distance. Loud cheers rose in reply, both from the foot of the mountain and from the castle itself – the hunt had officially begun.

'They mind their own business as long as they're left alone,' she went on. Her voice refused to grow louder than a muted whisper. 'They aren't particularly aggressive by nature, either. But the Mother introduced this hunt in autumn, and the Milk Moon challenge to steal a pup in spring, and the hounds very, very quickly learned to hate everything walking on two legs.'

'*Oh,*' Naxi said breathlessly. 'Oh, the poor things!'

As if in response, a harrowing howl emerged from the direction of Faewood, followed immediately by more cheering.

'Yes,' Thysandra said, every fibre in her body tensing at the sound.

'And no doubt she told you it was necessary for the good of the empire?' There was no mockery in Naxi's soft voice – no reproach, no *how could you be so blind.* 'That a simple execution by blade wouldn't do to instil duty and discipline in her people? Just a matter of strategy! Nothing to do with her own stupid, twisted sense of entertainment!'

Thysandra's laugh was like acid, biting and burning as it welled in her throat. 'You're starting to know her so well.'

'I dabble in being a heartless bitch at times,' Naxi said, her tone the epitome of humble innocence.

'Not like that.' It slipped out before she could think. 'You're not like that at all.'

This time, the world behind her remained silent. Ten, fifteen seconds, as exhilarated cries rose with irregular intervals from the distant woods ...

Then something fuzzy and pink moved on the edge of her sight.

Gaze stubbornly trained on the horizon ahead, slim hands shaking a little as she clutched her shawl to her chest, Naxi came inching towards the balustrade. The morning breeze caught her loose curls as she left the safe haven of the tower wall behind, sweeping them around her face in a dazzling dance of gold and rosy hues; her eyes, just a fraction wide, were the clearest, brightest blue.

Like the freedom of an open summer sky. Like boundless ocean depths in which one could sink and sink and sink and ...

Thysandra did not notice those clever little hands moving until nimble fingers curled around her own.

'You should come inside.' Naxi's voice trembled slightly. 'You've been thinking about terrible things for long enough now. Time to have a little fun before they make you sit through that terrible feast as well.'

*Fun.*

Her bones were much, much too heavy for fun. 'I don't think I should—'

Naxi rolled her eyes. 'Sashka.'

Oh gods. 'Yes?'

'It's really for the best if you come inside with me. I'm *this* close to making my way to Faewood' – her voice faltered briefly as her gaze dropped to the world below – 'and win the hunt myself by killing all of the others participating. So if you don't want me to turn your festival into a massacre ...'

'Ah,' Thysandra said with a feeble attempt at a smile. 'Blackmail and bribery again?'

Something tense flickered in Naxi's face. Just for the blink of an eye, then it was gone, and her fluttering lashes were as persuasive as they'd ever been.

'If it works?' she sweetly said.

It shouldn't work.

But hounds were howling down in Faewood, fae voices were clamouring their favourites' names, and she was so fucking tired of days spent on the brink of war. Naxi's fingers were soft against her palm. Soft like her lips. Soft like every other delicious inch of that little demon body: frail limbs, slim hips, pert breasts that fit perfectly in the palm of a hand—

'That's more like it,' Naxi murmured, tugging at her arm.

*Blackmail and bribery*

But Thysandra followed her inside.

Choosing a dress for the feast felt like picking the sharpest sword from a well-stocked armoury – like an act of war in itself. She postponed it until the sunset painted the world outside in shades of scarlet and the blaring of the horns approached the castle again; now, she knew, her absence would soon be noted.

And questions would be asked.

Telling the court she'd spent all day escaping the threat of violence – that she'd been busy eating marmalade buns on the bed and kissing soft, pink demon lips over and over again – was unlikely to go over well. Somehow, she suspected the rational, sensible explanation of securing loyalty might not make much of an impression.

She did not allow herself to wonder what that said about the explanation.

The dress she selected, finally, was one she hadn't worn in decades – a dress the Mother had acidly called *unremarkable* last time she'd worn it, and which she'd stashed away in the back of a wardrobe later that night. It was simple, admittedly. No glittering jewels or intricate embroidery; no bright colours or scandalous cuts. But the fabric ... it felt like woven shadows in her fingers, a red so dark it seemed black, showing the glowing sheen of its true colour only when it rippled and caught the light.

*She* had never thought it unremarkable.

And damn it all, she had no one left to serve.

As she dressed herself, Naxi lay sprawled out on the bed, idly picking sticky crumbs off her bare chest as she ogled Thysandra and cooed words of approval. Which was not markedly different from what she'd been doing the rest of the day ... and yet, with the armour of that dress in place, it was suddenly hard to endure it, that unabashed *softness*.

'Perhaps you should be getting dressed, too,' she said as she buttoned the slits beneath her wings.

Naxi pulled a face. 'I'm waiting.'

'What for?'

A shrug was the only reply. 'Did I tell you your tits look great in that dress, Sashka?'

Thysandra rolled her eyes and turned away, which was of course simply because she needed to find her jewellery box and not at all because she was blushing. Outside, voices were singing. Loud, off-tone voices – it appeared Orthea had not waited to serve the wine until they were all gathered around the tables for the more formal part of the festivities.

Which meant Thysandra would have to face a hall full of *drunk* hunters – quite possibly the only prospect less attractive than facing a hall full of sober hunters.

At least her tits looked great, though.

It was more of a comfort than it had any right to be.

She was still fastening her necklace – a single ruby pendant resting like a drop of blood against her bosom – when knuckles hit the door to her rooms. Nicanor's voice made its way in a second later. 'Thysandra?'

'A moment!' she yelled back, then turned to Naxi and started, 'Now you'll *have* to—'

Unexpectedly, Naxi had already darted out of bed.

In the blink of an eye, she snatched her discarded dress off the floor and yanked it over her head; one more blink, and she'd hoisted a blanket and a pillow into her arms, hauled them to the living room, and dropped them on the couch. Thysandra was still reeling from that cunning little bit of consideration after the door had been opened and Nicanor had stepped into the room, looking ever so slightly unnerved by the sight of a beaming Naxi ushering him in.

*Waiting*, she'd said.

For Nicanor? That seemed spectacularly unlikely. But the Lord Protector – dressed in impeccable Hunter's Moon colours, a black coat set with rubies and a blood-red ribbon in his hair – was holding a linen-wrapped package under his arm.

'Not sure what this is about,' he started as he closed the door behind him, uncharacteristically neglecting to greet either of them, 'but

Thorgedson showed up in the crystalline hall a moment ago, claiming this was to be delivered to—'

'To me!' Naxi brightly interrupted.

Nicanor narrowed his eyes at her. 'What is in it? If it's anything that might be remotely dangerous, I—'

'I don't need help to be dangerous,' she said, rolling her eyes at him. 'It's my new dress.'

This time Nicanor was not the only one to stare at her.

'What?' She snatched the package from his hands and clutched it to her chest, eyes challenging him to try and take it back. 'Hunter's Moon is black and red and silver, yes? I don't have any black dresses. Or red dresses. Emelin made me a new one. Now if you'll excuse me ...'

'*Emelin?*' Nicanor repeated, voice soaring.

'What?' Thysandra heard herself say.

'She's very good at that sort of thing,' Naxi breezily informed them both, then unceremoniously dumped the bundle of fabric onto the floor, dropped to her knees beside it, and began to tear the ribbons away as if they were eyes to be scratched out. 'I told her— Oh, *look*! It's so *shiny*!'

Nicanor was staring at her blankly now.

'It's shiny and *soft*!' A shimmering black creation emerged from the undyed linen, gossamer fabric rippling around those restless little hands. 'And the sleeves are puffy! And *fluffy*! Sashka, *look* at it!'

Thysandra was still too busy recovering from the notion of Emelin – godsworn, Mother-killing Emelin – spending her time sewing dresses ... but thankfully Naxi did not seem to care much about anyone's responses as she gushed and gasped and giggled, turning the dress over and over in her hands. Nicanor looked equal parts dumbfounded and disturbed as he cautiously backed away from her, making his way to the bedroom door instead, where Thysandra still stood frozen in her tracks.

Beneath his breath, barely audible over Naxi's squealing, he murmured, 'You're alright?'

That was even *more* of a shock.

286

Nicanor? Inquiring after her *wellbeing*? For a moment she found herself wondering whether this might be some delayed seduction attempt ... but then, if his goal was to get her into his bed again, why wouldn't he have started his campaign for her heart weeks ago?

'You're usually around sooner,' he clarified, not raising his voice. 'Before everyone returns from Faewood, at least.'

Oh.

He was *actually* concerned?

'I, um ...' She shook her head with a joyless little laugh, attempting to clear her mind. Naxi's elated giggling on the other side of the room held a little too much resemblance to the breathless sounds she'd made with Thysandra's head between her thighs. 'I ... I thought this might be a good moment to write to the Alliance with a quick progress report. Took me longer than expected.'

He considered her for a moment, then nodded and averted his gaze. 'Please be careful at the feast tonight, Thys.'

This was getting more and more unnerving.

'I'm always careful,' she countered, reflexively – the easiest shield to hide her stuttering heart. Worry was weakness. Weakness was death. Except that he should know the same thing, and it made it all the more unlike him to be so visibly anxious; the haunted look in those icy blue eyes was one she'd rarely seen before. 'Why? Did anything happen at the hunt?'

'Three people accidentally shot an arrow at my face,' he said, lips pressing together into a thin line. 'And someone was asking me why I visited Ilithia yesterday, although I don't think they actually saw me there – not sure who did, though. I know you said not to tell them anything about the arrests, but—'

'We're not going to tell them anything,' Thysandra sharply cut in. Fuck. The sounds of Naxi's exalted glee instantly faded into the background. 'The response to a breach of secrecy is to be *more* secretive, not less. And I'll be safe enough, thank you – having a demon around is helpful in these situations.'

He drew in a sharp breath, then hesitated – a glimpse of calculation breaking through the concern, as if he was trying to gauge just how much chance of success his objection would have. The answer, apparently, was negative. His breath escaped again.

'Alright,' he said instead, curt but not unfriendly – and then, so easily she had no time to be shocked or even surprised, his hand came up, landing on her half-bared shoulder in a single firm squeeze. Not a seductive touch. A reassurance, if anything, soldier to soldier, *friend to friend* – but that didn't make *sense*, did it, coming from––

He'd already let go of her again.

'Let me put some extra guards in place, then,' he said before she could react. 'See you downstairs in a bit.'

'See you,' she said reflexively, and then he was gone – leaving her to figure out for herself what in the world it had meant, that unguarded, almost *amiable* gesture. Old friends, yes, but that was a laughable explanation, wasn't it? Friendship was meaningless. Friendship lasted as long as it was mutually beneficial, and ended the moment it wasn't – so what was he doing, acting as if there was something like *affection* behind his movements?

What game was he playing?

*Was* he even playing a game? He ought to be, and yet––

'Sashka!' Naxi interrupted her musing, loudly, and only then did Thysandra realise this was not the first time her name had been called. 'Sashka, stop thinking about stupid things and *look* at me!'

That was enough to dispel every thought of Nicanor.

Because Naxi was standing between the monstrous begonias and braided heartleaf vines in a dress that–– Oh, gods help her.

Perhaps killing High Ladies wasn't even the greatest of Emelin's talents.

The dress was a *marvel*, matte black satin wrapping Naxi's slight form like a lover's embrace, puffed sleeves and cinched waist emphasising her delicate build. Dark red rose petals cascaded down the bodice, like luscious drops of blood; they tapered off along the skirt, merging elegantly into the silvery leaf motif stitched along the hem. Nymph-like, and yet not nymph-like at all – there was nothing sweet about this dress, nothing playful or innocent.

In it, Naxi looked like a tiny, sultry monster queen. Like a creature that had always belonged at the Crimson Court.

And only then did it hit Thysandra – that the little menace had made an attempt to *fit in*.

She swallowed.

Her mouth was suddenly dry as dust.

'That is the right reaction,' Naxi smugly informed her, skirt swirling around her slim hips as she turned and danced into the bedroom. The black and silver shimmered with the motion – like a night sky full of floral constellations. 'Don't tear it off me just yet, though. What did Nicanor have to say?'

'He— Oh. Yes. Nicanor.' It was almost a crime to be thinking of Lord Protectors – or *anyone* else, truly – with a little demon parading before her in a dress that seemed designed to cater to every hungry fantasy that had ever crossed Thysandra's mind. She shook her head, attempting to gather her scattered thoughts. 'He ... he was just concerned. About me being late. Warned me there've been some rumours making the rounds about the people we're arresting.'

By the wardrobe, Naxi stiffened.

'It doesn't appear that they *know* anything,' Thysandra hurriedly added. 'Just the suspicion that maybe they haven't all run off to join Bereas in hiding, but—'

'But they're whispering?' Another sharp turn had the night sky flaring out again. Naxi's eyes had narrowed to slits – a vigilance so sharp it was almost violent in itself. 'At the feast?'

'Yes, but—'

'At that same feast where a few hundred drunk, bloodthirsty hunters are going to get even *more* drunk?' The words stumbled over each other like clumsy feet, hurrying to catch up. 'With all their weapons still on them and their bodies full of red and black to better attack you – *that* feast?'

The shrillness of her voice was alarming, and sharp enough to snap Thysandra out of her satin-induced daze. 'Well, I'll have you there to guard me, won't I?'

'There'll be a few hundred fae there! And no plants!' A thin, high-pitched laugh. 'I can handle maybe two dozen of them at a time with just my demon magic, Sashka. Killing whole crowds at the same time is Creon's level of work, not mine. If they've truly caught wind of your plans—'

'Nicanor will bring in extra soldiers, too,' Thysandra brusquely interrupted – too brusquely, a hardness fuelled by the dread that came trickling down her spine. 'And I'm not *entirely* harmless myself, you know?'

Naxi plopped down on the edge of the bed, chest moving too fast with her breath, little hands balled into fists in the sea of satin pooling around her legs. 'I know.'

It did not sound convinced.

'So we're going as planned,' Thysandra stubbornly continued, more steel in her voice now, because *someone* had to be sure of herself here. 'It's not like I can just stay away anyway. I'm the High Lady of this court, and—'

Naxi snorted. 'You don't have to be.'

An icy, unpleasant silence fell.

Naxi looked suddenly small again, sitting on the bed in that gorgeous black and red dress, shoulders so tight even the puffy sleeves couldn't hide it. The room seemed to cool around them, to *tighten* – the discarded clothing on the ground and the crumbs on the pillows suddenly a mockery of trust, of their charade of intimacy.

They were standing in the Labyrinth again. *Come live somewhere else with me.*

'Let's not do this again,' Thysandra said, feeling her heart slink away from the conversation.

'Why not?' Something like despair shimmered in those wide blue eyes – something far too painful and far too genuine. 'I know you said you want to do this, but it's *hurting* you, Sashka! It might *kill* you! Saving the world and the court and the humans is all great and heroic, but it's hardly worth that sort of sacrifice, is it?'

The humans.

Standing paralysed in their own damn home, clutching their children to their chests, watching her like deer corralled by wolves. Anguish that Naxi must have felt in their hearts, too, and yet ...

'So you'd just run off,' she bit out, bitter disappointment welling in her throat as she abruptly turned away from the room. Away from that bed in which they'd slept together. 'Of course you would. Must be so gods-damned easy, mustn't it, to never feel love or loyalty to anyone?'

The rejoinder she expected didn't come.

Thorns clawed at the silence behind her as she paced to the overgrown kitchen counter and blindly began piling up plates and glasses, her own words stinging in her ears. Had that been too harsh? But fuck, it *chafed*, the brutal reminder of reality – of the idiocy of her own thoughts, having found an illusion of togetherness in something as meaningless as a demon's one-time choice of dress ...

Sweet words on the balcony didn't matter. Mind-blowing pleasure and marmalade buns didn't matter. It was embarrassing, frankly, that even after all these centuries at the Crimson Court, she had imagined anything else for even the briefest, most mindless moment – that she'd needed the reminder that Naxi was *not* going to be part of her life.

Just of the fun.

Just of whatever Thysandra would bribe her into.

A demon so blatantly dismissive of any form of selflessness ... it would be a miracle if she still attended the Hunter's Moon feast at all.

'I'm going downstairs,' Thysandra bluntly announced, her voice too loud for the confines of her quarters. The vines and flowers seemed to wince in response. 'If you decide to come with me, I'll try to make it worth your while, but—'

A scoff emerged from the bedroom. 'Stop being like that, Sashka.'

'Like what?'

'Like this is about meticulous bookkeeping.' Naxi skittered through the doorway as she spoke, dark and floral, a feral little nymph queen of the night. Her glare was vicious, her eyes a fraction red. 'Did you keep track of how many times you've had your tongue in my pussy? Want to tell me exactly how many dead fae that's worth, perhaps?'

Thysandra blinked. 'I just meant—'

'I know what you meant,' Naxi testily interrupted, rolling her eyes. 'That's the whole bloody problem. Are you coming, then?'

What?

*Wait,* she wanted to shout, the Hunter's Moon forgotten. *Tell me first what the hell you're talking about – what do you mean, the whole bloody problem?*

But Naxi had already flung open the door and bounded into the corridor beyond. On her way to the feast below – to that celebration that might just eat the both of them alive.

# CHAPTER 23

WITH THE BONE HALL destroyed, this year's Hunter's Moon took place in the slightly smaller crystalline hall instead – no towering throne presiding over the room, no skulls lining the high ceiling, and yet Orthea had skilfully crafted an atmosphere just as ominous against this unfamiliar décor. A small ensemble of violin players filled the air with their haunting melodies. Thick red velvet drapes hung like gushing blood behind the dais, and the light of thousands upon thousands of candles reflected in iridescent shimmers from the irregular walls, turning the crystals that dripped from the ceiling arches into moving, living things.

In the middle of the hall, the long tables lined up on either side of it, lay the carcass of the hound slain that morning.

Thysandra held her breath as she walked past it, trying not to inhale the smell of drying blood and ragged fur. The creature's dead eyes seemed to be following her on the long, long way to the head table, an accusation in them that even hundreds of fae glares from the surrounding tables could not begin to match.

*Thysandra!* her father screamed.

Her heart pounded in her ears, that familiar rhythm of *traitor, traitor, traitor.*

But no one lunged forward with a knife in their hands. No one raised their voice to denounce her. There were just their gazes, peering, scrutinising, as she stepped up onto the dais with Naxi at her side, as she sank into her seat at the centre of the table, as she forced a smile and congratulated the winner of the hunt to her right.

Once upon a time, Old Thysandra had wished to be seen.

New Thysandra could think of nothing worse than sitting here, hundreds of unfaltering gazes aimed in her direction, while she tried to remember how to breathe.

To her left, Naxi peered back at the gathered court with daggers in her eyes, unflinching under the weight of their gathered emotions. At the far right of the table, Nicanor was all silky smiles and haughty elegance as he chatted with the army commander beside him, no trace of tension on his whetted features. If they could do it, she must be able to manage, too – but it was *her* who people glanced at as they whispered among each other, and it was *her* their fingers pointed out while their glares went thunderous ...

*Traitor's daughter.*

They were courtiers and soldiers, all of them. Dreaming of war and glory, of restoring their lives of abundance and luxury. Not a single teacher or archivist among them, no cooks or sailors or gardeners – not a single person who might be quietly grateful for peace and three solid meals a day. How in the world had she never noticed that before – how many people had been excluded from the crowd with which the Mother had surrounded herself?

She'd always been one of the violent ones, of course.

She'd spent so much time striving for the top that she hadn't even realised not everyone might be running the same race.

Slowly, the tables filled up with black and garnet red to match the decorations of the hall. Orthea flounced in with the last groups of fae, her hunter's costume replaced by a flowing gown of star-flecked silk – and *she*, of course, was greeted with eruptions of cheers and applause, no glares for her and her scheming heart ...

Thysandra would have been furious if she hadn't been scared out of her mind, too.

The food was served as soon as the Master of Ceremony took her place at the head table, the dishes carried in not by humans as in previous years but by fae younglings in black frocks and coats, their faces tight with concentration as they performed their tasks. Plates of grilled venison, roasted onions and parsnips, steaming loaves of fresh bread ... The scents mingled with the aroma of spiced wine and a hundred different perfumes – a mixture that settled over the hall with almost physical weight, like the smothering blankets Thysandra used to hide beneath.

*Breathe in. Breathe out.*

She stared at the silver plate before her, honey-glazed plums and apples, and tried not to notice the empty eyes of the hound beyond.

Voices quieted down around the hall. At the head table, Orthea rose, goblet in hand – launching into a speech that should have been Thysandra's to give, but she no longer managed to care. At least she could just sit, now. Sit and smile and try to keep her head from spinning so violently. Naxi would warn her, wouldn't she, if someone tried to attack them?

'... on the memory of our beloved Mother,' she heard Orthea say, a small catch in her voice that might or might not be theatrics, 'who ruled our glorious empire with a wisdom and strength that will never be equalled ...'

Venomous bitch.

Glasses and goblets were raised around the hall. Thysandra grabbed her own just in time to hide the fact she had missed most of the speech so far, keeping her expression placid, unaffected, as she lifted it and drank.

The wine was too sweet. She barely suppressed a shiver as it slid down her throat.

'... and let us remember the thousands fallen at the Battle of the White City, who fought so bravely for our freedom ...'

Another toast. Another gulp of wine. *Freedom* – as if any freedoms had been taken from this audience since the battle, save for the license to kill anyone and everyone they liked without facing consequences. But she shouldn't scoff. She shouldn't roll her eyes. She was a traitor, but quietly, and she would *not*—

'... and finally,' Orthea continued, her purring voice growing noticeably louder, 'I would like to make a toast to the one hundred and thirty loyal patriots who have been dragged from their homes and locked up by our current High Lady, to be handed over to our enemies to die for the sake of her cowardice.'

The world froze.

A single moment of perfect stillness, like a glass about to shatter.

And then the hall erupted into raucous clamour. Wings flaring. Fists pumping. Goblets flying up with such violence that wine sloshed over their rims as voices shouted for justice, answers, blood – and all eyes, *all eyes*, aimed at Thysandra ...

Furious gazes.

Few of them surprised, though.

They'd known. They'd *known*. Not rumours at all – this was far too much knowledge, far too specific, too, for it to be a matter of rumours. Which meant ...

The thoughts rolled on, inevitable like an avalanche – even as her body sat paralysed at that loaded table, even as the noise swelled to a roar around her. Which meant someone must have talked.

And their audience had gladly believed it.

*Traitor's daughter.*

As if in a dream, she watched a handful of fae make for her table, still in their hunter's costumes, red smears on the fabric that might be wine or blood or both. Next to her, Nicanor was snapping commands. Around the hall, soldiers moved into position. There were not nearly enough of them, though, and even if reinforcements were waiting nearby ...

The fae jostling towards her were unsheathing their blades.

She had to move – she had to *move* – but her body remained stiff with shock even as her mind screamed at her to stand and defend herself, and—

And the first of her attackers started screeching.

He silenced the hall more easily than any commands or intervening soldiers could have done – that jarring, ear-splitting howl that seemed more animal than fae. His knees buckled. His hands went grasping, grabbling, for knives or anything sharp at all as gasps of *no* and *please* and *end it*. She'd seen it before so many times, decades and decades of studying the work of any demon to visit the court, and yet she could not stop staring now as the crimson-clad male before her jerkily managed to unsheathe his own dagger, sobbing in invisible pain.

'*Stop him!*' someone bellowed from the back of the hall.

No one dared to lunge forward.

The fae male was still screaming as his blade sank between his own ribs.

His voice died away in a wet gurgle as he went slack on the crystalline floor ... and then there was no sound left at all, the hall so quiet a pin-drop would have been a thunderclap. Around the tables, fae stood frozen. By the doors, Nicanor's people had stiffened with their swords half-sheathed. Only the dead male's companions moved, quiet like thieves in the night, as they inched back and away from his cramped corpse and away, most of all, from ...

Naxi.

Who sat leaning on the table with one thin elbow, chin in her hand, smiling serenely at the deadlocked hall before her.

Two chairs away from her, Orthea looked about to be violently sick.

It was no well-considered strategy that had Thysandra turning back to the gathered court before her. There was no diplomacy to it. If anything, it was a lifetime of battlefield training that moved her lips now – the instinct, ingrained in her bones by years and years and years of fighting for her life, to never let forward momentum go to waste.

'Thank you, Orthea,' she heard herself say through the numb spinning of her own thoughts, and somehow she said it calmly, placidly, raising her own glass again as if in genuine gratitude. 'And with that, I declare the feast opened. Enjoy your meal, everyone.'

Reckless audacity.

Then again, safe decisions didn't lead to victory.

And the slain hunter still lay before her table in the growing pool of his own blood. Naxi still sat smiling so saintly – unable to take on more than a dozen fae at once, perhaps, but *they* sure as hell did not know where that limit might lie.

Around the hall, fae began sitting down.

Not a victory. A stay of execution, if anything. But for now ...

For now, she was alive.

She did not sag back in her seat with relief. Relief was weakness, and weakness was death – more so now than ever. Instead, she scooped a generous helping of venison onto her plate, then took another sip of wine – anything to look as if she had matters well under control. Anything to make the few hundred fae around her believe *they* would be the ones on the losing side if they tried to attack her once again.

For now.

She did not dare to look at Nicanor. She did not dare to look at Naxi. Looking at anyone else for help would be weakness, too.

She stared sedately ahead instead, straight into the empty eyes of the dead hound, as hushed conversations slowly picked up again around her. She chewed venison and tasted dust.

*For the sake of her cowardice.*

*A hundred and thirty loyal patriots ...*

*Traitor's daughter.*

The heat in the hall was stifling, sticking to her skin like moist summer air. No matter how hard she tried to think and plan and *understand*, her thoughts kept sliding from her grasp – not so much scattered as bogged down, heavy like sluggish mud seeping between her fingers. She took another sip of wine. Her hand almost felt too heavy to lift the glass.

*Think, Thysandra.*

Someone had betrayed her. Not Nicanor's people, the ones tasked with arresting their targets – they had never known the intention was to deliver the captives to the Alliance in the end. But Orthea had.

So that left four.

Gadyon. Inga. Nicanor. Silas.

No, not Silas ... Silas hadn't been here when the news of the housing plans had leaked, hadn't he? And that must have been the same person ... or perhaps it hadn't been? Perhaps that *had* truly been an accident, and this had been her uncle making sure she would not be able to do without him for a while?

But then he should have been at the feast to save her, and he wasn't here.

Why wasn't he here?

Had he betrayed her after all, then run off to avoid the consequences?

The world swayed around her as she took another sip of wine. Her heart was a drumbeat in her ears, a hollow, strangely slow rhythm that blurred out all tinkling silverware and muffled conversation around her – *thump ... thump. Thump ... thump.*

What was she to do now?

Get out of this hall alive. That was the first step, even if ... even if her eyes strangely felt like falling shut ...

And then?

She drank more wine.

The Alliance – she needed to tell the Alliance. Needed them to come pick up their captives as soon as possible. Maybe she could pretend she'd never captured them at all, once all traces were gone? And even if she couldn't ... even if she couldn't, at least she'd have a hundred and thirty opponents she no longer had to worry about ...

'Thysandra?' someone was saying close-by.

She was so fucking tired.

The dead hound seemed to be crawling closer towards her. Its misted beady eyes were almost sympathetic – *we're in this hell together*, they said, and yes, they really were, weren't they? She'd seen the hounds as monsters, too, even if ...

*Thysandra!* her father screamed.

No.

No, that wasn't her father's voice.

The wine glass slipped from her hand, shattering against the table.

And then there was Naxi, tugging at her shoulder – pretty little mouth forming words that reached Thysandra's mind only an eternity later. *Thysandra*, she was saying, which was wrong. She wasn't Thysandra. She was Sashka. She was very, very tired, and her body was heavy enough to sink through the floor and into the cold, safe earth below ...

The hall had gone strangely quiet.

Other hands grabbed her shoulders. Thin, elegant hands. Nicanor hung before her, suddenly, which was vexing, because he was not nearly as pretty as Naxi was. He, too, was making sounds. *Thys, can you hear me? Can you tell me what you're feeling?*

Tired.

So tired that her lips wouldn't even move.

'She's feeling very tired!' Naxi was shrieking. 'She's feeling too tired to move – not paralysed, just *heavy* ...'

That was true, she wanted to say.

Her eyes were falling shut again.

'Cold?' Nicanor snapped – gods, there really wasn't any reason for him to be so angry ... 'Or warm? Any pain? Is she able to breathe?'

'No pain. Breathing is hard.' Naxi was rambling so fast Thysandra could hardly follow her words. 'Very warm, as if it's the middle of summer. Her limbs feel heavy. Don't think she really feels her feet anymore.'

Feet?

That was funny. She could have sworn she no longer had any feet.

The world tilted without warning. Arms hoisted her from her chair, and crystals swam above her, dazzling, mesmerising colours her eyes could no longer comprehend. Far too close, far too loud, Nicanor's voice shouted, 'Clear the way!'

Wings swept out. Not her own wings. These were blue, and there were no scars on them.

Did she still have her own wings?

She didn't feel them anymore ... oh, gods, had she lost her wings? Suddenly tears were running down her cheeks, because she *loved* flying, and now she'd never fly again, and she was so very tired it ached ...

'Thys,' Nicanor's voice was repeating, strangely urgent. 'Thys, stay awake. Just a few more minutes, alright? You can sleep in a few minutes. Stay with me now ...'

They were no longer in the hall, suddenly. Open sky above them. Dark blue, streaks of purple. Stars, so many stars.

They were flying

She didn't know how. She'd lost her wings, and either way, her body was so heavy she should be plummeting like a stone. So heavy ... so tired ...

'*Thys*,' Nicanor snapped.

So angry.

She was crying again.

They smacked down onto something. Then there was no longer sky above them but a ceiling, pale wood with burn marks in strangely green colours, and there were no longer arms around her but something ... what was the word again ...

A floor.

Yes, there was a floor beneath her. Good. She could sleep on a floor. She could ...

'Thys, stay awake.'

Why wouldn't he just shut up?

Glass tinkled. Drawers slammed. Then he was kneeling before her again, his face pale like his hair, something in his hand. A vial. Pink fluid. She liked pink. It made her think of Naxi.

'Open your mouth, Thys.'

She wasn't sure where her mouth was supposed to be again. He cursed and hauled her up from the floor – so strong, if he could move something as heavy as her ... Then the vial was against her lips. It didn't taste good. It didn't taste like Naxi.

'Don't you dare spit this out,' Nicanor told her as bitter horribleness slid onto her tongue, and she was so shocked she swallowed.

*Ugh* came from her mouth.

'Yes, yes,' he said, soft, almost *comforting*, as he chucked the vial aside. 'It's very ugh. Well done, Thys. You can sleep now.'

Thank the fucking *gods*.

She barely felt her head hitting the floor again.

# CHAPTER 24

'... GOING TO KILL them *all*,' the prettiest, loveliest, angriest voice in the world was saying.

'You know I'm the last to get in the way of lofty ambitions,' another voice – lilting, silvery – said, and only then did she hear footsteps pacing back and forth around wherever they were. 'I'm just saying we should possibly wait until she wakes up before we decide to massacre the entirety of her court, you know?'

*She*

*Wakes up.*

Thysandra became abruptly aware of her own body and immediately regretted that decision.

While she had never been run over by a herd of horses in her life, she was dreadfully certain that she knew now what the experience must feel like – every fibre in her body sore and bruised and aching, her head pounding as if someone had used it as an anvil. Her thoughts were clear, or at least close enough to clear compared to the utter wreck that was the rest of her ... but it took an arduous burst of concentration to figure out just how she'd ended up here, on someone's couch, while people were threatening bloody murder beside her.

Naxi.

That was Naxi talking.

'Then I'm going to torture everyone who touched that glass!' she was announcing, mere feet away. Her timbre was too high. Panic, even from the prettiest, loveliest, angriest demon in the world. 'Orthea will know who served the wine, won't she? And if she didn't put the poison in there herself, then—'

Poison.

And at once everything became horribly, perfectly clear. Wine. Warmth. Her thoughts turning into sluggish mud while fear should have kept her more awake than ever – and fuck, fuck, *fuck*, Orthea's speech before that ...

'No,' she croaked.

The voices went quiet.

And then Naxi again – 'Sashka?'

'Don't ... don't torture her.' Hell. She sounded like a wood saw had been blessed with the sudden gift of speech. 'Need her cooperation. To ... to rectify things.'

Nicanor cursed. 'Welcome back, Your Majesty. And maybe try a cup of tea first before jumping back into politics?'

'I can make tea!' Naxi squealed.

It seemed a little nonsensical to make a point of Nicanor not poisoning his tea when he had, by the look of it, just narrowly saved her life from whatever had been in her wine. So Thysandra merely opened her eyes, blinked at the ceiling stained with poison fumes, and tried to sit up straight on what did indeed turn out to be a couch.

Thank the gods they hadn't put her in his bed. She wasn't quite ready for *those* memories yet.

It took agonisingly long to get her body into a more or less vertical position. At least Nicanor's curtains were closed – no one to witness the humiliation but him and Naxi, which was presumably the best she could have hoped for. Soft faelights twinkled in corners of the room. A thousand bottles and jars reflected the light – the same menacing collection as always, and yet with the memory of that pink antidote against her lips, it seemed a lot less threatening than it had before.

She should have remembered from the start that her Lord Protector was not the *only* one with a knowledge of poisons in this castle.

It was hard not to curse over the stupidity of it.

Nicanor was sitting at his worktable when she had finally seated herself steadily enough to risk looking up – the red ribbon still braided into his hair but the ruby-covered coat gone, his slim frame strangely fragile in only the silvery shirt he'd worn beneath. In the kitchen corner, Naxi was bustling around, lively hands somehow in seven places at once as she prepared the world's least efficient cup of tea.

Night peered in between the curtains, quiet and black as ink.

'How long have I been out?' Thysandra asked hoarsely.

'*Forever!*' Naxi wailed without turning around.

'About two hours,' Nicanor amended, a wry smile flitting over his lips. 'We considered moving you to your own rooms, but it seemed better not to have you out in public with— Well ...'

'Yes.' She closed her eyes. 'Fuck.'

Naxi huffed. 'I could still kill them all?'

'Need to know what happened, first.' The hazy, strangely contorted images of her memories played before her mind's eye. The hound probably hadn't actually moved. The rest, though ... 'Are we certain it was in my wine?'

'No waiting for the cup of tea, then?' Nicanor said, interlacing his fingers as he rested his elbows on the table surface. 'As you wish. The poison is usually called *phyriga* – Fire's Kiss – and when ingested, its effects kick in quite swiftly. Near-instant sensation of increasing warmth. Ten to fifteen minutes before the tiredness and confusion become noticeable. Half an hour or so until death.'

Naxi gave a small whimper by the stove, stuffing fresh herbs into Nicanor's blackened teapot.

'Wine or venison, then,' Thysandra said numbly. *Half an hour.* Gods have mercy. 'And I probably ate the venison too late for it to be the cause – not to mention—'

'Yes. There would have been no way for anyone to control what piece you took.' Nicanor's lips pressed together into a thin line. 'Hence, the wine.'

'Fuck,' she said again.

'It's a pretty common poison, unfortunately.' He grimaced. 'Of course, if whoever did this had *truly* known anything about the subject, they would have picked a slower option to make sure I would be well out of the way by the time the symptoms showed up. Then again, we were only just in time as it was, and if Anaxia hadn't noticed you feeling odd ...'

'*Miserable,*' Naxi shrilly corrected as she poured boiling water over the herbs, then hauled the teapot off the counter and turned around. Her eyes were redder than the petals on her dress. 'As if you were dying!'

'Which, it turns out, was quite correct,' Nicanor added with a sour grin.

Naxi gave a choked sound.

The urge to pull her onto the couch and curl up against that soft, delicate body was almost overwhelming – but Nicanor was still sitting in the same room, and even if he'd just saved her life, snuggling up with demons might be a bridge too far even for the male who loved his bold decisions.

Instead, Thysandra rubbed her eyes and numbly said, 'So what do we do?'

They were clever enough, the two of them. They could hear what she wasn't saying, the space between the words – *how in hell am I going to survive this?*

*How do I still win this game?*

'I spent most of dinner trying to calm down the army commanders next to me,' Nicanor said, taking the teapot from Naxi and pouring three cups of tea. 'Lots of "no decisions made yet" and "not punishing anyone who did not do anything wrong". So they should be spreading that as we speak. Then again, all the soothing words in the world aren't going to help if ... well ...'

'If information keeps leaking,' Thysandra mumbled.

Nicanor grimaced. 'Yes.'

Naxi scowled at him. 'Why are you feeling so smug about that?'

'Oh, gods.' He gave a joyless laugh, slumping back on his stool. 'Bloody demon eyes.'

Naxi scowled harder.

'Alright, alright. Cards on the table.' His bitter smile slid off his face as he wrapped his hands around his teacup and turned back to Thysandra. 'I'm sorry. I should have talked about this with you sooner. It's just ... frankly, it always sounded unlikely to me, the idea that someone in the archives just happened to hear our conversation at the worst possible moment. Wouldn't the other archivists have noticed if one of them stood pressing their ear to the door for minutes, for one thing?'

Yes.

Yes, they would have.

But it had been such a blissfully convenient explanation, no guilty parties, no betrayal from any of the people whose cooperation she needed the most ...

'No apology needed,' she said blankly, falling back in the couch cushions to stare at the stained ceiling. 'I should have realised the same thing.'

'If I were a better person, I would also not feel so damnably satisfied about being right,' he countered, a sour note of amusement in his voice, 'so you're getting the apology anyway. I suppose the best we can do now is introduce some *very* specific bargains around confidential information as long as we don't know who—'

Fists banged against the living room door.

Thysandra's fingers already lay on her dagger when a familiar voice followed. 'Nicanor? Are you here?'

Silas.

Who had not been at the feast.

She swallowed and nodded, not releasing her blade. Only after that swift confirmation did Nicanor jump off his stool and yell, 'We're all here!'

Silas's muffled words were not entirely intelligible through the wood, but sounded suspiciously like *thank the fucking gods.*

He wasn't alone, it turned out when Nicanor unlocked his door and swung it open. Inga slipped in before him, in her servant's uniform again, a folded letter trembling in her hand.

'We only just heard,' she erupted before anyone else could get a word in, and for once there was no anger in her voice – just pure, breathless fear. 'News didn't make it to the human quarters until some guards told us. If we'd known – if we'd heard sooner ...'

She collapsed onto the couch's armrest, her breath coming in little panicked gasps, and for a long moment of silence, Thysandra had not the faintest idea what to respond. Was the girl afraid to be accused again? It seemed unlikely the mere news of Thysandra's near-death had her in such a frenzy, and behind her, Silas seemed grave rather than terrified.

'Tea?' Nicanor suggested cautiously.

'Fuck off with your tea!' Inga's voice fractured as she jerked up her head. 'Thysandra, *listen*. We made a detour past the archives on our way here. Wanted to make sure no one was attacking the place again, which wasn't the case, but then ... then ...'

Silas quietly shut the door behind him, then leaned against it, jaw set in a tight line. 'Looks like Gadyon is gone, Thys.'

Even Nicanor stiffened at that.

Naxi's eyes had widened, shooting back and forth between Silas and Inga.

'Gone?' Thysandra repeated warily, not sure what to make of the tears in Inga's eyes or the small muscle twitching at her uncle's temple. 'Do you mean you ... you couldn't find him, or ...'

'No,' Inga said, holding out the letter as if it was her own death warrant. 'No, we actually mean he's *gone*. Read it.'

The seal was already broken.

Thysandra took the letter from the girl's hands as if it might grow teeth and bite.

*Your Majesty,* it started, in that small, tidy hand she'd learned to recognise by now.

*I sincerely hope you survive to read this letter. The news of your poisoning just reached me, and I knew then that I would not be able to stay at your court any longer.*

*The leak of your housing plans was – unintentionally – my fault. Since I know I can be scatter-brained, I took extensive notes of our meeting for later reference. Only after the uproar at the archives did I realise they were missing from my office. Someone must have stolen them and spread the news on my behalf. I should have told you then and did not dare to, resolving to keep a better eye on my notes instead.*

*To my dismay, however, it seems I have somehow mislaid my summary of your agreement with the Alliance, too. I cannot find it in my office or my living quarters, the only safe places to keep such information. I can only conclude it was seen by unfriendly eyes in whatever place it ended up and is therefore responsible for this second attempt on your life as well.*

*I would rather go into voluntary banishment than wait for your retribution. I'm sorry. If you decide to send your army after me, I understand; I can only plead for mercy and ask that you consider my departure enough of a penance in itself.*

*With gratitude,*
*Gadyon*

She had to read the letter twice.

The second time was worse.

So she had her culprit after all – the head of her archives, who may have bargained to obey her orders but had still been able to *forget* despite his earnest intention not to. He had lied to her. He could have killed her twice over. He'd fled rather than face the consequences.

She ought to be furious.

And instead all she felt was ... shame? *Regret?*

She'd *liked* her kind, earnest, occasionally harebrained head of the archives – a sentiment that had no business intervening with her sensible politics but did so all the same. Who cared if he'd been an obstacle? Who cared if he could have been the death of her? He'd smuggled food into the humans' hands when they were starving – surely she could have found a way to keep him alive without losing face to the rest of the court?

And he hadn't dared to believe that.

He'd expected her to maim, torture, kill. Like the Mother would have done.

Was that what she seemed to be even to her closest allies – just another ruthless, unforgiving tyrant?

'Thysandra?' Nicanor was saying, and only then did she realise she hadn't lifted her eyes from those damning scribbled lines for minutes on end. 'Mind if I take a look at that?'

She handed him the letter, numbly.

He cursed as he scanned it. Silas was still looking at her with that same, stone-hewn expression on his face – attempting, it seemed, to see straight through the shield of her confusion.

'I ...' She wasn't sure why she felt she had to justify herself, and yet the shame wouldn't go – the knowledge that *others* had read that earnest plea, that *others* knew exactly in what light Gadyon had seen her. It should have been a triumph, knowing she at least had managed to be frightening to someone at this entire bloody court, and instead, it was the greatest humiliation of all. 'I wouldn't have killed him.'

No one moved around her.

No one responded.

Fuck. What was she thinking? This wasn't how the game was played. Assets and obstacles. Favours and payments. Simple, clear-cut calculations in which mercy shouldn't play any role at all ... and the others should know that, shouldn't they?

Except that there *had* been fear in Nicanor's voice as he hurried her to his rooms and pressed the antidote to her lips. Except that Inga's hands were still trembling. Except that Silas had almost knocked *through* the door a few minutes ago, and even now, the small muscle at his temple hadn't stopped twitching.

And Naxi ...

No love. No loyalty.

Yet there was no denying the redness of her eyes.

Nothing in the world made sense anymore. The quicksand of court intrigue was easy. Deadly but easy. Whereas this ... this felt like she was learning to walk all over again, so used to watching her steps and pulling her feet from the mud that solid ground sent her stumbling.

'Send out people to look for Gadyon,' she said, closing her eyes. It was easier that way. If the rest of the world did not exist, at least it couldn't hurt her. 'If they find him, tell him he can safely return to the court. We'll figure things out.'

Still no one spoke.

'I ... I'm not sure yet what to do about the Alliance,' she added, looking up, voice little more than a whisper now.

Weakness, to admit that.

She was so very tired of strength.

'From what I've seen outside,' Silas said grimly, 'your main problem is that the army itself is exactly the group most enraged by the plan. They are the ones who went out there and attacked the other magical peoples. They are the ones whose heads are on the line here. Which means you're not just gaining new opponents – you're also losing the exact group of people you need to deal with opponents in the first place.'

Nicanor made a soft sound of agreement.

Right. No more army, no more authority. The lingering threat of Bereas and friends they had handled, because that mob had consisted mostly of lickspittles and good-for-nothings who just did not want to lose the houses they had done absolutely nothing to deserve. *This*, on the other hand ...

Fuck.

She was much, much too sore to be dealing with violent insubordination.

'I'll see if the Alliance is open to negotiation,' she heard herself say, and even Inga did not scoff at the notion. 'Please send a messenger to the Golden Court. Surely Agenor has an alf or two around to let Thorgedson know I'd like a word with him.'

Nicanor sighed. 'Will do.'

She gave a nod as she dragged herself to the edge of her seat, allowing her wings to fold open behind her back. None of the others moved to assist her. Most days she would have been glad for it – glad to know they didn't think she needed it.

Tonight, she wasn't so sure.

She had things to do, of course. Things to kill. The Mother would have told her it was weakness to hide away and mope, that she needed to be stronger the more fragile she felt ... but then, the Mother had been a liar all this time, and the alternative ...

Her gaze met Naxi's.

Who couldn't love her, just like the Mother had never loved her. Who would leave her, just like her friends had done once she'd lost her use and standing. Simple facts, and yet in this mindless moment, she didn't *want* to accept them – because her head was pounding, her limbs ached like she'd been kicked around the court all day, and gods, how easy would it be now to pretend that softer, kinder world of sweet kisses and honey pastries was real?

She'd pay for it, of course.

She might just be able to afford it, though.

'Tell the court the leaked news is premature and incomplete,' she said, unable to take her gaze away from Naxi's red-rimmed eyes. The demon's watery smile was strangely encouraging. 'They can riot once the negotiations are finished, if they're still unhappy. Silas, if your bargains can do anything to calm them down, that would be appreciated.'

Her uncle and Nicanor nodded as if by some unspoken agreement.

'Thank you. Oh, and Inga ...' She couldn't keep down a groan as she hauled herself to her feet, more or less. The faelights seemed to split into different colours on the edges of her sight. 'You're hereby appointed as interim head of the archives. Let's talk more about that tomorrow. I'm going to need a few hours of sleep, first.'

Inga gaped at her, jaw sagging open in the most dumbstruck bewilderment Thysandra had ever seen from her.

'Thysandra,' Nicanor said, and for a moment she was sure he'd object to the nomination – that he'd remind her they were already close enough to war without half humans being granted such obvious favours. But all that came from his mouth instead was a weary, 'Are you sure it wouldn't be wiser to stay here for the night?'

Shaking her head was a mistake. The entire world seemed to shake with it.

'I'll be perfectly safe in my own room,' she ground out, struggling her first steps towards the door. It became easier once she was in motion. After all, walking was little more than continuously falling in the right direction; as long as she did not slow down, gravity kept her moving. 'Demons are helpful for that sort of thing.'

He hesitated behind her. 'Thys ...'

'*Very* helpful,' Naxi grumbled, the tap of her light footsteps suggesting she'd hopped off her stool. 'You can stop talking. I'll protect her. Might just kill anyone who tries to come between her and her own damn bed, actually.'

Not the moment to laugh.

Thysandra found herself choking on a chuckle all the same.

Wisely, no one else objected – not even Silas, for all his sensible warnings on demons and their games. She turned at the door, just as Naxi caught up with her. Three pairs of eyes were following the two of them, looking ...

No, not wary.

*Worried.*

'If nothing urgent happens,' Thysandra said, fighting to form coherent words, 'I'll be sleeping in tomorrow. See you around noon.'

And out she stumbled, Naxi like a shadow by her side – into the ominously quiet, ominously deserted corridors of the Crimson Court.

# CHAPTER 25

IT WAS A MIRACLE she even made it to her rooms.

Every step was a battle, every turn a deadly gamble. Her hands barely remembered how to open her locks. She crashed into her couch without remembering to wipe the heartleaf vines aside first; they slithered out from beneath her as she lay panting in the cushions, their cool caresses all that kept her from slipping into sleep within moments after her head finally hit the worn green velvet.

And it was Naxi, now, who checked her defences.

The lock on the door. The lock on the windows. Every single dagger in the room, and then the door and the windows again – Thysandra's own routine, and she had not realised just how painfully excessive it was until she saw someone else go through the motions in her place. Naxi was *never* fearful. It made it all the more unsettling to watch her now, moving around the room with a stillness that didn't seem her own, either – no fidgety fingers, no fluttering locks, her usual air of mischief replaced by a dejection that bordered on dread.

Like a wilted flower, having folded in its petals for the night.

She did not meet Thysandra's gaze.

Even when she finished her meticulous examination of every corner of the room, she didn't smile, didn't speak, didn't drape herself over the nearest chair with all of her usual breezy confidence. Instead, she scurried into the bedroom like some nocturnal creature fleeing the light, returning a moment later in one of Thysandra's bathrobes, clutching a pile of towels in her silk-clad arms.

Still without a word, she vanished into the bathroom. The sound of running water emerged a moment later.

Only then did she reappear and make for the couch, finally ... but she still did not look up even as she knelt and began to quietly unlace Thysandra's short boots. Her fingers were her own, and yet they weren't – small and rosy and nimble, but the *vigour* seemed to have seeped from their motions. She worked as if her life depended on it, not as if every twitch and pull was born from nothing but utter joy and excitement.

Thysandra hadn't realised until this moment just how much of that exuberance had seeped into the rhythm of her own heart.

The void it left behind ... it was more painful than even the lingering traces of poison.

'Naxi?' she tried, voice hoarse.

Those dull blue eyes stubbornly avoided hers. 'I'm running you a bath.'

'I ... I heard that.' Fuck. She'd rather deal with five more poison attempts than *this* – the stiffness on Naxi's face, the eerie flatness of her melodious voice. Was this about their last conversation before the feast? *No love or loyalty* ... but hell, an angry demon wouldn't be kneeling at her feet to strip off her shoes, would she? 'I can do that myself, if you—'

Naxi scowled and clasped her hands around the heel of the first shoe without another word, wrenching it off with swift, short movements.

'Look,' Thysandra said, fighting to feign an amusement she did not feel, 'this is a really bad moment to do me any favours, you know. I'm not exactly in a position to bribe anyone with—'

'Oh, shut up, Sashka,' Naxi bit out, yanking off boot number one.

It was the tone, more than the words themselves, that made her accidentally obey.

She watched in numb silence as those little demon hands took care of her second boot as well, then of her stockings. Naxi's face hadn't brightened, nor had her voice lightened, by the time she finally rose to her feet and curtly informed her, 'Your bath is almost ready.'

Without waiting for an answer, she marched into the bathroom.

Thysandra didn't move – from anxiety more than exhaustion now, the sensation crawling into her limbs like an army of ants. Something was wrong. Something was very, very wrong, and she no longer had the faintest clue of how to solve it – because demons lived for fun and pleasure, didn't they? For nothing but selfish desires?

So how in hell was she to placate *this* particular demon, if the little menace refused to selfishly desire anything?

And if she couldn't figure that out ...

Her pulse quickened to a sickening speed.

'Oh, for fuck's *sake*,' Naxi grumbled from the bathroom, her voice echoing against the tiles. The sound of running water abruptly cut off. 'What is it this time, Sashka?'

She shouldn't answer that truthfully.

It would be pathetic to answer that truthfully.

But she was sore down to the marrow of her bones. Her brain felt like it might drip out of her skull at any moment. Shields had crumbled that she hadn't even known she was wearing, and the world might crumble with them tomorrow.

And she was frightened.

Numbingly, sickeningly frightened.

'I just don't want you to leave,' she choked out.

It felt wrong, saying the words out loud. It felt right. It felt like spitting out her own unguarded heart for all the world to see, waiting for the first blows to smash it to pieces.

No answer came from the bathroom.

Then the door creaked open a few more inches, and Naxi reappeared in a whirl of steam, the golden bathroom light clinging like dew to her delicate features. Her robe hung half-open. Smooth black silk against flushed skin – like night brushing over the pale blush of dusk.

Her eyes were darker than Thysandra had ever seen them before, as blue as the iciest depths of the ocean.

'I know,' she said, weary voice excessively patient, as if talking to a whiny toddler throwing a tantrum. 'Which is why I'm not leaving. Now get into the bath, will you?'

'You— What?' What sort of response was *that*, to a confession that could have broken her? 'But I didn't even offer you any—'

'Oh, for hell's bloody sake, Sashka – *stop* talking about the gods-damned bribes!' A flash of fury flared in that melodious voice. Something that wasn't in any shape or form sweet or bright or playful – something heated and hard as steel. 'Isn't it clear enough by now that I'm not going anywhere? I've never been going anywhere! If you stop trying to bribe me, I still won't be going anywhere!'

Thysandra blinked at her.

'Which you should have known, frankly,' Naxi testily added before she could regain her good sense, turning to retreat into the bathroom. 'Notice how I stuck around for a century and a half while you weren't even around to offer me anything? Now—'

'Then why did you accept it?' Thysandra interrupted, voice too shrill, her words tripping over each other on the way out. Her thoughts were more jumbled still, struggling to keep up with every nonsensical twist of this night. 'The deal we made – why did you even go along with it, if you say you didn't need it in the first place?'

A scoff. 'Because you clearly needed an excuse to get over yourself and fuck me. Which I didn't mind, necessarily.'

Oh.

Oh, hell.

Had it been *that* obvious?

'So stop dithering and get yourself into the bloody bath already,' Naxi added with a crabby shrug, slipping back into that gold-lit room and adding from inside, 'You feel like utter shit.'

That much, at least, was true.

Thysandra blinked at the door one last time, then cursed and dragged herself off the couch, onto her bare feet. *Forward.* Towards the bathroom. Scented steam whirled towards her. She staggered over the threshold, onto the lilac floor tiles, and almost passed out at the sight of the plush white towels waiting for her.

'Need help?' Naxi said, looking up from the bottles of bath oil she'd been studying.

Thysandra's reflex was to say no. Help was always costly in the end. But she did need it.

She needed it, and Naxi had never been going anywhere.

'Yes,' she mumbled, shutting the door behind her. 'Please.'

She steadied herself against the wall, the edges of the gold and ivory mosaic tiles harsh against her fingers, as Naxi's quick hands unbuttoned the back of her dress, then the slits for her wings. They steadied her, those touches. Nothing sensual about them, nothing seductive; they trailed down her spine and over her shoulder blades feeling simply like ... care.

Like *tenderness.*

The dark red silk slid off, pooling around her feet like discarded skin. Her underwear came next, and then she was naked, the bath beckoning in a haze of steam and chamomile scent.

'Go on,' Naxi murmured, nudging the small of her back.

She stumbled forward. Her hands found the cool ceramic of the bathtub; her legs somehow managed to lift themselves. The water was almost painfully hot, a temperature so perfect she couldn't help but moan as she sank into it – letting it seep into every pore of her body, rinsing out the poison and sweat and the wine and the fear.

Rinsing out something older, too, a tightness that slumbered so deep in her bones she had not known of its existence until it uncoiled.

She was alive.

And somehow she was ... not alone.

It didn't make sense. Life was a solitary fight, each for their own and none for all – or at least that was what the court and the Mother had taught her. But the Mother had lied. The Mother had died. Her father *had* tried to save her, and even Creon had not torn her down for the cruel pleasure of it ...

Soft hands prodded her knees. 'Move over, Sashka.'

Only then did she realise she'd closed her eyes.

Naxi was already climbing into the tub when she opened them, her small, delicate body moving with swift grace as she lowered herself opposite Thysandra. Water sloshed over her small breasts, her shoulders, turning her pale skin pink. Their knees slid together for a moment, a gentle, fleeting touch. No seduction, still – no giggling propositions, no challenges, no skilful hands sliding up Thysandra's thighs ...

Nothing that could make this worth a demon's while.

And yet.

They lay in comfortable stillness for a few minutes, nothing but the lapping of the water and the rhythm of their slowing breaths to break the silence. Steam curled around the glowing faelights. Warmth misted the mirrors. The ripples of the water sent flecks of reflected light dancing across the ceiling, and Thysandra stared at them until she no longer saw anything else, too mesmerised by the dizzying patterns to remember to worry.

An eternity had passed when Naxi sighed, not lifting her head from the rim of the tub. Her voice was quiet, almost drowsy, as she murmured, 'My mother was scared of me, you know.'

There was a weight to that sudden statement. A sense of meaning – as if this was the answer to a question Thysandra had asked mere moments before.

In the soothing heat of the bath, it took her a few blinks to realise that in a sense, she had. That she had been wildly and helplessly confused. That she still was, really.

*Why are you still here?*

Demon senses. She had not needed to speak the words out loud.

'Your ... mother?' she stammered, belatedly.

'I didn't know it at first, of course. Before my demon powers developed.' Naxi's voice remained distant. Monotone. Her unseeing eyes were aimed at the wall. 'And then when they did, I didn't know what that feeling meant for a while, because my family members weren't scared of much else around me. Not until the war came. That was when I realised that what they felt for me was not unlike what they felt for the fae warships passing by our shores.'

Understanding rose – slowly and horribly.

'And they never told me just what my father did to my mother before he left.' A small, joyless smile curled around those soft, pink lips – a smile of resignation. Of a wound that would never fully heal. 'They still loved me, you see. In all the ways I could never love them. So they tried not to let me notice what I reminded them of ... but of course I knew damn well that there wasn't a pretty ending to that story.'

Thysandra swallowed. A painful lump had settled in her throat. 'I ... I'm sorry.'

Naxi just gave another wistful sigh, sinking deeper into the fragrant water until only her head still rose above the surface.

'I don't think I want to be like him,' she said then, suddenly.

Thysandra blinked. 'Like your father?'

'Yes. Old bastard.' In a surge of wet skin and soaked pink curls, she sat straighter again, wiping strands of hair off her shoulders with quick, impatient hands. 'I thought for a while that I wanted to be like him, because clearly I wasn't like anyone else. But when I found him ...'

She was silent for a moment, steam whirling around her, lips twitching with unspoken words.

There was something eerily unguarded about the look in her wide blue eyes – something that lay worlds away from her usual breezy cheer. That was innocence wielded as a weapon. This, on the other hand, the quiet, almost mournful contemplation in her gaze ...

An invitation. An unveiling.

Thysandra was suddenly – inexplicably, yet unshakably – sure that these thoughts had never been spoken out loud to any other soul.

'He didn't really care about anything,' Naxi whispered, finally. 'None of his friends did. And *I* don't really care about anything half of the time, either, but sometimes ... sometimes ...'

It hung heavy in the air for an infinitesimal moment, her faltering voice.

Then she pulled her bony knees to her chest, her small, mirthless huff abruptly self-aware again, and mumbled, 'Sometimes I wish I did.'

It was in that very moment that Thysandra realised she was in love.

A surprise, and at the same time, the opposite of it – not the abrupt emergence of brand new feelings in her heart but rather the sudden awareness of what was already there, lurking in the shadows, waiting for her to finally discover what was right in front of her. Not lust. Not the thrill of newness. She didn't care about the pleasure or the power or even the distraction from the deadly turning of the court.

She just …

She stared at the little demon curled up in her bathtub, frail, delicate, yet stronger than tempered steel, and wanted nothing but … *her*.

Naxi, who could support without subservience. Naxi, who could feel joy without weakness. A creature of opposites, of thrilling, terrifying unpredictability, and gods help her, Thysandra craved *all* of it – the bright colours, the infectious laughter, and every shard of unexpected hurt hiding behind that façade. A want so great it hardly left room for breath in her lungs. So great that it should have felt dangerous, that it should have been a betrayal of every lesson life had ever taught her …

And instead, it felt like the safest thing in the world – a sanctuary welcoming her with open arms.

She was in love.

Gods help her. She was in *love*.

With a demon who was by her very nature incapable of reciprocating the feeling, with a demon who should by all laws of her kind vanish one day and never look back … but also, with a demon who wished she cared.

It had to be fatigue, soreness, the poison still playing tricks with her mind, that all of a sudden it did not seem such a bad idea at all.

'You …' she started, grasping for words as the world rearranged itself around her. A whole new world, yet it felt startlingly familiar – a shock that felt rather like a relief. 'You still … can't feel love, can you?'

'No,' Naxi admitted, chewing on her bottom lip as she thoughtfully canted her head. The question didn't appear to surprise her 'No, I don't think I can. But on the other hand ... I can't juggle either, and Edored insists he could teach me if I just took the time to learn.'

Thysandra hadn't thought herself capable of laughter just now.

A chortle escaped her all the same.

Naxi sank back into the water with a small grin flickering around her lips, as if even that short burst of laughter had been a victory in itself.

Again they were both quiet for a while – a more hopeful silence, somehow, even though Thysandra's thoughts were still flailing like fledgling birds. She ought to feel more bewildered, shouldn't she? Or at least *Naxi* ought to, picking up on these bewildering feelings? Something, most of all, should have *changed* ... and yet, against all rational thought, it rather seemed the world had more firmly established what had already been, as if reality had finally settled where it belonged.

She was in love. The question was just ...

'What do we do now?' she muttered out loud, barely louder than the rippling water.

Naxi hummed a pensive little sound. 'What do you want to do?'

*Flee.*

For the very first time, it seemed a conceivable possibility to her mind.

She'd been minutes away from death, and not even Naxi had been able to protect her. The court knew of her plans, and even if they'd finally identified the leak, that damning information was still out there – which meant her only paths forward were to give up or to go head-to-head with her own damn army, and quite likely die in the process.

She didn't want to give up.

It seemed stupid to fall in love and die the next day, though.

Which didn't leave her with a whole lot of options.

'We could sneak away and hide somewhere,' she made herself say, even though the words lay bitter on her tongue, even though the thought itself made her want to shrivel up in the hot water. 'Your idyllic nymph isle, just as an example.'

She expected agreement. Cheerful triumph, quite possibly.

Instead, Naxi narrowed her eyes and said, 'But that's not what you *want* to do, is it?'

There really was no use in arguing against demon senses.

She *shouldn't* want to stick around at this hell of a court. By all laws of scheming and self-interest, it had run out of advantages: no more chance of success, and a towering chance of an untimely death. There were other ways to save the humans. Hell, she could move all of them to that nymph isle with her – surely they would agree to that, if the alternative was facing Bereas and his mob again?

Her heart wasn't that rational, though.

And the problem – the ridiculous but undeniable problem – was that she *cared* about this fucking place.

Not about the courtiers and the violence and the blood-soaked trees of Faewood. Not about the Mother's ghost haunting every inch of the castle. But she loved her rooms. The gardens and the hills. The shore, the beaches, the sea of which she knew every reef and islet. It was *hers*, this island, the soil in which her roots had grown, and she'd be fucking damned before she let another cutthroat conqueror burn it all to ashes.

*Do better.*

She had no one left to serve, and she was *not* bowing again.

'No,' she said, voice hoarse but unwavering. 'No, it's not.'

Naxi's shrug sent the water sloshing against the edges of the tub again. 'Well, then we're not fleeing.'

It was almost *too* easy.

'But you want to leave.' No use in beating around the bush here. 'You've been wanting to leave since we arrived.'

'Ye-e-es,' Naxi admitted, almost unwillingly, as she draped her arms over the ivory edge of the bathtub. Her wet skin shone golden in the deep, warm light. 'I suppose so. But I also don't want you to do something you regret and then resent me over the choice, so if you don't want to leave, I'm not going to *make* you leave.'

Bewildering, how a demon without empathy managed to be more considerate of her choices than most of her allies had ever been.

'We might die,' she said feebly.

'Hmm.' A devilish grin. 'We might not.'

They might not.

And at once the poison in her veins did not matter anymore – the ache slumbering in her every muscle, the exhaustion weighing down her mind. They might survive. She *had* to survive, truly, because how in the bloody world could she die after a hundred and thirty years of unwilling pining had finally turned into something as unexpected, something as utterly bemusing, as *love*?

'I suppose we have until noon tomorrow, then,' she said.

Naxi sat up straighter and squinted, rivulets of scented water running down her arms, her shoulders, her pale breasts. 'I thought you'd be sleeping.'

'Yes,' Thysandra said, unable to suppress something suspiciously akin to a smile. 'So does everyone else.'

A small beat of foggy, gold-and-lavender silence.

Then Naxi slowly said, 'Oh. You don't want to tell anyone else about it?'

'We've seen what happens when we tell anyone else.' Thysandra rubbed a wet hand over her face, then sat up as well, feeling the drops rush down her wings with the motion. Their legs tangled together again, deep umber and rosy pale, muscle and lithe boniness, and she felt weirdly like swooning at the sight. 'This time it was Gadyon. Next time it might be Inga. We really, *really* can't afford any additional trouble this time.'

Naxi looked doubtful, but did not object.

'So as long as we stay out of sight, we have until noon.' Something like energy was seeping back into her limbs. Something like, gods help her, *optimism*. 'Tared will probably show up as soon as he gets the message, which could be any moment after our messenger has reached the Golden Court, and once we tell him what's going on, he could get the representatives of the other peoples together rather swiftly, couldn't he?'

'Oh, probably.' Naxi's eyes were still narrowed. 'They're always quick when there's fae to be dealt with.'

'Right. So then we meet with them in secret. Get their official confirmation of the rates at which they're willing to trade. Have them take the captives from Ilithia – surely there'll be a few alves willing to handle that within a few hours?'

Naxi snorted a laugh. 'Minutes, if you need them to. But then you have a trade deal and an angry army, and—'

'Angry army,' Thysandra cut in, 'but happy everyone else, don't you think?'

Naxi fell quiet.

'We keep talking about the army as if they're the only force at the court that matters.' She drew in a lungful of humid, chamomile-scented air, pausing briefly to gather her thoughts. 'And they *are* a force. A significant one. But their numbers are ... maybe a fifth of our total population? Or even less, after the battle? Most people the Mother sent out during the war weren't permanent army members at all – people like all those teachers and archivists who were only called in when the need was high.'

It made so much sense, now that she was speaking the words aloud. And of course she'd never seen it before. She had *been* the army; it had shaped her entire world. Yet Inga had made a perfectly valid point: there *were* plenty of fae at the court with no desire to keep fighting at all, and ...

'And they've all had military training,' Naxi said slowly, blue eyes piercingly sharp now. 'The teachers and the archivists and everyone else.'

'Every single one of them.' A joyless laugh. 'No one survives into adulthood at this court without some skill with a weapon.'

'So what you're saying is ...'

'They aren't the majority, the people who were clamouring for my head at the feast.' There was no stopping the grin growing on her face now – the realisation, so perfectly crystal clear, of *whose* High Lady she wanted to be. 'And everyone else will be happy enough to have their peace and their daily meals. If I can rally *their* support, I frankly don't think the army stands any chance at all.'

It echoed a little against the bathroom tiles, that outrageous, triumphant conclusion.

Naxi, somehow, didn't yet smile – sitting perfectly still on the other side of the bath, a feverish blush on her cheeks, pink lips pressed together into a line of unspoken worries. 'So why do we need the secrecy, then? If you need the whole court to suddenly grow a backbone, don't you want to make the plan as public as possible?'

'I need the trade prospects to be a done deal before we ask for help,' Thysandra said, closing her eyes. She needed her focus, now, to keep track of the pieces moving in her mind. 'I don't think anyone will risk their life for just the *potential* of peace and security. And if the military knows we're moving forward with the plan before we meet with the representatives, they'll probably try to sabotage that meeting – so it has to stay a secret until the meeting is over, and *then* we can shout about it to every soul willing to listen, you see?'

A plan.

She had a *plan*.

To hell with Orthea and whoever had put that poison in her glass; to hell with the commanders champing at the bit to do away with her. She could still win this game. All she needed was a clear head and a few good hours of sleep, and ...

And Naxi.

Old Thysandra would have thought it a weakness – but hell, it felt a damn lot like a strength.

When she looked up, Naxi still hadn't moved on the other end of the bath, blonde head tilted like a clever little bird. Her blue eyes were swarming with thoughts. As if she was already making plans of her own ... and then she smiled, her own dazzling, sharp-toothed smile, and all glimpses of calculation were gone.

'Excellent!' she declared, rising from the bath and clambering out in an excited jumble of limbs, dripping all over the pale purple tiles. She shook the water from her hair like a stray cat shaking off the rain, then snatched a towel from the pile and wrapped it around herself. 'I'll get ready to shout at Tared if he makes a fuss. Shall we go get a few hours of sleep, then, Sashka?'

Too easy.

But for once in her life, Thysandra could believe in easy.

# CHAPTER 26

THE ALLIANCE WAS EVEN faster than she'd dared hope.

Mere hours passed between her request for a meeting and their collective agreement; from then, it was a matter of minutes. The sun was just about to rise when she donned the only dark blue dress in her possession – as close to a declaration of peace as her wardrobe could come – and left her rooms with Naxi, who had insisted on wearing a matching shade of frothy eggshell blue for the occasion.

A short night of sleep had not been nearly enough to feel all hale and hearty again. But at least Thysandra was able to walk without stumbling and talk without stammering; the persistent ache in her muscles, like the lingering effects of particularly strenuous training, was a mild nuisance in comparison. She'd fought under worse circumstances. And if all went according to plan, there would be no need for her to fight anyone at all – not for another few hours, in any case, and by then the poison would have worn off even further.

The castle was as quiet as it always was around dawn, even the prospect of violent rebellion not enough to keep most fae from their beds. Guided by Naxi's demon senses, it was almost laughably easy to avoid the few lone soldiers patrolling the corridors on Nicanor's behalf.

They reached their meeting spot within minutes.

Inviting five former enemies into one of the usual reception halls would have been asking for trouble. Instead, Thysandra had pointed her visitors to a location which she suspected Bereas and the majority of her army didn't even know existed: the statue gallery at the far end of the academy wing. The Mother had banished most traces of the fae rulers preceding her to that quiet, oblong hall, and these days it was rarely visited by anyone but groups of fae younglings during history classes – which meant that, no matter how publicly accessible the gallery might be in theory, it was significantly more private than the average meeting room.

They were the first to arrive. Only the rulers of old watched them walk between the haphazard collection of pedestals in the dusty morning light – their sculpted faces haughtily expressionless, shreds of cobwebs glinting from their marble wings and fingers.

'So many arseholes,' Naxi said wistfully.

Thysandra choked on a laugh, the sound echoing against the vaulted ceiling.

On the far side of the hall, surrounded by high, stained-glass windows on three sides, a semi-circle of marble benches had been erected. Most days, she'd likely have remained on her feet while waiting for her guests. This morning, she was too relieved to unburden her sore legs to care much about that little piece of etiquette; she plopped down on the nearest bench as Naxi ambled around her, studying fae faces and scoffing a little at the names and epithets inscribed in the blocks of marble beneath their feet.

'Please remember not to get involved in the discussion,' Thysandra said, even though she was well aware that she'd said the same thing four times already during their hasty breakfast, and that Naxi had miraculously not objected even the first time.

The response was a well-deserved eyeroll. 'Sashka.'

'Yes, yes, you already promised you wouldn't, but—'

'But you're nervous.' Naxi hopped from one stern fae lord to the next, sticking out her tongue at them both before adding, 'Which you don't need to be, because I'm here.'

Too easy.

Her wings unclenched a little nonetheless.

Because the simple fact was that she *had* done everything she could. She had her numbers, her arguments, her strategic little lies. She knew what the five representatives wanted, and she could give it to them. Yesterday she'd almost died, yes, but *they* didn't need to know that; as long as they did not know of her weakness, they couldn't take advantage of it.

As long as she did not tell them otherwise, she was still the powerful High Lady of the Crimson Court.

She still stiffened when the click of the door broke through the dusty silence. But Naxi was here and their opponents could not possibly know of this meeting ... so she sat still and waited without drawing her weapons, exposed and vulnerable on her marble bench as three pairs of feet made their way towards them through the shadows.

Tared was the first to emerge, the faint shimmer of alf magic flickering around his tall form all the more noticeable in the grey morning light. Sword on his shoulder. Hand in his pocket. Eyebrows halfway up his forehead as he glanced at the heroic sculptures around him, his thoughts visibly close to Naxi's muttered *arseholes*.

Perhaps, Thysandra realised with a mortified jolt, it would have been better not to invite the lot of them to a hall stuffed full of glorious fae history.

Too late to change that now, though. So she straightened her spine, forced a smile, and prayed her voice wouldn't tremble as she said, 'Good morning.'

'Tared!' Naxi exclaimed, bouncing towards him in an excited blur of eggshell blue.

'Morning, Naxi.' He ruffled her hair with a grin that looked perfectly genuine, but that paled the moment he turned to Thysandra. 'And morning, Your Majesty. Illustrious place you've found us here.'

She could hardly disagree with him on that.

'It's all the fae history the Mother tried to make us forget,' she said anyway, because better to pretend this was a little piece of intentional symbolism than to start the meeting by admitting she hadn't thought matters through that far. 'Figured we'd better have this conversation in the company of the rulers who *didn't* cause you centuries of trouble.'

'Ah.' He looked vaguely amused. 'I'm sure they'll be more than excited to witness this historic event, then. Don't suppose you've met Delwin before?'

Too easy, again.

Was it an act of mercy, his swift pivot away from her misstep? Or did he just ... not care that much?

It felt dangerous, proceeding without knowing. But the only thing that could aggravate her blunder was to linger on it, so she swallowed her questions and forced a polite nod at the tall human man stepping from the shadows. Dark-haired. Straight-faced. He wasn't wearing the white robes that came with his position, but his name was all the information she needed.

'A pleasure to meet you, consul,' she said.

Delwin inclined his head with the measured composure of a trained soldier, his voice pleasantly pragmatic as he said, 'Let us hope that will be mutual, Your Majesty.'

Tared bit down a grin behind him.

Which should have annoyed her, probably – but damn it all, coming from a magic-less human standing in the middle of the Crimson Court, she couldn't help but appreciate the stone-faced gall of that reply. The only mortal to attend their gathering, perhaps, but clearly the White City's consul was not a man to underestimate.

Their third companion came forward last, a more familiar face this time. Black hair braided into an intricate crown, pale features marred by two grisly scars – Nenkhet Bakarim, one of the first vampires to have openly joined the Alliance an eternity ago. Her presence was unannounced but unsurprising. It had been centuries since Bakaru himself had left the stronghold of Gar Temen; the true shock would have been the King of Kings attending this meeting.

Nenkhet's smile seemed solely intended to display her razor-sharp canines. There certainly wasn't any joy or fondness in it as she said, 'Hello, Thysandra.'

Oh, gods.

This was a bad moment to realise that they hadn't seen each other since the Mother had forced this same vampire to kneel at her feet, then laughed as she bound her magic – and much, much worse, that Thysandra had *assisted* her with the effort.

'Good morning,' she ground out all the same, because there were times and places to talk about regret and retribution, and this wasn't one of them. 'Take a seat, if you like.'

Nenkhet ignored that suggestion without even a sign of having heard it, standing by the side of the semicircle of benches with her head held high and her arms crossed over the leather-and-lace bodice of her dress. Tared similarly stayed on his feet, although he allowed himself to lean against the man-high pedestal beside him. Only Delwin accepted the invitation. It wasn't until he sat down and his trousers shifted that Thysandra realised he was wearing a wooden leg – a mark of the recent battle, no doubt.

An awkward silence loomed. Naxi, thankfully, filled it by chattering to Tared about other friends and how she was coming to visit them sometime soon.

Perhaps two minutes went by before the air flickered and turned into living matter again – this time right next to the benches, which meant this newly arrived alf female must have visited the gallery before. Thysandra did not know her name. She *did* know the white-haired, stiff-backed phoenix female who'd been faded along with the alf – Lady Yndrusillitha, second eldest of Phurys, here on behalf of the just-reborn Lord Khailan and the rest of their council.

Yndrusillitha's nod at Thysandra was curt and sharp. Her nod at Tared, surprisingly, was even curter and even sharper, and the smile the alf returned could have cut through solid steel – some history there, clearly, but Thysandra wasn't given the time to speculate. Before she could even greet her guest, a third alf faded into the hall.

This one didn't arrive quietly.

'Morning, everyone!' With the impressive amount of bandaging around his blond head, it might have been hard to recognise the new-comer – but that hot-blooded voice did the work instead. Last time Thysandra had heard it, its owner had been cheerfully hewing his way towards her on a battlefield. 'Bit early for important meetings, isn't it? Good thing I didn't go to sleep last night, because I'd never have woken up in time for—'

'Edored,' Tared interrupted, his voice calm, the corners of his lips trembling.

'What?' The alf whipped around, almost knocking over the nymph queen he'd brought with him – Helenka of Tolya, who seemed equally torn between unwilling laughter and heartfelt exasperation. 'Oh, right. Diplomacy. Although it's pretty early for diplomacy, too, isn't it? And— Oh, hello Naxi! Been a while!'

The gloomy, dignified atmosphere had somehow gone up in smoke. Delwin's shoulders were shaking. Yndrusillitha, who had sat down two benches to the consul's right, looked as if she was desperately trying to develop fading powers herself, and Helenka murmured something that sounded suspiciously similar to *madman* as she sank down on a low pedestal in her gauzy green dress.

None of them looked worried in the least, though.

And even Naxi – clever, vigilant Naxi, whose demon senses would not let a single flare of annoyance go unnoticed – beamed back at Edored without any sign of reserve or caution. As if this was perfectly acceptable behaviour for a peace-or-war meeting. As if there wasn't any need for mitigating measures at all, before she—

Well, Thysandra admittedly wasn't quite sure what she might do. She was hardly in a position to cause a stir and leave, was she?

But this wasn't the Alliance as she'd known it during the war at all – disciplined, competent, a united front that had driven the Mother to rage more than once. They had sounded so perfectly businesslike in that single, unanimous letter, too. So if they were at all interested in developing decent trade relations with her, then what in the world were they doing now – letting loose the alvish equivalent of an overly excited watchdog in this diplomatic equivalent of a porcelain cabinet?

'... another time,' the alf female who had brought Yndrusillitha with her was saying – her voice oddly colourless, her smile too faint to reach her pale blue eyes. 'I think they might prefer for the two of us to get out of here, Edored.'

'I was already leaving,' Edored sputtered, looking genuinely offended that she hadn't yet noticed his solemn dedication to his imminent departure. 'You all can't accuse me of ... of un-diplomacy, you know. Good luck, Nen! You'll do great!'

Nenkhet gave him a look Thysandra could only describe as a fond stare of death and muttered, 'Thanks, arsehole.'

'Hey!' Edored protested. 'I'm being supportive! That's not—'

They would never find out what it wasn't. The other alf female had unceremoniously grabbed his sleeve and faded him out of the gallery, leaving nothing but a slightly maniacal echo behind between the pillars and the pedestals.

Naxi was giggling uncontrollably into her sleeve.

'Apologies,' Tared said with a wry grin, although whether the excuse was aimed at Helenka or the company at large, Thysandra wasn't sure. He didn't sound particularly apologetic either way. 'Needed to quickly find someone who would keep his mouth shut to the other houses. Let's talk about—'

Yndrusillitha made a sound that could have been a scoff, if she had considered scoffing a proper activity for a lady. '*He* is supposed to keep his mouth shut?'

What in the world?

Were they going to start fighting with *each other* now?

'Yes?' The sudden politeness in Tared's voice was an unmistakable sign of alarm. Every single time alves had unexpectedly developed manners around Thysandra, hell had broken loose the next moment. 'Something about family being there when it counts – not that I'd expect that to make much of an impression on you, of course.'

'I beg your pardon?' The phoenix's widening eyes were the only outward sign of her outrage – but outrage it *was*, and she didn't seem to care in the slightest that she was in the presence of an ally-to-be. 'It was my impression that I'd been invited to a diplomatic gathering, not to a lecture from—'

'Um,' Thysandra interrupted, managing only with the greatest of efforts not to frantically look back and forth between them like a child trying to figure out the rules of some brand new sports game. What for the gods' sake was *happening*? 'Would ... would this be a good moment to return to the matter at hand, perhaps?'

Yndrusillitha's nostrils flared. 'An *excellent* suggestion.'

'Absolutely brilliant,' Tared dryly agreed. 'In fact, I vaguely recall proposing something similar myself, before we were regrettably interrupted. Let's get down to business, then. Where would you suggest we start, Your Majesty?'

Somehow, that title got more unnerving every single time he used it.

It sounded like a joke. Not even a malicious one, the way people like Bereas and Orthea had sneered it to her face – rather, the sort of casual quip one might exchange with fellow soldiers after receiving an unexpected promotion. As if her life didn't depend on the outcome of this meeting. As if he didn't bloody well *know* they were putting her right in the line of fire with the conditions they'd posited in their letter.

'Actually, I do have a place to start,' Helenka said, crossing her ankles on the low pedestal where she'd seated herself. Her shimmering, pupil-less green eyes were narrowed a fraction. 'Would the High Lady care to explain to us just why this meeting had to take place on such short notice? I'm still catching up on a few decades of lost sleep.'

'I'm sure certain alves agree with you,' Nenkhet muttered under her breath, and Tared snorted a laugh.

Helenka ignored the both of them. 'Thysandra?'

'The ... the matter is we're running out of cells.' She didn't dare to look at Naxi as she let the lie fall from her lips – a lie she'd prepared for, yet somehow it had sounded a lot more reasonable when she'd expected them to show up with stern faces and stiff shoulders, armed to the teeth with regulations and demands. 'Our efforts to arrest the individuals on your list have been unexpectedly successful. We could wait longer to capture the rest, of course, but we're already seeing people go into hiding, and ...'

333

'Really?' Helenka interrupted, tapping her chin with a dark, clawlike hand. 'How interesting. I assumed the Crimson Court would have more capacity than that to hold prisoners.'

An accusation?

Or merely a request for clarification?

If she had understood a damn thing in this entire conversation, she might have been able to read the queen's voice. Now she wished for the first time that she hadn't told Naxi to stay out of the discussion – because clearly Naxi *knew* these people in the capacity of messy, bickering allies, and why hadn't she thought to make use of that?

She glanced to her side anyway, hoping to catch the demon's eye. But Naxi had wandered a few rows of statues away and stood making faces at a fae lady with a skull in her sculpted hands, paying no visible attention to the rest of the company.

Leaving Thysandra to figure out all by herself why these people were suddenly treating her as if they'd forgotten they were enemies in the first place.

'Speaking frankly,' she said, taking the gamble before the silence could grow too damning, 'I think we all know the Mother wasn't in the habit of taking prisoners. She never seems to have had need for that many cells.'

Helenka quirked up a coppery red eyebrow, then shrugged, as if to say, *good point.*

'And I do understand correctly that you're willing to hand over these prisoners to us?' Tared added, hands in his pockets, but his grey eyes too sharp for the nonchalance to be at all convincing. 'Assuming we try to give them fair trials before we chop off their heads, that is.'

*Fair trials.*

How bad an impression would she make if she admitted she didn't give a damn about those trials at all?

'That is correct,' she said, drawing her wings tightly against her shoulders to keep them from flaring out. They didn't need to know how much it would cost her, speaking those words. How much she needed to do it anyway. 'The conditions posited in your letter did sound reasonable to me.'

'That is rather convenient,' Yndrusillitha said tartly, and although the words were approving, the tone was the opposite.

'I beg your pardon?' Thysandra said.

'You seem unexpectedly willing to grant our every request without significant negotiation,' the phoenix clarified – or at least her *expression* suggested it ought to be a clarification, while as far as Thysandra could see, it was mostly an expansion of the number of words used. 'Which is, one might say, a stark contrast to some of our previous interactions. It would be commendable, of course, if we could come to an agreement easily, but one cannot help but wonder what else might be driving you to—'

'What we'd like to know,' Helenka bluntly interrupted, 'is how desperate you are, exactly.'

Yndrusillitha gave a small, disapproving cough, but did not dispute that summary.

Nor did any of the others around the circle, five pairs of eyes watching Thysandra with eerily similar, sceptical anticipation – so *there* was the animosity after all, then. Messy and unpolished animosity, perhaps, but animosity all the same. And only then did it dawn on her – that they did not allow her to see the chaos behind their united façade because they no longer considered her an enemy.

Rather, because they no longer considered her a *threat*.

Gods have mercy.

How much did they know? Had Inga told her sister of the grain scarcity, perhaps? Or had the Alliance simply run their own calculations, based on the food tributes taken from their islands over the years, and arrived at the same conclusions as Gadyon and his administrators had?

Did they have the faintest idea that they could kill her by simply leaving this meeting without any firm conclusions?

The sun was rising outside, dawn colouring the historic events pictured in the stained-glass windows shades of orange and pink. A few hours to go before the court started looking for her. A few hours in which to arm herself against their fury, and the allies she needed might laugh in her face.

Sweat itched between her shoulder blades.

'It doesn't have much to do with desperation,' she said, forcing herself to speak impassively, a calm close to boredom. Panic was weakness, and they thought her much, much too weak already. 'The simple fact is that these fae used unprompted and unnecessary violence against your peoples. It seems more reasonable to let them bear the brunt of the consequences than to let the whole court, innocent members included, suffer on their behalf.'

'Very reasonable,' Nenkhet said in Helenka's place. A cold sort of amusement glinted in the vampire's dark eyes as she tilted her head. 'What if we added your own name to the list?'

On the other side of the hall, a small, barely audible, but unmistakable squeal of outrage rose from the direction Naxi had wandered in.

'I'm not sure I understand your meaning,' Thysandra said, her mouth dry. 'I hope I never used the sort of excessive cruelty against any of you that would justify my own arrest.'

'You did assist the Mother in binding every single one of us,' Helenka pointed out from Nenkhet's side, with a directness that wasn't so much unfriendly as unflinching. 'One could consider that a direct act of aggression against us, no?'

The worst thing was that it wasn't untrue at all.

Really, it was a miracle they *hadn't* come clamouring for her head yet.

'One could,' she forced herself to agree – necessary agreement, but it felt like laying her own neck on the chopping block. 'If so, though, it's an act of aggression I am trying sincerely to make up for.'

Yndrusillitha pursed her lips, sceptism drawn sharply in every line on her face. 'And as I've said before, your repentance is timed rather auspiciously.'

The silence that followed spoke volumes – the pointed lack of objections.

What in the world was she supposed to respond to that? *Don't worry, my regret is entirely genuine* – as if her word would convince a single one of them. *Just give me a chance, and I'll show you proof of my good intentions* – little good that would do, if they had already decided between the five of them that they wouldn't be giving her even the slightest benefit of the doubt.

The truth, of course ...

*I'm starting to learn this court broke so many versions of me I might have been. I'm finally picking up the shards.*

But they already didn't take her seriously, and admitting to being a flailing wreck would be the final nail in that coffin. They weren't looking for an ally who might collapse at any moment. They were looking for an ally they could trust – and hell, had she still not learned how much damage she could do by sharing too much with the wrong people?

'May I ask ...' Careful, now. She couldn't be too defensive. Not too offensive, either. 'May I ask what exactly the purpose of this meeting is to you? Because from your letter, I was under the impression we would be discussing trade agreements. If you'd rather dive into the details of my goals and motivations, I'd have liked to know in advance.'

'The trouble,' Tared said, still lounging against his pedestal, 'is they're the same thing.'

She blinked. 'Care to elaborate?'

'Our enthusiasm to work with you is entirely dependent on your goals.' He shrugged. 'Assisting the Crimson Court to make sure it isn't driven to desperate violence – that we can do. Assisting the Crimson Court so it can quietly regain its former strength and attack us again is ... a less attractive prospect.'

'Another war is the last thing I want,' Thysandra ground out.

'Well, that's good news,' he dryly said. 'And how about the rest of your court?'

Bereas.

Her entire army.

The poison in her wine.

Any moment, now, Naxi could speak up on the other side of the hall and inform her friends this place was a hellhole about to cause the rest of the world a whole damn lot of trouble. She *should* speak up, really. But the gallery remained painfully devoid of demon voices, and so the lies were all Thysandra's to tell.

'There are always dissenting parties,' she said – a laughable platitude for Symeon's knife diving at her, for a clamouring mob bringing her inches from death. Her voice did not waver as she added, 'For now, they are under control.'

Lies.

Filthy lies.

Then again ... why should she care? They weren't her allies. She didn't owe them her honesty any more than they owed her theirs.

'And you would agree that any treaties between your court and our people become voided as soon as any member of your court attacks us again?' Helenka said, and Thysandra could have sworn those shimmering gemstone eyes were taking note of every twitch of doubt to show on her own treacherous face.

Would she agree?

She *couldn't* guarantee a single thing – that was the ugly truth of it. She didn't even know where Bereas was hiding, for hell's sake! He might just have set up camp half an hour away from the nearest nymph isle, ready to raid it for food as soon as he felt like it. But telling them that much, admitting she was hanging on to her crown by the tips of her fingers ...

They would laugh in her face.

And she needed their pledges to save her own sorry life. She needed something, *anything*, to prove to the more peace-minded members of her court that she was the one who could give them what they so desperately wanted.

'Yes.' The voice coming from her mouth was Old Thysandra's voice, somehow – that voice that had assured the Mother time and time again that she was happy, really perfectly happy, to serve the Crimson Court with every shred of her body and soul. A voice she hadn't realised she *hated* – but gods help her, what else could she do? 'That would be a reasonable condition, I'd say.'

It was. That was the worst of it.

Did that mean *she* was the unreasonable one between the six of them?

But it was only a betrayal if she failed to keep the peace … and she could still very well succeed. She'd have to keep the Alliance's condition a secret, of course. Telling the court that a single attack would ruin the whole agreement was almost an invitation for a few rebel fae to go ahead and do just that. But if she kept it quiet, if she simply didn't tell anyone outside this hall …

'Alright,' a male voice broke through her frenzied thoughts, and it took her a moment to realise that it wasn't Tared's. Delwin had opened his mouth for the first time, healthy leg and wooden leg crossed before him, an expression of wary resolve on his tanned face. 'If that's where we stand, let's talk numbers.'

It took a moment for that to land.

Even the other four representatives seemed caught by surprise for a moment of stunned silence.

'Already?' Nenkhet said sharply, scarred face contorted in a frown. 'Isn't that a little quick to—'

'Finite lifespans,' the consul of the White City interrupted with a laconic shrug. 'You can go on bickering for two more decades if you like, but I might be dead by the time you're done. Also, I have an island to repair.'

Thank every dead and living god in the world. Never in her life had Thysandra thought she'd be so grateful for anyone's mortality.

'I'm willing to talk numbers,' she said and prayed the tone of her voice did not betray the truth – that she was not *willing* but painfully, shamefully desperate. 'Are there any proposals you'd like to make?'

'I can only speak on behalf of the White City and the dozen or so human isles I've visited so far,' Delwin said, a mild meticulousness to his words. 'That said, I'm willing to suggest these same arrangements to the others. We are willing to sell you a quarter of the grain and other crops that were taken as tributes by the empire – you're only a third of the full empire, and I'm sure you can do with a little less feasting.'

Her lips twitched up despite her best attempts to keep them down. 'We can, thank you.'

'Current market prices in the north of the archipelago are about ten coppers for a bushel of wheat, I've been informed.' His small grimace suggested this had been the first time in his life he'd been forced to dive into the minutiae of grain prices. 'We can stick to that, as far as I'm concerned. The only additional price I'd ask is at least one year of help restoring the city and other isles that were damaged over the course of the war.'

And that was all?

Gold and copper coins might be a valuable commodity for the human market, but not for the fae isles, where every metal could be forged with a single blast of yellow magic and the economy ran on favours and bargains. He had to know she could afford an endless supply of his money. And city repairs ... blue magic, nothing else. Finding a dozen mages willing to take that upon themselves, in exchange for appropriate rewards, should be a relatively painless affair.

Which meant ...

They had their deal?

Golden sunlight was pouring in through the stained-glass windows, the court was waking up around her, and she had what she needed to survive the day. The others might follow. They might not, and it would still be fine. The human isles had always been the court's primary source of food; this would tide them over until spring, at the very least.

'We can do that,' she heard herself say, relief pounding in her ears. 'We can absolutely do that. If there are no further caveats, I believe we're—'

The hall abruptly darkened.

As if a raincloud had pulled across the sun ... but it wasn't a *cloud* that moved outside the windows, dull shapes shooting back and forth behind the coloured glass. A winged silhouette— Another silhouette, this one closer—

'Watch *out!*' Naxi shrieked.

The sunlight turned a blinding red.

And with a deafening crash, every single gallery window exploded in a razor-sharp shower of glass.

# CHAPTER 27

SHE DID NOT EVEN have time to cry out before the mob poured in.

Dozens of them. *Hundreds* of them. Many, many more than had ever left with Bereas in the first place, a sea of black and red as they swarmed into the gallery – eclipsing the light of day almost entirely with the sheer number of them. Magic crackled, and two statues flew apart beneath the eastern windows. More magic, and the flagstone floor cracked open, a fissure running all the way from left to right.

No.

*No.*

This could not be happening. This could *not—*

A statue burst into pieces, a flying marble hand missed her head by mere inches, and her body reacted before her mind had even begun to process the pandemonium around her. Drawing from her dress was a matter of instinct. Midnight blue – at least there was *some* red in it, and it went hurtling at the face of a fae female diving towards them, cutting a bone deep gash through her forehead.

A dozen others were already filling her place.

Flames roared. Yndrusillitha had jumped to her feet with a speed that belied her physical age, a reflex older than this lifetime's body; fire spilled from her hands in a blazing cascade and billowed between her and the attackers. Thysandra aimed her next burst of red at a fae trying to sneak around the burning shield. He spun to avoid the magic, then swivelled straight into the dome of fire instead – and for one spine-chilling moment, his howl of agony drowned out every other sound reverberating through the gallery.

Then he went down, wings still smouldering.

The smell of charred flesh came a moment later, putrid and nauseatingly sweet.

No time to gag. No time to breathe. On the other side of the hall, Naxi screamed '*Sashka!*,' and her mind went blank for a moment – just a moment, and then the brightest ray of red so far exploded from her fingertips, taking down three fae at once. She tried to draw more and found there wasn't a sliver of the colour left in her dress. Why the fuck had she decided to wear *blue*?

Because there shouldn't have been an attack today.

Because there *couldn't* have been an attack – because the whole damn meeting was a secret and Bereas shouldn't have even been able to come anywhere near the island – and gods help her, where was Naxi?

There were no more cries.

Through the swarming masses of fae, she could barely see the other side of the gallery.

'You know what?' Tared said, suddenly close behind her. His sword lay loosely in his grip; with his other hand, he was holding a bleeding Helenka on her feet. 'Let's delay the rest of the meeting to another day. Lovely to have had a word with you, though, Your Majesty.'

No. No, no, *no*—

'Great idea,' Delwin panted, limping towards the two of them with a grimace of pain. 'Not in an urgent hurry to lose another leg, I must say.'

Feet away from them, a handful of fae dropped from the air without warning. Was that Naxi's work, then? But their faces didn't show that telltale demon agony, and only then did Thysandra catch sight of

Nenkhet – standing beneath the swirling ring of phoenix fire with eyes as dark as ink, a trickle of blood seeping from her pale, clenched fist.

Blood magic.

She hadn't missed the sight of *that*.

'Right,' Tared grimly said, no longer nearly so casual as he all but pushed Helenka into Delwin's chest. 'Time to leave. Drusa—'

The phoenix fire abruptly sizzled out as Yndrusillitha yanked back her arms, grabbed a blank-faced Nenkhet by the shoulder, and began dragging her towards the other three. A howl of excitement went up among the fae circling above them, and then they were diving down, down, down—

Delwin's hand clamped onto Helenka's bicep.

Yndrusillitha's fingers closed around Delwin's wrist.

'Oh, and Thysandra?' Tared's brief smile was joyless as the grave. 'Better keep Naxi alive, if you ever want to see a single kernel of that grain.'

And just like that, the five of them were gone.

Dissolved into thin air like wisps of smoke … and armed fae were still pouring in through the windows.

She didn't even have *time* to think about that last thinly veiled threat – about grain, about peace, about her hopes and plans shattering like the flagstone tiles beneath her feet. Magic was raining down upon her. She had nowhere to take shelter, and what little red had been mixed into the blue of her dress was gone. And Naxi …

A bloodcurdling cry rose from the other side of the hall.

*Naxi.*

The world stopped turning.

Because it turned out her decisions were so very straightforward after all, instinctive enough to pass for reflexes – damn the trade and the politics, the secrets she hadn't been able to keep. None of them mattered right now. What mattered was the simple fact that Naxi was there, and she was here, and if she didn't move right *now*, they would both be dead within minutes.

Her wings had already swept out wide.

With no other options left, attack was her only defence.

She shot towards the vaulted ceiling with such speed the maze of statues blurred beneath her, streaks of red whooshing past her like crimson lightning. Something sharp slashed her shoulder. She did not slow down, and above her, a white-haired fae male got out of the way a fraction too late; she smacked into him with the force of a sledgehammer, feeling the air rush from his lungs in an audible *oof*.

Her dagger dug into his wing as she spun around at breakneck speed, using their combined momentum to fling him sideways through the air. He slammed into a unit of other fae hurtling towards her, sending their attack scattering.

Temporary relief. A dozen others were already rushing closer on her right.

She dove to avoid their magic, eyes feverishly scanning the ground below. Cracked limestone and shattered marble. The occasional fae corpse sprawled across the rubble. Endless stretches of white and grey and crimson-stained stone, and ...

*There.*

A single fleck of pale eggshell blue.

In the northern corner off the hall, surrounded by a sea of broken glass, Naxi cowered between a pedestal and a knocked-down marble wing. A handful of dead fae lay strewn across the floor around her. None of them had been able to reach her, then ...

But a pool of blood was spreading around her bare feet.

Thysandra was already diving.

A sculpture of a sword-bearing fae queen blew to pieces beneath her, and lumps of marble hit her on the chest, the hip. She barely felt the pain. Down and farther down, a descent so swift she was practically plummeting – wings sweeping out in the fraction of a moment before she crashed like a comet into the floor, braking just enough not to break her legs. Her foot caught on a piece of debris all the same as she landed, and her ankle twisted sharply as the rest of her weight slammed down upon it.

Her muffled curse coincided with Naxi's 'Sashka!'

The piercing pain in her ankle vanished the next moment.

344

'Don't you *dare*,' she ground out, ducking as a flare of red shot by her face, then turning to face Naxi in her blood-smeared hiding place. The demon's skin was even paler than usual – the wrong sort of pale, greyish rather than blushing pink. 'You've got enough pain of your own to take mine, too. Where are you bleeding?'

The throb in her ankle did not return as Naxi choked out, 'Soles. Glass.'

Fuck.

'Alright.' That was a lie. Already their attackers were descending again. 'Give me your feet. At least I've got plenty of blue in this useless thing.'

Naxi let out a little sob as she stretched out one slender leg. 'You do look very nice in it.'

'That's *something*,' Thysandra rasped, cursing again as she caught her first glimpse of Naxi's wounds. At least a dozen small shards of glass were lodged in her calloused skin, some of them embedded so deeply she could only deduce their existence by the cuts they'd caused. 'Please go torture some fae to feel better. This is going to hurt.'

Eyes squeezed shut, Naxi obliged. Above their heads, one or two individuals who'd strayed too close began screaming; the rest hurriedly swept back, allowing the sunlight in again.

Thysandra gritted her teeth, dipped her left hand into the pool of blood, and drew out the red she needed to evaporate the glass shards. Just enough for the wounds. Too much for the *healthy* parts of Naxi's foot, though: where the glass hadn't been to absorb the magic, the red had torn open skin and calFuses, blood pouring free from a dozen new places now. Untidy work, and if she'd had time, she could have done better – but in this case, by the time she'd have taken out even half these shards, they'd both be dead.

She pressed her left hand against her dress. *Blue for healing*. Another swift sparkle of magic, and all wounds were gone.

One foot to go.

An arrow whizzed past her, piercing the floor behind her. Fuck. They'd finally realised they couldn't get her within magic's reach with Naxi covering her back – and so they'd taken up the more primitive weapons. If whoever was wielding that bow had even the least amount of skill—

A second arrow buried itself into the rubble by her feet.

'Fuck,' she managed, out loud now, as she shoved Naxi farther behind the pedestal and half-crawled after her. 'Alright. Give me your other foot. Keep them away from us.'

Naxi nodded, quiet tears pouring down her face as she squeezed her eyes shut again. Two more arrows whistled overhead while Thysandra repeated her healing routine with shaking hands, working even faster this time. A few fae tried their luck and flew towards them. Every single one of them ended up plummeting screaming to the ground.

Still ...

There were at least a hundred of them left, and as soon as they pulled off a single coordinated attack, she and Naxi would be done for.

'Fuck,' Thysandra said out loud again, crouching behind the dented pedestal.

Naxi sniffled in agreement.

Only now, with half a second to take a breath, did the pain of her own wounds catch up – the dozens of small cuts and bruises left by flying magic and marble. Her ankle had started throbbing again with Naxi's magic focused on the circling fae. Her head was spinning. Poison after-effects or loss of blood, she wasn't quite sure.

Either way ...

Either way, she was in deep fucking trouble.

More arrows were hitting against the floor around her, iron tips dragging flurries of sparks from the flagstone tiles. Useless warnings as long as they had cover, but as soon as she tried to move, there would be another volley waiting for her. So was there any way they could get out of here alive? Maybe if she broke a hole in the wall and made a run for it, although they would probably come after her, and carrying Naxi would slow her down. And even if she found shelter or a handful of allies willing to help her out—

Then what?

Her plan had leaked.

It had leaked *again*.

WITH WING AND CLAW

How was it even possible? She hadn't told anyone. She had covered up her absence. She had done everything right, and *still* it had all gone wrong – and now the Alliance thought her a liar, her court thought her a failure, and neither of them were wrong.

So what options did she have left?

Voices were yelling behind her, fae lining up for attack in the corners of her sight. Naxi was shaking her arm, saying something. She barely even heard any of it. Her limbs were so very heavy all of a sudden – her thoughts, too ... Perhaps she should just go hide in the deepest hole she could find and leave the whole fucking place to the wolves. Perhaps that had always been the best she could do, and—

A horn sounded, suddenly close.

'The army!' someone shrieked above her, the words punching through to her moments after. 'It's the army! Run!'

Nicanor?

Oh gods – had he found some people willing to come and save her?

She should have been relieved, yet even relief felt like too much of an effort as the sky outside lit up in fiery shades of red again. Stay of execution, if anything. Even Nicanor couldn't save her forever. The sounds of battle above her were a blur, feeling miles away – swords and dull thuds and a voice ...

A voice.

A far too familiar voice, yelling at people to get out, *get out.*

Bereas.

And at once, nothing was heavy anymore. At once, she was no longer out of options. Decisions made themselves in the infinitesimal moment between one eyeblink and the next – because he was *here*, the bastard who'd almost killed her three times over, and if she could do nothing else, at least she was going to get some gods-damned answers.

Her ankle screamed in protest as she jumped to her feet and staggered away from the pedestal. Naxi was crying out her name behind her – she ignored that as well.

Fae were hurtling out through the broken windows. And there, in the rearguard ... a flash of blood-red wings.

She launched herself into the air.

Bereas noticed her in the same moment, and gods help her, she could *feel* the grin growing on his face a hundred feet away – that same blinding-white smugness with which he'd intercepted her near her rooms weeks ago. *Enjoy that title as long as you manage to keep it, love ...*

'Thysandra!' he hollered, six feet of brawny arrogance as he swivelled around in midair.

He was baiting her. She knew damn well that he *would* be faster, with his prize-winning wings and his bulging shoulders – that when he ran, he'd do it well, and she would not see him again until the next time he came for her head. It didn't stop her from soaring towards him even faster. Around him, more and more fae slipped out of the hall and into the open air outside; fury thumped in every vein of her body, blinding her to their names, their faces.

In the distance, Nicanor's voice was shouting commands.

'How's life, Thysandra?' Bereas yelled, clearly enjoying the chase as he darted away from the reckless burst of power she drew from the black of her own wings. Hardly anyone else was left in the hall, now. 'Been busy kissing the Alliance's feet, I hear?'

She flung another crackle of red at him. He somersaulted over it, laughing out loud as he swept out of reach again.

'*Sashka!*' Naxi was crying, far down below. 'Sashka, let it *go!*'

She couldn't let him go.

Fuck him and his sleazy, cocky face. Fuck him and his warmongering hate. He was going to pay for every drop of blood he'd shed, for every sleepless night he'd caused her, and if she had to fly herself to shreds for it ... what the hell did she have left to lose?

Her wings slapped against the air so hard it hurt.

Somehow the bastard was *still* faster.

'Not giving up yet?' he sneered, circling tauntingly towards her and back away from her even as she flew fast enough to turn her stomach inside out. 'You'll have to give up on this pathetic show, *Sashka*. Your demon pet is calling.'

The burst of red exploded from her fingertips with twice the intended force.

She missed him by mere inches – hitting only the empty air behind him, underestimating his speed again as he pivoted without slowing down. The ray of destruction hit a pair of statues beneath them instead. Stone limbs, crowns, and sceptres burst in all directions at once, and Bereas laughed out loud, whirling around her one last time.

'Think I'll be going, love.' He blew her a kiss as he finally turned away from her, accelerating towards the broken windows. 'Say hello to the Alliance from me!'

He was still laughing as he flew.

There was no thought as she drew her magic one last time. Just rage.

It wasn't red, the colour shooting from her fingertips. It wasn't aimed at him, either. Because she still had her dress, which had paled to the sickly blue of sea algae ... and it was *that* hue she threw ahead of her with every magical fibre in her body, at the windows his friends had smashed to pieces when they entered.

*Blue for healing.*

The glass grew back into place inches before Bereas's face. Too late for him to change course. Too late for him to slow down. A last shriek was all that escaped him before he smacked into the window at his full, dizzying speed – headfirst, with a bang that reverberated all the way through the stone walls themselves.

For a moment he seemed to stick to the glass, as if his body had melted into the small leaded panes.

Then he started sliding.

His wings didn't so much as twitch on the endless way down. He thudded to the ground like a discarded bag of flour, sprawled out between the remainders of the statue Thysandra had blown to pieces a moment before – a crumbled crown beside his head, like a wry, mocking joke.

The hall was achingly quiet, suddenly. Outside, the battle seemed to have moved ahead with surprising swiftness.

She cautiously descended. Only when she'd landed and approached within a few feet did she see he was still breathing.

Her fingers curled around the hilt of her dagger. 'Bereas?'

He didn't move.

Fuck. Perhaps she'd been a little *too* successful in stopping him. Breath still gurgled through his throat, but the far side of his face was *crumpled* – as if his entire skull had folded in at the impact. Blood was trickling from his nose. From one pointed ear, too. One hazy brown eye blinked open as she tiptoed towards him, and there was no recognition in it.

'Bereas?' she repeated, louder now.

The hall was so dreadfully silent around them. There he lay, the male who might have brought her court to its knees with his reckless, violent pride ... bruised and broken, and heartbeats away from death.

Something curled around his lips. A sneer, even now.

'I can still heal you,' she heard herself say. A lie, quite possibly – but then, what had he ever done to deserve the truth from her? 'I'll heal you, if you tell me how you knew to attack this gallery.'

He blinked.

A spark of consciousness flared in his gaze.

'How ...' His lips moved almost without sound, nothing but a raspy whisper slipping out. 'How I knew ...'

'The *attack*, Bereas.' She fell to her knees beside him, as if she could glare the memory back into his battered mind. She had to know. She *had* to know. Nothing she'd done wrong, and yet ... 'Who told you?'

He blinked at her again, and then ...

Then he *laughed*.

'Oh.' Grating chuckles bubbled up from his throat, blood frothing out with them. His chest shook with the physical effort. 'So .... sorry to tell you, Thys. You're ...' Another wheezing inhale. 'You're fucking the wrong person, love.'

She stiffened. 'What?'

His breath grew more strained.

'Wait— Bereas, *wait*.' Trembling fingers. Bloodied skin. Blue, so much blue in her dress – but where should she even start? 'What do you mean—'

He blew out one last ragged exhalation under her hands.

And then he no longer moved.

*You're fucking the wrong person.*

She sat on the cracked flagstone, bleeding from wounds she no longer even felt, and stared with unseeing eyes at the ravaged hall around her. Shattered faces. Splintered limbs. Broken marble as far as the eye could see, the pedestals cratered, the names on them illegible. Millennia of fae rulers, fallen without so much as a fight – oh, she truly fit in well with them, didn't she?

An embarrassment. A liar.

A traitor, and hell, everyone knew it now.

*You're fucking the wrong person.*

They shouldn't have known to attack the gallery. They shouldn't have known she'd be making a last, desperate attempt to do better here. She'd told no one, she'd believed two minutes ago … and only now did she realise that was not true. That she'd merely wanted it to be true. That she'd wanted it so much, really, that she hadn't even allowed herself to see the crystal-clear facts before her.

That one person had known exactly where she'd be, and why.

That one person had known *everything* for weeks.

Four of them, she'd told herself again and again. Gadyon. Nicanor. Inga. Silas. One of them must have betrayed her secrets to the world, and only now did she realise she had entirely, completely overlooked the fact that there had been a fifth suspect on the list all along—

'Sashka?'

No.

Please, gods, no.

'*Sashka.*' Quiet footsteps, inching closer, and she did not dare to lift her head as that soft, soothing, spellbinding voice drew closer. 'What did he say? What is the matter? Why are you feeling so … so …'

Shocked.

Suspicious.

Furious.

All of them rational options, and all of them would have been so, so much more bearable than the truth—

*Heartbroken.*

Oh, she had been such a fucking fool.

'You,' she breathed, gaze immovable. 'You told them?'

The footsteps abruptly halted.

So very silent, this cursed, dead place – a silence in which she could *hear* her heart slowly, achingly crumbling to pieces in her chest. It made so much sense. It made *so* much sense, now that she was finally adding up the plain, ugly facts – the words that had been spoken straight to her face weeks ago ...

'What?' Naxi said.

At once her voice was no longer so sweet.

Looking up was the last thing Thysandra should have done, and she did it anyway, out of some twisted, self-flagellating desire to *see* the betrayal with her own eyes. Blue eyes. Pale cheeks. Small, dainty feet wrapped in strips of pale blue fabric. Sweet, so temptingly, lusciously sweet ...

Like poison.

Her wine had been sweet, too.

'You told them. While I was sleeping.' It wasn't even an accusation – rather, a conclusion. 'You were the one who stole Gadyon's notes and spread them. All those times you said you were gone to visit the Labyrinth, you ... you ...'

'Sashka, what are you *talking* about?' Too shrill. 'Why would I—'

'Because you wanted us to leave,' Thysandra said hollowly.

Blank blue eyes gaped back at her, and this time, no objection came.

'You wanted me to get out of here. The very first thing you told me in the bone hall, for hell's sake – that you were only biding your time at the court until I decided to come with you.' A joyless laugh burned like acid on her lips. 'But you didn't want me to resent you either. You didn't want to force me to run off before I could be well and truly sure that my time here was an irreparable failure – so you *made* it a failure, didn't you?'

So utterly brilliant. So utterly ruthless. The sort of scheme only a creature with no empathy at all would be able to come up with.

And shouldn't she have known from the start? Wasn't this how every interaction between them had developed? At the Last Battle, Naxi had toyed with her feelings to win the fight and save her own life. In the Alliance's cell, Naxi had toyed with her feelings to make her talk and win the war. So how, *how* had she somehow allowed herself to believe it was true this time, that all too perfect idyll the demon had so skilfully crafted between them?

Toyed with her feelings. Won her trust. Sold her out.

As always.

Like *everyone*.

'That's ridiculous,' Naxi said.

A scoff fell from Thysandra's lips. 'And that's the best you've got? When I'm only repeating the things you told me yourself? When—'

'I've been helping you! Why would I help you if—'

'—if it didn't gain you anything?' she cut in, voice growing louder. 'Exactly! You're a bloody demon! You're the last person in the world who'd be helping anyone just for the warm, fuzzy feelings! Of course you weren't going to sit around and just wait for me to maybe change my mind – of *course* you would be working for yourself first and fore-most!'

She'd thought Naxi's cheeks pale before. They'd gone almost translucent now, a waxy deathlike pallor. 'Sashka ...'

'And don't *Sashka* me!'

'I made a bargain.' It was almost a plea as Naxi staggered forward on her bound feet, arm held before her, wrist turned out. The mark gleamed pink and innocent in the morning light. 'You do remember our bargain, don't you? I couldn't betray you even if I *wanted* to, Sashka. You can't just—'

'You never bargained to not betray me,' Thysandra said hoarsely, barely feeling her own lips move. 'Just not to willingly harm me. And aren't you the one who told me it would be for my own benefit to get out of here?'

The silence was all the answer she needed.

It was as good as a confession, that silence.

Naxi was trembling. Trembling so violently that the pink tips of her curls shook around her slim shoulders, bottom lip quivering, blue eyes filling up – genuine distress, the panic of a thief caught red-handed with nowhere left to run, and it was shameful how even now that fragile-looking misery made Thysandra's arms itch to reach out for her. To apologise, to beg for forgiveness, to kiss those pink rosebud lips until they were smiling again ...

Like every fucking time she'd thrown herself to the floor before that bone of thrones, grovelling over any imagined slight and mistake.

Like every fucking time she'd been so numbly desperate for even the most pathetic excuse for love that she'd happily betrayed her own heart to get it.

'Make another bargain, then,' she breathed. 'For the truth. Then tell me it wasn't you who did this.'

Naxi stiffened.

A moment of stalemate between the dismembered, beheaded statues, the rubble of centuries upon centuries of history ... and then the demon stepped back.

Dropped her arm to her side.

And said, brittle voice choked, 'No.'

There it was.

Thysandra should have expected it, and still – *still* – her traitorous heart had the gall to feel disappointment at the confirmation. 'So you admit it?'

'I don't admit any fucking thing!' Another step back. Tears were welling in those blue eyes again, spilling over now. 'I'm telling you I didn't betray you. I've never spoken a word with gods-damned Bereas in my life. But if you can't trust me on that—'

'How am I supposed to trust you on that!' Thysandra burst out, swinging an unrestrained hand at Bereas's bleeding corpse. 'Do you know what he *said*? Do you know—'

'I don't give a damn what he said! And neither should you!' She'd never heard Naxi's voice break this way before, raw and thin and utterly wretched. 'I have given you every fucking reason to trust me, Thysandra, and he has given you absolutely none – I've supported you and protected you and comforted you, and I'm utterly *sick* of having to defend myself over and over again just because you can't comprehend that I might be speaking the truth, do you understand?'

Bullshit.

Sly, manipulative *bullshit*.

'Oh, so now I'm the one to blame?' she snapped back, struggling to her feet. Pain only made her anger flare higher, hotter, burning like fire in her veins. 'Now *I'm* the one who's too distrustful? Every other creature in the world is rightfully frightened of you, no one's even given you the *option* to defend yourself – but *I* must have it all wrong even if I've put more faith in you than anyone else ever has?'

Naxi's face had gone ashen.

'Tell me I'm missing something.' Thysandra's voice grew louder. 'You gave the Alliance every reason to trust you, too, didn't you? You stuck to their rules. You won them their war. And still they're wary around you – are they all wrong, then?'

'Don't you dare.' Those pink lips twitched up into a feral, sharp-toothed snarl. 'Don't you *dare* tell me—'

'You gave your family every reason to trust you, didn't you?' Thysandra spat.

Naxi went still.

Still like the statues on either side of her ... and something broke in that silence. Fractured like the heads, the hands, the wings that lay scattered between the pedestals.

'So tell me to believe you all you want.' It didn't feel good, allowing the words to spill from her lips. It felt like driving home a stake already wedged between those frail demon ribs. 'But you ran from the ones who relied on you before, and you've *told* me over and over that you wanted to do it again – to hell with the humans, to hell with the court. So if I know damn well that you don't care about hearth and home or any sort of family at all, then—'

'Shut up.' Naxi's hands twitched like claws by her side. 'Shut. *Up*.'

'But am I wrong? Am I—'

'I said *shut up*, Thysandra!' A shrill sob wormed its way out with the words. 'You have no damn clue what you're talking about! And you ... you ...'

She faltered.

Panting, heaving silence.

'And I?' Thysandra bit out, every muscle and tendon tightening.

'You have no right to talk about family.' Naxi spat out a bitter, burning laugh, staggering backwards. 'You wouldn't recognise family if you fell into their gods-damned arms. You'd be so busy distrusting them all that you'd rather lose them and feel safe again than put even the tiniest, saddest little bit of faith into *anyone* – wouldn't you?'

Hounds roared in the back of her mind.

Skin tore. Bone snapped. *Thysandra!* he had shouted, stumbling up the slope to reach her, dripping teeth dragging him down. *Thysandra,* again and again and again—

And she'd lost him.

Distrusted him and lost him – but hell, at least she had *survived*.

'Prove it to me, then.' She was pleading now, and she didn't even care; her legs were buckling, and she didn't care about that, either. 'Please. Make that stupid bargain. Prove me wrong. I *want* to trust you, I swear, but—'

'Oh, you don't,' Naxi said, voice quiet.

'I do! I really do!' Her knees thudded back to the floor. Her ankle twisted again, and then all of a sudden she was crying – pathetic hollow sobs wrenching out of her and reverberating through the empty hall. It felt like reaching for that non-existent memory again. Like grasping for something that should be so, *so* close, and simply ... wasn't. 'I'm *begging* you to let me trust you, don't you see? I just need—'

'That's not trust, Sashka.' Barely a whisper. 'Trust is scary. You're looking for the opposite of it.'

Survival.

Was she to blame for wanting to *survive*, now?

'Please,' she blubbered. 'Please, I—'

'I didn't betray you.' Flat. Apathetic. As if it could be that easy – a pair of teary blue eyes and absolutely nothing else. 'I don't know who did, I don't know how they did it, but it wasn't me. So are you going to believe that?'

She wanted to.

She really, *really* wanted to.

She knew what would happen if she asked again.

But the gallery lay in shambles. Her old allies might never respect her again, and her new ones had been driven away before they could even start respecting her. If she somehow survived this blow, she could never, *never* afford another defeat again, and Bereas's sneer was still there ...

*You're fucking the wrong person, love.*

How could she not wonder?

How could she not fear?

How could she ever sleep soundly at night with that irresistible threat of treason beside her?

'Please,' she choked out. 'Please just—'

Naxi turned around.

'Please. *Please!*' Not again. Not so *easily*, more than anything. She couldn't bear it, another heart shutting hers out without a wince – as if she'd never been worth the regard in the first place. She'd known of a demon's lack of ability to love. She thought she had prepared for it, and yet *nothing* could have prepared her for the sight of that slender back moving away from her now without a single stumbling step. 'Naxi, please!'

Not the slightest falter.

*Don't be so demanding, Thysandra*, the Mother had said, smile cold and scathing. *The arrogance, to think your tears are the first of my worries ...*

She had to stop crying.

She had to be strong.

So many ways to fail, and she no longer even had the strength left to get back to her feet, to pull herself together, to fight.

'*Naxi!*' It was pathetic, her voice – the desperate cry of a drowning creature fighting for air. It was all she could do. 'Naxi, please just talk to me! You *have* to talk to me! You said— You bargained not to harm me, and you're ... you're ...'

*You're harming me.*

She did not manage to speak the words as sickening suspicion rose.

The world was a blur. The floor swayed beneath her knees. But the inside of her arm was crystal clear when she opened her eyes and forced herself to look down, a vision painted in razor-sharp colours – dark skin, blood-streaked palm, and only a single, purple bargain mark lodged inside the hollow of her wrist.

No more pink.

*If you decide to leave the Crimson Court for whatever reason ...*

The bargain had been voided.

She folded over on the cold, hard floor, clutched her arm against her chest, and bawled like a lost, abandoned child.

# CHAPTER 28

DEMONS DIDN'T CRY.

Then again, Naxi had never been that good at being a demon, and her tears didn't give a damn whose eyes they were pouring from – just that they wouldn't, *couldn't* stop. The gallery was a maze of broken shapes around her. Shards of glass crunched beneath her linen-wrapped feet. The tidal wave of Thysandra's emotions was trying to drag her under with every step, and by the time she reached the door on the far side of the hall, she felt like she was struggling through knee-deep mud just to keep going – and yet she walked.

The alternative was running back.

The alternative was making that gods-damned bargain and resigning herself to being, once again, the monster lurking beneath everyone's bed.

Which she shouldn't care about! Being frightening was nothing new! And yet the tears kept coming and coming and coming as she slammed the door behind her, tore the linen off her feet, and staggered on through the deserted academy halls – because she *always* had to be the frightening one, whether she wanted to or not, and Thysandra ...

Thysandra should have been different.

For Thysandra, she had tried so very hard to be *safe*.

And still it was not enough. Still it ended with the same tired old story. She shouldn't care, she shouldn't care, she shouldn't *care*, yet demon heart or no, it hurt like hell. *You ran from the ones who relied on you before*, and the worst thing of all was that it was true – she had taken her revenge for the destruction of Mirova, lived with the shame and the regret for three hundred years, and still it was entirely, undeniably true.

Had she wanted to leave the humans to their own devices?

If she hadn't, why in the world had she said she did?

Didn't matter. None of it mattered. She was a demon, and she could run and never look back the way all demons did. All she had to do was find anyone with a ship, scare them into offering her passage to the Golden Court, then find an alf to return her to her friends – not a nice way of going about it, perhaps, but who cared about nice?

She was a demon. *She* sure as hell didn't.

If the world insisted on treating her like some child-eating, heart-breaking menace, she might as well lean into it.

Down the stairs. Through the gardens whispering at her to come and have a seat in them. It was unnerving how easily she found her way around the cursed place already, a maze of corridors and rooms that had etched itself into her unwelcoming brain – past the heavily perfumed gateway that led to the bathhouses, then down again, closer and closer to the main gate of the castle.

Out. Finally.

The relief of freedom did not come.

Why, for hell's sake? She *hated* this place. She'd wanted to leave from the moment she arrived, and at the very least that was finally happening – so why did it feel as though she was losing something with every step closer to her goal? There was little the Crimson Court had that she couldn't find elsewhere, except perhaps—

The Labyrinth.

*And Thysandra*, a vicious little voice whispered in the back of her mind. She wiped that thought away. She was a demon, after all. She did not stick around for what no longer served her. She was selfish and she did not care, and since Thysandra had hurt her by—

By accusing her of not caring?

Didn't matter, damn it! She was leaving the island, and she no longer wanted to think about Thysandra, because thinking about Thysandra hurt more than it had any right to. The Labyrinth, though ...

The Labyrinth hadn't done anything wrong.

And she didn't want the mountain to be angry with her if she never returned without any sort of goodbye.

She changed course mid-step, trotting in the direction of the bone hall at the heart of the castle. New plan, then. Leave the castle through the Labyrinth. Say goodbye to the trees of Faewood, too, while she was at it. Then make the walk around the mountain to the north coast, where the houses and the ships were waiting – a long walk, admittedly, but she had all day, and what else would she be doing with her time anyway?

She no longer had anyone to protect. There would be no more stealing lunch from the kitchens because Thysandra would forget to eat without her. No more sitting through meetings and making faces when no one but Thysandra was looking at her. No more of that unwilling smile, the amusement she could *feel* rather than see, and—

No.

The breathless sobs bubbling from her throat, the sticky tears misting her view ... they had gotten it all wrong. She did *not* care.

Bone hall. Labyrinth. Faewood. As long as she kept thinking very, very hard of her plan, she did not need to think of anything else.

The demolished heart of the Mother's reign was empty as always, although she could feel traces of a large group of people not too far away – shreds of triumph and joy emanating from their distant presence. Stupid Nicanor with his stupid army, probably. Would Thysandra be lying in his bed soon? Not that she cared, of course. If Thysandra wanted to waste that perfectly shapely body of hers on mediocre lovers, then—

No. *No.* Not the time to think about anyone's body – Thysandra's least of all.

She descended into the Labyrinth, still sobbing.

The mountains balmy concern was like a soft blanket around her shoulders, and even *that* couldn't stop her tears from flowing, as if some tap had broken inside her that could not be shut off again. She'd been here with Thysandra. Thysandra had told her she *needed* her in these same bejewelled tunnels. Thysandra had told her she wasn't scared, that she understood the demon mind, and even if that had turned out to be all wrong, even if it turned out she *would* in fact never trust Naxi no matter how trustworthy she was ...

It was still too happy, that memory.

Which was stupid. Demons did not do happy memories.

She staggered onwards over the warm stone floor, blubbering apologies at the silent walls of the Labyrinth. At least the mountain wasn't scared of her. At least she could pretend for another few minutes that she would never need to return to the world outside, where even the most genuine of smiles would always come with that little sting of reserve, where no one, *no one*—

Why hadn't she just made the stupid bargain?

Would it really be that bad to live the rest of her life under the constant weight of suspicion, to have to defend herself over and over again? To be reminded time and time again of who she was, *what* she was, and that there would be no way for her to ever escape the very nature of her own callous heart?

She no longer even knew.

She just ran.

Lingering was dangerous. Lingering might lead to pausing, and pausing might lead to giving in and running right back to where she'd come from – and so she kept moving and moving and moving, all the way to the Faewood gate of the Labyrinth. It felt like half a century had gone by since she'd stepped out of Thysandra's rooms that morning, and yet the light that welcomed her outside was still the pale sunlight from the east. The dew hadn't even dried on the leaves and petals yet.

She spoke her last teary goodbyes to the Labyrinth, then stumbled on through the tangles of Faewood. Yesterday's hunt had left its traces. Marred tree trunks, arrows sticking into roots and branches. Splatches of blood. The occasional tuft of animal hair left behind in thorns and brambles, and—

Voices.

*Familiar* voices.

Naxi did, of course, not care.

She did not give a rat's arse about the Crimson Court. She never had and never would. And Thysandra had accused her, insulted her, and deliberately flung the memory of her family's death into her face, which reasonably had to mean she did not care about Thysandra, either ... so she had no reason, no reason at *all*, to wonder why in the world Silas and Inga would be standing in the heart of Faewood.

Or what they were arguing about.

Or why they would be feeling worried and furious and ... nauseous? As unexpected as that may be, it wasn't her problem in the slightest. She did not care she did not care she did not—

She changed course.

The voices grew louder.

'... can't just stand aside and *wait!*' That was Inga, more vehement than Naxi had ever heard her before – no longer hindered, somehow, by the persistent wariness that usually lay over her every word and movement. 'At least it's still recent now. If we give it too much time ...'

Silas's answer was harder to make out, his voice lower and quieter.

'Well, there's only two of them left, isn't there?' Inga again. There was a pinch of *grief* mixed into the blend of her emotion, Naxi realised as she approached, and even if she still did not care, that was intriguing enough to keep her tiptoeing forward. 'And if we tell Thysandra, I'm sure she'll agree to—'

The girl stopped talking abruptly.

A surge of alarm peaked in the silence.

It was only then that Naxi remembered that a bright blue dress was not the most inconspicuous attire to sneak around forests in.

Two hasty steps back was all she managed. Then Thysandra's uncle lunged out from the foliage with much, much more speed than a male of his size had any right to – a slap of golden wings, a shimmer of gemstones in the morning light, and a solid, calloused hand fisted in the front of Naxi's dress, all but lifting her off her feet. Silas towered over her in a way that made her feel annoyingly like cowering. Most people towered over her, admittedly, but this male added a whole new dimension to the experience – a height and breadth to him that even most fae could only dream of matching.

His eyes were narrowed in fury.

Then narrowed even more in what was, visibly and tangibly, confusion.

Belatedly, Naxi realised she was no longer crying, but that her cheeks still felt raw and sticky, and her eyes ached with every blink. She wasn't sure just *how* pathetic she looked. The cautious ebbing of the Bargainer's alarm suggested the situation was dire, though.

She sniffled, because her nose was still a little runny, and squeaked, 'Hello, Silas.'

'Anaxia?' His frown deepened impossibly further. 'What are you doing here, exactly?'

'Saying goodbye to the trees,' she sputtered, considering whether she should be so merciful as to threaten him first or start draining his joy of life immediately. The first, probably. Thysandra would need him around the court. 'Let go of my dress, or I—'

'Goodbye?' he interrupted sharply.

Oh.

Perhaps he hadn't needed to know that.

'I ... I'm leaving.' The tears began trickling down again. 'I ... I ...'

He blinked, lowering her a few inches. 'Where the hell is Thysandra?'

'The statue gallery,' Naxi whimpered, unable to speak the words without hearing those pleas again, echoing through the ravaged hall behind her. 'There was an attack, and ... and ...'

'Were you away from her side at all, yesterday?' Silas cut in, fingers tightening around the bunched-up front of her dress. 'She spent the day in her rooms, yes? Did you leave those rooms at any point?'

She gaped at him. 'What?'

'Please.' As tightly controlled as his expression might be, the straining pressure within him was what Naxi imagined a volcano might feel in the moments before eruption. It was a testament to either his self-restraint or his fear of her that he wasn't yet physically shaking her. 'Just answer the bloody question: did you leave her rooms? Did you visit the Labyrinth?'

'No!' She was so bewildered she forgot to cry again. 'No, I told the Labyrinth I couldn't be there with the hunt going on – you can go ask it, if you like! It was very grumpy, so I'm sure it remembers all the details! I was with Thysandra all day until she got poisoned, and then again after—'

Silas let go of her dress so suddenly she almost toppled over.

'Why? What's going on?' She inched backwards, trying to peer around his looming posture and the near-endless span of his wings. 'Did anything happen during the hunt yesterday?'

Without an answer, Silas glanced over his shoulder.

Something went unexpectedly softer inside him with that movement. Or not softer but rather *mellower*, like that clenching, almost desperate anticipation of thaw after a long frost – a feeling of—

Oh, for fuck's sake.

Naxi barely kept down another miserable whimper. It would be unreasonably petty, wouldn't it, to torture a man to death just because he had the audacity to start falling in love right before her heartbroken eyes?

'Yes,' Inga said from behind that endless expanse of wing and muscle, voice a little choked. 'Let's show her.'

Show her *what*?

Never mind about the torment, then.

'Alright,' Silas said, voice grim as he turned away. 'Over here. Apologies for the distrust – we've been trying to figure out your movements for a while now.'

'What?' Her voice jumped. 'Me?'

'Don't take it personally,' Inga said brusquely, waiting for them on the other side of the clearing. Her eyes were red, her fingers and hair covered in mud. 'But I didn't tell anyone about the plans to move the humans, and I knew Silas couldn't be the leak because he wasn't at the court yet – so we figured it had to be Gadyon or Nicanor or you. We've been making visits, these last few days. Tried to get useful information out of everyone.'

Oh.

They'd been sitting in Nicanor's living room, the two of them, when Thysandra had walked in with the Alliance's demands – even Inga making unusual attempts to appear amicable in the Lord Protector's company. They'd been on their way to visit the archives together, too, when they'd found Gadyon's confession last night.

'But then there's no more need to be suspicious of me, is there?' she stuttered, trying to keep up with Silas's longer strides. *No reason except the gallery attack* – but they didn't know that much, and she had no reason to wince at the thought. She did *not* care. 'We know it was Gadyon who leaked the information.'

'Do we?' Inga said bitterly.

Silas didn't speak. Just held aside a curtain of vines for Naxi – not realising, apparently, that she could easily have willed them out of the way herself.

'He wrote that it was him,' Naxi said sheepishly, following as Inga turned and gestured at her to come along.

'Yes.' The girl's voice was back at its usual level of brewing fury. 'But that never made sense to me. He may appear messy, but his paperwork is always where it needs to be. And *if* he mislaid his notes ...' She sucked in a sharp breath as they passed between the next row of trees. 'He wouldn't have fled and never shown his face again. He would have dealt with the consequences.'

'So we've been searching all night,' Silas softly said behind them. 'And then half an hour ago, we found this.'

Inga stood still with a strangled sound – almost a gag.

Before them, half-buried in the soil ...

It was unrecognisable, the half-eaten corpse. Wings gone. Face gone. Nothing but bones left of the whole lower body. But around where the leg must have been, someone had meticulously brushed aside the mud and the leaves.

And there, pale and bloody, lay the twisted, misshapen skeleton of a foot.

# CHAPTER 29

'THYSANDRA?'

She didn't want to return to wakefulness.

It hurt too much, the world outside the safe, dark cocoon of her own scarred wings. Here, curled up within herself, she was invisible. Protected. A small, hidden creature that might as well not exist, that no one could reach, that no one could harm.

Outside was the blood.

Outside was the betrayal.

Outside was the game she'd played all her life, the game she no longer *wanted* to play and yet could never, *never* step away from again – the game she'd forgotten for one stupid, sentimental illusion of love, and look what had come of it?

She'd shattered with the dozens of rulers in whose company she found herself.

'Thys? Thys, can you hear me?'

A moan slipped over her lips.

'Oh, thank the gods— I'm so sorry, Thys, but I'm going to need you to wake up, alright?' The stinging pain in her shoulder dulled. She hadn't noticed it until it vanished. 'Wait, let me patch you up a little ...'

This time, eyes half-opened, she did catch the flash of blue. Her ankle abruptly felt like an ankle again, rather than a throbbing, swollen weight attached to her equally sore legs.

'There.' More blue. More relief. She couldn't even tell what parts of her body stopped hurting, just that the haze of agony cleared slightly with every burst of colour. 'Does that help?'

Yes.

No.

Without the physical pain, nothing was left to distract her from the vast and desolate void that had opened within her chest – the feelings she did not want to feel, because she might never emerge from them again.

She'd *believed* it. For one night of blissful insanity, she had really, truly believed the Mother may have been wrong, the court may have been wrong, the rules she'd bled to instil in her bones had been lies from the very start. That something like loyalty may just have existed for her after all. Sacrifice. Love, even.

And now she was back at the bottom of that pit.

That was the problem with taking off your armour. The blades of life cut so much deeper.

'Thysandra, listen to me.' Still no one touched her. 'I need you to sit up and talk to me. We might be in danger.'

*Danger* was a word she knew in every fibre of her body. Even now, it hardened something she hadn't even known was still there inside her; her muscles moved themselves.

Wings down. Head up. Spine straight.

Nicanor knelt before her.

'That's more like it.' His smile was strained with worry. 'Glad you're back, Thys. We need to have a word.'

Why was he even still here?

368

She'd lost. He had to know she'd lost. If he had any sense in that cunning fae mind of his, he'd already be miles away from the court – so what in the world was he doing here, tending to her wounds, *worrying*?

'What happened?' she managed to croak, reeling where she sat.

'That's what I wanted to ask you.' He sank down on the floor opposite her and crossed his ankles – his coat and trousers strangely unbloodied for a male who'd charged into battle minutes ago. Perhaps he'd changed before he came to find her. Honestly, she wouldn't put it past him. 'I understand that you killed Bereas?'

Bereas.

The window.

*You're fucking the wrong person ...*

'Yes,' she said hollowly, staring at her own dress with unseeing eyes. The first red was already seeping back into its dyed surface, turning pale blue into pale purple. She must have been out for a while. 'I ... I did.'

'Did you get anything out of him?'

There was a tension to the question – an urgency. The same desperate drive for answers she'd felt, until she heard the answers and realised she would much, much rather not have known.

'Naxi,' she breathed.

She saw him lean forward on the edge of her sight. 'Say that again?'

'Naxi— Anaxia, I mean.' Fuck. Too much familiarity. Then again, what did it matter now? 'She betrayed us. This meeting.'

*My heart.*

Nicanor's breath escaped in a rush ... of disappointment? An unspoken *of course*, perhaps? 'And where is she now, Thys? Anaxia?'

*Gone.*

It seemed the only answer that could even begin to explain. The empty spot on her wrist. The sight of a slender back moving away, away, away. That simple, deadly word – *no*.

That answer was all she'd needed, and she so desperately wished she'd never heard it.

'She has left?' Nicanor asked softly, and when she lifted her head, she found his gaze aimed at her wrist as well.

Thysandra nodded.

Somehow, he did not seem to need more than that.

For a moment, he was quiet, looking so eerily *tidy* against the background of rubble and dust – his spotless pale blue coat buttoned all the way up his throat, his silvery hair twisted into a meticulous braid. Not a scrap of mud on his boots. Not a fleck of blood on his hands. Only the small frown on his face betrayed what lay beneath the flawless composure – the smallest hint of the unending calculations always running through his mind.

'Alright,' he finally said, rising to his feet in a single elegant motion. 'There's something I need to show you.'

She blinked at the hand he held out to her. 'Now?'

'Yes. Now.'

She didn't want to move. She just wanted to sit here, stacked away with the other forgotten rulers of times long past, until she and her utter failures faded from memory with them ... but there was something reassuring about the sharpness of him. The cleanness of him. As if he existed in some parallel world where none of the violence and none of the chaos could touch him – as if she only needed to grasp that hand to join him there.

His fingers were cold to the touch when she laid her palm in his. He pulled her to her feet with effortless strength.

'Proud of you,' he said.

He sounded like he meant it, too.

She didn't think she could fly, and so they walked – out of the hall, through the academy galleries, back into the heart of the court. The castle was unnervingly quiet once more. As if every single soul around had done exactly what she most wished to do: locked the doors behind them and hidden beneath their blankets ... except that in the distance, louder and louder with every step forward, the clamour of voices could be heard.

Cheerful voices. Celebrating voices.

'Don't worry,' Nicanor said as she faltered, those panicked moments in the gallery returning to her with an alarmed stutter of her heart. 'It's our army.'

Oh.

Of course.

Did she think he'd have walked so leisurely alongside her if those had been Bereas's people lingering in their halls? Nicanor was many things, but careless wasn't one of them.

She followed him numbly – closer and closer, she realised a few minutes later, to the training fields. The heart of the army's territory at the Crimson Court. The place where she'd spent most of her first and second century, fighting and fighting and fighting, growing quietly stronger in the shadows while her brothers- and sisters-in-arms fawned over Creon fucking Hytherion and his unnerving skill in battle.

*Stop whining*, she heard Old Thysandra snap.

Bile welled in her throat.

It wasn't the fields themselves that Nicanor led her to, it turned out. Instead, they made for the floor above, where an open gallery ran along the full length of the level – a simple, sturdy wooden passageway from where mentors would usually be hollering instructions at their pupils below.

There was no one to be seen inside the building on this morning. Only the red marble walls of the castle rose up around them as they stepped outside, the steep spires and arches between which wisps of clouds came drifting by. And before them, on the stretch of sand and grass where the soldiers would usually be sparring – an army.

She didn't realise what she was looking at, at first.

They looked like any army in the minutes after a roaring victory – the boisterous laughter, the rough camaraderie, the display of weapons. She saw familiar faces among them, too. Imbros and the other commanders. Her own loyal warriors, the people by whose sides she'd fought so many times before. And—

The world seemed to stop in its tracks.

And Lyron?

The same Lyron she'd questioned after the attack on the archives. Who'd sneered that humans died anyway.

Whom she'd told Nicanor she never wanted to see again.

And by his side ...

Gods help her – those were two of her captives, weren't they? Two of the males who should still be sitting in that worn-down villa on Ilithia, waiting for the Alliance to come and get them?

As soon as she'd started seeing, she could not stop seeing anymore. More of Nicanor's soldiers. More of her prisoners. And there were two brown-haired females she was very, *very* sure had been among the mob attacking her outside the archives – *Bereas's* mob – and how could they possibly stand here, chatting and drinking and laughing with the very same force that was supposed to keep them off the island at any cost?

What—

How—

Her Lord Protector didn't speak, next to her. Didn't even glance her way. Just rested his pointy elbows on the balustrade and watched the crowd below them with a faint, content smile on his equally pointy face.

'Nicanor?' she said, unsure of what she was supposed to be seeing.

He didn't turn. 'Hmm?'

'Who— Who exactly are—'

'I told you.' He canted his head just a fraction. 'Our army.'

She opened her mouth to ask the questions.

Then shut it again, because the answers were already rising.

And slowly, ever so slowly, the ground started sinking away beneath her feet – the wooden walkway tilting, swaying, as if they were standing on the open ocean. Because this shouldn't be their army. This shouldn't be *her* army, in any case. And if it was *his* ...

No.

Dead and living gods, no.

'You've been working with them.' It wasn't even a question. '*You* have been ...'

He leaned against the wood even more gracefully. 'Mm-hmm.'

'You— No. No, that's impossible.' A feeble, lightheaded laugh stumbled past her lips. 'You made a bargain of loyalty to—'

'To the crown.' He clicked his tongue. 'Whomever that may belong to. Did you really think I'd so easily accept an Alliance-backed claim as legitimate, Thys?'

She stared at him. 'To ... to keep the court under ...'

'Control,' he finished, throwing her a glance as he nodded. It was almost *cheerful*, the quirk of his eyebrow – as if this was some harmless, mischievous trick he'd played on her. 'Didn't mention *whose* control it would be, though, did I?'

His own.

He'd bargained to get the court under his *own* control.

Too many locks were clicking open in her mind at once, too many thoughts hurtling in for her to be able to distinguish one from the other; she staggered through the sea of them like a ship caught in a sudden summer storm, swept in all directions at once. 'And Bereas knew—'

He gave a shrug. 'It's rather convenient that you killed him, I must admit. If I'd done it myself, it might have caused somewhat of a loyalty divide within our forces.'

She barely even heard that.

*You're fucking the wrong person, love.*

'He ...' The gall rose again, overwhelming in its acid bitterness. 'Bereas— He thought we—'

'Oh, that,' Nicanor said dryly, turning back to the fields. 'Frankly, I can't fault him for it. History and everything. Never confirmed it, never contradicted it – I assumed you'd prefer that approach, given that their assumptions at least kept them from realising who was *actually* spending her nights in your rooms.'

There was no leering innuendo in his voice. No triumphant mockery. Just the simple, matter-of-fact observation, and it was that pragmatic dispassion that truly made her heart go cold in her chest.

'You knew.'

'Of course I bloody knew, Thys.' A sliver of exasperation in his voice. 'If you're aiming for a secret tryst, try to avoid any canoodling in mid-air next time. You're lucky most people were distracted at the time.'

Naxi.

Oh, gods, *Naxi*.

Fear grabbed her by the throat, that one name piercing through the fog of her exhaustion, her confusion, her rising nausea. Naxi –

where *was* she? Had she run into this army on her way out? Surely she wouldn't have been captured or even killed so easily – but if she had, if—

No, wait.

Nicanor had *asked* her where the little menace was.

He couldn't know, then, could he? He couldn't have found her yet? Which meant Naxi was out there, *somewhere*—

And innocent.

For a single, chest-shattering moment, she could not breathe.

'I ... I don't understand.' She had to keep talking. She had to know just how much she'd messed up – how much she'd misunderstood *all* of it. 'If you wanted to get rid of me, why not just tell every single soul around the court? They would have done the job within the hour. No easier way to dispose of me.'

'Who says I wanted to dispose of you?' he said, and he sounded genuinely offended as he turned back towards her, white brows drawn together. 'I like you far too much to do away with you that easily, De-monbane. Figured I'd try to nudge you in the right direction first. There would have been no need for draconic measures if that had worked.'

*Nudge.*

Horrific certainty washed over her.

'Symeon,' she breathed, and the floor swayed harder. 'That attack on me – him calling me a traitor – that was—'

Nicanor shrugged, looking amused. 'He may have received some suggestions on the verbiage, yes.'

*No, Nicanor!* the boy had shrieked in that moment before the knife slit his throat, genuine panic in his eyes. *I was just—*

Just following orders.

Just scaring her into picking the safe path, the path that went along with what most of the court wanted her to do. Stay loyal to the Moth-er's legacy. Wage war against the rest of the archipelago. Regain con-trol, *somehow*, of the empire they had lost.

She barely felt her limbs anymore.

'And the leak on the human housing – telling Iaris, then killing her after she'd spread the news – that was you, too?'

'I took care to do it while you were away from the court,' he said, looking genuinely rueful as he grimaced. 'You weren't supposed to be in any danger at all, I promise. Figured I'd let the mob kill a few humans before I regained control of the situation, to show you that you were only causing *more* innocents to become victims with your incomprehensibly chivalrous decisions – but that admittedly went a little sideways when you returned earlier than I expected. Apologies for that.'

Apologies?

*Apologies?*

She wanted to hit him. She wanted to strangle him with his own fucking coat – *anything*, really, to break through that polished, uncaring breeziness. Her body wouldn't obey, her mind too busy catching up to remember her muscles' existence. Her heartbeat was a rambling gallop. Her hands were clammy with sweat.

'You told Bereas to attack the ships.' It all made sense now. Too much strategy for that smug fucking hothead, indeed. 'Another attempt to narrow my options. You ... you spread word of the agreement I was about to make with the Alliance and then poisoned me at the Hunter's Moon yourself?'

'Mm-hmm.' He threw her a quick grin. 'Painless poison, though. I promised you that.'

'*How*? You were never even near my wine!'

'Oh, it wasn't in the wine,' he said and beamed – an expression of *genuine* pride, a sudden spark of passion in his pale blue eyes. 'It wasn't Fire's Kiss in the first place. See, I developed this *really* intriguing substance that can spread the toxins through touch alone – so I took the antidote, then rubbed the stuff all over my hand. You may remember—'

That hand.

On her shoulder.

'Oh, gods.' Her breath came in shivery gasps now. 'Oh, gods – and then Gadyon—'

One purple bargain mark on her wrist.

No pink, and that was all she'd be able to see in the gallery ... but only now, with clarity of mind returning to her, did she realise there had been a *second* mark missing.

'Regrettable,' Nicanor admitted with the absent air of a man who's just squashed a fly. 'Necessary, though. You'd have gotten suspicious without anyone to blame.'

It wasn't even rage anymore, the white mist clouding her mind. It was a feeling so far beyond anger that all she could do was stare at him and *breathe*, draw the air deeper and deeper and deeper into her lungs and try not to physically explode with the raw force of her fury – Gadyon, who had been kind and loyal and now—

Dead.

How dare he?

How fucking *dare* he?

'And this morning—'

'I've learned not to underestimate you,' Nicanor said, tilting his head at her with a faint, almost *fond* smile. 'Figured you'd try something, so I had one of my people posted in the stairwell of your tower. They heard you discuss the plan with Thorgedson.'

Because she hadn't wanted to let Tared into her rooms.

They'd discussed it standing on the landing, like idiots, and when Nicanor had heard—

He'd attacked.

Worse than that ... he'd put up a fucking show for her. Bereas's host first, then his own army to play the part of her saviours. He wouldn't have done that if he'd only wanted to get the Alliance off the island. He could just have rushed in himself and finished the job, if he already knew he was about to make his final move.

But she'd have known it was him.

She'd still have had Naxi by her side.

Instead, he'd set her up to believe *exactly* what she'd ended up believing; instead, she had played right into his hands with her own unending paranoia. No wonder he'd been so tense about Bereas's last words. A single snag in an otherwise perfect plan, yet even that hadn't spoiled his schemes.

*You're fucking the wrong person, love.*

'You bastard,' she whispered, somehow, even though there seemed to be no air left in her lungs. 'You ... you ...'

'I swear I wasn't trying to hurt you, Thys.' He spread his hands, as if to say, *what choice did I have?* 'You kept digging yourself deeper and deeper into that hole. I figured if I could give you enough of a fright, you might finally agree to call off the whole thing with the Alliance and pick the sensible strategy instead. It seemed the kinder option.'

Kinder than killing her.

Which he could so, *so* easily have done.

'All of that work,' she choked out, 'all of those deaths, and all because you needed to have your fucking war? Really?'

'You *know* me, Thys.' A wry nod at the castle around them, the red walls gleaming like blood in the light of the morning sun. 'Did you truly think I would just accept it? Let the Crimson Court be degraded into some run-of-the-mill backwater castle?'

Nicanor of Myron's house, ambitious to a fault.

How, *how* had she ever thought he'd settle for Lord Protector of a single court alone? *Hungry*, Naxi had said – and she had stupidly, blindly thought it was her body he was hankering for.

Instead – her power.

'You're too intelligent for this madness,' she stammered, hand clenching around the wooden balustrade. Her stomach was churning; if she wasn't careful, she might end up spewing its contents over the unwitting soldiers celebrating below. 'You know damn well that we'd suffer nothing but blistering defeat if we went to battle now – that we wouldn't stand a gods-damned chance against an unbound Alliance with a godsworn mage on their side. Safe bets may not lead to victory, but asinine bets—'

'Who said I was planning to play fair?' he interrupted, looking wryly amused again.

She snapped her mouth shut.

'You gave me the perfect strategy, actually. Those prisoners they asked for.' He nodded at the fae on the fields below. 'Remember that nifty little poison of mine? All I need to do is send them to the magical islands as you planned and instruct them to get their hands on as many of the Alliance's rulers as they can reach. Don't think they'll be nearly as ready for war with half of their leaders dead within a day.'

Hell have mercy.

Would it *work*?

There had been a time, she was suddenly, keenly aware, when she would have been overjoyed with the ingenuous ruthlessness of it – a strategy! A chance at victory! They lay months, perhaps just *weeks* behind her, those days. Glory and praise. Strength and iron-fisted authority. What else had she had to fight for?

Now, she thought of a circle of frightened humans, cowering in her presence.

Tared, staying courteously out of her rooms. Creon, pouring her tea by the fire. Delwin, offering her grain at rates that were, frankly, a show of charity, and ...

Naxi.

Sweet, funny Naxi, who'd run her baths and fed her dinner. Who'd made her laugh and made her cry. Who'd kissed her and held her and fucked her into oblivion whenever she'd needed it most – who'd turned life, somehow, into something that could be ... *joyful*?

Naxi, she knew, would rather die than ever choose the side of the Crimson Court.

And at once nothing else mattered anymore. Because if she still had even the most minimal chance of repairing what she'd ruined, of making up for the unforgivable words she'd spat into that ghastly pale demon face – hell, even if she *didn't* get that chance – she would rather die than make an enemy out of the little menace ever again.

'No,' she said, her own voice miles away.

Nicanor raised his eyebrows. 'I beg your pardon?'

'No.' It came out stronger this time. 'No, you can keep your bloody poison to yourself. We're not going to war again.'

He sighed, turning away from the army below to lean back against the balustrade. His wings drooped over it, entirely relaxed. 'I'm not sure how to put this nicely, Thys, but I'm afraid we're rather past the point where anyone is going to keep your opinions in mind.'

Her stomach cramped violently.

'So why am I still here at all, then?' It should have been a sharp rejoinder but came out sounding rather like a whimper. 'Why not kill me immediately, since I'm of no further use to you anyway?'

'Gods be damned, Demonbane, how many times do I have to tell you I'm bloody fond of you?' He swung up his hand in a burst of agitation, only to drop it again with a mirthless laugh. 'We work well together, don't we? And plenty of people at the court respect your power and the role you played in the Mother's council, so—'

*So I could use you.*

'—I wanted you to have the chance to save yourself,' Nicanor finished, silvery and persuasive still, as if she wouldn't hear the glaring truth that lay beneath. 'A true chance.'

To play his game after all.

To be another ruler's sweet little pawn again.

*Your power. The role you played.* She would have killed for that acknowledgement once upon a time, and only now did she hear the hollowness of it – defining her only by the use she'd had, by her servitude and obedience. What he needed was a figurehead to obscure his own shameless grasp for power. The Mother's pupil, taking her beloved mentor's place; a much easier story to sell than an army commander taking a throne no one had offered him.

A figurehead, too, that he could blame when things inevitably went south one day.

'Really?' Her hands clenched into fists at her sides. 'How very moving. What do you want me to do, then – lead your army? Jump into your bed again?'

He glared at her. 'Come the hell on, Thys. You know me better than to think me *that* sort of bastard. Join me as a friend, if you wish. Join me as an enemy, for all I care – I'm sure we'll get over this little spat soon enough.'

*As an enemy.*

Could she?

Perhaps ... perhaps she could become a quiet traitor again. Pretend to have changed her mind. Warn the Alliance before the poison plan could come to fruition. Wouldn't that be much more useful than dying an undignified death on these fields and ending up in a nameless grave, while the rest of the world once again went up in flames?

'And if I did?' she said hoarsely. 'What would your next steps be?'

He hesitated.

'Nicanor.' Her voice cracked. 'No more fucking lies.'

'You're terribly efficient at this sort of thing,' he said, lips twisting into a sour smile. 'Alright, then. Poison plan can't leak, so dissenters need to be kept quiet. Probably best to get rid of the humans altogether, as unpleasant as it may be – they keep causing trouble wherever they go, and I wouldn't put it past Inga to get word out to her sister. I don't think I can let your little demon lover run around unchecked either, unfortunately. We'll have to get hold of her before she manages to leave the island.'

Naxi.

*Naxi.*

'You'd kill her.' Her lips were too numb to feel the words.

'See, this is why I'd rather not have told you,' he said, face twisting into a mask of unnervingly genuine regret. 'You have this awful habit of getting sentimental about things. It's a very simple choice, alright? I can get you through this alive and well, and I'm fully willing to make a bargain on that, if you wish – so what do you have to gain by resisting? You're not going to stop the wheels from turning either way.'

An offer of survival.

Plain and simple survival.

Old Thysandra would have grabbed the chance with both hands, she was distantly aware, the sensation of that desperate fright still lingering in the marrow of her bones. Old Thysandra had done this before. Safety over morals. Life over loyalty. She'd loved her father once, too, and had renounced him so gods-damned easily when the alternative was risking death.

And yet, no matter how many safe choices she made ... she'd never *felt* safe.

The realisation landed like the realisation of love had done. It had already been there, waiting for her to open her eyes and see it.

She had never been able to stop being vigilant, looking for movements in the shadows. It didn't matter how many doors she locked, how many daggers she hid in her plants. The fear had *always* been there, that little twelve-year-old girl still cowering beneath her blankets somewhere deep, deep within her, and the only time she'd felt really, truly secure in her life—

Naxi.

Always Naxi.

Gods, what had she *done*?

Even a creature with empathy might have abandoned her after that outburst, the accusations, the cruel rebukes. A demon, even a demon trying to care ... Naxi *was* still a selfish creature at heart. And what in the world did she have left to try caring about, when Thysandra had nothing to offer but distrust and delusions?

It would be so easy to be selfish in turn. To take Nicanor's bargain and save her own sorry hide. To survive, once again, the way she'd always survived in this cutthroat world – by discarding the right principles and serving the right people.

The problem, though ...

The problem was her awful habit of getting sentimental about things.

Fuck. She *did* care. And if Naxi didn't, she could still care enough for the both of them – because the little monster deserved the peaceful nymph island of her dreams, deserved to find her friends again, and what was the gods-damned use of survival if it meant sacrificing the one thing that made life worth living in the first place?

She wasn't going to stop the wheels from turning.

Perhaps she didn't need to, though. Perhaps she only needed to slow them down a little. Naxi was leaving the island right now. Every minute took her farther away from the court, farther away from Nicanor's inevitable attempt to find her and do away with her ... and the very *least* Thysandra could do was help her get away.

The opposite of a safe choice.

And yet it was the easiest thing in the world to step back and run her gaze over the packed field below her – to straighten her spine, steel her heart, and say, 'No.'

It felt very, very good, that word.

'Thysandra, *please*.' Nicanor finally came away from the balustrade, his wings tightening behind his shoulders. 'I'm begging you to see sense and—'

'You,' she said, calm and measured, a voice to hide a pounding heart, 'can shove that good sense up your arse, *Commander*.'

He did not flinch.

The stiffening of his face was unmistakable, though.

'I see,' he said.

Gone was the pleading. Gone was his mirthless smile and the hint of apology in it. Mercy he might do as long as it cost him nothing, but they both knew the look of a line crossed – and old friends or no, Nicanor of Myron's house was not a male to grovel, to look back and regret.

Just like that, they were at war.

In the blink of an eye, the space between them had become an imminent battleground.

'Marvelous,' Thysandra said, clinging to her ice-cold smile as she took another step back. No need to rush this. Time was all she needed, and every second might make the difference – so she leaned back against the red wall, deliberately languid, before adding, 'I suppose that makes us enemies, then?'

He shrugged, but it was no longer an indifferent gesture. Rather, the slow, calculating calm of a male waiting for the first strike. 'I suppose it makes you a traitor like your father, mostly.'

Once upon a time, she would have winced.

But the hounds did not howl in the back of her mind now. Her wings didn't itch to curl into a shield around her. Poison and wounds and exhaustion be damned, her bruised, bone-weary body was coming back to life again – the anticipation of battle breathing fire into every soldier's fibre of her.

If she had to be a traitor, at least she'd do it well.

She'd do it loud enough for all the court to hear.

'To you, maybe,' she said, and it felt like breaking out of a cage to finally speak the words aloud. A wild, reckless grin spread on her face. 'But not to my heart.'

And before he could move, she drew a burst of red from the wall and slammed the walkway beneath their feet to splinters.

# CHAPTER 30

NAXI WAS RUNNING HARDER than she ever had in her life.

Thorns and pebbles stung her feet. Brambles lashed her face. The gnarled trees of Faewood shot by in a blur of green and grey and brown on either side, their branches reaching out to her at every step – as if to snatch her hair and clothes. As if to stop her before she could do something hopelessly, monumentally stupid.

Like going back.

She did now slow down.

She should not be doing this. Even now, the voices were there in the back of her mind, reminding her that she was a demon, that she lacked compassion, that she *did not care*. She might die if she kept running. She might get grievously hurt. She had every bloody reason in the world to stand still and rethink her choices in life, and yet she ... didn't.

Standing still meant giving up on Thysandra.

And selfishness lost its meaning in the face of that thought.

Past the swords and arrows. Past the graveyard clearings. Up, up, up the hill, to where the mountain slope rose sharply from the earth. Her breath came in ragged gasps, her legs burned with the effort, and still she did not slow down.

How long would it take Nicanor to act?

The image of that mauled corpse wouldn't leave her mind's eye. She didn't feel sorry for Gadyon, or at least not in the way Inga or Silas did – that deep, nauseous sorrow, as if they needed to feel the dead male's pain on his behalf. But the archivist had been kind. He'd cared. Even if she couldn't share in whatever his feelings must have been, she rationally, intellectually knew that he should *not* have died – and much, much more importantly, that no one else could follow him into hell.

She did not think she would survive it, finding Thysandra in that same spot, the hounds gnawing at her lifeless face.

Why, *why* had she left?

Hadn't Mirova taught her what happened when she left?

It was the same old song all over again, a cruel, discordant tune that made her head spin. She walked, and behind her back, the world collapsed. Or not the world, even, but—

*Home.*

Where was that fucking mountain?

*Be quick*, Silas had told her, his face betraying the turmoil within him for once. *He may already have set his plans in motion. We may already be too late.*

She *should* have bitten off the bastard's fingers when he'd looked at Thysandra with those greedy eyes.

Thysandra. *Thysandra.* With her stupid sense of duty and her stupid distrust. With her stupidly stunning smile. With her locks and her daggers and her ever-ready supply of red – with her fiercely guarded heart that *had* begun to open up at last ... Perhaps it was selfishness, going back. Perhaps it was not that she wanted to spare Thysandra the pain but that she would hurt just as much herself, having to live in a world in which Thysandra was not happy.

Was that empathy?

Naxi no longer cared whether it was or not.

Because *there*, at long last, was the grey wall of the mountain's slope, looming between the foliage. And there was the gate she'd been looking for, its irregular shape dark, specks of light flickering in the shadows beyond.

She staggered into the Labyrinth half-sobbing with exhaustion, trickles of blood running down her scraped and scratched legs. Around her, the caves vibrated with worry. Relief to see her again. Most of all, growing steadily stronger as Naxi pushed herself farther into the mountain, the sort of fury that felt like a question.

*Who hurt you?* that feeling asked. *Who do we need to hurt?*

Despite herself, Naxi laughed. High-pitched, hysterical laughter, like a declaration of war.

'Let's kill some fae, sweetheart.'

# CHAPTER 31

HAD THYSANDRA BEEN TRYING to kill Nicanor, breaking the walkway would have been a ridiculous first strike.

Which was exactly the point.

The bastard had not seen it coming. His wings broke his fall before she could blink, of course; he did not plummet to his death, he barely lost his footing. But it was that moment of surprise – that single moment in which conscious thought had to move over for reflexes – that she needed more than his imminent demise, more than a brilliant first attack to gain the upper hand.

The upper hand was meaningless, with an army mere steps away.

What she needed was time, not blood. What she needed was to keep them busy – *all* of them – for just as long as she could. And a direct battle would see her dead within minutes ... so instead, as all heads on the field snapped towards her at once, she used that ephemeral moment of shock to do the one thing a clear-headed Nicanor would never have allowed.

Flee.

Like a coward – but a coward with a plan.

She soared back into the castle just in time. The doorpost flew apart in marble smithereens two feet behind her wings; Nicanor was already hollering commands, with that unflustered efficiency she'd once believed her ally. Now it only meant they were after her more swiftly, more orderly. Already the first winged shapes came shooting past the windows, and glass shattered around her as she flew ...

Their fucking problem.

This was *her* battlefield.

Her home. Her gods-damned court, and she'd spent four hundred years learning every nook and cranny of the place ... so let them follow. Let them try to lock her in. They would win in the end – but she could give them a hell of a chase, first.

More glass shattered. Fae came barging in from the side.

Thysandra dove through the doorway of the soldier's library.

It was a waste of space, this room. Not one warrior ever came here to study the tomes on battle strategy and military history. Except *she* had, of course, in her neverending eagerness to please the Mother with her knowledge and devotion – and so she knew exactly what to aim for, zigzagging through the maze of shelves and parchment as behind her voices yelled about splitting up and searching.

The little door wasn't on any official maps. She wasn't sure if even the Mother had known about it. Since it led straight to the castle's wine cellars, she suspected the tunnel had been created by a bunch of soldiers less committed to their studies – boozing idiots, but she muttered a word of thanks all the same as she swept aside the velvet curtains, unlocked the hatch, and squeezed herself into the unlit dark.

It would win her perhaps a minute.

For now, that was enough.

Even here, slipping between the castle's walls and floors, she could hear the shouts of the army surrounding her, the magic slamming into stone. She'd just reached the end of the tunnel as light flooded in from the other end and triumphant cries grew abruptly louder – an advantage of just about half a minute, then, but at least Nicanor wouldn't have surrounded the cellars.

Yet.

She gave herself no time to think as she darted through the pantries and larders, avoiding the kitchens and the fae working in them. The voices behind her sounded less confident now, unsure of their direction in the labyrinthine cellar system. Clearly, she grimly concluded, they'd never snuck in here in the dark of night to steal their evening meal, after having spent long enough on the training field to miss dinner.

She didn't dare take the exit near the harbour, the exit through which provisions were brought in – because if Naxi was leaving the island, she'd *have* to find a ship sooner or later, and it would be less than helpful to put the army in her path. Instead, Thysandra picked the corridor that led up into the heart of the castle – the one through which food and drink were served at the Mother's feasts.

Time to draw some attention again.

She didn't even need to make an effort. Two armed females raised the alarm behind her before she'd crossed the first hallway.

To her left were the archives – rooms she didn't know too well. To her right, however, lay the salons, the council chambers, the places where she'd spent hundreds upon hundreds of hours dealing with everything from looming rebellion to petty fae disputes. She made her decision in a split second, sprinting right and down the black-and-gold marble corridor as the roars of her pursuers swelled louder behind her – this was not the time for surprises.

At the far end of the corridor, winged shapes were sweeping in through the open arches.

Fuck. Faster than she'd thought.

Change of plan, then. She burst through the nearest door to her left, into an intimate little parlour exceptionally suited for threatening troublesome fae nobles – then out of the window, where five floors overlooked what was little more than a glorified air vent. She flew two stories up, scattering red at every window she passed. Her pursuers didn't need to know through which one she'd entered the castle again.

By the time she dashed into a fourth-floor office, the sky above her was already darkening with wings.

She was beyond panic, now. There was nothing but breathless, light-headed exhilaration left in her veins, driving her back into the maze of corridors. Around this corner and the next. Into the spiralling stairwell with its twisted, thorn-like railings. Outside, behind the open arches, she could see the throngs of circling fae, and—

And another target they were after?

She stumbled mid-step.

What in the world? More and more of the soldiers on her trail were looking away from the tower through which she was fleeing. Instead, their gazes were turning towards two lone figures circling just above the gardens, shouting insults at the force above them, flinging up red magic at anyone coming too close.

Wait. She knew those faces.

*Archivists?*

Why in Korok's flaming hell were two of Gadyon's assistants hovering there, taunting an entire bloodthirsty army on their own?

The soldiers began to dive before she could figure out the answer to that question, shouts of annoyance rising from their ranks – and for a moment, they seemed to have forgotten about their chase entirely. Not *all* of them, of course. Enough others were already swarming over the roofs. But at least a few dozen of them were going after the intruders – far, far more than a couple of clerks could ever hope to survive.

Which wasn't her problem.

She *really* had enough trouble to deal with already.

She dove after them.

It almost made sense, on some foolish, stupidly honourable level – because she would be dying anyway, and what was the use in dragging along the misguided idiots who seemed to be trying to *save* her? Even if they ought to know better, it was easy to draw the attention away from them again. The moment she swept into the army's view, they seemed to remember their hunt; new howls of triumph went up behind her as she soared through the nearest open gate and back into the castle's tapestry-covered hallways.

Too close behind her. Pinpricks of red magic bit the backs of her knees. A ruby chandelier flew apart above her head.

She was a fucking fool.

No time to slow down enough to open a door. No time to figure out an escape. All she could do was fly, fly, fly, faster than she ever had in her life, and pray for some miracle to save her for a few minutes more—

A wet *splat* sounded behind her.

Someone roared in fury.

She dared to throw a single glance over her shoulder and found her pursuers suddenly farther behind her, glancing wildly around as—

*Splat!*

—muck smeared a blond fae male's face.

Only then did she notice the handful of humans standing in the gallery high above her head, their faces pale, their jaws tight as they flung down a volley of eggs at the fae force hunting her. *Rotten* eggs, it turned out – the stench exploded with the cracking of eggshells against the floor.

What in hell?

A splatter hit another soldier's face ... and it was that hit that broke the baffled paralysis. With a series of furious profanities, the two sullied fae shot upwards, followed by at least half of the group behind them – after the humans, who were at the very least wise enough to make a run for it *then*.

Too late, if no one stepped in to save them.

Biting back a curse, Thysandra launched herself after the fools.

She reached the gallery simultaneously with the fae who had, moments ago, been following her; red flickered as she took the first three, four, five of them down, managing to sweep through the gallery arches first as they dropped screaming to the ground. Close-by, a door slammed. The humans, wisely making use of the distraction to get the fuck out of there.

She did not pause to see where they had gone.

Down the passageway before her, deeper and deeper into the heart of the castle. Behind her, fae soared into the gallery. Before her ... fuck, before her they came pouring from side passages as well, corralling her like cattle for slaughter. She slowed down – she had no choice but to slow down, trying to figure out which doors she had left to flee through ...

Something sharp hit her left wing.

*Fuck.*

She staggered, needing a moment too long to regain her balance. Laughter went up behind her. The first escape she could find, then – could she even still fly?

Problem for later.

She yanked open the door to her right, lunged into the room beyond. Before the windows, the sky was dark with fae.

*Fuck.*

Red magic filled the doorway.

No choice left but to attack – so she planted her left hand on the ebony table at the centre of the room, unleashed its every spark of red at the fae spilling in through the open door, and leapt back into the corridor in the moment of chaos. A fae male staggered against her. She drove a dagger into his guts, twisting him around to shield herself behind his wing.

A matter of minutes, now.

She gritted her teeth and struggled forward, dragging the dying male along.

Red tore through her boots, hitting her still vulnerable ankle. Red sliced across the back of her neck. With a gasp, she staggered back against the wall, drawing the colour from her own blood to strike, strike, strike … It was no use. They were crowding in on all sides, triumph glinting in their eyes already – the traitor queen of the Crimson Court, about to breathe her final treasonous breath.

Pain slashed her arms. Her chest. She managed to drag enough blue from her paling dress to heal a ragged wound just below her heart but lost a valuable fraction of a second in the process; the rhythm of her charges broken, she was too late, too slow, to respond to the onslaught of magic hurled at her from all sides. A dagger was flung at her, and she jerked her head aside just in time. A fae female stormed towards her on the left in a storm of red, and it took two attempts too many to hit her throat and take her down.

A sword rose to her right.

Thysandra already knew she'd be too slow.

Strange, how time slowed when she needed it to be over quickly – how the details of the world around her sharpened to almost unbearable clarity when she least wanted to see them. The sunlight glinting on the edge of the blade. The metallic tang of blood. Her heart, beating loud enough to drown out the howls and insults around her – as if even her pulse was counting down the seconds ...

This was it, then.

She closed her eyes and saw Naxi beaming back at her.

How long had she been running – thirty minutes? Please let it be enough, *please* let it be—

Steel scraped the wall beside her head.

*Beside* her head. Not *through* her head – and before she'd regained the presence of mind to process that unexpected development, before she fully realised she was still breathing, still thinking, still moving ...

Hell broke loose.

Her eyes flew open.

For a moment, she couldn't make out anything on the far side of the hall but the tangle of moving bodies and red crackling like lightning around them. Fae attacking fae. More idiots coming to her undeserved rescue? But these newcomers fought too well, too easily, to be clerks who hadn't seen battles in decades, and only then did she recognise that striking sweep of auburn hair ...

*Orthea?*

No, that did not make sense. Orthea wouldn't come to her aid unless her own life depended on it, and even then, it might be a close call. Yet it *was* the Master of Ceremony leading that charge, and next to her— Hell, was that Rhias?

The fucking harbour master? Who'd smirked at her so hatefully when she found him having breakfast with—

Oh.

*Silas?*

Gods have mercy. What was going *on*? This was supposed to be a lone battle, Thysandra Demonbane against the rest of the world – her own mistakes, her own damn penance. Why would any of her allies be mad enough to fight the inevitable when they should be running for their own dear lives?

And yet ...

First the archivists. Then the humans.

And now the barrage of red had all but dried up as more and more fae turned towards the uproar instead, where Silas's bargain-bound puppets were breaching the lines of Nicanor's army with too much success to ignore. Thysandra's head spun. Her wings ached. She barely had the presence of mind to draw the last blue from her dress and heal the worst of her injuries, and it did not even matter.

Others were fighting on her behalf.

The world suddenly seemed so ... *light.*

Someone lunged for her in a half-hearted attack, and she countered equally half-heartedly, stumbling along with the horde as it began to move. Already Orthea and the others were withdrawing. Thysandra tried to fight her way out of the crowd of wings and bodies but didn't manage – dragged along as if by the currents of the ocean, down the corridor, around the corner, fielding off blades and magic as Nicanor's force turned its focus towards the greater danger. Faster and faster did the attackers retreat. Into the east wing and—

Oh no.

Towards the bone hall?

'No,' she gasped, breathlessly, mindlessly, trying once again to elbow her way out of the throng. Hands pulled her back, tried to drag her down. Stumbling forward was all she could do to avoid crashing to the ground. 'No, wait! You can't— You—'

They did not listen.

What had she thought? This was the *last* group of people in the world to ever listen to her.

'No!' she tried all the same as they dragged her forward and the antechamber opened up before them. 'No!' as the damaged copper gate came into view. 'No!' as she caught her first glimpse of the eerily lit hall beyond, fae crowding through the doorway, pulling the lopsided doors farther askew ...

And then she was through them, too.

The bone hall was still its broken, damaged self, most of the floor gone. Dozens and dozens of fae had taken off into the air. Others had jumped into the cave below, where the fight was still raging – and there, at the farthest end of the hollow of the Labyrinth ...

Thysandra stiffened.

Fae continued to push into the hall behind her, shoving her farther and farther towards the edge of the crater.

'No!' she gasped one last time, knowing it was hopeless, knowing it would be too late even if she managed to start fleeing now. 'Stop! You need to *stop*! You—'

Because the earth had started rumbling.

The coloured gemstones were dimming one by one.

And that *was* Naxi at the far end of the cave – bloodied, dishevelled Naxi, who should have left, who should be miles away from the castle, emerging from the shadows with hands twisted into claws and murder shining in her bright blue eyes.

Thysandra's heart had a single stupefied, horrified, mesmerised moment to stop dead in its tracks.

Then those sweet pink lips moved, and the world erupted in a blaze of excruciating white.

# CHAPTER 32

HURT.

Everything hurt.

Her thoughts were lances of pain, her breaths ragged rips in the fabric of her consciousness. Her ears rang with a high-pitched whine. Her skin ...

Her skin felt like it was no longer there at all. As if the surface of her body was a single, all-consuming wound, raw and agonising.

A voice was talking.

She struggled to make out the words. *Alive*, they were saying. *Rooms*, they were saying. *Healer ... not just blue ... lucky she's breathing ...*

Hands touched her body, and everything became a thousand times worse.

'Sashka!' someone cried.

She clung to that voice. A good voice. A voice that shouldn't be there at all, even though she did not remember why it couldn't be.

'Sashka, I'm so sorry ...'

The pain subsided, and she was gone again.

Sunset. Bed. Soft ... soft blankets.

Sobbing.

Someone was sobbing.

Pain came and went, in pulsing, irregular flares. Like the sputtering of a dying flame. Like falling asleep but jerking awake again, over and over and ...

'Naxi,' a voice was saying.

She knew who it belonged to. She just couldn't remember, couldn't make sense of him here, by her bed, in the sunset. More than anything, it seemed a voice that ought to hate her.

'Naxi,' it said again.

More muffled sobs. Other voices were speaking in the distance. Thysandra tried to move her head and couldn't decide what side of her body it was on.

'Naxi, I've got her. You can let go. I've got ...'

The pain died away again.

Her mouth was dry as parched leather.

But she blinked her eyes open, and her mind was strangely, weight-lessly clear – a spring morning sort of feeling, as if the dew was still sparkling on her thoughts.

She was in her own bedroom. In her own bed. Plants smiled back at her from the walls and the ceiling. She no longer hurt, and her breath was slow, her skin smooth and unharmed; all her limbs were where they ought to be, moving at her command. The damaged blue dress she'd been wearing was gone, and instead a soft white nightgown had been tucked around her body.

A glass of water stood on the nightstand. She gulped it all down in a single swig.

Better.

What next?

Swinging her legs out of bed was an experiment. The rug was incomprehensibly fluffy against her toes, as if her feet had never touched anything like it before – and then she stood, warily, tentatively, and her legs held even as she turned and twisted to test her balance. When she didn't fall, she took her first step forward. Her knees didn't buckle.

From the living room, voices emerged.

*Naxi.*

A faint memory of bitter sobs rose in her mind, and all at once, her head was no longer so blissfully quiet.

She stumbled around to find her familiar green dressing gown, with awkward, clumsy motions, as if she was moving in a tangible body for the very first time. It wasn't Naxi's voice coming from behind the door, she realised only moments later. Still, it took her two more staggering steps to identify the person who *was* speaking—

'... told an actual *god* to stop fucking around?'

Emelin.

In her living room.

Sounding blissfully unconcerned, that rather puzzling question laced with barely suppressed laughter.

'Look, *someone* had to do it,' a voice she recognised as Agenor's said, sounding wryly amused, and at once matters began making rather more sense. 'And either way, he ended up rather agreeing with me, which solved the matter far more easily than the diplomatic approach would have done.'

Emelin's laughter, again. 'And this was around the end of the Conquest, yes? So you—'

Thysandra opened the door.

Their voices abruptly went quiet.

They were sitting on her couch together, father and daughter – Agenor lounging in the velvet cushions with his sleeves rolled up and a black snake curling affectionately around his shoulder, Emelin with her legs pulled to her chest, snacking on berries from a bowl she was balancing on top of her bare knees. No trace of Naxi. No trace of anyone else, either – but the collection of used glasses on the low table suggested more than just these two had entered her rooms during the however many days Thysandra had been out.

She should care about that.

The problem was there were about seventeen things she cared about *more* at this particular moment.

'What ...' she began, and then she no longer knew how to continue, staring at the High Lady of the Cobalt Court and the High Lord of the Golden Court exchanging stories of divine shenanigans on her couch.

'You're awake!' The sunny smile Emelin sent her seemed unnervingly genuine, the relief in her voice equally so. 'How are you feeling?'

*Bewildered.*

It wasn't even true, or at least, it wasn't the full truth. It felt like she'd skipped half a century – like she'd stepped through some mysterious portal and ended up in a world that looked like hers, smelled like hers, sounded like hers, but was nonetheless entirely and essentially different from the one she'd walked all her life.

*How are you feeling?*

They were looking at her like the answer *mattered* to them.

'Where ...' Her voice was a dry croak. 'Where is Naxi?'

'She's fine.' Emelin put her berries aside, hopped off the couch, and made for the kitchen corner as if she'd lived in these rooms for years. 'Creon took her down to the pavilion. She was drained to the point where she couldn't shield herself from the emotions of the court anymore, so we figured some distance would be helpful.'

Creon.

That was *Creon's* voice she'd heard in her half-dead delirium.

'Oh,' she stammered.

'Take a seat,' Agenor said, his smile faint but reassuring. *It's all under control*, that smile said. *No need to worry.* 'You've been out for five days.

Before you start dashing around the place again, I suggest you at least eat something.'

Five days?

Good gods.

She dropped into the armchair, head spinning. Agenor's snake idly slithered down over his arms, into his lap. From the kitchen came the sound of boiling water and a cloth bag opening; Emelin reappeared a moment later with a steaming mug of sharp-smelling ginger tea and two buttered sesame buns on a plate.

Tea.

Poison.

She stammered, 'Nicanor ...'

'Has been duly disposed of,' Agenor said wryly, lifting his snake back onto his shoulder before it could slip down onto the floor. 'The Labyrinth burned him to an impressively charred crisp. Most of them, really.'

That flash of white.

A shiver ran through her. 'And I—'

'It seems to have made an attempt to spare you,' Emelin said as she plunked herself back onto the couch and folded up her legs again. 'It's considerate like that. You still took some damage, though.'

'I ... yes.' Thysandra tried a grin. 'I noticed.'

Agenor was polite enough to chuckle at that feeble excuse for a joke.

The two of them were silent as she cautiously chewed on a sesame bun – a silence that wasn't impatient or awkward, somehow, but just *was*. Five days. How much of that time had they spent by her bedside together, waiting for her to wake up?

How many others had sat here in their place, watching over her?

'Did anyone else ...' She faltered. It felt like arrogance to even ask the question – to presume anyone had cared that much. 'Was anyone else ... here?'

'Not the alves,' Emelin said with a one-shouldered shrug, nodding at the door. 'They thought you wouldn't be too happy about it, them being able to fade into the room. Or was that not what you meant?'

It was not.

Her eyes started stinging a little all the same, though.

'No – no, I meant ...' She had to swallow to get rid of the catch in her throat. 'Are they alright? Silas and Inga and ... and ...'

Not Gadyon.

It would take a while for her to accept that failure.

Oh, Silas and Inga are quite well.' Something about Agenor's smile was more amused than she'd expected. 'Silas spent the last couple of days purging the court of a few more aspiring usurpers. Speaking of which – I'm well aware you could probably do without my unsolicited advice on the matter, but from the perspective of someone who's held the position for a while, *if* you are looking for a new Lord Protector ...'

She glared at him over her plate.

Emelin sniggered by her father's side.

Another comfortable silence ensued. The black snake familiar continued its attempts to be everywhere but on Agenor's shoulders. Emelin continued her snacking. Outside, beyond the vine-framed windows, the sunlight sparkled on the azure sea, not an army or rebellious mob in sight.

Thysandra had never seen the Crimson Court quite so close to *peaceful*.

Or perhaps ... perhaps it was not the court that was different. Perhaps it was rather that *she* had never watched the island with even half of the strangely serene calm stealing over her now. No alves in her rooms. No traitors in her halls. The worst had come to pass, yet somehow, *somehow*, those who ought to have deserted her hadn't – Silas and his bargains, Inga and her clerks. And Naxi—

Naxi and her Labyrinth.

Would it be too mad to take off for the pavilion the moment she'd finished her breakfast and just hope her wings would handle the flight?

But as she put down her plate, as she opened her mouth to announce it was time for her to put on some decent clothes and leave, Agenor unexpectedly cleared his throat and said, 'One more thing, Thys.'

He suddenly sounded more serious – almost *grave*.

Coming from most other people, that would hardly have been a cause for alarm. Agenor, on the other hand, had never in her lifetime turned grave unless the situation truly called for it, and her heart thudded accordingly as she fell back into her armchair. 'What is it?'

He hesitated.

'It's about your father,' Emelin said in his stead.

The world stood still for a moment.

She expected the hounds to howl – was already bracing for them to begin their ceaseless baying in the pits of her mind. Instead ... there was silence. Not a single snapping bone reverberating through her thoughts. Not a single whisper of his breaking voice – *Thysandra!*

As if all these years, he had only been shouting, *begging*, for her to open her eyes and finally see the truth.

*Traitor's daughter.*

She understood it now.

It had never been an insult in the first place.

'Did you ...' She drew in a shaky breath. 'Did you find anything?'

'It's not entirely pleasant,' Agenor said tightly, which from his lips she knew to be code for *you might lie awake for months because of this.* 'I just wanted to let you know that we found some answers, so you can tell us when you feel strong enough to—'

'What did you find?' Her voice had sharpened. 'Tell me what you found.'

He closed his eyes.

Emelin dryly said, 'Told you.'

Agenor's muffled curse suggested that she had indeed, and likely more than once. Rubbing his face, he tensely said, 'Thys, you spent the past five days on the brink of death. Even if you feel much better, you—'

With an eyeroll, Emelin leaned over him, nudged a hissing snake aside, and grabbed a leather folder off the floor by his feet.

'Ignore him,' she said with an oddly understanding nod as she handed it to Thysandra. 'He doesn't know what missing fathers are like.'

Agenor's next curse suggested that argument had come up before, too.

'Right,' Thysandra weakly said. 'Thank you.'

'Thought Creon was the ruthless one,' Agenor muttered under his breath as his daughter moved back into her seat, and she elbowed him in the wing hard enough that he winced a little.

The folder wasn't heavy. When Thysandra untied the strings and opened it, she found only a handful of documents inside, the faded ink revealing their age. One of them had been torn in two; it was only when she held the pieces together that she realised what it was.

A birth certificate.

*Cythera of Cyrigon's house.*

'Your mother's.' Agenor's voice seemed strangely distant. 'That is the state I found it in among the administrative documents we took from the court.'

'Why ...' The torn edges shook in her hand. 'Why in the world would the Mother have this in her personal files? Why not just keep it with the other certificates in the archives?'

He sighed. 'Read on.'

The next piece of parchment – she had to blink and blink again to be sure she wasn't going mad – was an academy report. Odder still, one *her* academy reports. Name scribbled at the top, in a meticulous teacher's hand: *Thysandra of Echion's house, Spring 2836.*

She'd been twelve years old.

This had to be her very first quarter at the academy.

Her grades had been excellent. Ridiculously excellent. Straight 5's all the way down, and for magic – the last on the list – a teacher had jokingly put down a 6, accompanied by a quick note on extraordinary talent. Of course it had been presented to the Mother. Promising students were always brought to her attention.

It had been a while since Thysandra had seen a report *this* excellent, though. Excellent enough that it seemed it had to belong to someone else.

'I— I don't understand—'

'Read on,' Agenor quietly said.

The last piece of parchment was a letter. She opened it as if a deadly scorpion might fall out from between the folds of the yellowed sheet.

*Your Majesty*, it started.

*It is a hallmark of my high esteem for you that I can even find it in myself to reply to your proposal with more than a simple "no".*

*Some, I presume, might have felt grateful for earning the honour of your royal preference. I am regrettably not one of them. The notion that I would abandon the love of my life, the mother of my child, to serve as a stud horse for the propagation of your bloodline is little short of an insult. I understand the offer was not made to be refused, but even so, I do.*

*I trust I need not elaborate further on the matter, though I am quite capable of doing so should the need arise.*

*Otherwise ever your faithful servant,*
*Echion*

She stared at it.

She stared at it for so long the letters bled together on the parchment.

'In hindsight,' Agenor said, so softly, so *gently* that she barely recognised his voice, 'I should have been able to put the pieces of the puzzle together long before finding this particular piece of correspondence.'

Pieces.

Her grades.

*Stud horse.*

She couldn't breathe.

'You did cause somewhat of a ripple during your first months at the academy. I'm not sure if I ever told you that.' He hesitated. 'The War of the Gods had ended only a few decades before you were born. There was this sense of excitement at the court, the notion of faekind being stronger than even the gods themselves, and then there was you – daughter of two extraordinarily powerful mages, the most powerful child born in quite a while. In a way, I suppose people saw you as a symbol of that new era of fae supremacy.'

Vaguely, Thysandra was aware of the disgusted sound emerging from Emelin's direction.

If she'd been able to speak, she might have agreed.

'So, looking back ...' Agenor slowly drew in a breath. 'I suppose your existence may have given Achlys and Melinoë the idea to have children of their own again. New world, new power, new players on the stage. They were the most powerful creature in the world at the time. A loyal lineage would have cemented that power.'

'And ... and so ...'

'Well, Echion had already shown he was capable of begetting exceptionally talented offspring.' A bitter chuckle. 'Why mess with a proven formula?'

*I did something entirely ill-advised,* her father had told Silas. *It may well be the end of me, and I won't regret it for a moment.*

Her hands were shaking.

'And so she killed him,' she breathed.

Agenor was silent.

'But ... but she couldn't tell the world he'd rejected her. Of course.' A manic laugh rose from her throat. 'So she branded him a traitor instead?'

'To their mind, he might have been,' Agenor muttered – and she was standing on that walkway by the training fields again, wounded, hurting, and surer of herself than she'd been in her entire life.

*A traitor to you, maybe.*

*But not ...*

'But not to his heart,' she whispered, staring at the letter in her hands.

Neither of them replied. When she looked up, finally, she found them still sitting side by side on her couch, watching her with eerily similar expressions – resignation, quiet anger, *sympathy*. Weakness, she would have thought once, to be sympathised with. Now all she could do was sink into it – let it wrap around her like the comforting softness of clean, warm, downy blankets.

'And my mother?' she said numbly.

Agenor looked at Emelin.

Emelin cocked her head. 'You still don't remember?'

*Didn't she?*

The hounds kept quiet. Her father's screams did not return. But even without them, there was no penetrating that blank hole in her memory – that hollow that should not be hollow at all.

She swallowed. 'I … I can't.'

'Alright.' Suddenly the girl opposite her no longer looked so young – barely two decades of life behind her, but she planted her feet onto the floor and leaned forward with the air of a scholar presenting centuries of painstaking research. 'What Naxi told Tared – to pass on to me – is that your attempts to remember your mother's fate felt a damn lot like my darling father's attempts to remember what had happened around the day of Korok's death. In that case, it turned out to be a binding-locked memory. We suspect the same might be true for you.'

Thysandra blinked. Then blinked again, at Agenor this time, and feebly said, 'She locked *your* memories?'

'Oh, yes.' A mirthless smile. 'Of that time I tried to kill them.'

Her jaw sagged open.

'He surpasses all expectations, doesn't he?' Emelin cheerfully said.

'You …' She shook her head, as if that would make the facts suddenly fall into place. '*You* tried to kill her?'

'After they blew up Korok to win the War of the Gods and sent most of the continent with him to hell. Yes.' It turned out the smile on Agenor's face could turn even bleaker. 'Didn't succeed, of course. They took away both my memory of the attempt and my memory of the events that had driven me to try in the first place, and I spent the next couple of hundred years having no fucking clue.'

Gods have mercy.

'But she didn't throw *you* to the hounds,' she said weakly.

He grimaced. 'No. Apparently rejection is a significantly more severe crime than the occasional murder attempt.'

She hated how much sense that made.

'Anyway,' Emelin interjected, with a pointedness that suggested she knew damn well that *some* members of the company might object to the words she was about to speak, 'we did find your binding in the halls of the Cobalt Court. I brought it with me, just in case.'

Agenor closed his eyes.

'You have it *here*?' Thysandra stammered, gaze shooting to the linen bag by the girl's feet. It didn't look like it contained any fragile crystal orbs. 'How did you—'

The object Emelin retrieved from her bag was not a fragile crystal orb.

A small, cubic piece of stone. A pebble, almost. It took a moment to make sense of it – *yellow for change*, and if the bindings had once been changed from humble pens into those glittering orbs that had been stored in the Cobalt Court, there was no magical law that said they could not be changed back into something sturdier again.

'For full transparency's sake,' Emelin said as she cautiously placed the stone cube between the glasses on the table, 'I believe I'm supposed to tell you it's bloody unpleasant, getting hours of memories planted back into your mind in a matter of seconds, and also, that the memories themselves are likely not the most uplifting of—'

'Give them to me,' Thysandra hoarsely interrupted. 'Please.'

Agenor let out a small, exasperated whimper.

Emelin, on the other hand, didn't bat an eye. 'Would you mind giving me an iridescent surface of some kind? I can't change textures any-more.'

Something to do with godsworn magic – Thysandra was too numb to ask. With a single flicker of yellow from her dark green robe, the table surface turned into shimmering mother-of-pearl; in contrast, the little stone binding looked even darker, even more foreboding.

Emelin's fingertips touched the tabletop.

Her right hand made a small, sweeping motion – as if to usher some-thing out of the way that only she could see.

And—

*It's dark. It's quiet. It's far past her usual bedtime, and she's never seen the island so still before, no lights burning anywhere around the court.*

*'We need to be very quiet,' her favourite voice in the world says.*

*Mother has said that five times already tonight.*

*Thysandra doesn't understand. Mother has been crying. She pretends she hasn't, but she has. Father isn't here at all. He left after dinner, but first he held Mother longer than Thysandra ever saw him do before.*

*It's a surprise, they've said. It's a secret. It'll all be fine, promise.*

*So she doesn't ask as they fly, faster than she's ever flown.*

*There's only sea beneath them. So much water, all of it dark in the moonlight. There are no birds. No breeze. Just Mother and the stars, and they fly and fly and fly.*

*Then she hears them.*

*Shouts behind her.*

*Mother whirls around. 'No,' she gasps, and something in her voice doesn't sound like it'll all be fine at all. It sounds like nothing will ever be fine again.*

*Thysandra wants to look, but Mother has already grabbed her by the arm. And now she's being pulled along, faster and faster through the dark, voices shouting behind them. She wants to cry, but she can barely breathe, so fast are they flying. Someone is shouting Mother's name.*

*'Fly on,' Mother says, and she lets go of Thysandra's wrist. 'Fly as hard as you can. Straight ahead, no looking back, all the way to Ilithia. Uncle Silas will be waiting for you.'*

*Thysandra has flown to Ilithia before, but never on her own. She says, 'I don't understand.'*

*'You don't need to understand. Fly, Thys. Fly!'*

*Mother is crying.*

*Thysandra doesn't understand. But she flies.*

*The ocean is so very large beneath her, and she's so very small. Her wings are so very tired. She doesn't look back, but she can see the reflection of colours on the waves beneath her – red, so much red. Red isn't good. Master Hyras said she has to be very careful with it, and the people behind her are not being careful at all.*

*Something falls into the sea. She hears the splash.*

*Still, she flies.*

*'The girl!' a voice yells behind her. Ophion's voice. Father never says it, but he doesn't like Ophion at all. 'The Mother wants the girl!'*

*There's even more red.*

*Mother's voice shouts, 'Not my daughter! Not my—'*

*And then there's a sound Thysandra has never heard before. It's a gurgle. It's a sob. It isn't loud, and yet she hears it as if it's coming from right behind her, as if for a single terrible moment, the entire night is full of it.*

*She looks back.*

*The darkness is full of wings, their movements blurs of grey in the moonlight. Beneath them, a single winged shape is falling. Falling. Falling. Like a broken butterfly, wings not even moving – wide and golden, the most beautiful wings Thysandra has ever seen.*

*There's a splash, and then she's gone.*

*Thysandra doesn't fly anymore.*

*They take her easily, and she doesn't even care.*

'Thys.'

A hand nudged her cheek. A voice pulled at her consciousness like a thread tugging at a seam.

'Thys, come back.'

With a gasp, her eyes flew open.

Plants. Couch. Wall. Her own rooms, yet it took her a moment to recall who *she* even was – some creature ages away from that night, that moon, that deadly dark. The smell of fresh tea hadn't been there, that night. The brush of linen and silk on her skin. All signs of here, of *now*, and yet each of them felt more like a figment of her imagination than that pair of wings still falling in her mind's eye.

Tumbling and tumbling. A plummet that had lasted four hundred years already.

'Thys?'

'Bowl,' she choked, and then she was vomiting, barely noticing the zinc bowl that was slipped into her lap with suspicious speed. There was little left inside her to throw up at all. Bits and pieces of two sesame buns, and then all that followed was sour bile and that sensation of mind-numbing terror – of a fear she'd forgotten but still felt, soaked into places of her that were more than memory alone.

'You'll be glad to know I did the exact same thing,' Agenor said wryly, his hand holding her shoulder steady as she retched and retched again. 'We came prepared.'

*The girl.*

*The Mother wants the girl.*

'Please tell me …' She gagged, gasped in a breath. 'Please tell me Ophion suffered *terribly* as he died?'

'Oh, he did,' Emelin grimly said.

'Good,' she heaved, and then she threw up again.

It seemed to take ages until her stomach finally calmed, until the images finally settled into the hollows in her memory. Hands pulled the vomit-filled bowl from under her. Someone carefully wiped her face with a warm, damp towel. She collapsed into the cushions of the armchair, eyes closed, body drained to the last drop, her mind feeling like the blood-soaked soil of Faewood.

Like a graveyard.

'Just breathe,' Agenor said, letting go of her shoulder.

That seemed like a decent suggestion. She decided to follow it.

Footsteps padded around her. A tap turned on and off again. Someone poured another mug of tea and pressed it into her hands, and she lifted it to her lips mechanically, the hot drink rinsing away the lingering taste of bile in her mouth.

*Fly, Thys!*

And she had never known.

Was that why the Mother had taken that memory but left her father's execution as a warning to remember? No way of twisting their desperate flight into an act of treason. No way to turn her mother's sacrifice into the act of a self-serving coward. *The Mother wants the girl*, Ophion had shouted – a simple but all-revealing truth, no reason for all that cruelty except for vicious, petty jealousy.

And the Mother had gotten her girl.

An almost-daughter of her own, the second-best thing to fill the time as she continued her quest for the true prize of her heart – only to discard that first hard-won child as soon as her coveted blood-born son arrived.

*Traitor's daughter.*

Fuck, and she was glad of it.

'Did she know?' The words emerged in a croak. 'Did she know I talked before she died?'

'She told us to spare her if we ever wanted to see the bindings broken,' Emelin said immediately, no questions or hesitation, as if these were perfectly normal things to ask. 'It didn't seem to occur to her that she wasn't the only one who could share the information, and she found out she was wrong before I slit her throat.'

It didn't make anything better.

It did make everything just a little less bad, though.

'Thank you,' she whispered. 'Thank you so much. I ... I'd like to be alone, now.'

A glass thudded onto a tabletop.

A snake hissed as it was picked up from the floor.

When she opened her eyes, an eternity later, they were both gone, having closed the door quietly behind them. Only their glasses were left on the mother-of-pearl table. Agenor's leather folder lay on the floor beside her feet. Where Emelin had been sitting, the little stone binding lay discarded on the couch, stripped of all its vicious power.

By the window, the plate-sized begonias pulsed gently in the sunlight.

Thysandra's mind was entirely her own.

# CHAPTER 33

THERE WAS ONE LAST battle she had left to fight, and she was both dreading it and craving it with a vehemence that made her heart hurt.

She made herself eat two more buns before she allowed herself to leave the room. She brushed her teeth. She brushed her hair. She put on a dress, took it off again, put on another dress, and found that one lacking as well; eventually, she settled on a gown she hadn't worn for ages, deep purple at the hem that blended into wine red, then vibrant orange, then daffodil yellow. It looked like a sunrise. Like a new beginning.

Two golden rings, one golden necklace, and she finally forced herself to turn away from the mirror. If she didn't give herself a stern talking to, she might dither until nightfall.

Out onto the balcony. Fresh air brushed her face. Chirping birds sang in the trees below.

She let herself drop into the briny sea breeze.

Only by flying over it did she realise just how much destruction the Labyrinth had caused in the Mother's bone hall. At the heart of the castle, a stretch of the roof had been torn away, edges curling like burned parchment. The single glimpse she caught of the interior was as black as that light had been white, every inch of the hall burned to charcoal by the force of the mountain's fury.

She remembered how her own skin had felt, open and raw, and shivered as she swerved away from the charred ruins.

Soon, she'd have that last reminder of the Mother's court torn down. Hell, she might smash the walls to pieces with her own damn hands.

Soon.

But first ...

She pressed away the cowardly urge to take a detour, making straight for the south of the island instead.

Creon's pavilion stood a little to the west of Faewood, where the trees were straighter and lighter and didn't whisper tales of murder to each other. The silvery roof gleamed blindingly in the sunlight as she descended. The roses curling around the stained-glass windows looked even redder than they usually did – nymph magic, perhaps, or else the flowers were simply reacting eagerly to Naxi's vicinity.

Which Thysandra quite understood.

It was bloody hard not to feel like a better, stronger, more *alive* version of herself with this particular half nymph around.

She stepped up onto the low porch and knocked lightly on the pale green window. Straightening her back was a useless gesture when every single person inside could read the nervousness directly from her heart, but she did it anyway – a fae had her pride, for hell's sake.

'Come in!'

Creon's voice.

For perhaps the first time in a century, her magic threatened to slip from her control as she drew just enough red from her wing to make the window vanish. Only a hurried addition of just the smallest drop of blue kept the shards from erupting into the home beyond.

She'd visited the place plenty of times in her life, yet it was rare for her to actually step inside – see the light birchwood floor, the intricate wood carvings around the windows, the plush blue couch and ready-made bed. It had always felt dangerous. Like stepping into enemy territory. Only now, the hate and the rivalry gone, did she recognise the pavilion for what it was: another safe refuge, another place to hide.

Creon still didn't look quite like the Creon she knew, peeling onions at the kitchen table with the ease of a man who knew his way around a knife.

Naxi, on the other hand, looked so very much like herself that it was hard to fathom she was real.

She was sitting at the short side of the table, rosy and golden, a half-finished flower wreath between her petal-stained fingers. A moment ago, she must have been chattering cheerfully. Now, her eyes had gone wide like saucers, her lips parted in a never-uttered squeal – as if she might have hidden beneath the bed if Creon had been just a heartbeat slower to reply to that cautious knock.

On the edge of Thysandra's sight, the bastard was looking very fucking content with himself. She couldn't be bothered to waste any thoughts on that observation.

Because Naxi was *here*. She shouldn't have been anywhere near the court anymore, shouldn't have wasted a single minute more in a place she hated to the very core of her demon soul – yet here she was sitting, radiant like sunlight, beautiful like the first rosy blossoms of spring, and even if it was silly and reckless to hope ...

Thysandra couldn't help it.

Just a tiny little sparkle of it, but enough to get her through the empty window frame. Enough to clear her throat, clear her throat again, and say, 'Morning?'

*You gave your family every reason to trust you*, she'd snapped at that dainty, delicate face. *Didn't you?*

She heard it again in the small beat of silence.

'More like afternoon, actually,' Creon helpfully pointed out, chucking his onion into an oven dish with the others and plucking another one from the unpeeled pile.

That was enough reason to avert her eyes and send him a blistering glare. He returned a smile that was a little too pale for the breezy carelessness in his voice – a smile that said *I know*, and *I'm sorry*, and most of all, *let's talk about that mother of mine later, when you're done sorting things out with the demon about to explode beside me.*

They must have heard she was awake.

He might have been the only person capable of keeping Naxi here in the time that had since passed.

'Right,' Thysandra said sheepishly. 'Afternoon.'

Creon shrugged and pointedly returned to his maiming of onions, as if to inform her that his job here was done.

'Right,' she said again, a little more lost now.

Naxi still hadn't moved.

It was almost unimaginable that this was the same bloodstained, sharp-toothed little avenger she'd seen emerge from the Labyrinth's darkness in those last frantic moments. Here, scrubbed clean and dressed in pale pastels, every part of her seemed crafted from the finest, most delicate materials – a fragile beauty that beckoned, *begged* to be cherished.

*You ran from the ones who relied on you before …*

Her words.

Her turn for courage, now.

'Would you, um …' Gods help her, it would have been useful if she'd actually decided what she'd wanted *before* opening her mouth – something more specific, at least, than *please don't hate me forever.* 'Would you mind going for a walk?'

There.

At least that would get them out from under Creon's chaperoning eyes.

Naxi turned even pinker than usual. But she rose, flicked a handful of bruised petals from her dress and fingers, and made for the open window without a word, blue eyes cast to the floor – a strangely demure posture, except Thysandra suspected it was likely a last, desperate attempt at restraint.

'Come by for dinner if you feel like it,' Creon said, not looking up.

Thysandra swallowed. 'Thanks.'

By her side, Naxi did not seem to have heard him at all.

Outside, the air was heavy with the scent of blooming roses, sunlight trickling through the foliage and flecking dancing patterns on the ferns and mosses. Thysandra walked onward aimlessly. Naxi followed quietly, her steps lacking their usual bounce – a stillness that became more and more pronounced with every minute that passed, morphing from flustered timidity into the implication of question, and then into an undeniable demand.

Even in this sun-streaked forest, the ghost of that gallery argument hung heavily between them. The words still echoed, sharp and vicious.

'I'm sorry,' Thysandra managed, finally.

A pathetic start. But it was a start, at least.

Naxi gave a small huff.

It was almost familiar. She'd been in a place like this before, begging for forgiveness in the face of unrelenting vexation – except grovelling before the Mother had only ever been a necessity, a betrayal of her own feelings for the sake of approval and survival. This ...

This was the gods-damned opposite. This was finally allowing her feelings to speak for her, approval be damned, survival be damned.

She didn't need anything in exchange this time. If the favour wasn't returned, the feelings were still just as true – and that realisation, somehow, made it a hundred times easier to open her mouth again.

'I was being cruel because I couldn't wrap my head around the possibility of kindness,' she said, the words coming mind-bogglingly easily – because she no longer needed to persuade, to convince, to prove herself true. She only needed to be honest. 'I was furious with myself for being weak, so I tore you down too. That was unnecessary and undeserved, and I wish I hadn't done it.'

Funny how frankness could feel so little like weakness. Far less so, really, than feigned strength.

Naxi sighed.

Then, long seconds later, she murmured, 'I was very angry.'

*Was*. Not *am*. Madness, to draw conclusions from a single small word, and yet Thysandra's heart couldn't help but stutter a little.

'Yes,' she said.

Naxi glanced sideways at her, face scrunched up a little. 'Maybe I still am.'

'Yes, that would be—'

'Even if you almost died in the meantime. *Especially* because you almost died in the meantime.' Her singsong voice was climbing higher. 'They didn't know if you'd survive it for the first three days! That was very rude, Sashka!'

Would it help to point out that *Thysandra* wasn't the one who had detonated a mountain right beneath her own feet? She decided the answer was a resounding negative and instead said, 'I'm very sorry for almost dying on you, too.'

Naxi huffed again.

The trees didn't stir, though. The ferns lining their path didn't develop any razor edges. It would have been so very easy for the forest to take bloody revenge on an aggrieved nymph's behalf, and yet it did not – a small comfort, perhaps, but this was hardly the time for complaints and grand demands.

At least a minute went by before Naxi suddenly said, 'I *was* going to leave, you know.'

Which shouldn't have been a surprise.

It landed like a blow to the skull all the same – the unspoken possibility, still so very much there. Perhaps she had only stayed around to ensure Thysandra would wake up from her near-fatal injuries. Perhaps she had hoped for a better apology. Perhaps she had needed more than honesty, and—

'Sashka.' A drawn-out groan. 'You're supposed to have the presence of mind to realise that I did not in fact leave, and then you're supposed to ask me why.'

Oh.

'Sorry,' Thysandra said weakly. 'I didn't realise there was a script.'

Naxi's eyeroll was a strong suggestion she figure out the rules of the game immediately, if not five minutes ago. 'It's not like it's hard. Just pretend you're actually good at trusting people.'

That was more helpful than it had any right to be.

'Alright.' She managed a nervous laugh. 'Why did you come back, then?'

'Because,' Naxi said, her entire body leaning into that word, 'I realised I was leaving you in the company of a backstabbing arsehole whose fingers I should have bitten off weeks ago, and you were going to die if I didn't do anything about it.'

It made all the sense, and yet it didn't.

'I was being horrible to you.' Why she was arguing, she didn't quite know. Not pointing it out felt like lying – as if Naxi might have overlooked the fact. 'Horrible enough that you decided I didn't have anything left to offer you. You weren't supposed to care about me anymore.'

'Yes.' Naxi shrugged, some of the springy lightness returning to her movements. 'That's what I thought, too.'

'Oh,' Thysandra said, because she couldn't think of anything better to say.

It earned her another glare. 'The *script*, Sashka.'

'I don't know the script!' Her voice cracked. 'I've never done this before! What am I supposed to ask – why you decided that you were going to run straight back into a fucking battlefield despite knowing damn well that it might be the end of you? Despite your having reminded me time and time again that you weren't going to risk your hide for anyone else's wellbeing? Is that—'

'Oh, pretty good,' Naxi brightly said, and all at once she was entirely herself again, the twist of her head swift, sprightly, as if her body could barely contain the energy bouncing within her. 'The reason for all of that is, of course, that I've always been a terrible demon.'

'You are certainly terrible,' Thysandra muttered.

'Oh, *thank* you.' A sharp-toothed grin. 'See? You're getting better at this already.'

The urge to throw something at that smug blue-eyed face was maddening and delightful at once. 'Am I supposed to ask what makes you so terrible now?'

'Well,' Naxi said thoughtfully, 'the thing is that I'm still a nymph, too.'

That was hardly news.

The tone of her voice suggested it *should* be news, though.

'Yes?' Thysandra said, entirely unsure what the script expected from her now.

'I've been thinking a lot about that, these days,' Naxi murmured, stepping gingerly over a fallen log on their path. Gone was the mischievous twinkle in her eyes. She was suddenly entirely solemn again, gaze drifting into the distance as if to puzzle out something far greater than either of them. 'I was never like my mother's family, you know, so I figured I had to be like my father instead. Except that my father *did* enjoy scaring people. He wouldn't feel lonely. He wouldn't feel envious of community.'

All of it made sense, all of it was entirely unsurprising, and yet Thysandra had not the faintest idea of where this line of reasoning was leading.

'Yes,' she said again.

Either it was what she'd been supposed to say, or Naxi had stopped caring about the precise course of the conversation. 'Demons are solitary creatures, of course,' she continued, expression not brightening. 'Nymphs are very much not, though. It was easy to forget that when I lived in the Underground and had friends around me every day. Here ... I realised.'

Thysandra's heart went cold. 'Are you saying you want to go back to the Underground?'

'What?' Naxi jerked her head around so violently that pink curls flew in all directions. 'No, of course that's not what I'm saying, for hell's sake! Don't be dense, Sashka!'

'But ... but you said—'

Naxi threw up her arms, whirling to a standstill on the path. 'I'm saying I want you, you idiot!'

That was not what she'd been saying.

Thysandra was really quite sure that was *not* what she'd been saying at all.

'But ...' Gods have mercy, why was she *still* arguing? 'But I ...'

'But you're stubborn and unreasonably distrustful and terrible at conversations?' Naxi finished, glaring at her. 'Yes, I know. So?'

'You don't love me,' Thysandra said faintly.

The forest was silent for a moment.

Green, gold-flecked silence, framing that pale little demon face as it softened into an expression Thysandra hadn't seen before – not the piercing knowingness of those all-seeing blue eyes, but rather pensive, self-observant, as if for the very first time, Naxi's demon senses were turning inward and reading the beats of her own twisted heart.

'No,' she admitted, tasting the word. 'No, I assume I don't.'

It didn't matter, and yet it did. Didn't matter, because Thysandra's heart had made its own senseless choices, and no lack of love could change a damn thing about that. Did matter, though, *because* she was already in far, far too deep. Because she didn't know if want could be enough. Because for once, just *once* in her life, she didn't want to be the one sacrificing, surrendering, giving more than she could ever hope to receive.

'No,' she repeated, and it felt like a lock clicking shut.

'Or at least ...' Naxi cocked her head, curls tumbling over her shoulders. 'I don't get those warm, fuzzy feelings in my stomach whenever I think of you. I don't feel your pain and joy like it's my own. I think those are the things you people with empathy tend to call love, aren't they?'

Did they have to spell it out like that?

It almost felt like mockery, coming from the person who knew perfectly well what warm, fuzzy feelings Thysandra still couldn't manage to suppress.

'I don't think there's any need to talk about this further,' she choked out. Not the script. Too hell with the script. Disappointment hit harder after hope; at once, she wanted nothing more than to get out of here, lock herself back in her rooms, and empty a bottle of wine on her own. 'Might be best if you—'

'It hurts not to have you,' Naxi said.

It didn't sound like a confession.

It simply sounded like a truth.

'It's hurt every single day since we first met.' A small, rueful smile that, despite everything, made Thysandra's heart twinge. 'And I told myself it was because of what you could do for *me*, what *I* got out of it ... but then you were in danger, and it had absolutely nothing to do with me anymore. I just didn't want you to be dead.'

Nymph blood after all ... but hell, did it really change anything?

'You already said you wanted me.' Disillusion made her voice tremble. 'That doesn't—'

'It's not *that*,' Naxi cut in, voice urgent, agitated, her hands fluttering the half-made point aside. 'Fine, I want you! But I also ... I want you to be well more than I want myself to be well, do you understand? I want to feed you tea and pastries after every stressful day. I want to hold you in the bath for hours and kiss you until you feel safe again. I want to bite the face off everyone who ever calls you—'

Was it a sob that broke from Thysandra's lips? Was it a laugh? She had no gods-damned clue anymore. 'You've made your point, I think.'

'No, but you don't get the point, Sashka!' There was a rawness about Naxi's voice. Something that wasn't soft or sweet at all. 'This *is* my sort of love. Who the hell cares what I'm feeling or not feeling? It's not as if you can read my emotions. And I don't think it fucking matters how *you* would classify what's in my heart, because ... because ...'

She wavered.

'Because what?' Thysandra whispered, and she wasn't quite sure her heart was still beating.

'Because what matters is you. Not me.' Naxi's lips twitched into a not-quite-smile. 'And even if I'm terrible at feeling love myself, I'm damn sure I can make you feel *loved*.'

Thysandra stared at her.

Felt, tangible on her skin, a blanket draped around her shoulders by gentle, feathery fingers.

Hot tea in her hands. A brush through her hair. Lips and hands on her body, coaxing her to sleep at night and waking her sweetly in the morning – laughter, danger, *always* by her side. Did it matter what feelings did or did not lie beneath?

It would be grossly inaccurate to claim *Thysandra* was the one giving too much in all those moments.

'You …' She had trouble shaping words all of a sudden as the world shifted in and out of focus – away from that single stupid word she'd put so, so much weight on, and towards the nameless, unspoken feelings that had been there all along, in every fight, in every tender touch. The things she *wanted*. 'You do make me feel … safe.'

'Good.' Naxi crossed her arms, jutting her chin forward. 'I intend to make you feel very safe and very strong and occasionally horny. Anything else?'

Her heart felt like it might burst.

Could it be that easy? Ridiculous, and yet so many things had become easy when she'd let them be – because people *had* helped her and saved her and wiped the vomit off her lips. She didn't want Naxi's feelings. She wanted what *she* felt around Naxi. So if she could believe it, if they could stay here and—

Oh.

*Stay here.*

Her chest deflated.

'You'll want to go somewhere else, though, won't you?' Even as she spoke the words, her shoulders were already tightening. Bracing for the next blow to hit. 'This is my home. It's never been *more* my home. So if you want to leave, I—'

'Oh, I don't want to,' Naxi lightly interrupted.

'You … you don't?'

'No.' A sudden, dazzling smile. 'I actually think I haven't wanted to leave in a while. Kept trying to convince you, but I was trying to convince myself just as much. I've come to the conclusion that I really like this court.'

It took several seconds of replaying those words in her mind before Thysandra dared to assume she had in fact heard them correctly.

'What?' she stammered.

'Well, the Labyrinth is lovely, of course. And not scared of me.' Naxi spun around, pointing to the east as if directing an invisible orchestra. 'Faewood needs some work, but I think I can fix it if you give me a few decades. And maybe we can domesticate the hounds? That would be pretty funny. Creon says there's plenty of good soil for gardening, and—'

'Are you *joking*?' It seemed unlikely, admittedly – but then, it seemed equally unlikely that any of this was true. 'You ... you really want ...'

'Well,' Naxi said, lips twisting into a wicked smile, 'upon reflection, idyllic islands are pretty boring, aren't they?'

A breathless chuckle slipped past Thysandra's lips, and then another one. And then she was laughing – wholehearted, unstoppable laughter – because the world was great, the world was *perfect*, and there were a million-and-one things she needed to do, but Naxi would still want her if she did exactly none of them ...

'So you want me to stay?' There was such light in those bright blue nymph eyes, such unguarded, un-demon-like hope. 'Do I make you feel happy, Sashka?'

'You make me feel stupidly happy.' She felt dizzy. Like she'd flown too hard for too long, drunk on the rush of the wind, spinning on the edge of lost control. 'I ... I'm not sure I've ever been this happy before. I ...'

'Oh good,' Naxi said, and her shivery little giggle sounded as delighted as it was surprised. As if even she hadn't believed life could possibly be *this* good. 'I really like it when I make you laugh. It feels like I've won something. You're really pretty when you laugh, do you know that, Sashka? Your eyes—'

Thysandra could not care less about her eyes.

One step forward, one dip of her head, and her lips smothered the rest of that breathless sentence.

# EPILOGUE

IT WAS A BRIGHT winter day at the Crimson Court, and Naxi was having the time of her life.

She was, admittedly, having the time of her life almost always these days – but this particular occasion was even better than average. Today, her friends were visiting her new home. And not in some faraway gallery either, stashed away like a shameful secret; Thysandra had called half the court together to witness the historic events about to take place in their midst. A horde of scribes and archivists. Farmers from the other fae isles. Every fae construction worker who'd spent the last few months cleaning up rubble in human cities.

Everyone, really, except the pitiful remains of the Crimson Court's army. The few commanders who had been invited for politeness' sake looked uncomfortably out of place amongst the many guests who'd arrived from the other magical peoples.

'... observe the sovereignty of each individual island as stated by its ruler or rulers ...' Thysandra was saying at the table at the centre of the hall, reading from the parchment in her hands, voice loud enough to be heard in the farthest corners.

She had to sit there with the rest of her visitors, of course, High Lady or no. It would be a grave insult to invite representatives from all over the archipelago and then have them stand before the brand new throne of the Crimson Court like children called to face the headmaster. Since that meant the throne in question was left vacant, however, Naxi had generously taken it upon herself to fill it; curled up in the comfortable seat of red-brown wood, fuzzy shawl around her shoulders against the chilly winter air, she was in the perfect position to observe both the proceedings and the exquisite curve of Thysandra's backside.

One had to treat oneself every now and then.

'Furthermore,' Thysandra continued, calm and unwavering as she flipped a page, 'the court pledges to lend all requested assistance to the ongoing investigations into wartime crimes committed by its inhabitants ...'

On the left side of what was now called the Labyrinth's Hall, dangerously close to a group of alves, a red-clad army commander stirred noticeably. Naxi narrowed her eyes at him, just in case he gave the impression he was in need of a sudden and painful death – but at the side of the representatives' table, Silas had already levelled a glare at the troublemaker and pointedly tapped a bargain mark on his forearm. The disturbance instantly melted away again.

Thysandra had noticed too, Naxi knew from the little spike of alertness stuttering through her veins. But she had not stopped reading, and the alertness was just ... that.

Not alarm.

Definitely not fear.

It had been a while since Naxi had truly sensed fear from her. She intended to keep it that way.

Listening with half an ear to the summary of the treaty the company was about to sign, she let her gaze drift past the table – Tared sent her a quick grin, Emelin a broad smile – and then around the hall, which was cold and resplendent in the clear winter light. Thysandra had wanted it razed to the ground at first, after Nicanor's timely and crispy end. The Labyrinth had been a little grumpy at the prospect, though, and Naxi had pointed out that the poor thing would be horribly bored without any company to listen to – so instead, they'd renovated the place.

The marble floor had been partly restored now, leaving a generous opening to the cave below. Blood-red, nymph-grown roses adorned the alabaster walls. The ceiling, burned away by the explosion that had killed Nicanor and most of his allies, had been replaced by a grand glass dome, allowing the Labyrinth to gaze at the stars at night.

Last week, Naxi had taken a small company of adventurous fae youths down with her for the very first time. They had gasped breathless compliments at every step along the way and meant most of them, too; the mountain had been enormously pleased.

It seemed quite pleased now too, judging by the bright white-blue light glowing in the cave beneath as Thysandra finally finished, '... for eternity, or until any of these oaths are broken. If there are any objections to these rulings ...'

The red-clad army commander wisely did not move this time. Nor did any of the seven other representatives around the table. A little cheer came from the ranks of the clerks who'd worked tirelessly for weeks to get every single word and number in the right place; a ripple of laughter pulsed around the hall in response, breaking the solemn tension.

'I'll consider that all the approval we need,' Thysandra dryly said, picking up the pile of parchment that contained eight copies of the meticulously worded, painstakingly negotiated peace treaty between the Crimson Court and not just the other magical peoples, but the two other fae courts as well. 'Shall we sign these things, then?'

'Thought you'd never ask,' Tared said, his grin almost entirely amiable. Thysandra had gone to great lengths to find the swords that had been looted during the massacre of Skeire among the court's significant alf steel reserves; returning those to the family had improved relations with remarkable speed. 'Pretty sure Em's getting hungry.'

'Oh, was that *your* stomach?' the High Lady of the Cobalt Court countered sweetly as she reached for a pen. 'I thought it was the Labyrinth grumbling.'

Delwin snorted. Agenor was making an unsuccessful attempt not to laugh. Drusa pursed her lips in obvious disapproval, then picked up her own pen when she did not find anyone else to share in her well-mannered rage; her fingers were stiff with displeasure as she signed her copy of the treaty.

For a minute or so, the scratching of pens and the clinking of ink pots was the only sound to be heard. Naxi decided it was time to hop off her throne, so she did – bouncing down the steps and then towards the others over the pleasantly smooth floor. A pile of half-signed agreements was piling up on the table before Thysandra, who needed to sign seven copies rather than a single one; Naxi recognised Agenor's messy hand, Emelin's slightly dramatic flourish, Bakaru's initials as noted down by Nenya.

'Can I sign too?' she asked, because now that she was seeing that list of names, this all looked like great fun.

'What?' Drusa said sharply.

'Of course you can sign,' Thysandra said, entirely unperturbed, as she handed Naxi a pen over her shoulder.

The phoenix eldest's eyes widened with outrage. 'This is *most* unprecedented and—'

'You can sign my copy too, Naxi,' Emelin cheerfully interrupted.

'Mine too, please,' Tared added, although the spark of spiteful glee within him suggested it was for the benefit of Drusa's fury as much as for Naxi's pleasure. She was perfectly alright with that. She'd never liked any of the phoenix rulers, and Drusa made Lyn feel terrible, which meant a little anger was the least she deserved. 'Can't hurt to have a demon on the treaty.'

Naxi glowered at him. '*Half* demon.'

His smile went a little rueful. 'Sorry. Half demon.'

So she signed three copies, and then Agenor's, Helenka's, and Delwin's too, making sure her capitalised *NAXI* was just a little larger than any of the other names. Nenya regretfully suggested Bakaru might make a fuss about an additional name on his treaty, so Naxi kept her hands off that one. No one even bothered to check with Drusa what her preferences might be.

Then it was done: seven copies, seven signatures with a little demonic bonus, and for the first time in over a thousand long years, the archipelago was officially at peace.

None of the rulers at the table allowed themselves to show it, but in the sudden and weighty silence that fell, Naxi sensed more than a few stinging eyes and catches in throats around her.

'There.' Helenka broke the silence, chucking her pen onto the table with a characteristic brusqueness. 'Time for a drink?'

The hall collectively started breathing again.

'I must be on my way,' Drusa said stiffly, tucking her copy of the treaty into a neat pile of parchment. 'If any al— If *anyone* would be so kind as to take me back to Phurys ...'

'Almost sounded like you were asking your favourite northern barbarians for help there,' Tared said, his grin at her broad and full of heartfelt loathing. 'Don't worry, I'll be overjoyed to get you out of here at the earliest convenience.'

Naxi saw Emelin mouth something at her father – *So much for the peace*, it seemed – and Agenor choked on an unwilling laugh. Thankfully Thysandra was already intervening, thanking Drusa politely and sincerely for her presence and the pleasant cooperation during all these weeks – because that was Thysandra, determined to do things well and fairly even when the things truly deserved nothing better than a good bout of laughter, or perhaps a good punch in the face.

Some days, Naxi despaired of her. Then again, it was damnably attractive, too.

Somewhat placated, Drusa took her leave of the company and haughtily offered Tared a thin hand in order to be faded out. He returned about five seconds later, the tight-lipped elderly lady on his arm replaced by a much smaller, much brighter, much more welcome bundle of red hair and freckles. Lyn had, as usual, requested that no one try to put her in the same room as the older phoenix who ... well, Naxi wasn't sure what exactly Drusa had done, but she was quite certain it warranted biting off several fingers and perhaps a nose.

Not that she was going to speak that thought out loud, because last time she had, Lyn had somehow started crying.

'Excellent,' Thysandra said beside her, resuming her role of hostess with resolute ease. Her moss-green gown shimmered around her hips and legs as she rose; along the walls, the gathered court finally started moving too, as if they'd needed the departure of one of the negotiators to signal the officialities had truly ended. 'Time for a drink, indeed.'

The celebratory dinner was hosted in the crystalline hall, where Thysandra had almost died a few months ago, and where Naxi had been stupid enough to mistake the tension and grimness in Nicanor's heart for genuine distress.

It didn't look nearly as ominous today. No dead hounds to be seen, no blood-red velvet drapes on the walls. The Crimson Court's new Master of Ceremony, a young fae by the name of Calaria, had received Thysandra's instructions and thrown every ounce of her considerable imagination into their implementation; the hall was covered in white flowers now, the light glinting off the iridescent walls unmistakably alf magic. Behind the dais, an embroidered map of the archipelago filled most of the wall, the colours matching the newly drawn borderlines to the tiniest stitch.

Most of the nymphs still sat with the other nymphs, of course, the vampires with the vampires, the alves with the alves. But some of the fae and human scribes who'd spent the last few months working on negotiations gingerly took seats between the other magical creatures, and the main table was the usual hodgepodge of all Naxi's friends.

She ate very, very happily.

Thysandra was doing High Lady things and doing them very well as always, having serious conversations with everyone who approached her, shaking hands and remembering names and laughing at nervous jokes that really weren't all that funny. Naxi decided not to disturb her, because she was slowly coming to grasp that Thysandra *enjoyed* being dutiful. Instead, she ate a second helping of rhubarb pudding, then bounced off her chair and went to look for someone else to talk to.

Nenya seemed a bad candidate; she was sipping a goblet of blood and chatting with a greying, red-haired clerk named Rinald, who had volunteered to oversee the vampire negotiations a few months ago and seemed *overjoyed* every time he got himself close to a pair of fangs. Naxi was a little surprised to see the vampire was humouring him and his obsessive fascination at all, until she realised that Edored had seated himself on the opposite side of the table, and that Nenya was mostly extremely busy not looking *his* way for even a second.

Edored, oblivious to the fact that he was being aggressively snubbed, threw Naxi his broadest grin as she passed and yelled, 'Catch!'

She squeaked but caught the fork he flung her way just in time, managing by some miraculous new reflex not to get herself injured in the act.

'*Edored!*' Lyn snapped, two chairs away.

'What?' the alf sputtered, looking indignant. 'She wanted me to teach her how to juggle!'

'Yes, and does that need to happen with *forks*, Edored darling?'

'Why not? Safer than' – he interrupted himself to snatch the fork from the air as Naxi hurled it back at him – 'than to start with knives, yes?'

'That does sound entirely sensible to me,' Thorir said next to him, face deadpan.

Lyn's reply was somewhat hard to interpret due to the arms she'd buried her face in, but it did seem to contain the phrases *fucking idiots* and *lucky you're still alive* and *not my responsibility if any of you kill yourselves tomorrow*. That last part was of course a lie, because *everything* was Lyn's responsibility according to Lyn's brain – but Naxi figured there might be better moments than festive dinners to point that out.

Empathically, of course.

She was practicing empathy. And juggling. And, bit by bit, love.

She exchanged a few more forks with Edored, then bounced on to where Lyn had reemerged from her own arms and resumed her conversation with Tared – her wildly gesturing hands and the flurries of sparks spilling from her fingers suggesting the topic was related to her research on magic. She was feeling the way she always did around Tared, happy but *cautiously* so – as if that happiness was a fragile thing she couldn't possibly afford to drop. And below that, buried so deep it had taken Naxi years to notice it ... that perpetual small, smouldering thread of brewing anger, unwanted and neglected, biding its time.

It would be very good for Lyn to finally be angry for once.

That, too, would be better discussed on literally any other occasion.

Naxi didn't interrupt the two of them. The last months had been fraught enough – no sense in disrupting things while they were going well.

She found Inga and Agenor near the end of the table, accompanied by two empty seats and a tanned human man who looked to be in his late forties. Inga broke off their conversation the moment Naxi appeared, her face pink with either happiness or tipsiness or both, and there was only a small and habitual wince of fear inside her as she beamed one of her rare true smiles. 'Naxi! Have you met Russ? My sort-of-brother?'

'You have a lot of sort-of family members,' Naxi observed, squinting at the man in question. His sturdy build didn't resemble Inga's slender form in the slightest, nor did he look like Allie; it seemed unlikely he was her brother by birth. 'Is that a human thing?'

'More of a vampire thing, these days,' Russ said with a faint grin, and Agenor almost choked on his wine beside him. 'Pleasure to meet you.'

'The pleasure is mutual,' Naxi said politely because that was what one was supposed to say, and anyway, she didn't think she was going to have a problem with him. Inga seemed to like him. Agenor seemed to like him. If those two agreed, it quite had to be justified. 'May I take this seat?'

'Go ahead,' Inga said, nudging back one of the empty chairs with her foot. 'We're mostly waiting until Al is done interrogating Silas about his honourable intentions, but that could take a while. She's only been going for ten minutes or so.'

Russ and Agenor grimaced in perfect synchronicity.

Only then did Naxi spot the Lord Protector of the Crimson Court in a quieter corner of the hall, six and a half feet tall and about half as broad, looking decidedly sweaty about the unimpressed glares the thin-limbed, sharp-fanged Lady of the Golden Court was levelling at him. Naxi hadn't seen him this unsettled since Thysandra had bestowed his new position upon him a few months ago, and that might have had more to do with Inga threatening to gut him if he didn't stay and accept the office.

'He'll survive,' the girl now said, airily. 'At least he didn't actively *serve* the Mother in the last four centuries, you know? She's been known to forgive people for worse.'

Agenor winced. 'More wine, anyone?'

They drank more wine.

Silas was called away to deal with a disturbance a few minutes later; Naxi had rarely seen a male so deeply relieved by the prospect of potential danger. The small tussle on the other side of the hall looked rather harmless – a few rowdy alves getting on the nerves of their fae neighbours – but she quickly checked Thysandra's emotions regardless. If there was any fear there, it would be time to kill a few people and make a point.

There was no fear, just awareness and a pleasant layer of trust in Silas's ability to handle matters. Excellent.

Naxi turned back to her wine just in time to see Allie fall into the seat beside Agenor, her smile still showing a hint of fang. The full extent of her assessment was a measured, 'Well, that could have been a lot worse.'

'I knew you'd like him,' Inga said fondly.

'I've just come to accept that I sent the whole family down a path of terrible taste in men,' Allie said, throwing her a grin. 'Speaking of which, where did my beloved daughter and her own terrible man vanish to?'

'Thys had something to discuss with them.' Agenor gave half a shrug. 'I'm not sure where they went next.'

Thysandra?

Naxi frowned and glanced at the other side of the table. Her High Lady was engrossed in an animated conversation with two nymph

432

queens; there was no trace of either Emelin or Creon to be seen around the hall.

Shame. Then again, Naxi could ask Creon about important topics like kittens and the domestication of hound puppies later. If Thysandra needed to get something done, she presumably had good reason for it.

Naxi nestled herself more comfortably in her chair and let the cheerful sound of voices wash over her.

It was past midnight by the time the last visitors left the Crimson Court; even most fae had vanished to their beds by then, and only Calaria's army of organisers was still swarming through the hall, clearing out dirty plates and glasses. Emelin and Creon had reappeared shortly before leaving. They had exchanged a last few words with Thysandra, then run off again with nothing but a wave at Naxi by way of goodbye – mysterious, but she was drowsy with wine and good company, and sooner or later she'd get her answers anyway.

Thysandra found her then, exhaustion in every fibre of her, but the light in her dark eyes no less bright for it. There was, Naxi had come to realise, a world of difference between the exhaustion of losing a game and the exhaustion of working to win one.

Thysandra was winning a lot these days.

She did not sit down now, instead resting her hands on the back of Naxi's chair so she could press a kiss to the top of her head. 'Feeling happy?'

Naxi suppressed a contented yawn. 'Are you reading emotions now?'

'Not at all,' Thysandra said dryly. 'You just look like you're about to start purring. Do you think you can handle one more surprise for the night?'

Faster than expected. Naxi tilted her head back, squinting up, and said, 'What sort of surprise, exactly?'

'That's not how surprises work.' A small pause. 'I can promise you it's nothing dead, though.'

Naxi's squint turned into a glare. 'I don't know why you keep bringing up that ratty clerk. It was just once! And he deserved it for—'

'—helping to trap Gadyon – I know.' Thysandra gave a grimace that looked more like a grin in disguise. 'All the same, I didn't necessarily need his severed head on my dinner table. Are you going to come with me, or do you need to argue a little longer?'

A good question. Upon reflection, perhaps this was not the moment to defend that moving gesture of demonic devotion in any more detail.

'*Fine*,' Naxi said, dramatically yet happily, and hopped off her chair to follow.

Their path through the castle was uneventful, murder attempts having become increasingly rare after some public demonstrations of what could happen if one really, *really* pissed off a demon. Naxi had vaguely expected they would be making for some unusual location, like the bathhouses or the gardens – but Thysandra led them straight up the usual stairs, towards the tower by the Faewood cliffs and the rooms she'd stubbornly refused to move out of no matter how many luxury apartments had been suggested as more suitable replacements.

There was nothing particularly surprising to be seen in the stairwell. Nothing on the landing either, save for the familiar redwood door with its familiar flower carvings and the invisible magic shields it contained.

Naxi bounced up the last steps and paused, waiting for Thysandra to open the lock only she – and admittedly Creon – could open.

Thysandra did not open it.

Instead, she stood and studied the door for a moment, the emotion within her a hard-to-parse mixture of curiosity, nervousness, and an unmistakable whiff of smugness.

'Shouldn't we' – Naxi cleared her throat – 'go inside and see the surprise?'

'Oh, we should.' But Thysandra stepped *back* – wings folding in, green dress pooling around her feet as she sat down on the winding stairs leading to the next floor. 'So why don't you open the door?'

Naxi blinked. 'Because I can't—'

She faltered.

Thysandra tilted her head, a small smile tugging at the corner of her lips, and Naxi blinked again.

*Open the door.*

Which was impossible. Because only three people in the world knew how that lock worked, an ingenious magic invention that turned at the spark of red magic in the right place; two of them were fae, and the third was Naxi, who did not have colour magic to operate it. There was no other way to get in. The Mother had made the door immune to the workings of magic in all other spots, and to physical attacks as well – a shield tested thoroughly by dozens, if not hundreds, of attacks over the course of the centuries.

But there was one other fae mage with godsworn magic in the world, and that same mage had just been suspiciously absent from dinner for hours. As had the one other person able to operate these locks.

Rather an ideal combination if, hypothetically, one wanted to ... well, *alter* the mechanism.

It felt dangerously hopeful to even think it. More dangerous still to look at the door, look back at the stairs, and say, 'Did you ...'

Thysandra's expression didn't shift. 'Mm-hmm.'

'You changed the *lock*?'

'Just an idea I had.' The minuscule twitch upward of those sweet, sweet lips was nothing compared to the ocean of brimming satisfaction that lay beyond. 'It's wood, you see. I figured your nymph magic should be able to manipulate it. So I asked Emelin to modify the protections a little, and she *thinks* ...'

Naxi blinked again, at the door this time.

It was a bit of a challenge, finding the soul of the wood. It had been cut off from its living tree for such a long time, cut into shapes, subjected to all sorts of strange magic. But it was still *there*, and the moment she grasped it—

She found the hollow within it.

Most of the wood was touching the cold, hard, lifeless iron of the lock. One small patch was left free, however, and she whispered at it to grow just a *little* bit bigger, just for a very short moment ...

A click.

A sense of movement.

Naxi barely dared to touch the doorknob. But she did, and it *turned*, and the door to Thysandra's rooms – no, to *their* rooms, damn it – opened without a creak of the hinges.

'Oh,' she breathed.

Behind her, Thysandra was emanating waves of pride and relief and the faintest hint of nervousness.

Naxi should have looked around, of course. She should have smiled and said thank you a thousand times over – but she stared at the room that had opened up before her, lit by glowing faelights, at the kitchen corner and the arched windows and the plants growing contently over all of it – and something was burning like hellfire behind her eyes.

*Home.*

Thysandra's feelings went a little more concerned behind her. 'Naxi?'

She opened her mouth and managed nothing but a feeble little sniffle.

'Naxi? Are you crying?'

'No!' she sputtered, sounding blubbery.

Footsteps behind her. 'You *are* crying, aren't you?'

'I'm fearsome!' she protested, hearing the quiver in her own voice. 'Of course I'm not crying! I'm deadly and—'

'You're utterly adorable,' Thysandra said, arms wrapping around Naxi from behind, hoisting her off the floor. 'And very much crying.'

They were strong and warm and gorgeous, those arms, and it was hard not to melt into them instantly, because Thysandra had said *adorable*, not *scary and occasionally homicidal*, and Naxi wanted to bask in the sound of that word forever. She buried her face into a muscular shoulder and grumbled, 'I could reduce you to pleas in a minute.'

'Really?' Thysandra stepped into the half-lit living room, nudging the door shut with her foot as she carried Naxi inside. 'I'd love to see you try.'

'I won last time we fought!' Naxi sputtered, sending a slightly teary glare up at her.

A mesmerizingly wicked grin. 'I'm pretty sure I won. I seem to recall I ended up with a knife against your throat.'

'Well,' Naxi said and defiantly sniffed again, 'I ended up with you, so you're not going to beat that with all the knives in the world. Checkmate.'

Thysandra wisely did not argue with that.

Instead, she lowered Naxi to her feet and kissed her.

No bribes needed. No vines, either. No pretences of courtly duty and obligation and whatever justifications she had spent so long giving herself. There was just desire inside that beautiful fae heart now, bright and hungry and unrestrained, and Naxi gave into it the way she did everything these days – with all her heart, and just a little bit of teeth.

It earned her a hissed curse and a red-hot sting of arousal.

Demons got bored, but *this* never got boring – the sweet, hot taste of being wanted, a sensation of longing so bone-deep she could have wept from it. Thysandra's fingers raked through her hair. Fisted around handfuls of curls. Tilted back her head, positioning her just so, and deepened the kiss with an intensity that sent the last of Naxi's sensible thoughts scattering – and then they were staggering into the room, towards the bedroom door, hands frantic and breath a shared, gasping mess. Naxi fumbled with green satin. Thysandra clawed at her hair ribbons. Buttons and lacing and clasps, the slither of fabric over skin, and they never even made it to the bed; Naxi went to her knees on the plush white rug, and Thysandra followed without question, pulling her farther down.

'Should maybe ...' She gasped as Naxi clawed at her thigh, arching back against the rug with wings splayed wide. 'Should maybe close the curtains.'

'Alternatively,' Naxi mumbled, out of breath, 'the curtains can go to hell.'

The plants were already moving around her, vines and leaves weaving across the glass. She'd barely even needed to ask them.

Thysandra let out a strangled laugh as she let her head fall back – that beautiful surrender, given so easily these days. 'So useful.'

'And powerful,' Naxi merrily suggested, crawling over her, the pink tips of her hair brushing over dark skin, pebbling nipples. 'And extremely pretty. And—'

'Naxi.' A throaty laugh. 'You don't have to earn this.'

A good point.

Really, a *very* good point.

Naxi bit her lip. 'Can I sit on your face, then?'

Thysandra's strong hands had already wrapped around her thighs, dragging her forward, head coming up a fraction – and then her mouth was on Naxi, and the world shrunk to touch and need and a single, all-consuming *yes*.

Once upon a time she'd thought there was no better feeling than revenge.

She knew better now. Revenge was all about loss. About not having. It was nothing, absolutely nothing, to being *had*, thoroughly and enthusiastically, and Thysandra's lips were doing exactly that – sucking and skimming until Naxi thought she might die from it, and then she was still not stopping. Drowning herself in pleasure as much as she was driving Naxi mad ... and only then did the realisation dawn.

Treaty day.

Months and months of work, culminating in the greatest victory yet, and where Naxi loved to think about it, Thysandra was undeniably looking for a well-earned break from thinking about anything at all.

Good.

Mindless oblivion was a demon's specialty.

Naxi did not move, kneeling over those ravenous lips. The hands clamping down on her thighs wouldn't have let her. But her nymph magic swept out, her demon senses sharpened ... and when the vines cascaded down, when the first of them curled around Thysandra's wings and thighs, she was ready for the heady burst of pleasure, the startled gasp against her pussy.

'Fuck.' Hoarse. Raspy. 'Naxi ...'

'Don't stop,' she murmured, her own voice a little slurred as she fisted her hands in Thysandra's glorious curls. 'I'll be very cruel if you stop now.'

A breathless laugh, and Thysandra's tongue slid into her, nails clawing into Naxi's thighs. The vines followed the example, wrapping around Thysandra's legs with just the smallest scrape of thorns, and for a single moment of mesmerising unity, there was no telling whose pleasure was whose. Naxi's legs were shaking now with the effort of keeping her upright, with the unfaltering onslaught of tongue and teeth and lips working her in unison. But she focused her attention on the thicker vine skimming over the rug, smooth and thornless, and called it closer, closer, closer ...

Thysandra gasped again as it slid between her legs.

Naxi didn't wait for her to recover, probing deeper.

Sensations mingled, as if her demon senses were getting dizzy, no longer sure of up or down, of *you* or *me*. She felt the tongue dragging along her own soaked lips. Felt the wet heat clenching tight around that vine. Felt its sweet intrusion, Thysandra's shock and lust and brazen pleasure, and thrust deeper.

A breathless moan brushed over her wetness.

'Sashka,' she gasped. 'Don't *stop*.'

Then she thrust again, before those clever fae lips could resume their work, and Thysandra cried out, actually *cried out*, as her mouth closed on Naxi once more.

It was agony, having to think as pleasure cascaded over her through all senses at once. It was *glorious*. Thysandra writhed beneath her, fucked slowly but unrelentingly as her tongue fucked Naxi in turn, panting and moaning, wings tightening with need. Naxi threw her head back. Closed her eyes. Sank into the sensations, into the overwhelming, incandescent bliss of everything at once, and reached back.

Found the plump swell of a breast under her fingers, the rock-hard peak of a nipple, and – sweetly, viciously – pinched.

Thysandra came apart beneath her.

It was the last straw. The last nudge over that tempting, looming edge. Naxi followed gladly – twofold pleasure, rippling through her in cascading waves, echoing back and forth across her demon senses, until she was out of breath and out of sense and she no longer felt anything at all but the sweetest, most savage *rightness*.

Rolling herself onto the rug felt like coming home. Snuggling into Thysandra's arms felt like coming home. Breathing in the scent of sweat and sex and joyful flowers felt like coming home, or perhaps, even better, like *making* her own home.

Tomorrow would be yet another day at the Crimson Court.

Tomorrow she would be having the time of her life again.

But right now the world was quiet and lit only by warm, glowing faelights. Right now the High Lady of the Crimson Court was lying drowsy and debauched on her own living room floor, and Naxi wasn't moving from her arms, wasn't even *thinking* of moving, because she might be getting a little cold, and she might be exhausted and in dire need of sleep, and her left foot might be developing just the slightest cramp ... but more than anything else, she was by Thysandra's side, in Thysandra's arms.

And she was exactly where she ought to be.

Haven't read the story of Naxi and Thysandra's first meeting yet? Check out In Love and War through: mybook.to/ILaW

The main Fae Isles series, starting with Court of Blood and Bindings, tells the story of the war against the Mother – and of Naxi and Thysandra's romance in between their first meeting and the start of With Wing and Claw. Get book 1 here: mybook.to/cobab

More Fae Isles books will be coming! To be notified of my new releases, you can:

- Sign up for my newsletter: www.lisettemarshall.com/sign-up

- Follow me on BookBub: www.bookbub.com/authors/lisette -marshall

- Follow me on Amazon: www.amazon.com/author/lisettemar shall

# OTHER BOOKS BY LISETTE

**They call him the Silent Death, because he kills without sound and leaves none capable of speaking in his wake...**

When the empire's deadliest fae murderer catches her wielding forbidden magic, twenty-year-old Emelin believes her hour has come. Instead, her inhumanly beautiful captor spares her life, but carries her off on his velvet wings – into the one place from which no human ever returns.

The heart of the Fae Isles. The treacherous Crimson Court, where the Mother of faekind has ruled unchallenged over fae and humans for decades.

The Silent Death is supposed to be the Mother's loyal servant, her invincible warrior, her ruthless, soulless killer. But in the shadows he is playing a game of his own, and he needs Emelin's magic to win it.

If she agrees to work with him, she could free all of humanity. But can she trust a fae male with so much blood on his hands? Worse, when his smouldering dark eyes and dangerous secrets reveal glimpses of the heart behind his murderer's mask... can she trust herself?

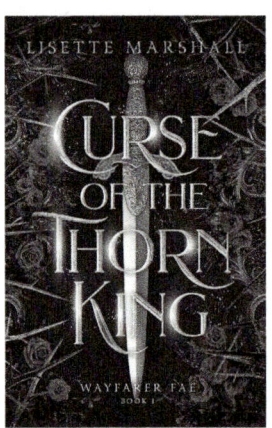

**Killing a fae king is hard. Doing so politely is even harder.**

Briannis Iavi – well-bred lady and accidental assassin – is so close to securing the life of her dreams. All she needs to do is complete one last challenge: make her way into fae territory, sneak into the enchanted halls of Rosethorn Keep, and kill the king of Faerie.

But her plan goes disastrously wrong, and Briannis finds herself a captive at her target's mercy instead.

Cursed to a life of loneliness and slow decay, the monstrous fae king seems hell-bent on revenge – and if he can't hurt the human rulers who sent her, he'll amuse himself with her instead. Unable to escape his sentient castle or to disobey his commands, Briannis has no choice but to fall back on her sharpest weapon: her wits.

Tricking fae is a dangerous game, however. And miles away from the respectable life she thought she knew, even her knives and poisons may not be enough to protect her heart ...

# ABOUT THE AUTHOR

Lisette Marshall is a fantasy romance author, language nerd and cartography enthusiast. Having grown up on a steady diet of epic fantasy, regency romance and cosy mysteries, she now writes steamy, swoony stories with a generous sprinkle of murder.

Lisette lives in the Netherlands (yes, below sea level) with her boyfriend and the few house plants that miraculously survive her highly irregular watering regime. When she's not reading or writing, she can usually be found drawing fantasy maps, baking and eating too many chocolate cookies, or geeking out over Ancient Greek.

To get in touch, visit www.lisettemarshall.com, or follow @authorlisettemarshall on Instagram, where she spends way too much time looking at pretty book pictures.

Printed in Dunstable, United Kingdom